I0831875

# The Bat Coronel

AND THE

# Bloodless

BOOK 5
HEALING FATE SERIES

ASHA NYR

ISBN: 979-8-9885350-3-4 (ebook)
ISBN: 979-8-9924739-4-0 (paperback)
ISBN: 979-8-9924739-3-3 (hardcover case laminate)
ISBN: 979-8-9924739-2-6 (hardcover dust jacket)

Copyediting by Misha Carlstedt, Verity Ink Editorial

Dedicated to my late grandmother, who passed when I started this novel. Ancient, youthful, and fiercely independent until the very end. These are words she'd said to me a hundred times:

"Sometimes life is so crazy that you just have to laugh."

Also dedicated to my beloved Mogget, who passed when I finished editing this book. He was my best friend, my family. Now, he is pure starlight, forever in my heart.

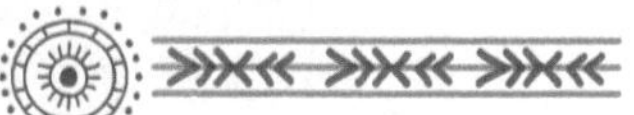
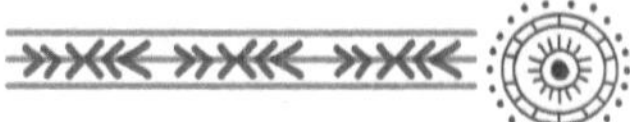

# Content Warning

Dear new readers, this novel contains adult content with scenes describing explicit sex, sexual assault, violence, human trafficking, and references to passive suicide ideation. Reader discretion is strongly advised.

*The Bat Coronel and the Bloodless* was originally exposure therapy for the sexual assault and abuse I survived. Due to popular demand, I've decided to publish it. More information is provided in the Author's Notes about why this was written. Please note it includes spoilers.

More information can also be found in the Author's Notes of *The Mistake and the Lycan King*, *The Dragon Knight and the Coveted*, *The Packless and the Fae Prince*, and *The Tiger Pariah and the Runaway*, the first four books of the Healing Fate series.

## Disclaimer

Keid does not represent all individuals with albinism. The group of disorders has different types with a variety of presentations, and a person with this genetic condition may experience different social, medical, and emotional challenges.

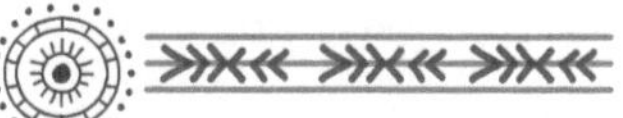 

# Chapter 1

## Keid

Free. My coven was free. After six years of imprisonment, all our witches and menfolk were finally free.

And I tried not to feel.

My mind simply ruminated on facts, desperate to focus on positives while I escorted the sick and elderly out of the prison beneath the arena. They were a devastating sight. One day was unacceptable, but six years in a small space put a brutal toll on the body and mind. Behind me, thin and unwashed bodies followed, cold feet scuffled, and weak legs trembled.

I maintained a rigid expression, keeping stony to prevent turbulent emotions from showing. I'd been the lucky one to have lived in the castle, not stuck in a cell for years, and only I had the stamina to be my people's pillar of support.

My footsteps were lost in the stony, dirty stairwell as I marched the last fifty out into unfiltered daylight. I'd formed teams to move certain groups, wanting to avoid a stampede to freedom. Anxiety plagued them, understandably, and some were on the very cusp of losing their… mental stability. This particular group had been treated inside for a couple days to stabilize and comfort.

Our old enemies assisted us in our exodus. The lions who'd imprisoned us had fallen to the females, ones fed up by some… internal issues. There had also been a kingdom-wide revolt, and the other cat-shifters were now forcing the lions and lionesses to return all the stolen territory. In summary, the lions' power had crumbled, their occupation ended, and we were liberated. Soon, we'd be going home, and I tried not to think about the state our coven grounds would be in.

I walked my group under the gate leading to the open wilderness and prepared encampment. We passed lionesses—and the occasional lion loyal to their cause—and both our groups tensed from the proximity. We humans weren't strong enough to retaliate though. They'd done well for themselves in keeping us weak. Returning what'd been wrought also wasn't wise, and witches were not a foolish people. An eye for an eye led to blindness, and our scryers very much coveted their vision—though some might tell you otherwise.

The rest of the coven received the group, but not the final person. I had to go back for her… carefully. I pulled the hood farther over my head, trying to avoid the burn of the late autumn sun, and turned back to deal with the last imprisoned person. Only my lone footsteps accompanied me as I descended back into the prison. The noises of my gait scraped and scuffed like raspy breaths, echoing down the steps and into the chilly corridor where I'd left her.

The woman, the old witch, sat in the cell that had been her home for all these years. She didn't speak as I approached her open cell, just smiled blankly at me while she shook with elderly trembles. When her odor hit my nose, I held back a gag and called upon all my muscular control to keep revulsion off my face. It wasn't her fault. It wasn't anything even a bar of soap could fix.

I extended a hand out for her bony, liver-spotted one, purposely not looking at the fingers and nails that were a little too long to be considered human. I didn't want to touch her, and I didn't want her smell to get on me, but she was positively ancient and could use the support. Though our kinds did not associate, to put it lightly, I didn't have it in me to be disrespectful to a dying woman.

The others might not have any qualms with that though, and I needed to bring her out a different exit to keep her from being harassed. One of the lionesses assisted me with this, making sure we were able to leave safely through the arena's gate, which was quite a ways from the castle's main gate. Well, it was a ways for me, but for the witch tottering along next to me, it might as well have been leagues.

As her hand shook in mine, I cringed internally, picturing it breaking off into my grip the way it was said they fell apart at life's end. Fortunately, it stayed attached to her wrist, and I did everything I could to distract myself from my wicked imagination.

Forcing my senses away, I picked sound and hummed softly as we passed through the arena's gate. Once we entered the rolling hills and shrubland, I aimed for a small shady grove, wanting to deliver her to cover instead of leaving her out in the sun. If the Sun God glared upon me with prejudice, I couldn't imagine Him sparing the old witch.

Once we ambled over there, I released the old witch's hand and faced her. She'd never spoken before, and it didn't seem like she ever would. She simply smiled up at me with slightly mad, watery eyes. Her wiry grey hair stood out like the dry grass that surrounded the nearby shade. Much about her appearance was rough, nearly violent in its wildness, but she'd never acted violently. Her behavior over the years had always been harmless—a bit unstable, but harmless.

Her kind was anything but harmless though. I didn't need to remind myself; it was ingrained into my very being. What was worse was her age. These creatures were stronger before death, and it was very possible this feeble-looking one could end me with the twitch of a finger. She'd likely die too though.

I sighed and looked around, not sure what to do with her. "Where is your home?" I asked, already knowing I was never going to get her name. I probably wasn't going to get an answer either. The old woman's eyes unfocused, and she cackled in a throaty, gurgling laugh. Amused for gods-knew-what-reason, she shifted her weight from side to side, making her sackcloth robe swish stiffly in the undergrowth.

I pressed my lips together into a thin, tight line, mildly aggravated. I couldn't tell what her mental acuity was. She could be whip-smart and simply playing me for a fool, or she could be in the grips of deep dementia. I knew better than to underestimate her ilk.

"Can you point in a direction? Do you have a place you can go to?" I resisted the urge to tap my foot in impatience.

The witch continued with her odd, pleasant smiling, and her left hand twitched northward. I wasn't sure if that was an answer or an involuntary spasm. Her eyes slowly left mine and roved to look blankly into the scenery, like she was lost in a wondrous daydream.

"North? Is your home north? Is it far?" I received no answer to my question. "Do you have someone we could reach out to? To help you home?"

Now that inspired a loud bout of cackling from her. It was sharp and shrieked across the fields, startling me with its intensity. I winced and shushed her, not wanting to attract attention. It was best she departed separately from the coven, my people. I wouldn't put it past one of them to try to kill her—not that it looked like she had much more time left.

I snorted and gazed down at my feet in thought. After a moment, I placed my hands on my hips, regarded her, and said, "Look, I have many people to coordinate. I have to leave, but I can bring you food and water later. Maybe then you can provide some answers?" I arched my left brow and was only met with her blank, elderly smile. "Alright, well… I'll be back. Just don't"—I hesitated, trying to pick diplomatic words here—"go toward the main gate. It'd be best to keep some distance from the Stellar Coven… for your own safety." With that warning, I spun on a heel and stepped back into the burning gold light.

When I turned the corner of the great stone wall, a witch came running up to me, and I hastily cast a scent-masking spell to hide the lingering… 'presence' of the person I was just escorting. I likely reeked of her. The old woman's existence wasn't a secret, but it was best not to remind the others that she was still nearby.

The other witch, my twin sister, reached me in seconds and threw her arms around me for the second time today. "Say you're done going back in there, Keid! Tell me you're not going back into that place!" she implored rather vehemently.

She wasn't normally so emotionally vulnerable, but she had spent the last six years searching for me. Now that we were reunited, she rarely let me out of her sight. I squeezed her tight for a long minute, just holding her and absorbing her love. I'd missed her so, so much. She was my only family—the only light in my life.

"I will likely have to, Tsisana," I replied, mumbling into her dark brown hair, so unlike mine. I smiled as the beads and trinkets in her ponytail and hair clacked against my nose and brow. "There will be more assistance coming our way, and I need to facilitate." She sighed miserably and nodded, rocking a little as we stood in our embrace. "You can come with me if you want."

She barked out a laugh. "No, you couldn't curse my feet to walk past that gate."

"I imagined as much," I replied and released her as something foreign came to my face—a smile. I placed a hand on my rounded cheek at the odd, tight, bunching sensation. I rarely smiled. I'd had little reason to in the course of my lifetime, especially the last six years of it. I supposed that if there was a proper time to smile, it'd be now.

"You're still so pretty when you smile," my sister said, speaking as though no time had passed, and looped her arm through mine to walk me back to our encampment. I immediately stopped smiling, uncomfortable with the compliment. "You should do it more often, especially now."

"Do we have all the tents set up?" I asked tersely, changing the topic. "Do we have enough?" I stared ahead, able to see the answer for myself.

"Yes, but we're expecting more nomads to come help." With a dry, husky laugh, she added, "We're used to camping out though. I mean, we've been without a home for six years too."

"Are you returning to the coven with everyone else?" The only witches who weren't captured when our coven was invaded had to live on the run this entire time, like her, finding work where they could to survive.

My sister lowered her hazel eyes, eyes so different from mine, and twisted her lips in thought. "I'm not sure. I guess it's been the last thing on my mind. Being able to go back… it never felt like a possibility. I guess I'm still having a hard time processing all this." She squeezed my hand, acknowledging that she was as overwhelmed as I was. "Been a long time since I was around so many people. I think I know how you feel now," she said with a laugh, then cringed and fumbled to apologize.

I held up my other hand in placation. Yes, it'd been insensitive, but it'd been a long time since I'd felt that way. I didn't know who I was now. I certainly wasn't the same person who was captured all those years ago. Time in the pride had… done things to me. I no longer had the same relationship with my emotions.

"What a-about you, Keid?" she stuttered, her face ruddy from embarrassment. "Are you going back?" The way she asked it told me what her assumption was, and she was right.

"Probably not." I sighed, and her grip on me tightened. "You were the only thing that kept me there, Tsisana. You know that."

"Maybe things will be different? You made an impact taking charge the last couple of days," she said quietly as we walked into the encampment toward the tent we'd been sharing. "Everyone is older too. Maybe…"

I almost laughed. “No, sister. I’ve had a taste of life without that kind of harassment… though it’s been a whole new kind of nightmare. You know how I almost lost my hand for disobeying the lions’ doctor”—I rubbed my wrist at the uncomfortable memory—“but I don’t want to be that person ever again. I don’t ever want to hear that nickname again or see those looks. Those buildings only house bad memories, and what if people return to who they once were? The menfolk… No, Tsisana, there’s no future there for me.” I kept my face set in stone, not wanting her to see my feelings, ones I didn’t want to feel either.

“Then where will you go? Maybe I’ll go with you?” she asked, her face twisted in a complicated expression of worry and hope.

I lifted the tent flap to let her go in first but froze when a loud commotion erupted at the castle’s front gate. Someone was yelling, aggressively so, and I stood on my tiptoes to try to see over the other tents. I recognized one who’d just stormed out of the gate, a female bat-shifter who’d come here to represent her people’s gripe with the lions. Her name was Lisa or Luza—something like that. She was arguing with someone, another male shifter I think, but I couldn’t see them very well.

“I told you she wouldn’t be out here!” he snarled, and his attractive tone sent prickles down my neck.

I scrunched my nose and shoved my reaction aside, knowing no good ever came of developing feelings for men. I came off my tiptoes. I no longer wanted to see what he looked like.

His disgust was palpable. “She wouldn’t be one of… these!” he snapped impatiently.

Ah, he seemed to not like witches… or maybe humans in general. I wondered who ‘she’ was. Maybe I could help Lisa… no… Lu… no, it was Luzia! Maybe I’d ask Luzia who they thought was missing. Perhaps they knew someone who’d been imprisoned here too. We had several people who were still unconscious.

“Just bleedin’ say you don’t scent her, you clot!” she growled back. A loud smack made it sound like she’d slapped her companion upside the head. “You’re making a scene!”

I snorted as their arguing voices faded. I supposed they'd continue their search in the castle now.

"Looks like things will be a little messy for a while," I murmured to my sister, who'd been staring in the direction of the scene like me. "Let's get our people strong enough to travel back home, then we'll see about our own next steps."

## Ferrer

I was going to lose my bleeding mind. I couldn't find her. I couldn't find her! I couldn't bloody find her! Where in the bleeding skies was she? Where was my mate? Was I crazy? Was I imagining her scent? It was everywhere! It'd been in the throne room, the hospital, the dungeon, the halls, the arena, but I couldn't find her!

I leaned against a wall as I punched it, but a different kind of pain sent a signal to my brain, and the grey fog that clung to my vision dissipated. My right hand had found its way through a mirror, and I stared in horror as my trembling arm vibrated off the bits of glass that had fallen onto my skin. An aggravated sigh accompanied the tinkling of the glass, and I closed my eyes, praying to the Sky Gods for calm.

*Don't kill Luzia. Don't kill Luzia. Don't let me ki—*

Her inevitable low chuckle snapped me from my chant, and I growled a warning over my shoulder. "Don't!" I hissed through gritted teeth. "I swear to all the gods above us, Luzia, that if you laugh one more bloody time, I will piss in every ration you get for a year."

*I miss Nofre,* my bat said with a sigh. *She's sooo much worse when he's away.*

I didn't have anything to say to that, but my bat piping in gave me enough clarity to start cautiously pulling my arm from the shattered mirror. More glass fell, and without my arm holding it up, the entire frame separated and crashed loudly to the ground.

*Blood clots.*

Luzia cleared her throat. "Alright, I'm sorry… it's just…" She laughed again, and that was when I noticed how unbearably tight my shirt was. My wings had come out, but my shirt hadn't ripped, so one wing was painfully bunched up under it, its clawed thumb jutting out the neck, while the other wing had shot straight down and out the bottom. "Do you want me to cut you free?" she offered, her voice full of mirth.

I didn't answer. Instead, I shut my eyes and tried to will them away, but they stayed adamantly out, my body too agitated to calm and control. With shaking hands and a furious growl, I grabbed my collar and ripped my shirt down the middle.

"I'm going to enjoy watching you suffer when this happens to you, Luzia," I grumbled and stretched out my trembling, cramping wings. There was far too much adrenaline pumping through my accursed blood, and I thought I was going to have a heart attack, such was its speed.

I turned to face my female comrade, a fellow bat-shifter who was a third cousin—one of many. "I don't think anyone is going to suffer quite like you are right now, you romantic, piney little pup," she replied, crossing her arms and shifting her weight onto to the other foot. Her teasing words sounded like an attempt at levity, but she was giving me a wary look. "I'm not nearly in a rush. I'm just glad to be enjoying our new freedom in a new home where we're not starving to death. I'm happy with the number of unrelated males out here to sate myself with."

Her gratitude just irritated me further. Luzia had simple wants that were easily met. Mine had not been, and now that I had proof of my greatest desire's existence, I couldn't stand how it evaded me. If I had to watch one more couple experience recognition before I could, I'd bind my wings and toss myself off a bloody tower. My creators only knew how frustrated my heart and balls were.

"What in the name of the Sky Gods is going on in here?" an aghast voice demanded, and I stepped hastily back from the pile of glass. I turned to find Tumidia, a highly respected lioness, glide in with a look of reproach. Her brows furrowed as she stared at the destroyed mirror, and her blue gaze snapped back to me. "Why am I still getting complaints of your behavior, Ferrer?"

"I promise he's not becoming violent," Luzia jumped in hastily, waving her arms to get her attention. She hesitated, glanced at the mess behind me, then added, "To people."

Tumidia snorted through her nose and tossed her greying dark blond hair over her shoulder. "Do you still scent your fated mate? I'm assuming you still haven't found her or figured out her species?"

I set my jaw, annoyed and embarrassed at how I was bringing attention to my very personal problem during a diplomatic mission. When I realized I was bare-chested before this important lioness, I gripped my shirt tightly, white-knuckling it. I then cleared my throat and replied slowly, choosing my words carefully. "I… have not. There are too many scents here from too many species. I can't tell." I straightened my posture in an attempt to at least look more composed. "I humbly apologize for the commotion I've caused. We will most assuredly leave after sunset." It killed me to utter those words, and my stomach cramped from stress. I'd run out of time.

"You said that yesterday, but—believe it or not—I am understanding," she said and looked briefly at her sleeve to casually adjust it. "Seeing my own daughter find her fated, and seeing many of my lionesses finding their fated… I am not unsympathetic. I am seeing it everywhere now. I see how it changes one's behavior."

"Yes, he is definitely… not normally like this, Madam Tumidia," Luzia asserted, straightening as well with her hands behind her back. I could tell she was holding back a jibe at my expense, but she seemed to successfully resist the temptation.

*Maybe only piss in one of her rations,* my bat suggested.

"I have no issues with you staying until you find her, Ferrer, so long as you're kept under watch," Tumidia offered. "We are very busy with moving our pride out after seeing to the witches."

Ugh, I could hardly stand hearing that word—witches. Still, my heart leapt at the opportunity to linger.

"We can't," Luzia declined, and I shot her a glare. Before I could argue, she added, "We have an important event back home to help with."

"They hardly need us," I said, trying to keep the anger from my voice. "There's four hundred of us already there."

"What sort of event is this?" Tumidia asked in innocent curiosity, tilting her head. "I admit to being very curious about you, our new northern neighbors."

I sighed and gestured to Luzia, preferring she explain. I was becoming bleedin' cranky.

"It was the Wolf Queen's idea. She suggested we regularly host an open party for all unmated, inviting people from other kingdoms to mingle—see if we can get a large percentage to find their fated so we can start rebuilding our population. Some are definitely willing to settle down with a chosen should the opportunity arise."

"Regularly because you definitely wouldn't be able to fit every single unmated into one party," Tumidia inferred with an understanding nod, smiling slightly. "It sounds like a good idea, but your security will have to be tight. That's a lot of people from different kingdoms."

"We are resourceful, but thank you for the suggestion," Luzia replied with a nod in return. "We're building good relationships."

"We would like to as well," the lioness remarked, looking over her shoulder at two lions moving down the hall. "There is much damage to repair here first."

"And our contractual offer still stands," I said, more put together now. "Blood donations for protection. You know there will be many targeting the lions now that they've been weakened. We look forward to hearing from you."

"We are grateful." Tumidia appraised us both. "I will leave you to your devices until you leave. Please do stop frightening my lionesses though." She raised a stern brow and glided out of the room, leaving me with my comrade, who narrowed her eyes at me.

"Have you forgotten who you are, Ferrer? We're coronels now," she chastised. "We have to show our faces. Our people need to feel like we want to find their mates too. You're not the only one who wants one, Ferrer."

Perhaps I should have felt ashamed at being called selfish, but I didn't. "Nothing's changed," I responded dryly. "Stop acting like we're more important than we were before we came here. It's just a bloody title so other kingdoms have something to call the leaders of our colony. It's superficial. Don't let it fly you too high, Coronel Luzia. You'll get tired and fall." I growled and prodded her in the forehead with a finger.

She wrinkled her nose and snarled back at me, furious. We would continue to not see eye to eye on this subject. I was focused on results, not frivolity. Egos caused problems.

"Look," she snapped and jabbed me back in the forehead—much harder than I did to her, might I add. "We need to go back and report to our colony. Our mission is over. Let's just… Ugh, follow me!"

She stormed in the direction of the throne room, and I followed, asking, "What are you doing?"

"Just… just bleedin' wait," she answered, annoyed.

We turned into the massive throne room to find Tumidia with her daughter, Niusha, and her daughter's mate. The intimidating tiger-shifter noticed our approach, particularly my shirtless one, and his face hardened into a frown.

"Can we help you?" Javed inquired, and Luzia bowed. I copied her bow, doing it rather stiffly.

"Your Majest—" Luzia began saying, and Niusha waved her hands to interrupt her.

"Not royalty, Luzia," Niusha affirmed. I sighed inwardly. They might as well be. This realm, with all its titles, was so confusing.

"I have a small request," Luzia said, "if you would hear it."

"Proceed." Tumidia gestured with a hand.

"The event we mentioned. Can you extend our invitation to all the unmated who have been within these walls?" she proposed, and I hissed under my breath. We should have discussed this beforehand! She couldn't possibly mean to include the bloody witches!

"Luzia!" I whispered to get her attention, but she ignored me.

"Ah…" Tumidia said with a lift of her chin. Her daughter sent her a questioning look, and the lioness nodded slowly. "They're having an event to try to get mates for their people, you know, being endangered," she explained to the two leaders. Looking back at me, she answered, "We'll discuss it, but I see no issues at this time informing them of its existence if you provide details. I will warn them that we cannot guarantee their safety if they're leaving cat territory. They'll know they're going at their own risk."

"I believe that is very fair," Luzia replied with another short bow. "We'll send more information as soon as we return home."

I opened my mouth to try to say something, but nothing came to me. Luzia turned away, leaving me to hesitate before the leaders of the cat kingdom.

"Thank you for having us. I look forward to bettering our relationship," I said shortly. "Please forgive my appearance. There was an incident." I immediately rushed out to catch up to Luzia, fuming.

"I can't believe you did that without discussing it with me first! And you can't possibly mean to include the witches, right? And what if she doesn't come?" I asked, throwing my hands up in the air.

"Then just come visit here until you find her! Clots, you're driving me mad, Ferrer! You've got time! You're not exactly on death's door!" she seethed, gripping the sides of her head. "And yeah, witches! Some of us might be fated to them! Yeah, that would suck, but it's not up to us!"

A pair of lionesses passed us, not hiding their bewildered staring. Gods, we must look like such stupid bickering little pups.

*I don't want to go,* my bat said truculently.

*I don't either,* I replied. I ran my hands through my hair, then scrubbed them down and over my face.

"It's not like you've made progress. It's been days, Ferrer," Luzia continued to argue. "She could have already lef—"

"Fine. Fine!" I snapped, interrupting her on our walk back to our guest chambers. "Shittin' stars! We'll go." I then mumbled under my breath, "Just to bloody shut you up." I placed a hand on my stomach, loathing how sick I felt having to give up the hunt here. Where was she? Where was my fated mate?

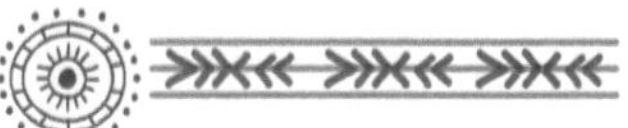
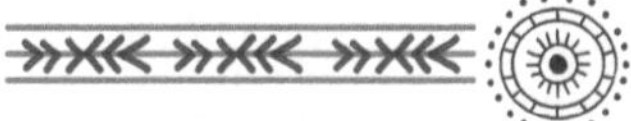

# Chapter 2

## Reid

"Shhh!" I shushed the old witch as I approached with her hot meal. She'd cackled in delight when she'd spotted me entering her little campsite, lightly clapping, before holding them out wide for the food… or for a hug. It was weirdly hard to tell. She looked like a grandmother excitedly welcoming home a granddaughter she hadn't seen in ages.

Her laugh faded into a pleased hum when I handed her the bowl of hearty, fatty beef stew. Wherever she was going, I wanted her to at least leave with a full belly. Speaking of bellies, stinging bile rose from mine to my throat. The sound of her noisy slurping and mastication did not mix well with her wretched smell.

I turned my head and placed a hand to my mouth, prepared to dry heave, but I managed to keep the reflex at bay. Of all the things I'd done over the last handful of days, this was my most impressive accomplishment. I swallowed hard and leaned my face against my fist, making it look like I was just paying attention to her instead of trying to block the smell.

The witch would giggle occasionally, and at one point, she dipped a mushroom into the broth before eating it. I had no idea where she'd gotten it. That particular fungus didn't grow around here.

"Where did you find that? Wait—are you high?" I asked, remembering the properties of that particular species. The witch just leaned back, kicked her feet a couple times like a toddler, then hunched over her dinner once more. I dragged my hand down my face and simply stared at the elderly mess before me. "Curses," I muttered. "What am I going to do with you?"

I watched the witch finish her meal and wondered if I should confiscate her store of mushrooms. I dismissed the thought as soon as it came to me and sighed. I was worrying too much over things that weren't within my control. If she wanted to waddle on out tomorrow as high as the stars, then that was what she'd do.

"Are you headed north tomorrow?" I asked, not expecting an answer. The witch rocked back and forth while bobbing her head in an odd manner. I supposed I'd take that as a nod.

Perhaps this would be the last time I'd see her. I stared down at my cotton leggings and picked small bits of nature off them. My tunic and pants were my only clothes, but they were significantly nicer than what the other witches and menfolk had to wear. I had this old creature to thank for my garments, but I had to thank her for something much bigger than that—something incomparable. I wondered if she would remember.

I opened my mouth to address her and hesitated when I didn't know what to call her. I didn't know her name or if she'd ever been given a coven title. I cleared my throat and skipped that part. "I don't know if you remember, but I wanted to thank you for… doing what you did all those years ago. Do you remember that day when I was taken to the castle?" I asked, but the witch just continued working on her meal, smiling in her oblivion.

I stared at the small fire she'd made and frowned. She made it with some damp, rotten wood that she must have dug up from somewhere, and a good deal of smoke plumed from it. Was she trying to draw attention? There was a ton of dry wood around to use. I growled quietly in aggravation, tightened my ponytail, and just went on to say what was on my mind.

I took a deep breath. “If you don’t recall, it was just after the evening shift had arrived at the prison. Several of the guards were older and hadn’t liked the sight of me since day one. You remember them? Both maybe middle-aged? One had a rather crooked nose…” When she didn’t react, unsurprisingly, I just continued.

“Anyway, I imagine you must’ve seen and heard how they spoke to me from your cell. I was next to yours, remember? They wanted to put us ‘scary’ ones together.” I laughed and rubbed an eye in my mirth, but there was a sharp pang in my chest. Though it still hurt to some extent, my overall feelings weren’t as bitter as they used to be. Laughing—albeit bitterly—and the passage of time had helped.

I stared down at my pale pink hands. “You know how they changed though. At first, they were just anxious to patrol past me, then they became paranoid. They knew what you were, but they didn’t know what my ‘deal’ was.” I frowned. “The lions aren’t some backwater people. You’d think with their age they’d recognize albinism when they saw it. But I suppose superstition overpowers reason, doesn’t it?

“It was awful when they started talking about just getting rid of me. I very much believed them when they said no one would investigate if another witch was executed for misbehaving. They could make up any number of excuses for killing me and would likely just end up with a slap on the wrist.” I spat out that last part bitterly and drew my knees to my chest. Saying all this aloud for the first time had resentment crawling back into my heart. I hadn’t really gone into detail with Tsisana about my captivity, not yet.

The witch finished eating and put down the bowl. I eyed her as she started filing her long nails with a stone. A muscle in my face twitched at her delicate, sophisticated movements. Whether or not she was listening, I continued.

"Th-then the doctor came. He strolled through the prison looking for someone to help in his office. One of his peers had passed away, and he needed someone to assist him at the castle. He asked witch after witch if they knew healing, but no one volunteered. You, however," I accused in a wry tone, "volunteered me like a rabid animal. By the gods, how you hollered at him, screaming and pointing at me like the liar you were…" I sobered and suffered a sharp jab of pain in my gut from the next memory. "You know, the doctor liked how I looked too. He knew about the condition, but he said maybe I'd intimidate some of the difficult patients into behaving better."

My shoulders slumped. The witch had stopped filing her nails. She blew a fine dust off them, her dry hair trembling from her elderly vibrations.

"Thank you," I said quietly and fingered the hem of my tunic. "If you hadn't made such a ruckus, I wouldn't have been dragged out of there—out of immediate danger. Still, that put me in a rough situation. Maybe you weren't aware, but I didn't know more about medicine than the average witch. The doctor thought I was just being rebellious. That had a three-strike rule placed on me by the advisor, you know. If I misbehaved enough, he'd cut off a hand." I shuddered and rubbed my wrist. "That was incentive enough to pick up every accursed medical journal in the place.

"The doctor… I wasn't fond of Doctor Gris, but he'd never mistreated me. He was actually rather reasonable for a lion. Didn't want conflict and neither did I. He even allowed me to take the journals back to my room at night so I could get caught up on 'their type' of medicine. Great gods, that was a stressful—and sleepless—period of my life." I rubbed my eyes. "Turning pages is hard when you're shackled, by the way."

The witch was just staring into the fire now, her hands folded in her lap.

"But I was alive and safe… enough," I murmured, staring at her. "So… thank you." I swallowed heavily and asked, "Do you remember? Volunteering me?" I didn't know why I was nervous. I supposed it meant more to me than I thought for her to know. Slowly, as I waited for her response, I realized what I felt was kind of like a life debt.

The witch just rubbed her nose and yawned. My cheek twitched again, feeling compelled to do a half-smile. Well, at least I felt better for having thanked her. Even though I'd been a slave, my last six years had been relatively luxurious compared to everyone else's stay in the prison. Only Fate knew if I would have survived without her raucous interference.

I stood and bent down to collect her bowl, needing to return it. "Good luck on your journey, witch," I said softly. "May your remaining days be peaceful."

The old lady cackled and yawned again. When I turned to leave, I was startled by a smack on my bottom. I closed my eyes, gritted my teeth, and took a deep breath. Had she just sent me off with a spank? I resisted the urge to whirl around and glare at her, then promptly marched out of her campsite to the sound of her giggles.

I cast a scent-masking spell again and made a mental note to wash my leggings tomorrow. That wicked hag! That spank was going to linger. Ugh.

I returned to the starlit tent I shared with my sister, then stripped down to my underwear before crawling under a blanket. I could barely see Tsisana blink at me in the dark, not yet asleep.

"Everything going well here?" I asked quietly, decompressing to the sounds of the breeze, autumn insects, and nearby snorers. It was a cooler evening, and the crickets were lazy in their chirping. "Got everyone fed?"

She hummed a yes and rolled over to completely face mine. "Rumor spread like wildfire over dinner though."

"Oh?" I asked, fisting the front of my blanket and raising it to my chin. "What's that?"

"Those new shifters are hosting some kind of huge recognition banquet… or ball… or something," she answered and scooted closer to me. I slipped a hand out of my blanket to push a hair from her brow, then covered my mouth to yawn.

"Well, I suppose that would be an effective way to find a bunch of mates all at once. If they got lucky with their guests, that is."

She stared meaningfully at me and added, "They're apparently inviting us too."

"'Us' as in our group of witches and menfolk?" I did not like the look on her face. That was the expression she adopted right before bullying me outside of my comfort zone. "Seems rather desperate, don't you think? We're all exhausted. I think everyone just wants to go home and start healing. I can't imagine anyone thinking it was time to go to a party. These shifters must also know they'd be inviting a lot of injured, exhausted, and traumatized folk."

Her nod was slow, cautious. "I can't say I know their thought process, but why wouldn't they be desperate? Heard they're endangered. Maybe if they had mates among us, they'd be dying to take care of them. I mean, if my future spouse had been enslaved and abused, I'd want to rush in and nurture him within an inch of his life."

I snorted in a slight laugh. "I suppose that makes sense."

She was silent for a moment, then spoke softly, "I think you should go, Keid."

"Why?" I asked flatly, shutting down my emotions. *Don't do this to me, Tsisana.*

"Don't you think that the one person who'd never judge you, who you could completely trust, would be a fated mate?" she asked quietly.

I pushed down a flare of anger. I wasn't necessarily mad at her, but I hated the topic of spouses and mates. "Shifters are the ones who get them, not us."

"But shifters have been fated to humans before," she argued. "You could have one out there, and you'd never have to worry about them cheating on you or talking behind your back…"

I struggled to swallow past the lump in my throat. This topic was resting heavily on my chest, and I could barely breathe. I'd gotten my hopes up once, and the letdown had been crushing. I rubbed at my chest and focused on taking slow, deep breaths. Emotions bottlenecked, trying so fervently to fill my lungs and drown me.

My sister went there. She went where I absolutely hadn't wanted her to go and said, "Not everyone is going to be like him…" She put a hand on my shoulder when I stiffened. I couldn't speak because this time my mouth had gone dry. Only my sister could do this to me, and she took advantage of it. "Isn't it worth one evening just to try? You don't even have to think about finding a mate. Just go for the free food for all it matters."

My mind and heart couldn't follow her, to go where she wanted me to go. Everything in me had gotten stuck. I crumbled into tears. "I g-gave him everything." I was too tired and too worn out to keep my stoic act going. I had hoped with the passage of time, that memory would hurt less. I supposed my twin just knew how to draw the pain out of me.

She sighed and pulled me into a hug, shushing me while I cried into her neck. "He was a right bastard, Keid, but we've got a fresh start now. I bet even he regrets it. People see you differently now, I'm sure of it."

"Don't defend him, and I don't want to get my hopes up again," I said through my weeping, shutting my eyes tight enough to hurt.

My sister just withered and rubbed my back as she held me, nuzzling her cheek into the top of my head. "Wasn't trying to defend him," she muttered, patting me. "I'm just saying that no one is who they were before the lions came. You're a lot more confident now. You're quite cool and calm. I hardly recognize you."

"Yeah, well, it wasn't easy hanging on to my left wrist," I muttered right back at her, bitter, but my crying had subsided. I sniffed and shuddered, completely drained now… but somehow lighter.

"What if I went with you?" she offered. "I could see if anyone else wants to make the journey. I heard it's about as far from here as it is to the coven. They're just in different directions."

I shrugged, unwilling to admit that I was somewhat intrigued. But did I have it in me to face disappointment again? I held my breath for a handful of seconds as I considered. When I released only my held breath, Tsisana realized I wasn't going to answer.

"It's not like we were planning on returning to the coven. This could give you time to think about what you want. I don't know about you, but the thought of going to a feast with a bunch of hot bachelors sounds like a good way to celebrate getting my sister back."

Her line of thinking surprised a weak laugh out of me, and both of us relaxed.

"I'll think about it…" I relented.

"Promise?"

"Yes, Tsisana… Good night. Starlight on your dreams."

"Yours too."

"This seems excessive," I stated as Tsisana draped a gown over my head. Multiple pairs of hands worked to pull the dress down my body and straighten the fabric to check the fit. I was standing in the old Jong Harem's dressing room, swallowed by lavender until my head popped out the dress's neckline. Behind me stood two lionesses and a witch, the latter having finally caved in and stepped foot into the castle.

"Well, you're going to tolerate this because it's the only reason I'd ever walk into lion territory," Tsisana said just as flatly. "The lionesses left a mountain of finery behind, and I intend to cover you in it."

"Ex-lion territory," Niusha corrected. "Cat-shifter territory with equal representation."

"Doesn't make it easier." Tsisana attempted to make the words more polite by speaking in a milder tone.

Niusha's mother, Tumidia, said, "You've done much to care for my lionesses during your forced service, Keid." She pulled the velvet sleeves down to my elbows and untucked the lace. "You saved Niusha's marking and pregnancy—the queen's cubs."

"She saved her own cubs," I repeated for the third time since being freed. "I just gave her an opportunity to do so." I kept a straight face and tried not to think of the nightmarish things I'd been unable to prevent. Too many young ones had been forced to carry to term, and too many who'd illegally dallied with cheetah servants had been forced to have their pregnancies terminated. It was going to take a long time to forgive myself for things I hadn't been able to control. At least the lionesses cared fiercely for their own; their support of each other had been nigh unfaltering. It seemed to run particularly deep in this species of shifter.

"Not a queen," Niusha said of herself.

"Well, if not queen, then what?" her mother asked.

"It's not decided yet. Some want something humble like 'Chieftain' and 'Chiefess,' but others are suggesting something more modern like 'Ambassador.' Javed doesn't care at all, and I don't ei— You know what? Let's not talk about work," Niusha replied and squatted to pull on the dress's skirts. "We're focusing on Keid right now."

"Yes. My sister deserves it," Tsisana asserted, putting heavy emphasis on the word 'deserves' and stood back to regard everyone's handiwork. "I don't know. The lavender is pale. It kind of washes her out with her light pink skin."

"I agree," Tumidia hummed, placing a finger to her lips. "Maybe we should go with something dark to offer contrast, but that'd call for some dark face paint. Our palest blondes often complain about not having a face."

I felt a flare of both embarrassment and anger at that statement but forced the pain into the tiny box that I kept in my mind. She didn't know better, and it was too exhausting to explain it to every person who let something insensitive slip. Tumidia, however, wasn't just a regular person. I changed my mind and opened my mouth to say something, but Niusha addressed it first.

"Mother," she cautioned, "she has a very visible, very lovely face." Aside from my sister, who knew everything about my feelings, Niusha was the only one I'd confessed my insecurities to, though it hadn't really been intentional. She'd taken me off guard.

That being said, part of me wasn't sure if her defense of me was worse. I sighed and tried to keep my posture from drooping. The gods of the skies and earth knew that there didn't seem to be a right way to talk about my appearance. A hand rubbed my arm, and I turned my head to see my sister's uncomfortable smile. It was obvious that she knew what I was thinking.

Still, I was being cared for with good intentions. I had to be grateful for that. I cleared my throat and stopped thinking about things that got under my skin. I was older, wiser, and tougher now. I didn't want to think about the small child in me that was somehow still hurting. She hadn't piped up in ages.

"Still, do you not think this style is too…" I searched for the right word that wouldn't offend. "Formal?" I played with the lace that hung from my elbows and stared at how the tight top clung dramatically above skirts that flared wide at the hips. I frowned at the faded acne scars on my shoulders, feeling insecure about more than just my albinism. "Maybe something with shoulders and longer sleeves?"

"Shifters are libidinous. You will have the most success getting a mate with the least amount of coverage. I think we should go with less," Tumidia urged and turned to dig into the other options with my sister.

"It won't matter for fated mates," Niusha pointed out defensively. "They go crazy just finding the person they're supposed to be with."

"I suppose you would know," her mother said thoughtfully, and I wondered if there was some envy there. I couldn't tell. Niusha's mother was an extremely strong, independent female.

"Still, someone might want her as a chosen. Ferrer and Luzia mentioned many wanted to take a chosen if they didn't find their fated."

I stared thoughtfully at my hands. Was Ferrer the one I'd overheard that didn't like witches or humans? "Were they the only two who came?" I inquired subtly, slightly berating myself for letting my interest sneak through my defenses.

Niusha answered, "Yes, they left a few days ago. That poor male was going mad looking for his mate, but I suppose she'd left with the other lionesses… or perhaps she'd been one of the Proudless who'd been here during the takeover." She glanced over and waited for my sister and Tumidia to pick out another option.

Ah… so he was already spoken for… in a manner of speaking. I accidentally let a frown slip onto my face and immediately got rid of it. Though, I couldn't keep my cheeks from flushing, which infuriated me to no end. It was stupid. He didn't want a witch, and I'd only heard his voice. I'd liked it, but that was not enough to justify my odd, curious crush. How could one get a crush on a voice? Stupid. This was stupid. I wrinkled my nose and shook my head, but this time Niusha noticed my reaction. All I could do was pretend my nose had itched.

"Yes, we heard that hullabaloo, I believe," my sister intoned dryly. "I think the whole coven heard his racist remarks. Fucking idiot."

"Yes, I was surprised to hear them extend the invitation to the witches. Well, Luzia had delivered the request. Ferrer looked like he was going to slaughter her," Tumidia said with a chuckle.

Niusha frowned. "I don't think it's fair to treat other witches like they're somehow related to rot-witches. I don't know much about them, but it doesn't sit right with me."

"Prejudice is born from fear, Daughter, as you've witnessed firsthand." Tumidia sighed, pulled out a black-and-gold gown, and held it up to my chest. "All our females will be introduced to it soon too. The rot-witches put millennia of torture upon those poor bat-shifters. They still suffer, endangered because of what they did. I think it's understandable even though it's ultimately unacceptable. I fear that only time and education will change that. Lions will have to prove themselves just like the witches, unfortunately—though we lions inflicted that upon ourselves with our occupations. Foolish males. Think this is too warm for her pink skin?"

The change in topic was jarring, and it pulled me from my thoughts of this Ferrer. I needed to let it go, so I finally embraced the topic of finding something to wear. I wanted to leave. "It's fine," I said hastily. At least the sleeves were longer.

"I admit, I'm curious about how this event will turn out," Tumidia said while my sister quietly pulled the lavender dress up and over my head. "Recognition is so new to us lionesses. I'd love to see the bats find their mates. Can you imagine living such long lifespans as virgins—surrounded only by those too closely related to mate with? Skies, what a misery. What an opposite life from ours—breeders as soon as we were of age."

"They must be quite pent-up," my sister said with an amused snort and helped me try on the black-and-gold gown. Niusha couldn't seem to suppress her smile and seemed lost in an old memory. I didn't really understand what was that great about sex. It had been okay the couple times I'd done it, but it wasn't something I looked forward to anymore. I more so craved affection than anything else. Well, I only craved it when my emotions slipped. I'd become better at controlling them, and a serious mindset helped to focus on other tasks.

"Are you going, Tsisana?" Niusha asked, and my sister hummed an affirmative.

"I've been without male companionship for far too long," she drawled. "I'm mostly going for Keid though. These shifters better be fine specimens."

"If Luzia and Ferrer are any example, I imagine their males are attractive and virile. I've seen Ferrer without his shirt," Tumidia shared with a wry smile, and Niusha released a bark of laughter.

"I still can't believe he tore his shirt. Their wings must pop out the same time as their…" the younger lioness started saying, then faltered as her eyes flickered to her mother. She promptly shut her mouth in conservative embarrassment, and my sister cackled wickedly. I pursed my lips as I focused on smoothing my sleeves. I did not want to think about Ferrer's erections. This conversation was getting a little too intimate for my liking.

Without any warning, emotions slammed into me. They struck like a sharp slap, weakening my legs and winding me. Panic seemed to hit me out of nowhere. I resisted the impulse, but I was desperate to escape and crawl into a closet somewhere.

My thoughts raced along with the emotions, as if the uncontrollable wave dragged them through the dirt. This was altogether too embarrassing. What was I doing here? Why was I picking out a gown to wear? No one would want me. This was stupid. This entire idea was incredibly stupid. I was only going to get hurt and be embarrassed. I'd go. I'd hang around by the banquet table and nibble on food until it was time to leave. I'd be alone the entire time because no one would be attracted to me and approach me.

I placed a hand to my belly, wan and sick to my stomach. I reeled. The edges of my vision blurred. Too much.

"Stop it," my twin said sharply, knowing where my mind had gone. Sometimes, I wished she wasn't so good at reading my body. Scratch that. I always wished she wasn't so good at it.

"Tsisana…" I murmured quietly, feeling myself spiral out of control. "They won't want me. I'm defective."

"Stop. It," she snapped harshly, standing in front of me to grip my shoulders and glare into my eyes. "That's not true. You're a woman. You're beautiful. You're worth loving. You have so much to offer a spouse or mate."

"No, I don't," I whispered, feeling my wide, unblinking eyes dry. This had been a mistake. I hadn't crumbled this hard in over a decade. I'd gotten stronger. I'd grown more independent and confident. This subject was my weakness. I shouldn't put myself in situations that would make me lose my grip of my newfound confidence. I was proud of my survival.

"I know you've always wanted our family to be bigger," she whispered back. "I know that you feel like finding someone is impossible. Give yourself a chance. You have a big chance here. This is a real opportunity."

Tumidia said, "We've never had many opportunities for love here. Most lionesses never really felt it with our males, and we didn't know what fated mates were." Niusha nodded in agreement, approaching quietly from behind to wrap me in a hug. The older lioness continued, "You must learn to love yourself."

My stomach flipped from a hot bout of anger. That phrase always cued a rage in me. I'd heard it so many times that I wanted to scream. At the end of the day, when my emotions slipped, I still went to bed feeling cold and lonely.

Though it was offered through affection, the sympathy around me was stifling, and I forced my emotions to shut down immediately. I straightened and gave the dress a good stare in the mirror. "This is fine. I'll borrow this one," I said in a detached tone. "Hopefully it won't wrinkle on the journey over."

"We'll give you a nice travel bag…" Niusha murmured and frowned, likely from my change in countenance.

I was no longer sure that I was going anymore, but I definitely didn't want to stay and argue over it. I had to see off the remaining witches and menfolk, then swing by where I'd dropped off the declining witch to make sure she'd left before I decided my next steps. It was absurd to think of all this spouse stuff when there were other more important tasks to complete.

Curses.

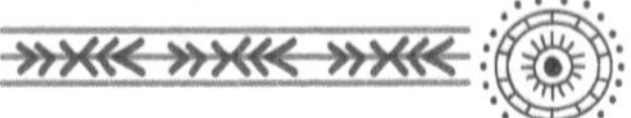

# Chapter 3

## Ferrer

Ettor and I stood over the border of the party grounds, watching the line of guests back up for what seemed like well over a mile. Through the thick woodland, it was hard to tell exactly how many stood waiting. From what I could see though, the faces of our guests were expressing a myriad of emotions from excitement to nervousness, and I could guarantee that my people's faces were mirrored in kind.

"What is causing the delay?" I asked Ettor, bringing his attention to the rate our guests were trickling into the recognition grounds.

"It is part of the intake process suggested by Queen Hekla and her mate," he replied with an impatient sigh. "It has been brought to our attention that our reaction to recognition is too aggressive. You recall Nofre's experience, do you not?"

"Of course I do. I had to restrain him when it happened, Ettor. His bloody wings springing out nearly knocked me unconscious."

Ettor failed to hold back a chuckle and continued his explanation. "The guests are required to sign what's called a 'release.'"

*Aw yeah,* my bat responded inappropriately, making me grunt in irritation.

*Sheathe your tiny dick,* I snapped.

"—ich states that each guest has been made aware of the risks upon entering the grounds."

"So they are informed that we've trained all our participants to interfere if they see something forced, correct? Any misbehavior will be pounced upon by all nearby bat-shifters," I inquired, tilting my neck to the side to crack a bone. My back had been stiff all evening. The thought of my mate being out there was enough to risk ripping another shirt. Fortunately, the fae had been generous in providing us with clothes that would prevent such embarrassments. Our females had been given open-backed dresses while our males had been given shirts with slits, though we weren't exactly confident our wings would line up with the openings in time.

Ettor nodded. "Yes. That and any females currently menstruating must stay on the downwind outskirts of the celebration so those with less appetite mastery can find some reprieve. They bleed more than our females apparently."

"Or rather ours bleed less than them. Another side effect of our forced evolution. Don't forget that we're the strange ones here, Ettor."

"It is rather hard to forget," he replied, picking thoughtfully at his shirt cuff.

"Does it appear like everyone followed the fasting rules?" I asked and leaned over to try to see our own waiting participants.

"Yes. No blood for twelve hours prior to prevent libido spikes, like we all agreed. The guests have been made aware of that instinct as well and have been asked to not cave into pressure if asked for a taste."

I nodded in satisfaction. We couldn't afford to scare off our priceless guests. This was our first event, and it was crucial that everyone left with nothing but good things to say. The future of our species depended on everyone's good behavior. We needed mates… badly.

I sighed and mumbled, "I can see now why it's taking so long. We need more people down there to help with intake, Ettor."

"I've already assigned a team that's assembling now. I'm aware that the night is only so long."

"Patience is not a virtue we have much of," I stated, drumming my fingers on the cool stone railing. "I admit that I've never felt so alive since arriving back at these ancestral lands."

"I think we all feel it. We owe much to our Queen Hekla."

"Don't call her that to her face," I replied with a snort and turned to use the stairs instead of jumping off the balcony like I was itching to do.

*I would think our flying would impress our guests,* my bat replied sullenly.

*The dragon-shifters, maybe,* I replied. *Best not intimidate them, Iron.*

*I would still like to feel like I'm participating. Let my wings out, Ferrer. Come on.*

*Well, if our mate shows up, I won't be able to stop you,* I said, annoyed at his willfulness. He'd been particularly chatty all bloody day, but I supposed I couldn't be too hard on him. We'd lived too long without the taste of a female—our entire life. I held my breath through a rush of excitement and tried to calm myself. The thought of spreading a pair of legs tonight was too much to handle at the moment. I had to focus. If my mate was here, I had to show her my best side. My heart was just as hungry.

*Whatever you do, get into a female tonight. I can't take it anymore,* Iron ordered.

*You're doing the opposite of helping. I'm only interested in our fated,* I snapped, losing my patience with him as I strode onto the recognition grounds. I fought to ignore him and tried to mentally prepare myself for the night.

Taking a deep breath, I made an effort to enjoy my surroundings. Our people had done well to charm our guests with the decoration. Our redwood forest was sprawling, and the lanterns were aplenty, dim enough to not bother our eyes—eyes that had evolved within the Night Court, a place of eternal starlight. The ground was soft beneath boots, layered with pine needles and rich soil. Decorative red-and-gold cloth hung between trees, a display of finery that Queen Hekla deemed important. Wind chimes made from gold and something called abalone occasionally clinked from the night breeze but were mostly drowned out by the growing chatter.

The fae had also sent a team of chefs, knowing that we had no idea how to feed this many people. Some of us already had non-bat mates who were provided with their type of food, but we definitely required help for everyone else tonight. Now, the banquet tables were nigh encumbered with treats and fine beverages.

I lifted my nose to look for Luzia, then followed her scent to the southern edge of the grounds where she was setting up tents with the others. I approached and gestured to the many that were already erected. "I thought these were completed days ago," I said, frowning in confusion.

"Some thought fit to celebrate early," she gritted out through her teeth. "Stole their mates from the line to find a little privacy. We've punished them, but I doubt they even care."

"Are their mates alright?" I asked. It was appalling, but I wasn't entirely surprised by the impulsive behavior.

"Yes, they were only upset they were separated from their bats, so I doubt we'll receive complaints about anything but the guests wanting their fated back. We stuck the bats in the dungeon until tomorrow night. They knew the rules."

"Seems easily forgotten in the midst of recognition," I murmured, troubled by the lack of self-control.

"It will be easier when everyone is out to keep an eye on everyone else." She shoved the last pole into the dirt and brushed her hands on her tunic. "I'm done here, and I need to get ready. Go finish your rounds."

This had been my last errand, and I wracked my brain with something to do to keep my anxious mind occupied. I glanced up to try to find a glimmer of my gods and spied a couple stars peeking through the crowded, needled canopy.

*Please. Please, Sky Gods, have my mate show up tonight.*

The stars winked in their twinkling, and had that not already been in their nature, I would have assumed they were communicating awareness of some secret. A shudder ran down my back, and I turned my gaze from the sky, not wanting to think of anything going wrong tonight.

*You're not superstitious. Don't start now,* Iron chastised. *Go take a peek at the line. I want to see if I can scent the end of our virginity— I mean our mate.*

*We can't go doing what we told others not to,* I countered.

*Alright, well, just keep on doing what you're doing.*

That brought my attention back to where I was walking, which was in the direction of the guest line. Bloody clots, I needed to get myself under control.

Fortunately, a distraction named Borredan was headed my way from that direction. I smiled and nodded in greeting, but the expression was knocked clear off my face when I saw how pale my friend was. Well, we were all pale, but I could clearly see that his blood pressure was suffering from some shock. Since he had been working at intake, I was concerned that something had occurred with our guests.

"Borredan?" I asked, turning to walk next to him as he strode past me. "You don't look too goo—"

"She's a witch," he blurted out flatly. Movement at the corner of my vision grabbed my attention, and I took note of his shaking arms and quivering hands.

"No…" I murmured more to myself, unable to believe what he'd just said. Borredan was a good male. He didn't deserve this. "Maybe you didn't get a clear scent. There are many types o—"

"No, I got a good whiff, Ferrer," he replied, nearly choking on the words. His voice thickened, like he was about to cry, and I'd never witnessed him so much as sniffle.

"Well, where are you going? Aren't you going to reje—" I started asking but was interrupted by his swinging fist. I grabbed his hand and gawked, aghast at the rage in his eyes. That anger wasn't directed at his fated mate; it was directed at me.

"Don't!" he shouted, his face flushing as his neck corded in fury.

"Blood clots, Borr! Ground yourself!" I growled hotly and pushed his fist away from me. "What was that for?"

"Don't tell me to reject her!" he yelled again, stepping closer to get into my face. I scowled and pushed him out of my personal space. Despite my assertion, he was still as aggressive as a frothing animal.

"I'm confused," I snarled warily, eying him up and down to see if he was an immediate threat. "She's a witch. Just pick someone else... unless she's... drugged you or something..." I squinted and tilted my head, trying to get a good look at his pupils. "There are plenty of females now."

"I don't... I don't want..." He stared down at his clenched fists, his broad shoulders heaving. His eyes shut tight, and he all but screamed his confession. "I don't want to reject her, Ferrer!" He scrubbed his hands over his face, launched into the air, and rampaged through the canopy to get to the safety of the sky.

*What... in the shitting stars... just happened?* Iron asked in shock as I took a step back to avoid leaves and falling branches.

"Borr hates witches..." I murmured, staring where he'd disappeared. I bent to pick up a large branch and leaned it against a tree so no one would trip on it.

*Most of us do,* Iron replied. *That was unexpected.* He was nervous now, and I admit that I was shaken myself. How was it that the mate bond...

*He's just surprised. He needs some time to come to his senses. I'm sure he'll pick someone who'll make him happy,* I said and shook out my nerves, swinging my arms to get rid of my jitters.

*At least we know the shirts work now.*

I burst into nervous laughter and nodded. I hadn't even noticed. When I turned, I saw that some bats had arrived to see what had caused the commotion.

"Fated to a bloody witch," I said in dismissal. "Borr needs some space to come to his senses."

"Better watch how you address other bats' mates, Ferrer," a male named Cegri warned. "We must adapt or we'll fall farther."

There were murmurs of both agreement and disagreement, which left me perplexed. Too many voices had agreed.

*That was unexpected as well...* Iron mumbled as the others turned to leave.

I shuddered and looked up at the patch of sky that was now more visible thanks to Borredan. I don't know why I waited for it, but I did. The stars winked again, giving me the feeling that the warning I'd felt earlier was actually real.

"How long have we been in line?" I asked my sister. I have never been skilled at estimating time.

"Only about an hour," Tsisana said, her face dimly illuminated by the pretty lanterns hanging from the trees. The orange glow was steady for there was hardly a breeze in the woods now to disturb their suspension. I thanked the gods for that. It had been a relatively mild evening, but once the sun had set, the temperature had dropped with it.

I pulled my golden silk shawl tighter, hopelessly fighting the growing chill that came from the higher elevation. The colony was nestled between the mountainside and the thick forest, likely shielded from the sun at any time of day. I could sympathize with a people who were sensitive to sunlight. The Sun God Himself knew very well how badly I could burn. I allowed myself a moment of vulnerability, briefly fantasizing about living here with a spouse. Yes, I'd very much like that.

The night and trees blocked most of my view of the broad stone castle, but I could see that it was still in the process of being constructed. It was also nerve-racking to see it built into the mountainside. What if there was an avalanche or an earthquake? Did they have witches assisting them to protect against such things? Perhaps the fae?

I sighed as pain brought me back to the line. The closer I got to the front of it, the more I began to fidget in discomfort. My lower back and legs were already exhausted from the days spent traveling here, and I was thinking more about eventually finding a place to sit than finding a spouse.

The black-and-gold dress wasn't particularly comfortable either. My sister had tied the middle too tight, and the skirts were heavy. I'd been naive about the time I'd spend in this dress, not realizing it'd actually become taxing.

"Yes, they're a little cumbersome after a while, aren't they?" Tsisana muttered from behind me, and I turned my head to catch her adjusting her top. The royal-blue fabric did her bosom justice as she put her cleavage on proud display. I sighed and turned away, wishing I had her confidence. I tried not to think of the names I'd been called. I didn't need my brain to remind me of all the proof I had that people wanted to see as little of my skin as possible.

"This is weird," I murmured, discomforted with seeing my sister dressed up after all we'd been through. It was as though we were continuing to pretend that the last handful of years had never occurred. "I was a slave working for a doctor not long ago, and now I'm dressed as fancy as a dandy."

"At least you're not as foppish as one," my twin said with a laugh, smacking my arm to try to lighten my mood. I raised my brows and pressed my lips into a fake smile that fooled no one.

The line moved again, and when we came out from behind a colossal redwood tree, we could finally see the front of the line.

The female in front of us muttered to her friend, “Oh thank the gods. The end is nigh.” If I hadn’t been so out of sorts, I might have been visibly amused by her comment.

Seeing the entry to the event suddenly made it more real. This was happening. I bit my lower lip, took as deep of a breath as my dress allowed, and tried not to have another panic attack. I was here, my sister was here, and there was no turning back now. If I ran, she’d chase and curse me with something regrettable. I was certain of that. I didn’t want to risk her wrath for losing both our places in line… not when she had a chance to get male attention.

Out of nowhere, she took my arm in a bruising grip, nearly squeezing a yelp out of me. “Ouch! Tsisana! Why a—”

“Look!” she hissed, leaning into me while simultaneously yanking on my arm so we almost knocked heads. She nodded to the front of the line where bat-shifters were making guests sign in at multiple tables. A burly bat with dark brown hair, a delicate cleft chin, and shadowy, deep-set eyes had locked gazes with her. His pale face was fighting a strained expression, and his mouth was hanging agape. “Did he say what I think he said?” she whispered. “He mouthed something!”

“Tsisana… did he just recognize you?” I gasped, completely thrown off-kilter. My stomach clenched in pain, but I was far too distracted to pay attention to it.

“Oh, he’s leaving!” she lamented, talking over me and sounding… nigh devastated. I started in surprise when she moved to run after him, but I succeeded in grabbing her.

“No, no, no, no!” I hissed, wrapping my arms around her waist before she could take a second running step. I yanked her back into the line, my face heating up from the wild, creative profanity streaming from her mouth. “You need to stay in line to get in! Shh! You’re making a scene! Be patient!”

She calmed after trying to buck me off a couple times. We were well matched, and she knew I could probably tire her out before she could escape. I tentatively took my remaining hand off her, apologized profusely to the alarmed people behind us, and gave my sister an assessing stare. She blew a strand of hair from her blushing face and shoved it behind an ear with an impatient hand. She was scowling now, and it was honestly scaring me a little.

"What was that?" I asked in a severe tone. The question was largely unnecessary, but I gawked at her all the same as we took another step forward to keep pace with the line.

"I think..." she stammered, fumbling for words. This behavior was so unlike her.

"He recognized you?" I inquired once more. "Was that what he'd mouthed? That was... quick! We haven't even gotten inside yet!" A short, nervous laugh burst from my lips, and I embraced it to hide the pain in my heart. I wasn't jealous. I wasn't envious. Good for my sister. This was good. This was a good thing! I pressed my lips into a thin line as the people ahead of and behind us in line congratulated her.

Tsisana was just babbling now, and I could barely keep up with half of what was radiating from her mouth. "K-Keid, I hadn't expected this. I thought tonight was just fun. I thought it'd just be fun, you know? Just a night out with my sister. Maybe find someone for a casual time while I'm at it. No big deal. Nothing serious, you know? Tonight was about you, Keid. You and me, reunited and celebrating. We were gonna just find you a man an—"

"I guess you better go find him when we get in. I wonder why he ran?" I asked, interrupting her never-ending speech as I stood on my tiptoes to see if I could spy him nearby. Maybe he hadn't gone far. If I focused on this, I wouldn't feel the pain of not being the one recognized. I didn't want to feel pain over something so stupid.

"He looked scared! Maybe he thought he needed to change so he could meet me inside..." she considered, putting a finger to her pondering lips. "He can't run from me," she added with a shaky grin.

I tried to focus on relaxing, realizing that her colossal discovery might actually take some pressure off of me. If my sister spent the whole night with this male, she wouldn't be around to push me at people. I could just go hide by the banquet table and wait for dawn.

I worried at my lip again, staring at the dirt, needles, and crushed bark under my feet. After all this, I was still convinced I'd leave tonight with an empty-handed heart. It just felt like such a… fact. I checked in with my emotions and verified that my assessment wasn't being fed by a significant amount of depression. My relatively calm heart was pretty accepting of my assumption. I was ready for disappointment. The math was sound. The odds of both of us finding someone tonight were infinitely low.

My sister was practically vibrating by the time we arrived at the front of the line, and I wasn't certain that she'd completely absorbed all the warnings we were given. Some of them had been rather shocking, and I repeated them over and over to my glassy-eyed sister when we were finally allowed entry.

As soon as we stepped foot onto the recognition grounds, my sister broke into a run, disappearing into the growing, raucous crowd of humans and shifters. The sights, smells, and sounds immediately oppressed me. I'd suddenly found myself completely alone, and I scampered over to a redwood tree, fearful. I thought I'd wanted her gone, but now I desperately wanted my sister back.

My fingers dug into the flaky bark, and I felt a little faint as my eyes took in the sea of people. My brain had pretty much stopped working, and I was unable to find the steeled, conditioned person I'd become over the last six years. I couldn't even get my analytical brain to work as I struggled to pick up on the little cues that told me who was what species. In that moment, all I knew was that I was surrounded by gorgeous females, stunning women, strapping men, and intimidating males, all looking their very best. I clutched my shawl tighter, feeling an intense urge to cry as I slid behind the tree.

Memories came unbidden to me, and I blinked hard in an attempt to scatter them. I placed a fist on my chest, trying to will my heart to slow and my breathing to even, but everything was mutinying. Too many times I'd been put in this situation.

Too many times I'd been in crowds and felt both exposed and invisible. It was one thing to not be noticed, but to be stared at like a novelty, then rejected was a different kind of pain. It made me feel like an object instead of a person.

Could I risk looking at someone's face? Could I handle it now?

Why was this so accursedly difficult? My life had been on the line for years, and though I had a greater perspective now because of my time with the lions, being at parties still had me quaking. It made no sense. It had no reason!

I fought the compulsion to run and took deep breaths until I could form a plan. I needed steps. Steps were simple. I could do steps. I could do one thing at a time. What did I need right now? I needed my sister. Where'd she gone? I peeked around the tree and scanned for where she'd disappeared—just to the right of the farthest banquet table.

I braced myself against the tree with a palm, then forced myself to stand straight and square my shoulders. I picked up my skirts, hating that I couldn't see my feet, and carefully walked out from under the tree to stride in the direction my sister had run. I kept my eyes straight ahead and didn't look at any faces. If I didn't see them, I wouldn't feel that spark of terror. If I didn't see them, I wouldn't know if they were staring.

*I couldn't be that strange, could I?* I debated with myself, knowing exactly what phase of tonight I was experiencing. This was the part where I started second-guessing how repulsive I really was. That was usually when I prematurely let my guard down, right before I'd get humiliated. Now, I was moving into the phase of overanalyzing, which was usually right before I started spiraling.

I couldn't afford to spiral—especially not here and definitely not now.

I meandered forward until the crowd thinned, but I still couldn't find Tsisana. I blushed furiously when I started hearing some telling noises farther out in the lantern-lit woods. It seemed like some of the guests had gone off with a partner in search of privacy, and I hesitated, not wanting to walk in on anyone's intimate moment. I brushed a bead of sweat from my brow, the droplet from nerves and not the temperature.

I almost tripped when I thought I heard my sister's voice but not in a manner I was used to hearing. Concerned, I followed it, but I couldn't tell if I'd be walking in on something I should stop or not. Considering the warnings we'd gotten, I just wanted to make sure she was ok.

I turned around a corner to find my twin pushed up against a tree, mashed into it by the bat-shifter we'd seen earlier. I choked on a shriek and ducked behind the redwood. They were clothed, but with how they were fumbling at each other, it didn't look like it was going to stay that way…

"A-are you ok, Tsi—" I shouted out to her, but she interrupted me.

"Get out of here, Keid!" The yell was at the very top of her lungs. Yup, she was fine.

"I'm sorry! I'm sorry!" I ran back to where most of the people were gathered, wishing I could just disappear forever. Oh gods, why had I done that? Why'd I have to look for her? Was I that pathetic that I couldn't handle being alone at a party? I cringed in embarrassment and was only more horrified when tears blurred my vision.

Food. Eating food was something I could do to pass the time. I slowed and approached a table covered in delicacies. Yes, this would be a good distraction. I grabbed a plate of fine porcelain and filled it with appetizers and little desserts, knowing that I probably looked quite gluttonous. It wasn't that I was hungry—in fact, I was extremely nauseous now—I just knew that the more food I had to eat and the slower I went, the more it made sense for me to be seen not interacting with anyone.

I moved to a nearby tree and focused completely on my pile of treats, not daring to look elsewhere. The party was growing quite loud, and voices filled the air in celebrating recognitions between fated mate after fated mate. I did, however, hear the occasional tussle. Some bats were reacting too strongly—as we'd been warned—and I witnessed firsthand how their own people had to restrain them.

When I noticed my hands shaking, I stopped and questioned everything. What was I doing? I was losing control here. I should leave. I'd already made a complete idiot of myself. Curses, I was spiraling already. I missed myself. This wasn't who I was anymore, was it?

That was when I heard the only thing that could stop my spiraling—Ferrer's voice.

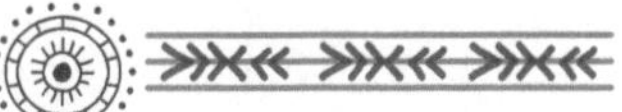
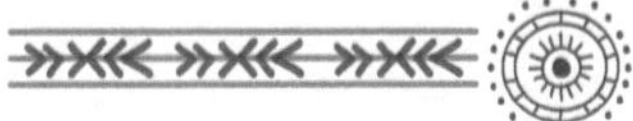

# Chapter 4

## Ferrer

"If you're not careful, Ettor, these woods are going to become home to an orgy," I snapped at my peer as I yanked a wolf-shifter off a she-bat. He'd been grinding her into one of the banquet tables, and some nearby humans weren't looking too pleased by their public… courtship.

*Feel free to join one,* Iron piped in crankily, as frustrated as me. I hadn't had a lot of time to perform my own search for my mate, having been constantly interrupted to deal with one issue after another. I thought I'd scented her once, but it faded as fast as I'd discovered it, so I shrugged it off as my imagination being a mischievous bastard.

"Go someplace private!" I roared into the new couple's faces, sending them off with a violent gesture. They didn't have to be told twice. I stared in disgust and amazement as the wolf slung the she-bat over his shoulder and ran like he was chasing the blood moon. "These other shifters—always carrying females. You notice that, Ettor? It's like they think they can't walk for thems—" I said, then realized that he'd wandered off, and I was talking to myself. "Shittin' stars. Could've warned a bat."

I rubbed my brow as I scanned the crowd one more time, relieved to see nothing else requiring my immediate intervention. Some of us bats were on the alert, but I was dismayed to see that others were too distracted to keep an eye out for misbehavior. The peer-regulation wasn't as active as I'd hoped.

Still, maybe the worst was over for now. We'd made some good examples, and separating several mates temporarily seemed to sober a number of individuals… to some extent. We left alone any pair that made an effort to find privacy. There really was only so much we could do.

I blew out a held breath and coughed on my next inhale. I had no idea how so many were able to find their mates in the pool of aromata. It was like I was wading through a fog of sweat and pheromones. The scents of excited wolves, cats, dragons, lycans, and humans all seemed to melt into one cloying mist. Then there was the food that was laid out on the tables. Roasted meats and freshly baked desserts announced their own presence as potently as a musky dog.

*Come on, let's look!* Iron hollered, losing his patience. *Stop worrying about everyone else! You're not the only coronel!*

The tiny bastard was right. I sighed and went to find a small section of personal space by a tree to free my wings. My back was aching incessantly now, and I couldn't tolerate it anymore. I slowly grew them out and craned my neck to see if they were lining up with the slits in my shirt, but of course they weren't. I frowned and tried to adjust it, but it was like trying to scratch an itch I couldn't reach. I gave up with an irritated growl and put my wings away, accepting that I'd just have to deal with the discomfort.

I took in a deep, calming breath, then released it. I took in a second, willing my muscles to grow lax. After I took in a third, I found her.

I found her.

*Mate!* Iron screamed. His presence flapping wildly in my head. *Left! Left! Go left, you son of a backed-up blood clot! Go left!*

My head snapped in that direction, and I forced my way past dozens of bodies. I pushed through the thick crowd of humans and shifters, ignoring complaints as I followed the faintest, sweet scent of birch. I knew there was more to her aroma, the scent incomplete through the fog of hundreds of people, and I couldn't wait to bury my face in her neck. I couldn't wait to breathe all of her into my lungs. I couldn't wait to taste her sweet flavor on my tongue. I swore I'd die if I spent one more second away from her.

When her scent thickened, I slowed down a little. The birch sweetness had been joined by something earthy. I swallowed hard, telling myself that she was probably just standing near a witch.

*What do you think she is?* I asked my bat as I pushed through the crowd, my heart starting to pump from mild fear instead of excitement. *Wolf? Dragon?*

*I hope dragon so we can fly together,* Iron said hesitantly, distracted by the same thing that was bothering me.

*Yes, that'd be nice... wouldn't it?* I tried to imagine a sultry she-dragon waiting for me. By the stars, I was so ready for her. I was so ready for love, for sex, and for tying my soul to another forever.

*You bloody r-romantic,* Iron teased half-heartedly.

I grew uneasy as the earthy aroma became sickly sweet. No... no, no, no. Impossible. "You're not getting away from me this time," I growled loudly, pushing my fear away and focusing on the birch part of the scent.

I finally nudged my way past two conversing humans to find a woman standing by herself, staring down at her plate like it was a mirror. I slowed to a shamble as I faced my worst nightmare. This couldn't be her.

I gazed past her, looking desperately for another figure. Perhaps there was someone on the other side of the tree? My stomach lurched as my senses made their final confession. There was no one else.

The woman stilled but didn't look up, not even as I took a deadened step toward her. Though I stared her up and down, my horror and shock blurred my vision. Was this what the Moon Goddess had chosen to give me? Now that I was within feet of her, I could finally discern the subtlest hint of rot. That had been the source of the sweetness. Had the Moon Goddess given me a young rot-witch? This had to be a sick joke. Was Luzia playing some kind of disgusting prank? If so, I didn't know how she did it, but this was going too far.

My nose wrinkled and my lips curled up in instinct-driven revulsion. I could barely tolerate the smell. The last rot-witch I'd seen had decomposed before my very eyes, and that had been bloody traumatizing. To imagine a future with such a creature, to grow old with such a creature, it made me want to vomit. The humans couldn't seem to smell it, but it was no wonder that the other shifters had given her a wide berth.

The witch finally looked up and met my eyes, but again, I could barely see her through my spiraling mind. A cold came over me—a chill so thorough it settled into the marrow of my bones. I shook my head slowly at this manipulative, deceptive creature, telling her without words that she was not my desire. My eyes fell on a glint of silver near the bottom of her gown. It was a grey hair. She was a young rot-witch, and she was already greying? How much longer would she live?

"How could they have possibly let you in?" I asked in a low voice, speaking mostly to myself.

The woman flinched at my words, her face reddening in response. Aside from the trembling in her hands, she didn't move. She was frozen in her spot like a helpless animal, which was a laugh. This creature was anything but defenseless. I was there when one manipulated an entire regiment of fae. No, this was a bloody farce.

"You make every other witch here seem like a gods-given prize," I seethed, and the people around me quieted, finally noticing what was happening. How had no one escorted this creature out of here? How had they allowed our mortal enemy to sneak past our defenses? Rot-witches had cursed us into what we were today! They were the reason we were forced to drink blood! Clotting, vile, disgusting, gods-forsaken blood!

"Ferrer?" Luzia's voice called out as she approached the scene of my humiliation. I could barely scent Ettor through the reek of rot, but I could tell he had joined us as well.

"What is that smell?" He gagged, then said, "Oh... What in the..."

"Someone get an escort!" I yelled off to the side, nearly screaming the order in my state of near madness. "Get this out of here!" Against my instincts, I took a step toward her, our kind's mortal enemy. I leaned forward, needing her to know that she couldn't fool me. Her kind must have known she was my mate and sent her to get into our territory. That had to be it. She'd just been able to sneak in with the other witches, probably when Borredan was distracted by his own discovery. I knew we shouldn't have invited them.

"She's young..." Ettor murmured to Luzia. "We've never seen one this young. That must be why the rot is barely discernible. Should we kill her?"

"I..." Luzia faltered, sounding uncharacteristically uncertain.

Castanon, another coronel, must have joined us because he whispered, "I don't feel comfortable killing any young thing, even if it is our enemy. Let her go. She got no information from us. We just got here. There are no secrets to find. If this evil thing returns, then we'll kill her."

The more everyone spoke about her, the more I boiled over with fury, but I couldn't say what it was that triggered me so. I took several fast breaths, building up to the worst moment of my life. My bat had gone silent, knowing what was coming. He curled up in the shadows of my mind like a dying spider, devastated.

I opened my mouth and forced the words out in a yell. "I, Ferrer Galvan, rej—" My throat closed up, and I couldn't finish the sentence. The rot-witch looked more horrified by the second, and in half a heartbeat, tears trickled down her face. Why in the name of the Sky Gods was she crying? I guessed she realized she'd failed her mission. May her rotten coven have mercy on her.

I tried again, nearly hyperventilating as I fought to get the necessary words out of my mouth. "I reject y—"

"Ferrer, wait! Let's th—" Luzia interrupted, and Ettor's hand clamped over my mouth. My eyes flew wide in disbelief as my fellow coronel censored my rejection. I lashed out and elbowed him in the gut. The rot-witch dropped her plate, and the shattering distracted me enough for Luzia to wrap her arm around my neck, attempting a headlock.

I didn't know who they were because I was swaddled in madness and heartbreak, but several more bats got their hands on me, which just made me more violent in turn. How dared they interfere? This was my business! How could they judge me for what any of them would do? This wasn't even a normal witch! This was the enemy! Never once had they done any species any good!

My wings shot out of my back but tangled painfully in my shirt. I screamed in agony, my bat's voice joining mine in my head. Everything hurt, but the true pain was coming from my soul, which felt like it'd been brutally stabbed by the goddess who'd received all of my devotion. How could She do this to me? I'd been practically pious! Was this punishment for how I envied others finding their mates? Was jealousy the one thing She wouldn't tolerate? Perhaps I failed Her in some other way?

I barely heard Castanon yell, "Get her out of here!" and Luzia's headlock became a chokehold. As I fell into a sweet, blissful black void, my last thoughts were a prayer to the Sky Gods asking for this to be the very last time I closed my eyes. That way, I'd never have to face how I'd actually loathed making my fated mate cry, rot-witch or not.

Nothing… nothing in my life could have prepared me for this moment.

There was no happiness in Ferrer's approach. There was no joy or lust, and yet I knew by how he stood at my side that I was his fated mate. They had told us humans didn't feel it strongly, and it was often mistaken for infatuation, but I was able to connect all the facts. There was no denying the sudden pull I felt from his proximity. As I stared at my plate in fear, I felt the same thrill I'd felt when I first heard his voice, but I knew it'd be short-lived. His tone radiated nothing but rage and disgust.

I knew he didn't like witches, but his vitriol threw me into shock. It was more horrifying than someone threatening to remove my hand and felt far more traitorous than a false lover. No, it was worse because under all the numbness, I could tell that the pain was going to be everywhere—my body, my heart, and my soul. I'd never thought it was possible to feel my own soul, but I could tell that the bruises were already forming, and like bludgeoned skin, I needed but time to see it.

When he came through the crowd, I thought I'd be excited to see what he looked like, but had I known the cost of him seeing me… I would've run. I should have run. I just hadn't anticipated that he'd been looking for me, of all people. Though… I supposed running would have been pointless. There was no outrunning a shifter, but maybe I could have at least reached a place without a crowd.

I also shouldn't have looked at him, oh gods, but Fate had dragged my eyes up to lock onto his. I'd been frozen, stupidly excited to see his face, but then I was trapped under his furious scrutiny. If anyone's eyes had ever felt heavy before, his were like an anchor, ripping me under the waves and dragging me into the deep, dark below.

I couldn't possibly be underwater though, because I could feel my tears wetting my cheeks. In between shouts and orders, and over the void of the crowd's collective silence, I could hear the droplets hit my broken plate. I felt bad about breaking it, but that had nothing on my heart. I thought it'd been broken before, but it turned out that I didn't know what broken meant until now.

We were too different, and I couldn't process how I'd been picked for him. It turned out that Ferrer was roguishly gorgeous, and I should have known from his voice alone that he'd be too attractive for the likes of me. There was no way I could've competed for his attention had I not been a witch. If he was forced to stick with me, I bet he'd always have someone on the side.

Despite being furious and off-kilter, he moved with a beauty that suited him—a hypnotizing grace. And even though he was slightly leaner than a lion, he still appeared powerful, lithe, and just as lethal. Whatever was odd about him was beautiful too. He had strange thick white streaks in his dark taupe locks that didn't seem to be from age, just like my entire head of hair, and I was curious about them. They definitely weren't grey hairs.

But I'd never know. I'd never know anything about him because he was rejecting me—rejecting me with the force of a deadly curse. In front of everyone, he'd given me the answer to a question I'd have never dared ask.

"You make every other witch here seem like a gods-given prize," he'd said. He'd practically announced my condition disgusted him, and for some reason, I couldn't shut down my emotions. It was brutal. It should have let me turn to stone, but I couldn't. I didn't know why my mind cruelly decided to block my one mental escape. My body was on fire from humiliation, and I couldn't even seek the simple solace of a locked heart. It was almost as heartless as Ferrer's words.

I thought I was going to faint from them, but despite my fuzzy vision and nausea, I unfortunately stayed upright and conscious. It was a good thing I was crying because I could hardly blink in my wide-eyed despair. I actually couldn't do much at all. I was almost a statue, and as much as I willed my joints to move, they only threatened to collapse in their duress. If I moved, I feared I'd fall apart just like the old rot-witch. Before Ferrer's own kind had tackled him, he had certainly looked at me like I was one.

But move I must. That was what one of the bats had said. They'd ordered me out like a stray. I tore my eyes from Ferrer's fainting body, envious that he was the one who'd been knocked out instead of me. I'd throw all the gold in the world at someone to put me into that same black sleep.

Several bat-shifters coming out of the crowd gave me the motivation I needed to stumble into my first step. Sharp fear got my other foot moving, and it wasn't long before I was rushing toward the exit. One of the shifters would occasionally snap at me when I got confused and went in the wrong direction, which made me all the more embarrassed. I didn't know what they expected from me. I'd only been here once!

The farther I got from the scene of my emotional demise, the more confused the partygoers seemed to be. Murmurs filled the too-quiet woods as I rushed, and the eyes grew heavier with every passing heartbeat. I couldn't look at any faces. I'd made the brutal error of looking into Ferrer's earlier. I'd never forget it. That had been my biggest mistake besides coming here altogether.

My nerves buzzed as if a nest of wasps had settled under my skin, growing more frantic the longer it took to leave. My flat shoes slipped on some bark and detritus, nearly making me trip. This escape felt like it was taking an eternity. Would I ever get out of here? Perhaps this was a nightmare.

A sob of relief flew from my lips when I spotted the table where they were still letting in guests, and I ran. I shot out past the paper-shuffling bat-shifters and raced in the opposite direction of the line, not capable of being within anyone's eyesight. I had to escape the eyes, so I went toward the darkness.

Everything bubbled to the surface now that I was freed from faces, and the footsteps of the bats following had long since stopped. I let out a shrieking sob, screamed at the top of my lungs, and lost control of my lungs. I fell into hyperventilating. Nothing could have prepared me for that encounter. Nothing!

I cried and cried as I was sucked deeper into a dark pit of black emotions. I didn't know what I was doing or where I was going. My mind was blank, and all I could do was feel. My stomach was a twisted mess, my lungs were iced over from my rapid inhales, and my heart… oh gods, my heart!

He hadn't wanted me. He was from an endangered species… and yet I was still the last person in the world he wanted. I barked out a crazed, heartbroken laugh. If only he knew.

But I thought I'd try anyway. Tsisana had been accepted! When I saw how that other shifter embraced my sister… I thought… I thought that maybe… A strange, choked, grieving noise tumbled from my lips. I'd thought wrong. I'd been so mistaken.

When my encumbering dress snagged on a stump, it slowed my body and mind enough to come to the present. What was I doing?

Looking around, I swallowed heavily. Confusion was muddying my ability to think about the simplest things. What did I need to do now? I needed to find where my sister and I had stashed our bags. Where in the blazes had we left them?

I panicked when I forgot the spell we'd set up before leaving, and I turned in circles, worrying at my dress with sweat-soaked fingers. When panic started crawling into my numb brain, I stopped and slapped myself in the face—hard. After that, I just stood for a while, laboring for breath in the dark, focusing solely on the vibrating stinging in my cheek. I let out a crumbling exhale when my body slowed from its rush, but it took another handful of minutes for my memory to peek out from its shelter.

When I was ready and could remember how to do it, I set off my half of the spell on my arm and ran in the direction of my belongings. When I started crying again, it was different. It was the world-weary, bone-deep crying of complete and utter exhaustion.

Despair also did not assist in my mobility. The third time I tripped on my dress, I screeched and started yanking it off. I fumbled at the ties, and I ended up ripping the delicate fabric in my haste to remove it. When I pulled it over my head, I screamed again and ripped at where it'd torn, wanting to show the accursed garment how much pain I was in and how much I hated myself.

I choked on another sob and threw it into the dirty forest floor, now half naked and not giving a single shit. I spun around and continued running, accepting how wretchedly cold I was. Who cared if I got sick? I certainly didn't.

When I reached my belongings, I threw on my normal clothes and swung my bag onto my back. A grimace trembled on my face as I stared at my twin sister's bag. I tried desperately not to hate the only person I loved. It wasn't her fault that, after a lifetime of her being pretty enough to go from man to man, she'd now found someone who would love her the way I'd always deeply and desperately craved.

I wiped away more tears as they streamed down my face, utterly devastated. Would she be embarrassed when she found out what happened—that her sister was rejected by a male of an endangered species? Would she say anything? What would my coven say? Would they be surprised at all? Did I care if they were surprised?

Suddenly, a heavy fatigue tried to pull me down to the ground. I leaned against a redwood and braced myself with a palm to let my tears fall silently. There was no way I could show my face again, and I realized that, right now, I was saying my final goodbye to my sister. I squatted down and grabbed her bag, riffling through it until I found the pen and paper she kept. I left the short note just inside her bag, on the very top so it'd be the first thing she saw when she opened it.

It made sense for us to part ways here. It likely would have happened anyway. There'd be no more traveling for her if this was where her future spouse had to stay. We wouldn't know what to say to each other, and this would save her the pain of not knowing how to comfort me. It always killed her when she didn't know how to ease my pain, and this time, it wasn't possible. He'd taken one look at me and…

Even though I stood slowly, a head rush tipped me to the side. I caught myself on a tree and took three deep breaths. This was it. I stared sadly at her belongings as I started putting distance between her bag and me. My destination was anywhere but the bat-shifters and the coven, so I checked the stars and turned northeast. I'd met a couple dragons during the end of my stay at the cat-shifters' castle. The cats…

There was another pang in my heart at the thought of the cats. Niusha had tried so hard to help me. I couldn't return to tell them of my failure, and there was no way I was spending the rest of my life in the castle where I'd been enslaved, so I forced my thoughts back to the dragons.

Perhaps I could apply for citizenship in their kingdom, find a little town to settle in, and do some witchwork? Everyone could always use a witch. The idea should have sounded good, but it didn't. Nothing sounded good, but I needed a direction. If I died on the way there from an animal attack, injury, or illness… well, so be it. I wouldn't try hard to fight it.

So, I began my journey with the stars as my guide. I couldn't tell how much time had passed, but after a while, I started smelling something familiar. Instead of repelling me, it tugged at me. Gods knew why, but something about it lifted my spirits. Perhaps I'd gone insane, but I chose to follow the gross aroma, moving like an old dog who couldn't smell anymore.

Fortunately, the old witch was terrible at hiding, and it wasn't long before I caught sight of her campfire smoke. I would have smiled had my heart not been in the process of rotting like the damp firewood she'd chosen to use.

# Chapter 5

## Ferrer

*Someone's at the door...* Iron mumbled helpfully, but I didn't know what he was going on about because I certainly didn't hear anything.

Another minute or two passed before I did hear something, but it wasn't knocking. I thought someone was slapping at the door. Not sure why they were assaulting it like that, unless it'd done something unsavory. I'd never known a door to grope a person.

*Would you please, for the sake of all the stars in the sky, get that?*

"Try harder," a voice at the door said.

Harder? Why would slapping a door har—

"Ah!" I shouted, slapped straight out of slumber. My hand shot to my stinging face, and I glared up at my assailant. Castanon rose from his squat before me, frowning for a reason I couldn't discern. "Shittin' bloody stars! Castanon, what is your problem?"

"You mean, 'what is our problem?'" he asked, offering a hand to help me up. Despite my wounded pride, I accepted his assistance because my inner ear was saying I'd been slapped more than once.

"How many times did you hit me? Bloody stars…" I placed a hand to my head and shook it.

"Enough to wake you, but not enough to satisfy our irritation," Luzia piped up from behind the male with the short tan hair. Castanon was the same species as me, but the white streaks in his hair were barely noticeable.

"With wh—" I started saying, then I recalled what'd occurred. I shut my mouth, speechless, and resisted the urge to rub my aching chest. My mood plummeted as more memories trickled in slowly, but it didn't matter… I already felt like dying.

I took note of the bats around me, suddenly wary. They'd apparently taken me to the Palaver on the first floor of the castle, the circular room we coronels used to discuss colony matters. I noted that only a couple coronels were here, and I was surprised to see that Ettor was missing. It was unfortunate because I had a handful of choice words for him. I also had a handful ready for his face, and it was called my fist.

"Why did you all stop me? You would have done the same," I growled at everyone and took a seat at the round table. The others settled, but before anyone could answer me, the door opened to reveal Ettor… and Borredan, of all people. I wrinkled my nose at the scent of a female witch on him. There was no need to ask what he'd been up to tonight. Guess he didn't reject her after all.

Ettor took a seat, but Borredan walked straight up to me and said, "Sorry." I opened my mouth to ask him why he was apologizing, but he immediately slapped my face.

"Stars!" I recoiled and rubbed my abused cheek. "What the shit?" I eyed Borredan as he grabbed a chair and crossed his arms, excessively grumpy.

"That was a message from her sister, my mate," he rumbled, not looking at all sorry.

I sent an alarmed look to the other coronels, who didn't appear surprised by this bit of news. "Tell me you kicked her out as well," I blurted, aghast.

"Do you smell rot on me?" Borredan asked with a touch of attitude in his tone. I bristled at how he'd asked it, but I faltered when his question sank into my thick skull. No, I didn't.

"Rot-witches… are they born that way or is the rot-witchery learned?" Luzia asked, tilting her chair back precariously. "Perhaps her sister is one, but she isn't?"

"I don't think we know enough about them," Ettor said.

Castanon rested his chin on his fist, deep in thought. "What does her sister have to say about it? Assuming she can be trusted, of course."

"What does it matter?" I interrupted, not wanting to discuss the topic anymore. "I needed to reject her. I don't want to be mated to a bloody rot-witch!" I snarled and leaned forward to show a fang. "You had no right interfering in my private matter."

"Rejection is something we've never discussed. I can't even think of an instance in our history where one was rejected. They're so precious," Ettor stated in a far-off voice as if searching his memories.

"That's because we faced a shortage of potential mates as our population declined," I argued. "There are plenty of others we can mate with now. We're not desperate. We have the luxury of being picky. Besides, we've deemed it acceptable for those of us to mate with a chosen if fateds weren't found. Do I not have that option as well? Are you saying you're going to force me to mate with her?" I slammed my fist down on the table, furious. "She's. A. Rot. Witch!"

"Stars, you're always so dramatic, Ferrer," Luzia drawled, rocking in her chair. "Not at all, but it all happened too fast for comfort since it's practically never happened before. Do we know that rejection has the same effect on us as it does on other shifters? A mate dying can kill you."

"Not after rejection," I pointed out to her.

"I don't think he's being dramatic, really. I don't think any of us could tolerate having a rot-witch mate," Castanon interrupted before Luzia could release whatever nonsense was on her tongue.

"But that's not the only thing we have to discuss. I did notice something when Ferrer was busy shouting at her, and fortunately, Borredan was able to help me with it," Ettor said, and gestured to the aforementioned bat.

Borredan dropped a burlap sack onto the table and slid it over to me. I raised my brows and looked at him, waiting for an explanation. Borredan glared at me as he started his report. "When my mate mentioned she'd left her bag in the woods, I offered to pick it up for her because it'd be quicker. I came across a torn gown that had the scent of rot on it, so I brought it back. I found it alarming. Her sister saw it and lost her wits. It's her sister's dress! She's scared out of her mind for her twin."

I didn't like the thought of the dress being torn, but, with a great deal of effort, I dismissed it. What did I care if a rot-witch was attacked? They were all evil creatures.

Then I realized what was in the bag. "Why in the bloody skies are you shoving this shit at me, Borredan? Is this the dress? I don't want to smell her for the second time tonight. Are you mad?" I pushed the bag back across the table, but Borredan threw it at me this time. I growled when I caught it. "What's your point? Great gods!"

"We took a closer look, and we noticed that the only thing that smelled like rot was a single hair on it," Ettor explained calmly, and Luzia nodded along obnoxiously. They all stared at me, waiting for me to come to some realization. I opened the sack and didn't smell any rot coming from it.

"Before putting it in the bag, we removed the hair and whatever fabric touched it," Castanon informed, leaning back in his chair and crossing his arms. He stared at the bag in my arms as I pulled out a sleeve. I didn't need to bring it to my nose to understand.

"She wore this," I murmured. "The whole thing should smell like rot..."

"Exactly!" Borredan exclaimed, pounding the table with his fist. "And now my mate's twin is somewhere out there, possibly injured, because you got rash!" His face flushed with anger, one shade above murderous.

"But why was that hair on her to begin with?" I asked, bewildered but annoyed that he was missing that important fact. "Does that not seem suspicious to you?"

"It definitely does," Castanon agreed and glanced over at Borredan.

I continued, adding to my own point. "Your mate could be lying if she's covering up some kind of relationship her sister has with rot-witches."

"She's not lying!" he roared in outrage and knocked his chair over as he stood. Simultaneously, there was a pounding on the door, and Ettor jumped up to see who was causing the ruckus. When he opened the door, a witch stormed in, livid, and another snuck in quietly behind her. I could tell that the first one was Borredan's mate. They smelled strongly of each other.

"How dare you accuse me of lying!" she yelled at the room, scrutinizing every face. "Which one of you assholes said that?"

Like the traitorous bastard he was, Borredan pointed right at me. I dipped my head in annoyance and turned to face the furious witch. She was a tall brunette with an assortment of natural trinkets woven into her hair and looked very much the part of a protective sister. I wanted to ask if she was an identical twin, but I was too ashamed to admit that I could barely recall what her sister looked like. The scent of rot and my rage had mostly blinded me. My memories were simply too foggy to help.

"How in the world did you hear that? This room is supposed to be soundproof," Castanon asked, furrowing his brows in confusion and displeasure.

"Don't underestimate witches," she spat.

"Woo!" Luzia interjected. "Borredan, you've got a shootin' star! Good luck chasing her around."

"For gods' sakes, grow up, Luzia. Now's not the time," he reprimanded, scrubbing a hand over his face.

"Did you ask about a search?" the witch asked her mate, and Borredan shook his head.

"We haven't gotten to that yet."

"And which one is Ferrer? I never got a chance to see what his ugly mug looks like!"

I laughed at that, gods knew why. Perhaps I was going a little mad. On top of everything else, I was extremely tired and hungry from fasting.

Luzia, the other traitorous bastard, pointed at me in answer to the witch's question. I tilted my head and asked the witch, "I don't think I got your name."

"I don't think you think at all!" she retorted, still fuming. "It's Tsisana! Look, if you're not going to take responsibility for your stupidity and send a search party, I'm leaving right now to look for her!"

"I think we need to find her for interrogation," Castanon asserted with a grim expression.

Tsisana gaped. "You cannot be serious! She's done nothing wrong!"

Castanon tilted his head to give her a severe, challenging look. "With all due respect, you're a stranger to us—in our territory. We do not owe you trust."

"Well, I want to find my sister! I just fucking got her back!" she yelled, her face flushing red as tears trickled down her cheeks. Borredan stood and placed a firm hand on her shoulder, showing support. I gritted my teeth at the scene before me, annoyed for some reason.

"I think Ferrer should go get her," Luzia said, volunteering me.

"That is a terrible idea," Ettor said in complete rejection.

"Maybe he needs to learn to clean up his own messes. I don't see why anyone else should lose sleep over this stupid debacle." She glared at me.

I absolutely did not want to admit it, but I was anxious to find out why the dress was torn. I did not trust my fated, but the longer I sat with it, the harder it was to do nothing. I hated it, but it made me itchy to end this meeting.

"Fine. Just to shut you all up. I'll go," I said quickly.

"I don't trust him. Send someone with him," Tsisana barked, jabbing a finger in my direction.

"Fine. Ferrer, take two bats and leave," Castanon said in dismissal and glanced at the other coronels. "Agreed?"

"And don't reject her until we get her into interrogation. I don't want complications. Take her to the hospital if she's injured. If she dies before you can find her, return her body to her sister," Ettor added, and I sighed, slumping a little in my chair. These people would be the death of me.

And yet… something in my gut twisted painfully at his words.

"Also, who is this?" Castanon asked impatiently, pointing to the quiet witch. The woman fidgeted and inched back towards the door.

"That's Leilani," Tsisana said flatly. She seemed annoyed at the other woman's presence as well. "She's from my coven. Followed me in, and I almost told her no. Wanted to say something to Ferrer, but I don't know why she'd want to talk to that asshole." The twin shifted her weight to her other leg and crossed her arms. "Speak up, Leilani. Don't make me regret this."

The timid witch pushed her blond hair back and gazed demurely through her lashes at me. I sighed and waited for her to say her piece so I could leave. I caught my knee starting to bounce in impatience and stilled it.

"S-so, I was there when you recognized Keid. We grew up in the same coven," she started saying, and I almost stopped listening to her. I hadn't known her name was Keid. That was an odd name. "I-I just thought that you should know something about her if you decide t—"

"That is not yours to share!" Tsisana yelled, returning to fury in a heartbeat. She moved to the other witch and raised her hand to slap her, but Castanon yanked her away and nodded for Leilani to continue. "Don't you dare, Leilani! Leilani, no!"

"Let her speak or we'll remove you," Ettor said and gestured for her to hush. I frowned and turned my attention back to Leilani. I had a feeling I wasn't going to like this.

The blonde folded her hands in front of her and took a deep breath. "Since you're endangered, you have a right to know that sh—"

"Leilani, don't you dare, you bitch!"

"—e can't have children. She's barren."

My lips parted in surprise, not sure what to make of this. The entire table seemed to go quiet as everyone digested this piece of news. My head quirked to the side as I tried to make sense of what I was feeling. What was I feeling? I was going to reject her anyway. There was no doubt of rejection, especially if she was involved with rot-witches.

"That was not yours to share," Tsisana said in a trembling voice. I thought that she was livid at first from the waver in her tone, but when my eyes went to her, she looked absolutely crushed. "Why would you do that?"

Leilani's hands shook, like her nerves were starting to catch up to her. "I came here because I didn't want to go back to the coven. I wanted to start fresh, but I didn't f-find a fated." She gestured to me. "Keid can't give him children, but I could. If he stays with her, perhaps I could do that for him… that way she'd get to keep her fated ma—"

"You're a real nightmare," Tsisana said, her voice dripping with hurt and disgust. "You need help. I know you were in the prison with everyone else, but this was an unbelievably fucked-up thing to do."

The other witch pursed her lips and looked down at her feet. I couldn't tell what she was thinking. Gods, I didn't know what I was thinking.

"This is your personal business, Ferrer," Ettor said with a wave of his hand and got up from his chair. "I recommend you go start the search for Keid."

"Certainly wish you'd thought that about my rejection," I murmured and stood with the rest of them, still in shock. Leilani sent a hopeful glance my way, but I just strode past her without a word.

That wasn't how I'd planned my future. The gods knew… they knew how much I'd wanted a fated mate to breed and grow old with, and yet they'd chosen to give me a barren witch who conspired with the enemy. I simply couldn't fathom what the Moon Goddess had been thinking.

*She must have fancied a laugh,* Iron finally said, sounding as numb as I felt.

## Keid

When I stepped into her little campsite, the rot-witch didn't look particularly surprised to see me. Taken off guard by her calm gaze, I hesitated but held my hand up in a shy greeting all the same. I wasn't necessarily scared of her, but I didn't exactly trust her either. Did I trust her? Why was I here?

The witch quivered in her usual geriatric fashion and offered me a nigh toothless smile. Had she lost teeth since I last saw her? I supposed I shouldn't be surprised. Stars, it was impressive that she was still alive with all her limbs attached.

"I see you've made your way pretty far north," I enunciated in a gentle, clear voice. I had no idea if her hearing was fine or if it had long since departed, but I made it easy for her to read my lips regardless.

The witch began rocking back and forth from her seat on a soft, rotted log. It was odd how comfortable it looked if one didn't mind the fact that it was riddled with fungus and possibly mold. The old woman was obviously not bothered… as such rot was her lot.

I took the rocking as a nod and gestured to the opposite place by the fire, trying like mad not to gag from her smell. There just wasn't any getting used to it. "May I join you?"

The old woman continued rocking but opened her arms as if to offer a grandmotherly hug. I waved her off as I settled, which made her cackle. The rot-witch dropped her arms after delivering her joke, still chuckling wickedly. Though her eyes were slightly wild and red, they held genuine mirth.

"I see you trying me make me stink," I chastised half-heartedly, clinging to our conversation as a distraction. "Like how you smacked my bottom, you wicked creature. Don't you dare try that again."

The witch pouted and leaned over her cooking pot to stir something that looked positively revolting. I didn't stare too closely at it, having a feeling that it was probably just an entire animal dumped in boiling water, guts and all. It certainly wasn't helping me breathe, and I moved to be more upwind of both her and her dinner. My stomach was beginning to roil.

I wasn't just nauseous from the smell. The trauma of the night ate at my entire body, weakening it, painfully twisting it out of sorts. There was a sudden prod, and I looked down to find the witch poking my arm with a long stick. She tapped me a couple more times before stopping. I hadn't even realized my arm was shaking.

My eyes filled with tears.

"He didn't want me," I said through a sudden, bursting sob. I didn't look at the witch as I confessed the cause of my presence. "I'm so humiliated!" I broke down in front of her, drawing my knees up to my chin so I could hide my face.

I wailed for a while, destroying my throat and lungs, a sharp contrast to the silent witch. I hadn't exactly expected her to laugh or anything, but her lack of reaction almost made me feel like she'd known it was going to happen. I had no idea if rot-witches were able to scry. Perhaps she'd seen it in her disgusting soup.

When my head throbbed painfully, I forced myself to stop crying, and I groped around in my bag for my water canteen. I'd get a migraine if I kept this up, and I was already beyond miserable. I didn't need to be spending the rest of the night throwing up as well. The gods knew I wasn't that far from vomiting just from my proximity to the witch.

I fought to steady myself with a long drink of cold water, then I wiped my mouth and stoppered the canteen. I had to get it out. The night boiled like poison in my belly. "The bat-shifters were having an event to encourage recognition. They need mates, so they invited a number of unmated to attend. I…" I hesitated, feeling somewhat embarrassed for the reason I'd attended. Did I care if I sounded pathetic? No, I guessed I didn't.

"I was lonely," I confided and rested my cheek on my knees. "My sister convinced me that shifter mates were genuinely caring and completely faithful. I thought that if I had one out there somewhere, he'd accept me and see me as a person, not a condition." I glanced up at her and knitted my brows. "Should I not have gone? Was it wrong for me to seek out a mate when I'm barren?"

The witch began laughing, and I slumped, burying my head back into my knees. I tried not to take it personally, but it hurt. I could hear her slapping her legs as she choked on a gurgling cackle, and I sighed. "Yes, I know it's amusing. A barren being fated to an endangered male."

A follow-up giggle broke out of her one more time, but it calmed. I rubbed my swollen eyes in misery. "Truly though, was I wrong?" I asked again, but I was addressing the campfire this time because at this point, it was rhetorical. Yes, it had been wrong. "I shouldn't have let her convince me. Tsisana can be pretty convincing when she wants to be. I know they need mates… I just… I just thought that maybe one not being able to reproduce might not be a huge deal for them. And certainly there must be some who prefer their own sex, I would think. Maybe he'd be happy just to love me? Maybe he'd be happy just to have someone to love?"

I winced as I recalled Ferrer's expression. "I'm never going to forget that face, you know. That will be the last thing I see at night for the rest of my life." My stomach clenched from a wave of almost excruciating emotional pain. "You have no idea how much I just want to give up and die," I confessed honestly through fresh tears.

It took a few seconds, but dread settled in like frost on a cold morning, and I peeked up at her. Had I really just told a dying woman that I wanted to die? I was horrified. That had probably been the most insensitive thing I'd ever said in my life.

"I-I-I—" I stammered, completely unable to get a sentence out in apology. The witch just smirked and ladled some chunky soup into her mouth. I looked away as my body threatened to heave. Gods, why was I here? I sighed, tucked my head, and mumbled an apology into the dark of my knees. "I'm sorry… it hurts too much to have been born with multiple conditions. One was bad enough, but two? And everything else? It's like the gods specifically made me to not be anyone's spouse. I know I'm otherwise useful… I can do witchwork like the rest of them, but I crave love so badly!"

It was easier to talk into my knees, especially now that I knew I hadn't hurt her feelings. That smirk had said a lot. She didn't seem to care about any of this. I must look like such a young fool.

I calmed and finally my emotions rolled into a deadened state. "Are you still headed north?" I asked emptily, not sure if I cared or not. I didn't really care if she answered me because she likely wouldn't.

I turned my head a little as she nodded during her rocking. Huh. That was the closest to an answer I'd ever gotten out of her. It slightly grabbed my attention.

"How much farther?" I inquired, curious to see if she'd offer more information. The witch shrugged subtly, and my brows drew in confusion. "Well," I informed, "we're a little ways northeast of the bat colony…" I scratched my brow as I stared at her, not sure if that'd help. I mean, I didn't know how it would. I hadn't even heard of the bat-shifters before the lions' occupation and my coven's imprisonment. All of this was new.

The witch motioned weakly with a hand, pushing at the air several times as if to say she still had a long ways to go. "Days?" I asked. "Weeks?" She only shrugged. I hesitated before my next question, not sure how else to word it. "Are you going home to be with family… before you pass away?"

It was the first time I saw her looking anxious, and I cursed myself for asking. I was in a terrible mental state for this, and I was being horribly insensitive. I shouldn't have come. I was just causing more pain. I couldn't even be useful to a dying woman.

I stood abruptly to leave, but the witch held out her stick to stop me. She looked over her shoulder, a little wilder in her countenance. An uncomfortable, soggy laugh sprang from her chest. "Bone eater," she gurgled wetly.

My mouth gaped in slack-jawed shock. She'd just spoken! It had been almost incoherent from whatever condition her throat and lungs were in, but she'd spoken!

Then her words sunk in, and I asked, "Did you mean blood drinker? Are you talking about the bat-shifters?" I asked in alarm.

She cackled sharply, then shook her head before spitting out a tooth. I eyed it sourly and tried not to retch. Gods, she was disgusting. I knew she couldn't help it, but I didn't think I could sit here much longer.

"Not blood drinker?" I asked, then worried at my hands, looking around to see if there was anything lurking in the dark. My eyes spotted nothing, but that kind of silence only spooked me. A chill tumbled down my back like an icy fog.

I certainly didn't think she was referring to fellatio… unless she was simply a mad, perverted old woman. I frowned and eyed her suspiciously. I wouldn't put it past her to be a little degraded.

Still though, bone eater was an incredibly creepy combination of words. I didn't like it. What if something was stalking her? Did rot-witches have enemies that were unknown to us?

"Are you in danger?" I asked quietly, leaning forward to make sure she heard me. "Is something stalking you? I can't help you if you don't talk to me!" I quickly looked over my shoulder again, no longer comfortable having my back to the darkness.

When I glanced back at her, the witch started choking and coughing. I grimaced and leaned back helplessly, worried that if I patted her on the back, she'd just fall to pieces. After a wet hack, something large and wet fell from her mouth. I shrieked when I realized what it was, and scrambled away from it in horror. I couldn't stop it; I turned and heaved, then scrambled from the fireside to empty the contents of my stomach.

I caught my breath after my last unwilling hurl and stayed bent over my mess, traumatized by what I'd just witnessed. A scraping noise told me that something was being slid over, and I glanced to my right to find my water canteen. The tip of her stick left my peripheral vision, and I thanked her hoarsely.

I rinsed my mouth, spat it out, then took a long draw from the canteen, nearly emptying it. I was barely able to stopper it because of how my hands shook. I closed my eyes, tried to calm and slow my breathing, but all I could see was her tongue laying there in the dirt. She'd used her very last words to warn me about the bone eater.

I cringed, squeezing my eyes shut to block the impending tears. I was scared now. I was hurt, my soul was dying, and now I was terrified of something that might be searching around out there in the dark. I'd never heard of anything called a bone eater. I wiped away a rogue tear, wishing I could die now more than ever.

But I had one more thing left to do. After a couple stabilizing breaths, I got up weakly and trudged over to the witch, who was delivering more soup into her now tongueless mouth like nothing had happened. I tolerated the smell for just a moment more, praying to the Sky Gods for help settling my stomach.

"I'll make sure you get home," I told the old, dying woman. "I'll get you to your family, ok? I promise I'll help keep you safe. I know you're powerful right now, but I don't want you casting anymore if it'll be the last thing you do."

I sighed as I stared down at her, but she'd just returned to her clueless behavior, slowly rocking and smiling vacantly. I shook my head, scrubbed my hands over my face, and fought back another urge to sob. This was overwhelming, but what other purpose did my life have at this point? She was a rot-witch, my kind's enemy, but she was also a dying woman in need of help—though I imagined she might argue that last part if she could.

I no longer cared if I was stepping into a grey area. I'd help her. Perhaps it'd help distract me from the agonizing pain of being completely unlovable.

Making my way around her campsite, I worked to hide her smell. It wasn't easy, and I knew she'd left a scent trail, but there was only so much I could do. I warned her she should put out her fire, wished her a good night, then walked several minutes away to find a place to sleep. I couldn't bring myself to rest near her. Harmless or not, she still made me uncomfortable.

I tucked myself under a small outcrop and set up a couple spells to tell me if any creature bigger than a squirrel approached. I shuddered and curled up in my blanket, barely able to hear the sounds around me because my scared heart thudded too loudly in my ears. It was cold too. The chill of the wilderness knew quite well how to seep past cloth, an adamant kind of reach that pervaded all. It'd been a long time since I felt this kind of cold, and I no longer had Tsisana to keep me warm.

Thinking of her had me remembering Ferrer, and I numbed in body and mind until I finally relaxed. I'd forgotten that I didn't care if I died. It was weirdly comforting, and I drifted off into an uneasy sleep.

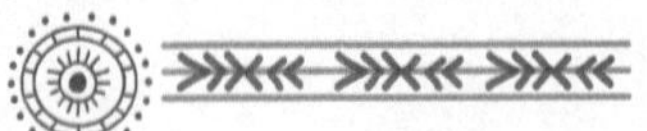

# Chapter 6

## Ferrer

Getting out of the castle and grabbing two bats for my search was an ordeal in and of itself. With Leilani dogging my steps for an answer to her offer and Tsisana pursuing like a raging vixen—which meant that Borredan wasn't far behind—we were an absurd string of confusion, hurt, rage, and… something else I couldn't recognize.

I didn't know what I was feeling, so I focused on the task at claw and ignored the bickering behind me. Perhaps I could have calmed everything by telling Leilani to go find someone else, but I was too fixated on my goal to even bother looking at her. My mind was loud with thoughts of Keid and her ruined dress. As much as I told myself that I didn't care—because I was so beyond bloody disappointed—the truth was much more complicated than that, and I had a hard time facing it.

"Yuca, Aldonica, follow me," I tersely ordered the pair of bats standing on the outskirts of the recognition grounds. They'd swapped places with two other guards who'd found their mates and looked relieved to have something to do. "We have a guest who went missing, and we suspect they may be involved with rot-witches," I informed as they picked up pace beside me, giving odd looks to the three people in tow. Wait, they were still following?

I spun around and held up a palm, forcing the two witches and Borredan to halt. I narrowed my eyes and addressed Leilani. "You. Go home. I thought maybe you should find someone else here, but I just realized that a good person does not target someone else's mate. I don't want your selfish genetics in my offspring or in my people. We can afford to be picky now. We want good people here, and to be honest, witches are absolutely the last thing we're looking for. Go home."

Leilani paled from my speech, but I had no remorse. I was as cranky as the soil under a fallen star. I turned to Tsisana, pointed a finger, and snapped at her, "Go home with your mate. You are lucky that he accepted you because many of us wouldn't have. Know that your sister is not dead. Since r"—I choked angrily on the word and continued past the stutter with a wrinkled nose and an irritated scowl—"r-recognition, I would have felt her expire. If I find her alive, she'll return here alive. I'm not a murderer. I'll do my job and no more. Be thankful that you will be here for her because I still intend to reject her."

Tsisana's face did the opposite of Leilani's and reddened from both blood and rage. "But why? She's the best person I know! At least get to know her first! You have no idea what she's been through!" she screamed at me, taking a step forward so her nose was just an inch from my pointed finger.

I leaned down to get in her face the way she was doing to me, and Borredan bristled in the corner of my eye. I ignored him and hissed, "And you don't know what we've been through! My rejection of someone I don't want is nothing compared to the millennia of suffering we've experienced as a people! Open your eyes, take your entitlement, and get out of my face. You're wasting your sister's time."

I left her there to stand in her speechlessness and stormed off, furious at everything and everyone in this bloody realm. I was free now, and I wasn't going to have my choices made for me. I had a right to decide my own destiny, and that was what I was going to do.

*So hungry,* my bat complained as we hurried from the recognition grounds. I launched off the dirt, clawed my way up a tree, and released my wings. Cracking my stiff neck and spine, I jumped into the moonless sky and flew over the woods in the direction she'd gone.

*We'll eat when we get back but only when we get to our chambers. I don't want to risk that libido spike. Mating with... that...* I was about to say 'creature,' but I couldn't seem to do it, so I stopped talking to Iron altogether.

I caught Keid's potent scent near the front tables and snapped a thin branch off a shrub that'd been in her path. I passed it to Yuca and Aldonica. "This is her. Notice that rot-witch odor? That will likely go away, so try and remember her scent without it."

They nodded, wrinkled their nose in disgust, and didn't say a word. They just seemed happy to be away from the event. Perhaps they didn't want a chosen and were waiting for the next gathering to find their fated mate. How lucky they were.

I tracked Keid's trail down the slope and past a creek. She'd run a considerable distance, and it took us a while to find the spot where Borredan retrieved her dress. I checked the stars and oriented myself in the direction he'd said his mate's bags were. He'd only found Tsisana's belongings, so Keid had likely returned for her own.

We ran slightly southwest and arrived at a thicket that contained both the sisters' and the rot-witch's scents. I sniffed around and drew my brows up in confusion as I tried to get some kind of story from the smells, but gods, it was messy. The twins had come from the south, from the cat-shifters' castle, and their old trail verified that. Somewhere in between their arrival and tonight, a rot-witch had arrived from the east—maybe more like southeast, but they had definitely not arrived together.

"It's so strong. Can you verify this southeast trail is fresher than the southern one?" I asked my comrades, who squatted and pivoted their heads in concentration. Aldonica picked at some debris on the ground, noticing what I had. Game had always been scarce in our old territory, and these two were good trackers. I was relying on them to help me discern the truth here.

"Yes," Yuca agreed, then turned to gag after taking a particularly deep whiff of a piece of bark. "I wouldn't use the word 'fresh' though."

Aldonica held a hand up to her mouth and nearly sympathy-retched. "Maybe it's good we haven't eaten," she muttered, patting Yuca on the back. I snorted and nodded. It wouldn't do to waste a precious, freely donated blood ration.

"Do you think a human would have noticed this smell? I can't tell how bad their noses are," Yuca asked with an arm over his nose. Aldonica twisted her lips in thought, and I just shrugged.

"The humans at the event didn't seem to smell what was on our target. This is perhaps a little more potent than that but not by much." I scratched at my jaw with a hand. "Let's go. There's a trail going northeast that has our target's scent all over it."

As we tracked Keid, I couldn't tell if I was feeling my comrades' eyes on my back or not. Had they heard what'd happened? I couldn't imagine that the news hadn't spread like a forest fire. Shame pricked at me; they'd probably found out I was fated to a witch and not just any witch. Were they embarrassed for me that my fated smelled like rot?

I had a weird impulse to defend that it wasn't her scent but someone's that she'd associated with recently. I didn't know who I was defending though, her or me. I grunted silently and placed a hand to my heart—it felt bruised. The wretched waves of disappointment hit again and again, and the lurching sickened me. All I wanted to do was go home and sleep for a year.

When Keid's scent led us straight to her sleeping form, it was mixed with the scent of a doused campfire, but there was no pit near her. Before getting any closer, I gestured for us to take to a tree to discuss what we were seeing and scenting.

"I don't smell anyone else," Aldonica said as we conferred in hushed whispers. "The campfire smoke is pretty faint. Maybe we should go against the breeze to find it."

"Take Yuca and go see who's there and how far away they are," I ordered. "Scout only. Do not engage."

They nodded, but Yuca sent me a reluctant look as he moved to follow Aldonica. I held back an annoyed growl and jerked my chin to tell him to hurry. I'd be fine here. I had enough self-control.

Once they were gone, I climbed into another tree to get a better vantage. I absolutely was not curious, but I looked down to verify that she was an identical twin. When I craned my head, I realized that she was… not.

*Mate…* Iron repeated involuntarily, but I was too flustered to retort with something scathing. *Mine…* His depressed tone was steeped in misery.

I settled where I could look at her sleeping form and experienced despair equal to my bat's. Now that I wasn't blinded by shock and fury, I could get a proper look at her. I hated how beautiful she was. I absolutely loathed it. The Moon Goddess, as if She hadn't done enough already, had given me a star-kissed, and I was stricken. I looked up at the moonless night sky and almost laughed. Of course She was hiding tonight. She'd thrown this at me and ran.

*Careful how you think of the goddess,* Iron murmured nervously.

*Star-kissed,* I countered, too emotional to heed him.

Like how all the colony had described our previous star-kissed, she had the lightest pink skin, and her hair—held tight at the back of her head by a strip of leather—was a soft, lucent wave running over a shoulder. A little taller than the average witch, just like her sister, she was curled in her sleep like a scared prey animal. The swelling around her eyes and blush around her nose told me she'd been crying… a lot.

Even in her sleep, she looked strained. Her lips, only a shade darker than her cheeks, were stretched taut, like she was reliving the last handful of hours. I brought a hand to my face, realizing that my expression mirrored hers. The tension had settled in so deeply that I'd almost gotten used to how it felt. Perhaps that was why Yuca had stared strangely at me. Had I looked more sad than angry? That couldn't be right. I scrubbed my hands over my face, trying to relax all my muscles and start fresh.

I couldn't see much of her body under the blanket, and I wondered if it matched my preference the way her face did. Perhaps I shouldn't eat until she was completely out of bat-shifter territory—period. I didn't know if the desire for her would disappear after my rejection. I sharply wrinkled my nose in anger at where my line of thinking had gone and resisted the temptation to slap myself. I did not desire her.

*Please don't,* Iron muttered. *We've been slapped enough tonight as it is. Our inner ear might cave in, and I'll never hang straight ever again.*

I didn't trust myself to talk, not even to Iron. If she wasn't a witch… I couldn't even handle ideas like that. It would have been so much easier if everything about her had been undesirable. I didn't want to vocalize that she was visually… ideal to me. An image of both our pale bodies writhing under starlight came unbidden, and I wanted to tear my eyes out from how excited it made me. I shut my lids tight, feeling myself start to go a little mad from my splitting mind. There was no way I could handle this much longer.

I swallowed hard as I became more uneasy with my thoughts and behavior. I considered myself lucky that I didn't have detailed memories of her devastated face, but I was definitely staring at the echo of it. I brought my wings in closer to comfort myself and forced my eyes away until my comrades returned.

I was eventually joined by Yuca and Aldonica, who had much to share from their scouting. I kept my face hardened as I listened to their report, but my expression slipped into shock when they explained their findings. I placed a hand to my jaw and stared back down at Keid, feeling a crushing wave of disappointment I hadn't expected.

There was an old woman at the campsite that didn't smell like anything. When they backtracked her route that'd come from the south, it eventually smelled like rot. My fated mate was sleeping not that far from our mortal enemy. They'd met secretly at the southern site, a hair got on Keid, and now they were meeting again. Or perhaps they'd already met? Was she going to report and just got tired before reaching her? Were they meeting tomorrow?

Had some part of me hoped that Tsisana was right? I didn't know how else to see this. My fated mate was conspiring with the enemy.

"Roost for now," I ordered. "I'll take first watch. When she moves tomorrow, we'll follow her and see if they meet. If they do not, we'll kill the rot-witch and take the other one in for questioning."

"We should get reinforcements for the rot-witch, Ferrer," Yuca warned and Aldonica nodded nervously. "She looks ancient. If she's close to expiring… she could kill us all, you know."

"Do not forget that we are immune to curses, but I have heard you. We don't know what else she is capable of. The gods know I don't want fire thrown at me like a dragon," I replied crankily. I hated the unknown, but I was not afraid of it. Nothing but the Sun God's fire could falter me when I had my own to protect. I'd been put into a position of power for decades, and I refused to disappoint now.

Still, the future looked grim for me. I made an effort to harden my heart, but I knew it wouldn't be enough to survive this. I had to kill what pumped my pain through me. There could be no sympathy for the rot sympathizer.

I swallowed hard, sick from the notion, and turned to stare at Keid one more time. I was no longer certain I could handle this. My mind was breaking in two.

Aside from the angry struggle to keep my gaze off Keid's sleeping form, the night had been uneventful. I'd switched out watch duty with Yuca and went to roost for the precious few hours that were left in the night. None of us trusted sleeping on the ground with the rot-witch nearby, so we chose to hang from whatever high, sturdy branch we could find in the redwoods.

An irritable Aldonica woke me a little after dawn, shading her eyes as the orange sunrise filtered through the trees. I squinted, immediately suffering the stinging pain of daylight on my pupils, and cursed the diurnal nature of humans. Even being in the shade was too bright.

I massaged my temples, relaxed the locked tendons in my legs, and swung off the branch to land upright on a lower one. I flapped a couple times to keep my balance, then leaned against the tree to rub at my eyes.

"I already have a headache," Aldonica mumbled as Yuca joined us.

"We're going to have to track by scent," he whispered. "I can barely see. We can't risk using sound."

"No clicking then. They could hear it. I will never say that I miss the fae's Night Court," I grumbled, "but I do miss perpetual darkness. I fear I'll never get used to this."

"It's better than how we were starving to death," Yuca replied, placing a hand to his stomach. "Though I don't exactly have a full belly at the moment." Aldonica nodded sourly, but I patted the bark next to me with the side of a fist to get their attention.

"This is nothing compared to that," I reminded both of them. "I don't need you distracted today, so either remain or return. We have to stay focused. Will you be alright?" I asked Yuca as I offered my wrist to Aldonica. I didn't flinch as she bit it and partook of my blood, only taking enough to prevent weakness. I was used to it. Like Nofre, Luzia, and Castanon, I'd donated countless times when we'd all been starving to death in the Night Court. The strong had to feed the weak. If it was preventable, bats never let others die from hunger. It was too deeply imbedded in our instincts, even if we hated the other person.

I could not offer any blood to Yuca though, and he knew that. Aldonica was safe to feed because she preferred males, and when her libido spiked, she would not be tempted to force Keid. Like all the bats, Yuca and I were too closely related to her to be enticing.

Yuca's face was dubious as he said, "Yes… I'll be ok for another day. I could perhaps travel away for game and return later."

I shook my head but continued to keep my arm still for Aldonica. "Not taking the chance. I don't want a commotion if you catch scent and return feral. Look, let's just follow the witches. If we decide to kill the rot-witch and return home with the other one, we don't need to worry about extending this trip."

"That's fair," Yuca said, and Aldonica removed her mouth from my wrist with a murmur of gratitude. I applied pressure to where she'd bitten to fight her anticoagulant and nodded to where Keid had been sleeping.

"She still there?" I asked Aldonica, whose eyes had dilated with her libido spike. She shifted her weight on the branch, looking crankier than ever, and nodded.

"I can hear her moving though," Yuca added.

"Alright, let's follow but only at hearing range." I rubbed my eyes one more time, scowled at how degraded my vision had become, and turned to keep my ears on Keid. Aldonica temporarily left in search of privacy to take care of her pressing issue.

*Time to focus, Iron,* I told my bat, moving carefully to the next tree.

*Too bright,* he complained. *It's confusing me.*

*Focus,* I repeated, nearly missing a branch that I thought was closer. *Blood clots!* I dug the thumb claw of my left wing into the bark of the redwood and took my boots off, quickly tying them to my belt. I needed all my claws right now so I wouldn't end up falling like a gods-forsaken branch during a windstorm.

Yuca and I listened to Keid's movements as she started traveling in the direction of the rot-witch, and my heart plummeted. I rubbed at my chest in denial, telling myself that I was only disappointed because this meant we might have to stay out here longer. I followed her sluggishly as she moved, my depression worsening by the heartbeat.

When Keid arrived at the rot-witch's campsite, we perched to listen.

"I see you're ready to go," Keid said with a sniff. Her voice was weak, rough, but she cleared her throat. "Let's get you home, shall we?"

*Home?* I looked over at Yuca, whose confused expression mirrored mine.

The rot-witch released a disgusting, gurgling chuckle in response and started shuffling. We cautiously followed their footsteps through the woods, staying high up and out of sight. They were traveling abysmally slow, but all we could do was track them and gather information.

"I need something to call you," Keid said with a sigh.

*How doesn't she know her name?* Iron asked. *Augh, watch out for tha—*

I pivoted my head, and my temple smacked right into a branch's protruding knot. *Blood clots! Bloody, clotting shit stars! Augh!* I cursed internally, getting infinitely more annoyed with this mission. Yuca stabilized the branch I'd ran into and kept it from making more noise than it already had.

"Thank you," I grumbled as we continued our stalking. Gods, that'd hurt.

"—an?" Keid was saying, and the witch chuckled breathily. "Alright, what about Aldegund? Genista? Valli?" Her voice turned dry. "I'm going to pick something utterly stupid if you don't like any of these. What if I started calling you Mother Mushy? How'd you like that?"

The rot-witch sounded like she was going to either fall over or fall apart with how much she was laughing. I scowled at the camaraderie my fated mate seemed to have with the hag, but I was confused. If they knew each other, if they conspired, how did Keid not know her name? I puzzled over that as we listened.

Keid's tone strained when she pushed more suggestions. "Bituin? Setareh? Ila?" The hag only grunted, and the young woman gave up.

"Alright, well... never mind," Keid said on a sigh. "Ah, careful!" It sounded like the witch fumbled with her footing. I hazarded a peek through the branches and spied the woman stabilizing the old crone. She seemed to hesitate a little at touching her, which didn't surprise me. I wouldn't touch that disgusting old monster except to kill her. I'd reek for days.

We updated Aldonica when she caught up with us, but we had nothing to report. The rot-witch hadn't said a single thing, and based on her gurgling noises, I was starting to wonder if she was mute.

"They're traveling directly east," I said to the she-bat. "They must be making an escape to dragon territory."

"And if that's their goal, we need to stop them," Yuca murmured. "We can't enter their kingdom uninvited."

Aldonica ran a hand through her hair in frustration. "We can't risk a diplomatic incident so soon. We just made friends with them."

"Should I go back and report?" Yuca asked quietly. "Or are we engaging?"

I sighed and scrubbed a hand over my face, thinking about our options. "I want more time," I stated decisively and gestured back in the direction of our castle. "Yuca, go report to the coronels and ask for reinforcements. Make sure they know they'll be engaging with a rot-witch. Also make sure they only send us well-fed bats that aren't attracted to females. Have them send a coronel to the Summer Court to ask Queen Hekla for assistance and her counsel. I recommend Luzia. She knows her better."

Yuca's shoulders fell in relief. He nodded once and departed for home, likely excited to both eat and put distance between him and the rot-witch. I then gestured for Aldonica to follow, and we continued our mission in silence.

"—uld tell me what they are? Or it is?" Keid was asking when I refocused my ears on her. Shitting stars, had I missed something? The rot-witch stayed silent after Keid asked her question. "Ok, so is it a beast or a person?" She glanced southward on occasion. What was she looking at?

The rot-witch grunted and continued her shamble down a hill, holding her robe away from her bare feet with a couple ugly, clawlike nails. She didn't look where Keid stared, only focusing on where she stepped.

"If I don't know what's stalking you, it could keep me from effectively protecting you," Keid said, her voice projecting irritation, but the subtle wavering in it suggested fear.

I turned my degraded vision southward and redirected my hearing. "Do you scent anything out there?" I asked Aldonica. "I don't hear a thing aside from birds, lizards, and rodents."

She shook her head, and I sighed in acknowledgement. All I could do right now was gather information while we waited for reinforcements. If all went smoothly, we should get some by dawn tomorrow. We had enough time. There was no way that they were going to make the border by then, not at the speed of their ambling. If worse came to worst, Aldonica and I would attempt an ambush to capture Keid and kill the rot-witch. I couldn't say who'd win though. It'd have to be fast.

We listened to Keid's own interrogation of the rot-witch, but the old hag never answered any of her questions regarding the stalker. It was becoming apparent to me that she hadn't known this witch for very long.

"You're being quite difficult," Keid muttered under her breath. "Well, I guess I'll ask this bone eater for a quick death."

The hairs on the back of my neck stood on end at those words. Bone eater? I obsessed over that name for hours as they traveled in silence. I stared southward every time Keid did, which was often, but I never sensed a thing. The breeze wasn't always in my favor, but I knew that whatever was chasing them hadn't caught up yet.

Though she wouldn't admit it, I could tell that Aldonica had gotten spooked. I didn't need to ask her why; I knew that neither of us had heard of bone eaters. I wished I had researched more of this realm's creatures after arriving. I wondered if Queen Hekla knew of such a thing.

The witches stopped several times throughout the day to rest and ended up camping early when they came across a small stream. A humble campfire was built, and the rot-witch waddled off to forage for food. Keid made a sound of dismay when the hag returned with a half-eaten rabbit that had been dead for quite some time. It was dropped into a pot of boiling water, and the preparer excitedly rubbed her hands together.

I watched Keid run away to gag behind a tree, obviously disturbed by the sight and smell. I didn't look too closely at the carcass in the pot. I had a feeling it was infested with other life-forms that Keid had seen more clearly. I glanced over at Aldonica, whose face had gone a bit pasty.

I signaled for her to rest, and I perched on a branch where I could safely spy on the two witches. Night was falling, and my vision was slowly becoming more helpful. I exhaled quietly in relief and rubbed my exhausted eyes. I hoped my people got here soon. This mission was turning into a waste of time. We were learning absolutely nothing.

I leaned against the tree as I lazily watched them go about their evening. Keid was eating some kind of grainy bar from her bag and would move to a different place by the fire whenever the subtle breeze shifted.

*That's what you get when you conspire with a rot-witch,* I thought petulantly as she covered her nose. I'd lost track of how many times she'd done that.

I was not comfortable watching her. She'd been visibly miserable all day, except for moments when her face would go blank. It was starting to look blank again now, actually, like she was going somewhere far away in her mind. The witch slobbering over her fetid meal no longer had Keid grimacing, and it wasn't long before the occasional tear started trickling down her cheeks.

My stomach turned in discomfort at the sight, a response that made me angry at myself. *No sympathizing for the sympathizer*, I thought vehemently. I scowled and chanted the words of rejection in my head. I repeated what I was going to say to her once we brought her in for interrogation. *I reject you,* I snarled in my head. *I reject you. I hate witches, and I hate you. Once you tell us what we need to know, we're done with you. I'm done with you.*

My body didn't like any of those thoughts. Nausea roiled hot inside my belly, and my skin broke into a cold sweat. I wrapped my arms around myself, then added my wings, discomforted by the sudden illness.

*L-let's not think about rejection until we g-get back,* Iron said, sounding woozy as well. *F-focus…*

*Focus,* I agreed, swallowing hard to get saliva down my throat. My body was slowly rebelling on me, more and more.

"Somehow," Keid said quietly from below, still looking lost in thought, "even though you're here, I feel so alone." The rot-witch merely trembled as she took another slurp of her grotesque meal. Keid picked up a twig and tossed it into the fire. "I thought that, for once in my life, I'd have a chance to not ever feel alone again. I'm such a fool. I've lost everything."

I furrowed my brows as I listened. I had to assume that she was talking about the recognition event, but there was no way she'd been there for herself. If she was with this witch, she'd been up to something. I just hadn't figured out what yet.

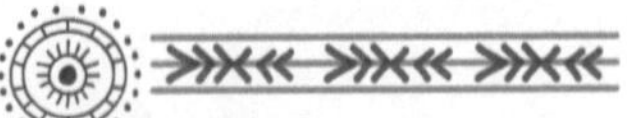
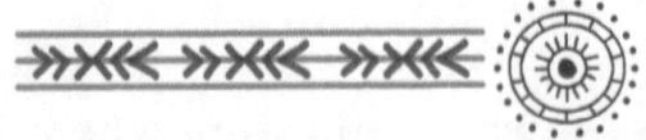

# Chapter 7

## Reid

I sniffled emptily as I took another bite of my granola bar. Except for the popping of the fire, the night air was quiet. Neither insects nor breeze stirred my false peace, and I was especially grateful when the old woman stopped her noisy slurping because I was minutes away from leaving. I simply focused all my senses on the little nuts and pieces of dried fruit in my bar while firmly eschewing the memory of the maggot and rabbit stew she'd concocted. I needed food in my stomach, and I needed it to stay there.

I rubbed my eye as another stubborn tear trickled off an eyelash. I couldn't help it; my body simply wouldn't stop grieving for what it'd never had. Perhaps it would have been better if he'd been able to properly reject me.

"Maybe I'll go back after I take you home," I murmured to her as I unwrapped more of my food. "Maybe they'll kill me, but maybe it'd be worth the risk to get a proper rejection, you know?" I wasn't expecting a response to my musing, and I didn't get one. "Give us both closure? What do you think?"

I picked at my teeth and smiled at her mad giggle. I had a feeling she was going to drive me crazy, but I welcomed it, gods help me. I glanced at the ground when she made a sweeping gesture, poking the grass and dirt with a stick. What did she want now? Frowning, I crouched where she was pointing, and she made another gesture, this time like she was yanking at the grass.

I pulled some grass out and held up the clump for her to take, but she waved away my hand and once again made the sweeping gesture. I disposed of the grass and plucked out more, realizing that she simply wanted to see the dirt. Curious, I worked to remove the plants from where she pointed, and the witch appeared to be very happy with my efforts.

When she started drawing in the dirt, I was hit by a spark of excitement. Could she talk to me this way? Was she going to write her name? Maybe she could explain what the bone eater was!

I nearly held my breath as I crouched near her, watching every quivering stroke she made with the stick. She drew a long line, then another. I tilted my head when she drew a circle… I was waiting for the moment I'd recognize anything, and when I did…

I gasped, appalled, then berated her. "That's a penis! I thought you were going to write something meaningful!" I raised an eyebrow at it though. It was startlingly accurate.

The witch doubled over, cackling so hard that I thought her head was about to pop off and traumatize me for life. I shook my own head, unable to tell if I was smiling or scowling. All I knew was that I had an extremely odd expression plastered to my face. There was no describing my emotions.

"You know, I was wondering whether you were degraded or not," I grumbled caustically. "You are biodegraded"—I tapped the side of my head—"right in the noggin." I crawled back to where I'd been sitting, crossed my arms, and snorted humorlessly. "You're a mad, mad woman, Mushy," I chided, throwing in the new nickname. She'd earned it with her antics.

The rot-witch eventually calmed and wiped away some milky tears of mirth. I grimaced and tossed my gaze away from her face. Tears should definitely not be that color.

With the sound of scraping, I risked a glance over to find her erasing her penis. She started another drawing, and I lazily watched its progress, expecting a pair of breasts this time. When it ended up being a symbol I recognized, I frowned. Why had she drawn that?

She stared at what she'd drawn, her stick quivering as she settled. I looked between her and the drawing, waiting for something, anything. Then she started rocking and tapped it with her stick.

"Why'd you draw that?" I asked.

She tilted her head toward me but kept her eyes on the symbol, her rocking uninterrupted.

"No, I don't have one," I said and gestured to her. "Do you?" I didn't see how she would.

Frustratingly, she didn't answer with a nod or anything remotely helpful. She tapped it again, and I threw my hands up in the air. "I don't know what you're saying!" I expressed, getting progressively more frustrated with her.

When I stood up to leave, she scraped away at the symbol and started drawing something else. My shoulders slumped, and I waited. She'd get one more chance; otherwise, I was retiring for the night, far away from her.

This time she illustrated the process. "Why are you showing me the steps to summoning a familiar? You do know it takes years of study to be able to pull it off, right?" I leaned in as I addressed her, trying to gleam any ounce of information from her old, leathery face.

She waved me off with a dismissive hand and started fake crying. Deeply offended, I frowned at her and snapped, "Don't make fun of me, Mushy."

Her head lolled to the side to stare just past me. Unnerved, I checked over my shoulder, then regarded her once more. No, this wasn't a brainless old hag. This witch still had a razor about her wits, and it was clear she still sharpened it. I nibbled nervously at my lower lip, feeling my own mind falter out of anxiety. An errant breeze had my skin prickling, and I shuddered, then hugged myself out of both coldness and insecurity.

The rot-witch then gestured to the ground and cleared away her drawings. Tiny little brown mushrooms had sprouted in the recently disturbed soil. They were so small that I wouldn't have noticed them had I not been following every move the witch had made. Yes, that was a particularly reactive patch of earth… Indeed it became more apparent by the second.

I raised my gaze to hers. "That doesn't mean it's possible. I don't have the skills to d—" I started saying, but there was something in her eyes that made me shut my mouth. "Fine."

I stood abruptly and cleared away foliage to make a larger patch of dirt. I ripped out weeds and tossed away the biggest rocks—and I did so angrily. The witch giggled when I threw a rock close to her head. It'd been a joke, but a part of me might have been satisfied had I missed and conked her right in the face.

Once I cleared and prepared the patch of dirt, I started removing my clothes. The old witch's attention wandered, and I caught her gazing idly up at the shadowed canopy, a grin on her face. Had she already forgotten what I was doing?

"Why am I doing this?" I asked her as I kicked off the last of my clothing. "Really, Mushy. Why?"

When her gaze swung to meet mine, there was something in her expression that shattered my defenses. Something cracked within me. In that moment, looking at her felt like looking into a mirror.

She was lonely.

No… I knew I was projecting that. I swallowed hard, knelt, and avoided looking at her again. "Familiars aren't summoned to be a cure for loneliness, Mushy," I said in a thick voice, fighting tears and wrinkling away the stinging in my nose. I lowered myself onto all fours, then lay flat on the cleared patch of dirt. I tried so hard to prevent them, but my teetering control collapsed. A puddle of tears formed beneath my face, and sobs racked through my body.

*I'm so lonely.*

The rot-witch stood and shuffled over to bury something close to my head, which caused several more mushrooms to start pushing through the dirt. I could barely see through my tears, but sprouted the mushrooms did… right before my eyes. What had she put in there?

*Do I care?*

No, I didn't care. I closed my eyes and let my face rest on the cold, damp dirt. I dug my fingers into the ground to root myself and connect to my gods. Though I served the Sky Gods—or I did when I belonged to the Stellar Coven—the gods who made women and menfolk were the Earth Gods. We drew from the earth, and our gods gave freely. The Earth Gods were pure love, the union of an earth deity and a wandering stellar goddess who collided mega-anna ago and birthed the Moon Goddess.

I let my toes wiggle their way into the dirt and relaxed as the earth grew warm. I forgot about how stupid this was. I knew it wasn't going to work, but at least I could enjoy connecting to this particularly active patch of dirt. The gods lingered closer than I'd ever felt Them. I could almost imagine myself reaching out to Them and feeling two hands touch me back in response. The Earth Gods didn't have hands, but if They did, they'd be warm… loving… giving…

My thoughts meandered as I let myself connect deeper to the soil. Did I want a familiar? Of course I did. Every witch wanted one, but not every witch would get one. It took years of dedicated study to learn how to get close enough to our gods to ask for one. To learn how to pluck at a piece of one's soul in exchange for another. It was no small thing. Many who dedicated themselves to the task found themselves living an entire lifetime without one and passing on alone.

One had to have a deep capacity for love to be gifted with such a companion. I wasn't sure I had it. How could one love if they were unlovable? Or was it the other way around? Certainly, the goddess had given me Ferrer to make it clear that love was not in my destiny. If anything, the gods would not waste a soul on me.

The ground beneath my face was now mud from all my tears. I was lonely. My heart felt so empty. I couldn't take it anymore. When I raised my elbows to remove myself from the dirt, a force pulled at my chest, and my breath was stolen from me. My ribs smacked painfully down into the dirt, and try as I might, I couldn't move. I'd been anchored to the ground, and panic smothered me.

I screamed as something delicate inside of me snapped, like someone had harvested a twig from my soul. The ground went from a calming warmth to an unbearable heat, forcing sweat through my skin. My limbs began shaking, and as soon as I thought the earth beneath me had turned molten, I was freed from the encounter.

I was back on cold, packed dirt again and catching my breath. My arms and legs wavered like gelatin, and I struggled to prop myself up onto my elbows. Unable to brush it away, I blew aside a strand of my white hair, but it irritatingly settled back onto my nose and became glued by a wandering tear.

Movement past the strand caught my attention, and I spied a small patch of dirt vibrating, like there was something rising under it. I scrabbled at the dirt, gasping through my uncontrollable crying.

*It simply isn't possible*, I told myself as I dug feverishly, unable to believe my eyes. Was I dreaming? Had the old crone fed me one of her mushrooms? Was I hallucinating?

I barely heard the rot-witch chuckling as I tossed aside chunks of dirt like my life depended on it. No, my life didn't depend on it, but someone else's did. Some kind of limb stuck up through the dirt, small and twiggy. I choked on a manic laugh and dug around it, trying to free it before it asphyxiated. It had been upside down, and its tiny foot wiggled about in its struggling.

"It's ok! I've got you! I've got you!" I sobbed and finally pulled it out of the Earth Gods' embrace.

When I registered what was in my hand, I froze. Its tiny black eyes blinked slowly open as I tried to keep the horror off my face. A brittle laugh came out of my throat, but it distorted into a low, grieving wail of despair. I hugged it to my chest and rocked in place as I cried and screamed.

The Earth Gods had gifted me with a familiar, and I'd barely done any of the steps required to do it. The Earth Gods had given me a companion, and it wore the face of my heartbreak. The Earth Gods had sent a soul to me to aid my witchwork, and it manifested into the form of a tiny, delicate blood bat. I'd done the impossible, and all I could think about was Ferrer.

I was having issues.

*She's naked! She's naked! She's naked! Go! Go! Go!* my bat screamed as I clung to the bottom of a branch with my hands and feet, flapping wildly and hanging on for dear life.

*Shit! Shit! Shit!* I tried to claw my way back up as quickly as possible. Scrambling back onto the relatively thin redwood branch, I winced as I accidentally dislodged flakes of bark and lichen. Gods, I prayed that they hadn't noticed any of that. I flopped against the tree and sunk my claws into it to anchor myself, breathing harder than I should from that fiasco.

I tried to suppress my bat, but he was uncontrollably crazed and slippery. When Keid had started removing her clothes, he'd taken over my wings, and in his haste to get me down there, knocked me right off the branch. He'd noticed that she had what he thought I liked and shoved at me like the tiny bastard he was. Iron had the personality of something much larger and more stubborn than anything he had the right to act like.

I brought my palms to my eyes and tried to forget the split-second view I'd gotten of her. She was not at a tall, ideal height to bend over before me. She did not have soft-looking, perky breasts. She did not have perfectly round, small areolas with generous longer nipples that deserved oral attention. She did not have a lovely, confident back that curved out into a dimpled, mature rump with plenty to grab. She did not have broad shoulders, a small waist, and wide, well-boned hips that would all make perfect handholds. She had nothing. She was a witch. Undesirable. Completely undesirable! Not my ideal in the least!

I'd barely gotten a glance, so when under the accursed blood moon had my memory suddenly become so flawless? Shitting stars!

*You backed-up clot!* I cursed at my bat. *You almost ruined this entire shit-of-a-mission. Get a hold of yourself!*

*Get a hold of that rump! Or your dick! I can't take it! We're a bat. We're designed to explore caves!* he yapped, struggling against me.

I wrinkled my nose in disgust and glanced down at my tented pants. This gods-forsaken fated mate pull was a complete disaster. I'd only gotten a peek at her body, and my own had gone absolutely crazy. I certainly could better understand Nofre's reactions to his mate now. It was bloody blinding—worse than the sun.

I thumped a fist against my chest, trying to slow my heart by sheer force of will. I needed my blood flow to calm the shit down now.

After a couple minutes, there was a different pull. Keid's crying below became more desperate, and my thumping at my chest turned into an uncomfortable rubbing. I grimaced, but I refused to look down there again. *No sympathizing,* I chanted and shut my eyes tightly. Oh, the suffering was so very real.

Tilting my head back, I took a deep breath of the sappy tree needles around me. I either needed to focus or switch out with Aldonica. I couldn't let my dick spoil this mission. There was too much at stake… or so I'd thought.

I plucked a nearby leaf off a smaller branch and methodically pulled out the needles in my anxiety. The more I listened to Keid's bizarre, one-sided conversations and interactions with the witch, the more I suspected this was just an escort mission. She'd plainly said that after getting the rot-witch home, she was considering returning here to accept my rejection.

I swallowed hard at that. I hadn't expected to hear those words considering how upset she'd been. I didn't like being taken off guard either. She mentioned risking death for it. Did she not fear death? Would she rather die than live with an incomplete rejection? She said she'd do it for the both of us.

This information wasn't being digested well. It didn't sit right in my belly, which cramped with unease. I'd expected her to keep running. It was easier to stay angry and detached that way.

I should be relieved that she wanted to cut all ties to me. I was, wasn't I? It'd make things easier for everyone, including Borredan and his mate. We could all move on as soon as possible. Tsisana wouldn't fight me on getting to know her—not that I would ever consider that. I'd never allow a witch to pressure me into anything.

Keid had also said 'home' instead of some rot-witch's coven name. Didn't they all have names or something? Maybe I was reading too much into that, but she didn't make it sound like she was returning to a location to make a report. No one else was even mentioned—no other names, nothing.

I rubbed at my temple as I tried to make sense of such little information. Everything was moving slower than a living star, and I was impatient for answers. I wanted her in that interrogation room.

Well, I wanted her in that interrogation room with plenty of other people… not alone. I definitely didn't want to be alone with her at all. Someone would need to comfort her when I rejected her, which would be the first item on the agenda. No, who cared if she needed comfort?

There was a throb in my head. I'd never… I'd never been such a shit before now. I… Castanon always appreciated my sensitivity… In fact, I was often made fun of for being a bloody romantic. Who… who was I anymore? Wasn't it… ok to be a shit to a sympathizer? It was… wasn't it? Why was I the only one aiming to treat her like she should be treated? Maybe they just hid it better? I'd always been terrible at hiding my emotions.

Or maybe they just wanted to be better than our enemies. If we didn't abuse our captives, it made us better than the rot-witches. Maybe I needed to be more neutral… maybe that was the professionalism that others relied on to survive this.

Why was that so hard?

*Hard,* my bat lamented unhelpfully. *Still hard.*

*Shut it.*

I adjusted my seating and pants to get more comfortable while I sorted through my emotions. I also wanted the worst assumption to be true, which wasn't very neutral, but it was so much easier that way. Rot-witches were our enemy. That was a simple fact I could handle. They were everyone's enemy. No one who'd ever encountered them in our entire history, in anyone's history, had anything good to say.

Queen Hekla had slaughtered one. I quite clearly recalled carrying that wolf-shifter's battered body to the hospital after her encounter, and she was a vessel of the Sky Gods! If she'd struggled, what chance did anyone else have in a solo encounter? It was ingrained in my memories. Normal witches had been spoken of with respect by the other shifters and were supposedly not associated with them, not officially. What happened in the shadows though? Witches were witches. Their ilk had to overlap at some point… right?

I was startled out of my internal debate by an unpleasant sensation that seemed to tug at the back of my mind… or perhaps deeper. I peered down without thinking and caught sight of Keid splayed out on the ground, screaming. I dug my claws into the bark as I watched her suffer, fighting an instinct to go down there.

*No sympathy.*

I'd heard them mention familiars, but I didn't know what that meant. Perhaps it was similar to King Belenus's wolf. Was

Keid going to change now? I grimaced and stilled when her body went limp, but I could still hear her heart pounding, so she was alive. Why had she collapsed? I was definitely no longer aroused, but I was experiencing something much worse, something that I didn't want to acknowledge.

*I don't like what we are feeling, Ferrer,* my bat murmured.

*Don't talk about it then,* I advised heatedly, but I wasn't angry with him. I was anxious. *No sympathy.*

I watched Keid suddenly lurch forward and dig at a disturbance in the dirt. A chill came over me at how unnatural this seemed. What was going on down there? Was she summoning some undead monster?

The answer was no.

I recoiled in horror at what she cradled in her palms. She'd found a bat… underground. She'd dug up a living, breathing bat. She'd…

*What?* Iron gasped. *That is not where we come from! Ferrer, my human, my other half, did you steer me wrong? Why did you do me like that?*

*Don't be stupid. You recall the day you awoke in my mind. You were born when I was born. You have my memories. You know you didn't come from the blessed ground, you tiny, webbed heathen.*

Iron hummed a disbelieving note while I simply stared down in disbelief. Keid had plucked a blood bat from the ground like it was a gods-forsaken turnip. Our reactions, however, were quite different—she was devastated.

Keid stilled, brought the small mammal to her chest, and wailed at the top of her lungs. The depth of the pain in her sobbing… There was another unwelcome pang in my chest as I watched her grieve… something. The whole scene was incredibly bizarre. I hated it.

A subtle wobbling of my branch told me that Aldonica had landed nearby, and I turned to see her settling cautiously onto a neighboring branch. "I'm hearing a ban-sìth, Coronel," she grumbled under her breath. "What did I miss?"

I explained everything as she stared down at the witches. "And you kept yourself from going down there. She's naked. Very pretty for a human. Admirable restraint."

I groaned quietly. So, they did know who she was to me. "Clot your gob," I snapped irritably. "You have no idea."

Aldonica winced, knowing she'd gotten on my bad side now, and sat by me in silence. Then we just watched Keid cry over the tiny thing, who was slowly becoming more alert.

*It's like us,* Iron noted. *It's a blood-drinker.*

*I know,* I spat. *I noticed. I don't know why that animal specifically. It's suspicious.*

*Can you let me out soon? Someone needs to lose our virginity.*

I remained silent for a moment as I tried to formulate some kind of response—any kind—to what Iron had just said. While I searched for some kind of inner equilibrium, I stalled by ignoring his request.

*Wh-what do you think that is? Think that's some kind of... evil spirit in animal form?* I asked him. *This was obviously some kind of witchual—ritual!* I couldn't even speak properly in my own head.

*Whatever it is, it looks like a pretty female. I am a handsome male. I could charm her. I could charm her and get some answers. They called it 'pillow talk,' Ferrer. I don't have a cushion, but I think I could pull it off with just my pecs.*

*I...* My bat was utterly destroying my ability to think. *What nonsense are you... What do you mean by 'they?' Where are you hearing these th—*

*Then, after making sweet, sweet interrogation. Bam! Lose our virginity. It's brilliant. We resolve two issues with one mission.*

*I...*

*Look, that bat is clearly starved for companionship. If I was a female who'd just emerged from the dirt, I'd immediately look for the comfort of the wings of a strong, warm male with nothing but poetry coming from his mind-lin— Shitting stars, I'd have to mark her first so we could tal—*

*There will be absolutely no marking! Are you mad? You cannot mate us to a bat, yo—*

*What? You human halves mate with pure humans, and we don't get to have any! And this bat isn't a witch. Why can't I h—*

*I cannot believe we're talking about this right now. Clot. Your. Gob!* I hissed and shoved at him so hard, I was finally able to block him.

My nerves were shot, gods help me. I was fighting opponents from all angles, and they were not going to win. I glared through my pants at my now-calm cock.

*That includes you.*

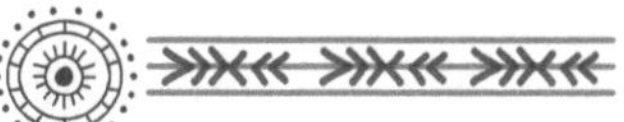
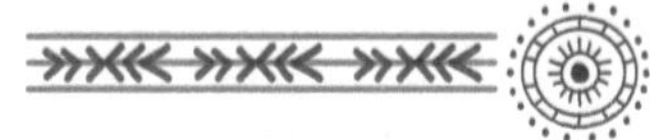

# Chapter 8

## Reid

"I'm sorry," I whispered down at the blood bat after I'd spent the last of my tears. I had none left to give as I became swaddled in numbness. Though I couldn't feel anything, I knew I owed the newborn familiar an apology. I should not have lamented its existence. Its form wasn't its fault. It had a right to exist as it was without judgment. "I was hurting, and I took it out on you. I'm so sorry."

The small blood bat shivered as it tried to balance itself in my palms. It was testing its limbs and taking its first steps. It was a precious moment, and I wished I wasn't feeling so detached so I could appreciate it more. Everything about this was surreal. How had this been possible? It defied all reason.

"You must be hungry," I said softly and settled the blood bat on my right palm while offering my left wrist. "At least you'll be easy to feed," I added, wishing I could smile at the words. I wanted my familiar to know that I wasn't normally like this, though to be fair, I rarely smiled in general.

I resisted jerking when the tiny thing bit my wrist. Yes, it felt like the jab of a needle, but a very tiny one. It barely hurt at all. After it prodded the wound with its tongue, the anticoagulant in its saliva prompted a little bleeding, and the bat lapped hungrily at the flow. I rested my arm on my knee when I realized that this was going to take a while and just watched it feed.

The more I studied it, the more I realized that the fluffy tan bat was the cutest thing I'd ever seen in my life. Its ears weren't as large as other bats I'd seen and were shaped like little spades. It had large eyes for a bat, and its little pug nose had one wrinkle just above it. Its tiny mouth was curled up at the corners, which gave it the illusion of having a happy smile.

Its cuteness further fueled the protectiveness I was developing toward it, and I twisted my lips in thought, becoming worried about its fragility. I would have to think of some spell to protect it. Even a wild hawk or eagle could easily kill a blood bat, and I wasn't about to lose the most precious gift a witch could receive.

"Perhaps I'll make a charm for you," I murmured thoughtfully. "You're too small to receive a symbol, but I'm not quite sure where I'd pierce you…" I looked over its tiny body and frowned. I didn't want to pierce its ears in case that affected its hearing, and I was afraid that piercing any webbing would affect its flight. Perhaps a dermal piercing, but those were tricky to apply. "It might have to be a collar." I sighed, knowing it wouldn't be very comfortable. "I'll try to think of other options."

I admired the little thing as it fed for… maybe thirty minutes? I forgot about everything in my fascination. Thoughts of Ferrer, my sister, and the rot-witch were pushed into the back of my mind. It was a luxurious reprieve, and when I realized that the familiar had offered some comfort, I wondered if maybe survival was possible. I would always have a gaping hole in my heart, but maybe I could scrape by without the love of my sister or a spouse.

Having a familiar meant that I had to survive now. If I died, this little one would die too. I blinked rapidly when that thought provoked a shocking realization, and I couldn't bring myself to look at her, especially when my cheeks flushed. I was shocked, yes, but embarrassment had also crept into me.

Would I be giving the rot-witch too much credit if she'd actually initiated this whole thing to make me value my life again? I pursed my lips as I spied her vacuous rocking in the corner of my vision. If so, that'd been incredibly calculating.

It wouldn't be wise to drop my guard around her. I definitely knew now that she wasn't as senile as she appeared. She wouldn't fool me again with another silly penis drawing.

*All done...* The blood bat sighed over our bond as it moved its head away from my arm. The incision was barely more than a scratch, but it did keep bleeding, so I cleaned and bandaged it. *Thank you.*

I forced a smile onto my face as I brought the blood bat up to eye level. "My name is Keid. It's a pleasure to meet you," I greeted as warmly as possible.

*I'm Vain,* the blood bat said tiredly. Based on the voice, I surmised that it was a female. I didn't exactly feel like it was polite to ask or check.

"Certainly, you can't be all that bad," I responded, and the bat stayed silent for a moment.

*No, that's my name. My name is Vain.*

"As in artery or vanity?" I inquired, and she hummed tiredly.

*My birth was traumatizing... I'm fatigued...*

"I know. I'm so sorry I didn't get you out of there faster. I wasn't... expecting you. You were a surprise," I admitted, and her delicate chuckle fluttered in my mind. "Let's go to sleep then."

*Away from the smelly thing?* Vain bemoaned. *Please say we are.* I glanced over to the old woman, who was staring blankly into the woods, and I nodded silently to my familiar before addressing the witch.

"Good night," I said to her. Pushing aside my fear of how she might have manipulated me, I grew thoughtful and fumbled to express my thoughts. "I... don't fully understand what happened this evening. To be honest, I think I'm still in shock." I swallowed and fought tears that threatened to spill anew. "Thank you though. This never would have happened if I hadn't met you. I don't know how to express what I'm feeling other than… thanks. It's too… overwhelming."

She snorted, but then she smiled as she rocked in her seat. My eyes flickered down to where she'd buried something earlier. Part of me wanted to dig it up to see what it was, but the other part of me didn't want to know. I felt like whatever it was might give me nightmares. I could only hope that the Earth Gods were not offended by whatever the rot-witch had done to the soil.

I frowned when I thought more about it. Had she cheated in order for me to acquire Vain? Would I be punished? Would Vain be taken from me? The more I thought about it, the more anxious I became. What occurred tonight had been far from normal.

Like last time, I walked a fair distance to find fresh air and comfort. Even if she didn't reek, I still couldn't bring myself to sleep close to the old woman. I didn't necessarily feel threatened, but I just wasn't comfortable being vulnerable around her.

I angled my bag against a tree and helped position Vain so she could hang under it. I was too paranoid about her getting snatched up by an owl. Her safety was now my priority. It wasn't because she could make my magic stronger and last longer; it was because I simply cared about her. I'd always felt closer to animals than people anyway. They'd never treated me poorly.

After casting the same spells as the other night, I curled up protectively by the bag and stared at Vain while she slept. There was a spark of warmth in my heart, and even though it was only akin to a candle in a snowfield, I embraced it.

## Ferrer

Aldonica and I continued our stalking of the two witches the following day, knowing that we were getting closer to dragon territory with every tree passed. I cracked my knuckles anxiously and looked over my shoulder to get my comrade's attention.

"I'm going up to see if I can see anything," I whispered, and the she-bat grimaced through already squinted eyes.

"What if you get blinded?" she protested, shading her face with a cupped hand.

"I'll heal," I replied and hoped that would be the case. I ascended to the treetops and knew that I'd broken through the canopy with how a direct layer of heat slathered my brow and shoulders. White encapsulated my vision, and I clapped a hand over my eyes. Blood clots, the sun was brutal. I sucked in a breath as I slowly opened a gap between two fingers and tried to push through the pain of strained eyes.

*Stop,* Iron hissed. *It's pointless!*

It was true. My vision was far too degraded to see anything under the Sun God's fire. The backs of my eyes ached, and I blinked frantically to erase the black dots that sprinkled the scenery. I had to give up the attempt. When I climbed back down into the more forgiving shade, I found Aldonica waiting patiently.

"Can't," I grunted, irritable now.

"They wouldn't be traveling at this hour, would they?" she inquired.

"I have no idea," I replied as we caught up to the witches. "If they were, I would have hoped to see some disturbances in the treetops. Also going at this sludgy speed, it's difficult to tell how far we've traveled. I wanted to see the castle."

"What should we do? They should have been here by now. We're not exactly able to outrun them come nightfall."

"No, we're not." I stared at the old witch's excruciatingly slow amble. "If nothing changes by tonight, I might ask you to backtrack to see how far away they are. I don't know what could possibly be slowing our people down."

"Maybe I should go now," Aldonica suggested. "Then I won't have to backtrack as far."

I frowned and stretched out an achy wing. After a moment, I nodded reluctantly. "Alright. Go but be fast about it. I don't know how far we are from dragon territory. We should still be fine, but I really want to wrap things up here. Tell them to hurry."

The she-bat, like Yuca, looked relieved to get away from here. She nodded and said, "Will be done, Coronel."

I stared after her until she became too blurry to focus on and then turned back to my task. I did not feel comfortable being the only one tracking the rot-witch now, but I'd made the decision.

*Let's just increase our distance from them,* Iron suggested. *I can't see Vain anyway if she's tucked away in that bag.*

*You need to get over that obsession,* I growled.

*You're the one eavesdropping on their conversations.*

*Do you not understand what we're doing here?*

*Not having sex.*

My caustic reply to that was prevented by the unexpected return of Aldonica. I frowned as I turned to face her. "They're here?" I asked, cautiously optimistic.

She shook her head with a worried expression. "When I backtracked, I noticed our scents were gone, Ferrer!"

I quirked my head, taken aback by that observation. "Gone?"

"They won't be able to follow our scents. They'll have to look for visual cues but maybe that caused some confusion? Maybe that's what's slowing them down?"

"Blood clots," I cursed and glared in the direction of the witches.

"Think they're responsible? I never saw the rot-witch do anything."

"I saw the other one wander around the area last night," I answered, referring to Keid. "If she's hiding their scents, maybe it got rid of ours too."

"The area just smells like woodland, but I haven't tested the radius," she agreed, nodding and rubbing at her own strained eyes.

I released more curses through my teeth as I tried to think of a solution. I ran a hand through my hair and emptied my lungs in a frustrated puff. "Sun sleeps in the west here. Use that if you get turned around, Aldonica. I need you to backtrack. Leave cuts on the trees so you can lead them back here. I'll start marking my route as well." I dug my claws into the trunk next to me and dragged them down, leaving five long gashes in the bark. I shook off the splinters and sent the she-bat a severe look. "Get them here fast!"

She nodded and scrambled away, fumbling almost blindly through the trees. I scrubbed my hands over my face and groaned in frustration. This was getting ridiculous, and I was getting bloody hungry.

When the witches retired for the night, Aldonica still hadn't returned. I set my lips into a grim line as I ascended the tree and poked my head out of the canopy and into starlight. A soft, cold breeze ruffled my hair, and I sighed as I took in the scenery. The castle was as far as I'd feared. Nestled against the mountain, the very top of it looked like a tiny island in an ocean of redwoods.

I turned to look over my shoulder and scanned the twinkling skies for dragon silhouettes. They patrolled their borders heavily, but not in fear of us. They'd recently raided a massive number of slaver dens and were now hunting any slavers who were trying to escape their kingdom. I had no idea if they'd be as strict as letting in visitors as they were about letting people out without an interrogation. Would they simply wave in the witches?

I gritted my teeth and released the nigh feral growl clawing within my throat. I tried to stay calm and collected, but even I had to admit that I was running out of time. I'd have no 'jurisdiction'—a word they'd taught us—once we passed the border. I could make requests to leave with any captives, like they did with us, but that would require time and an investigation on their part. I could probably get it escalated, being a coronel, but I'd rather avoid the whole mess altogether.

"Things were so much simpler in the Night Court," I whispered and tucked a flapping strand of my hair behind the point of an ear. "No neighbors to worry about. None of these fancy words or titles."

*Isolated. Unable to get mates. Starving to death,* my bat hummed. *Yes, very simple.*

I smiled as I plucked a leaf and mindlessly peeled off each needle. "Yes. Simple in its misery. It's a new kind of misery now," I said, and my smile faded. I wiped a tear from an eyelash and was grateful for this moment alone. It was the first I'd truly had since trying to reject Keid. I didn't have to worry about Aldonica or Yuca walking in on a vulnerable moment. Luzia was already a pain in regards to my sensitivity.

"What in the shitting stars am I to do, Iron?" I whispered. "We've waited decades for her. I don't understand. If we can't tolerate the one we're meant to be with, how could we possibly pick a chosen? I've never felt so… sick over a thought before. I'm literally queasy. I feel like throwing up. I thought it was a momentary ailment, but it's being persistent."

*Ask the goddess,* Iron replied darkly. I plucked another needle off the leaf and stared up at the Moon Goddess. She was starting to show Herself again, peeking out in a thin crescent. It was like She was checking to see if I was still mad at Her, and I chuckled at the thought.

Was I mad? I wasn't so sure about angry, but I might be going a little crazy. I was more confused than anything. The more I watched Keid, the more I felt myself softening toward her, and that scared me. That fear led to frustration because my hands were tied. I had to reject her. Even if I could tolerate being mated to a witch, she was still aiding a rot-witch. That made her a criminal. I couldn't be with a criminal.

"Why are you doing this to me?" I asked the Moon Goddess quietly as She sat suspended in the silent, glittering sky. "Is this some kind of test? I have to put my people first, you know that. I can't blindly follow your lead if it puts my kind at risk. We're endangered. You know we have no lives to spare."

The moon didn't answer me, but talking to Her made me feel a little better. It helped me organize my thoughts. I flicked aside the rest of the leaf and climbed back down the tree. I had to do one thing at a time. I didn't need to agonize over rejecting the woman because that time hadn't come yet. I just had to do my job and not think about it.

Moving to a redwood near Keid, I carved several deep grooves into a high, sturdy branch so I could tuck my feet into them to roost.

*Just don't think about it,* I repeated to myself as I hung upside down and crossed my arms. I wrapped my wings around myself and locked my tendons in place. I took in a deep breath and focused on the beautiful scent of redwood, not beech. *Just don't think about it.*

My thought was echoed by Iron's bitter laugh.

## Keid

The witch seemed to put on speed the next day, and I studied her with renewed suspicion. Even strolling down another hill, she didn't slip as much on the loose needles and detritus as she had before, and my familiar made note of that too.

*You said she was a rickety old thing,* Vain chirped.

"I did indeed," I muttered, and the witch wobbled in her footing but giggled when she caught herself. "I mean, she's not exactly spry, but…" I left the thought hanging there. Vain and I would just have to remain vigilant.

*May I eat?* she asked politely.

"You may," I replied and waited for the sting of her nibble. I hadn't put my hair up in a ponytail today, deciding that I'd let Vain perch on my shoulder where the hair could block any bird's view of her.

I winced slightly as she made a small cut in my neck and began prodding it with her tongue, licking at the slow flow she'd created. I knew I'd get used to it, but I certainly hadn't yet. I definitely felt an urge to slap her like I would a mosquito. Between this and my growing skill at not gagging so much around the rot-witch, I was starting to realize I had considerable restraint.

"I guess it comes from years of tolerating bullies," I murmured thoughtfully. "It's incredibly difficult to restrain yourself when all you want to do is punch someone in the face."

Vain hummed a question, so I started telling her a little about myself. "I'm a twin, Vain. I was born with albinism, but my sister was not. Albinism causes decreased or no melanin production. Melanin… uh… it's a pigment. It makes the skin darker. See how my hair and skin are light?" The blood bat hummed again, and I continued. "So, because it's rare, I stood out as a child. I was made fun of by the other children, which didn't stop after I reached adulthood. Though it lessened, it mostly changed its form. It became subtler.

"My poor sister was torn. She had her own friends but didn't like seeing me alone. I told her to enjoy her friends. Despite my jealousy, I certainly wasn't going to force myself into her little social group. I'd tried it before, and it never ended well," I said with a self-deprecating laugh.

"So, I just watched everything from afar. I tried to hold my head up high, accept who I was, but for some reason the boys loved to make fun of me for that. I mean, no one was asking them to bother me." I snorted. "They say that boys like to torture little witches they have crushes on, but I have the experience to say that's complete and utter shit."

What I had to say next had me feeling a bit ill. "I wasn't even approached by a man until I was twenty-three, but I suspect that was only because word got around that I couldn't get pregnant." A pang struck my heart from all the attached memories. "I never found out who'd been responsible for sharing that very private diagnosis with the whole accursed coven. There was no way it'd been my sister. I didn't show my face for a whole week. I was so humiliated."

It had been painful too. There'd been many agonies that day. I breathed through a wave of sadness and held my head a little higher, careful not to dislodge Vain. Crisply, I continued, "I'm not the same person anymore, Vain. I'm stronger now. I don't let others decide my personality for me. I could have grown up cold and hateful, but I never turned my back on anyone, and I never will. I know how much it hurts to be re…" I hadn't intended on that word sneaking its way into my speech, and I choked on it. "Rejected," I said calmly and repeated myself, shifting the topic to the rot-witch. "No, I've never turned my back on anyone. Though I'm not certain she truly needs it."

*I'm still undecided,* Vain admitted. *I'd say she's more like a troublesome child who could benefit from a nanny.*

I snorted humorlessly. "Your assessment is probably more accurate than mine."

*I still don't know where she got her cooking pot.*

"Well, I'd be afraid to ask, but you know she wouldn't reply with so much as a fart." I said it loud enough for Mushy to hear. She knew she was difficult, and I made a point to remind her.

*Please don't say that word. She already smells bad enough.*

That was wise. I didn't want to inspire any more bad behavior. Mushy was already too creative for her own good.

*Keid?* my bat prompted suddenly, and I froze in my steps. Something like a warning flickered from her soul to mine, and it grabbed my attention like a slap to the face.

"What?" I whispered, staying still and listening to the woods.

*Something is following us. Your soul is helping me hear and smell farther. There is another heartbeat nearby that does not belong to something small.*

"How not small?" I then tried to get Mushy's attention by hissing at her to stop.

*Bigger than you.*

"Oh gods." I whimpered and tried to think about spells I could use. My mind had gone blank, and I could barely think of anything helpful… unless whatever was stalking us had an urgent case of foot fungus.

*Curses? I'm feeling for your magic... What about your numbing spell for surgery? If they lost feeling in their body maybe... Let's find a branch.*

I nodded slowly, letting her know I heard her idea clearly. I glanced up through the tree branches but couldn't see anything. "Is it approaching?" I squeaked and started slowly following the rot-witch again. I made every step as soft as possible so I could hear over the din of my frightened heart.

*It hasn't moved. It's keeping its distance, I think,* she answered.

I nodded curtly and caught up to Mushy. "Something is following us," I warned her and looked over my shoulder again. I couldn't spy an accursed, abnormal thing. There were no swaying branches or disturbed shrubbery. "Is it the bone eater?"

The witch tilted her head back and laughed loudly. She shrieked and hooted as if I'd just told the world's funniest joke.

"Quiet! I'm serious," I hissed at her, furious. "My familiar warned me! You're the one who wanted me to summon one!" The witch continued laughing, and I lifted my hands in surrender.

*Hide our scents in case it only tracks by smell,* Vain ordered, assisting my flabbergasted brain. I held my breath out of sheer anxiety and started masking both our scents, then I set out to remove our older scents from a wider area. Vain kept her ears and nose open while I worked, warning me if I was getting too close to the stalker or if it ever moved.

"Can you tell what it is now?" I murmured when I placed the last spell down on the forest floor. I retreated hastily to catch up to Mushy, the back of my neck prickling like someone was watching me. Something probably was. I shuddered.

*Not yet.* She gripped me with her claws while I squatted to pick up some soil. I rolled the dirt around in my hands as I walked alongside the witch, trying to reabsorb some magic from the earth. I wanted to replenish what I'd just spent because I had no idea if this creature was going to attack or not.

"I am not a warrior," I mumbled as I searched around for a long stick I could sharpen. My expertise was in making charms, not warfare. If I made a spear, I could place a transferable curse on one end. Why hadn't I prepared for something like this sooner? "Perhaps…"

My planning was interrupted when I nearly ran into Mushy's back. I sputtered out an apology, but when I looked up to see the cause of her halt, I froze once more. This time, the freeze trickled in to not just stop me but to chill my very soul. I could hardly breathe with its grip on my chest alone.

The thing that had been stalking us was here, and he was blocking our path with his wings spread wide, blocking the light from ahead and casting a shadow upon us.

"Ferrer," I whispered and suffered the sense of ice slicking down my spine.

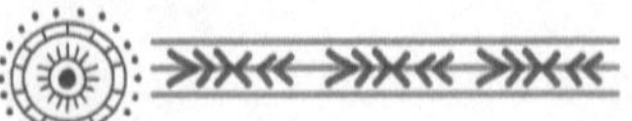
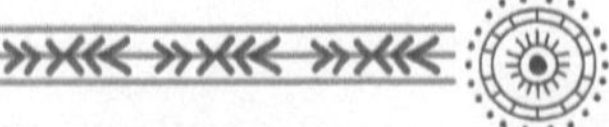

# Chapter 9

## Keid

I stepped around the rot-witch to address Ferrer, feeling the most indescribable hot-and-cold hodgepodge of emotions. Half of me wanted to yell at him, half of me wanted to cry, and the third half wanted to tackle him to the ground and ride him. The fact that I had three halves to contend with was a sign that close proximity to Ferrer had a wretched effect on my brain.

*Thirds! For fuck's sake, Keid!* I screamed at myself.

"What… Why are you here?" I asked sharply, biting back tears. I hated that I was already so close to crying. The way he looked at me nights ago was still so fresh in my mind; however, he was not looking at me in the same way now. What could he possibly want? I scowled and girded my loins. "Coming to properly reject me? Well, get it over with then. I've things to do!"

Ferrer was dressed in the same clothes he'd worn at the party, as if he'd left the very night I did. He tilted his head to regard me, significantly more calm. He didn't curl his lip this time, but his nostrils did flare in contained agitation. Most of the heat of his gaze seemed reserved for Mushy though, so I slowly inched in front of her.

I pressed my lips together, painfully tight, and my eyes unwillingly flickered to and from his gaze. It was hard to look at his face. He seemed more handsome now that he wasn't scowling at me, and I couldn't help but admire his fine features. Despite the roguish cut of his hair that fell about his cheekbones and strange pointed ears, he had an elegance about him. And now that I could study him for more than a second, I noticed that what was coming out of his back was an aesthetic match to his hair. The enormous dark taupe bat wings should have been frightening, but they actually had a bit of majesty. The white tips looked like they'd been dipped in porcelain, and that pale color streaked along the rest of the edges like a cloud's silver lining—obnoxiously beautiful.

So, surprisingly, it was his relative composure that unnerved me.

He jerked his finger in the direction we'd come and said, "I'm not rejecting you until we return to the castle, which is what you must do. Your sister is worried about you, and the colony has questions."

From his tone, he seemed less concerned about what my sister wanted and only mentioned her to destabilize me. I was about to give him a piece of my mind when the rot-witch waddled around and picked up a pinecone. She brought it to her lips like she was muttering a spell and tossed it at Ferrer.

His eyes widened, and he jumped away from the projectile, startled. His wings flapped haphazardly as he caught his balance, blowing a small breeze toward me. Mushy ambled past him now that her path was clear, giggling like a toddler. She leaned in Ferrer's direction and clawed at the air to spook him, which worked—surprisingly.

"Aaaeeeuhh!" she cried, tongueless, then started laughing again as she continued on her merry way. Little did Ferrer know that she couldn't say any spells. That pinecone had been nothing but a seedy trick. Perhaps I would have laughed, but I was in too dark of a mood to be properly amused. I followed Mushy past Ferrer and made an effort to not look at him.

"The only place we're going is this woman's home," I said and frowned at the emotional waver in my voice. Vain clawed gently at my neck, reminding me that she was here, and I slid a hand up my shoulder to stroke her. Her sweet gesture, unfortunately, only weakened my emotional dam. Now I was at risk of crying out of gratitude.

"You mean coven," Ferrer growled, catching up to us but keeping his distance.

"Nooo," I replied, drawing out the word. "Home. We just got freed, and now I'm taking her home! Haven't we gone through enough?"

I was starting to get angry again, and I held on to that. If I couldn't push away my emotions, I'd rather bite back than cry. I'd already spent too many tears, and my body couldn't take much more of that.

"I cannot let you leave!" he snarled and moved in front of us again.

"Oooeee, oooeee!" Mushy raised her long fingers as if to tickle him, and again he stumbled back with wide eyes. Clearly he was scared of her.

"You're wasting both our time," I scolded, shaking my finger at him. "I have nothing to say to your colony! I went to find a spouse, and he didn't want me! What more is there to say? Do you want to know how it felt because that's the only thing I can tell you that you don't know!"

He made a visible effort to compose himself before interrogating me, all but speaking through his teeth. "What we don't know is why there is a rot-witch on our land, and why you're assisting our enemy! You didn't come to us to find a spouse. You came for something. What was it? We have no secrets to steal!"

"Are you stupid? Did you get into some position of power because someone felt sorry for your tiny brain?" I yelled rudely, then balked. This wasn't like me at all, this childishness, and I felt ashamed for the first time in ages. I shook it off and glared at Ferrer. "You can thank the lions for abducting all the witches in the region." I jabbed a finger at him again. "It's not her fault that she got pulled into a dungeon with the rest of us! I'm just trying to help an old woman get home. Unlike you, I don't live a life of prejudice!"

I spun away from Ferrer and realized I'd lost sight of Mushy. "Oh shit." I ran to catch up to her. She seemed to have no interest in Ferrer's appearance. "Don't run off like that," I said breathlessly.

"Don't you do that either," Ferrer said from behind me. A large hand grabbed my wrist and jerked me to a stop. A tingling sensation peppered my arm where our skin met, and we recoiled from each other. He took a step back and brushed his hand against his pants, like he was wiping away the sensation.

I loathed how good it'd felt. I hated that I wanted more.

"I'd forgotten about that," he grumbled, then looked angrily up at me. I set my brows and mouth into a firm line, challenging his next words. At Vain's reminding scratch, I stood taller and raised my chin. I was not in the wrong here. I was doing a good deed, and Ferrer could suck it.

I called whatever bluff was about to tumble from his lips. "It seems to me that you can't touch either of us, so we'll be on our way. You might as well reject me now while you can."

His face contorted into something undecipherable for just a moment before he warned, "I have more bats coming, Keid. Don't force us to become hostile. They won't hesitate to kill your friend."

Despite the context, I tried to ignore how blissful it was to hear my name on his lips. My sister must have told him.

"Like you won't kill her anyway?" I finally shot back, taking a step forward in my accusation. "No, I think not. I think you're panicking because we're close to dragon territory, and your people won't get here in time. Why show yourself otherwise?"

The ire on his face told me I'd hit the truth, so I pushed my offense. I strode right up to him and reached for his hand. He jerked back and growled, "Don't touch me, Keid!"

"Or what?" I challenged and took another step forward, darting to poke whatever I could reach. Ferrer was too fast though, and I kept hitting thin air. "Seems to me like you're scared of me!"

When he backed up into a fallen branch and tripped, he bared his teeth in irritation. Though he'd lost his balance, he righted himself immediately and glared at me. For a heartbeat, I balked at the look on his face but kept pressing my attack. Maybe I could keep him busy while Mushy put some distance between us… or just drive him off entirely.

"I know what you're doing, woman," he snapped. "She won't reach the border in time."

"Or so you say!" I countered, lunging for him again. "Why can't you just leave us alone? Just kill us if we return because we don't plan on coming back! What harm could that decision do?"

"Because maybe it won't be you that returns but an army of rot-witches!" he accused and dodged behind a tree to put it between us.

"You're giving a feeble old woman a lot of credit!"

"If you know rot-witches so well, you know she's anything but powerless right now!"

I was running out of arguments. He just wouldn't understand. I leaned against the tree as I shook my head at him. "You'll never get it, Ferrer. You'll never know what it's like to be targeted because you're different. She has a right to go home and die in peace."

"Don't act like it's the same." He mirrored my pose and leaned down to stare me down with his intense red-brown gaze.

This night denizen's irises and pupils were so large and alluring that I was drawn into them for just a heartbeat. I hated how pretty his accursed eyes were. The reddish color reminded me of the clay I used to collect from the creek to make little friends for myself. Ferrer was no friend though. I grappled to return to our argument, but I'd already forgotten what I was going to say.

"What?" he asked, eying me warily.

"Nothing!" I growled, it obviously being my turn to make a stupid animal noise. I wasn't very good at it, and the corner of his lip twitched like he wanted to laugh. I reached out to slap the amusement off his face, but he simply ducked to avoid my furious hand.

I had no idea what we were doing. This was definitely immature behavior on both our parts, and I kept chasing him away like a little girl fed up with her bully. Still, I could only go so far.

Winded, I stopped and placed my hands on my hips. I supposed I'd driven him far enough away for now. What mattered was keeping Mushy safe. Annoyingly, the bat-shifter wasn't short of breath at all.

"Leave us alone," I ordered as I caught my breath. "Just let us go. You'll never have to lay your eyes on my ugly face ever again." I used my wrist to wipe away an angry tear. "If you won't do it then I will."

He looked alarmed after I uttered those words and took a step forward. "Keid? This is not the order to do things in…" he warned.

"Like shit it is!" I cried and opened my mouth to reject him. I couldn't take it anymore. I wanted the torture to end.

Ferrer lunged forward and clamped a hand over my mouth before I could utter a sound. The movement startled Vain, who fluttered out from my hair to hide behind a branch. I yelled for her, but Ferrer's rough palm muffled every sound I made.

"Do you really want to do that now? I've heard that rejection weakens you for a while. You really think you can protect your filthy charge in that state?" he asked with a terrifying intensity. It seemed like he was tolerating the fated touch just fine now. I was not doing so well.

An ache formed between my thighs despite his aggressive hold on me. I blinked rapidly from the puffs of his breath on my face and tried to get a hold of myself, but it was a struggle. My imagination pictured his heavy breathing as a result of lovemaking, and arousal fluttered in my abdomen. I swallowed hard and tried not to look at his soft, parted lips, but it was like they had their own gravity. I glanced at them for a second, and that was when Ferrer let me go, practically pushing me away from him.

I stumbled back, tripped on a root, and fell painfully hard to the forest floor. "Ahh!" I hissed and rubbed at my tailbone as I crawled to my feet. I glowered at a somewhat stricken Ferrer and turned to find Mushy. "Just leave us alone, and you'll never have to see me again."

"And your sister?" he called after me. "What about her?"

That had been the wrong thing to say. I whirled around, furious, and nearly screamed, "I think she'll be just fine because her bat accepted who she was! At least she'll know love in her lifetime!"

His features tensed, but he seemed at a loss for words. I turned around for the last time and called to Vain. She flapped into my embrace, and I returned her to my shoulder, apologizing profusely. I made a mental note to start on her collar. I wanted to think about anything… anything but Ferrer. Feeling eyes on my back though, it seemed he wouldn't even let me have that.

I cleared my hoarse throat. "The bastard is still following, isn't he?"

*Batstard,* she corrected. That was all the answer I needed.

## Ferrer

If Keid had been right about anything, it was the fact that, yes, I was panicking. I was panicking because we were approaching dragon territory, and my backup was nowhere to be found.

*The only backup you were thinking about was pushing her back up against a tree,* Iron accused gleefully.

I couldn't respond to that, so I ignored him. I had no intention of taking the woman who'd teased me mercilessly through a game of tag, but her stubborn attempts to touch me had ignited something that I didn't want to acknowledge—that I'd kind of wanted her to succeed. Gods, I did not know why. It simply must be the bloody mate bond.

It'd been a good thing that I'd already covered her mouth when she'd looked at mine. She'd gotten me too stirred up with her feisty game that I was afraid I'd end up kissing her to shut her up instead. I couldn't see her as well as I could scent her in the moment, and it didn't help knowing that she'd gotten excited as well.

My only regret was shoving her back, and I wished I hadn't. I hadn't meant to be a brute. Contrary to my behavior at the event, I didn't enjoy hurting her.

A part of me was also relieved that she still had a flicker of starlight in her. The more I'd thought about how she could have easily taken her life after my attempt to reject her, the easier it had been for the guilt to seep into me. If this project of hers, this escort mission, was as she claimed, then I supposed I could be grateful that she'd found purpose. I just wished she'd picked anything but helping a rot-witch.

But was what she said true? I was pretty good at reading people, and now that I'd gotten to engage with Keid in a relatively sane way, she seemed to at least believe her words. It left several options after that. One, all of what she said could be true. Two, the rot-witch was using her. However Keid wanted to explain it, the woman was still a stranger to her. She knew it. I knew it. I'd seen Keid's wary glances across the campfire, and her nightly retires were farther from the crone than necessary to simply be running from the stench.

The worst-case scenario would be the easiest to resolve. If Keid was cursed into helping this rot-witch, I could easily cure that. I did not want to do that around the rot-witch though. I doubted they ever learned the side effect of their curse on us, and I wasn't about to ruin my people's secret. No, I'd have to get her back to the castle before attempting to clear any curses inflicted upon her.

*Would you be ok with her sucking on someone else?* Iron asked curiously.

I bristled at his question as I followed Keid through the trees. *I really wish you'd use your brain to think of more helpful things, Iron.*

*I'm just wondering who she'd be sucking, that's all.*

*Please, for the love of nightfall, stop wording it like that!*

*Like what? I just want to know if you're ok with her giving Castanon a good suck. Probably not Ettor, though he looks like he could reaaally use it.*

I scrubbed a hand over my mouth, closed my eyes, and took a deep, calming breath. My bat was becoming increasingly more belligerent since my refusal to let him 'play' with Vain. He was growing significantly more vulgar as well.

None of this was helped by the fact that I was bloody starving. I hadn't eaten in days, and that led to another serious problem; I was worried about assaulting Keid if I tried to get a little food in me. We were going to have to have a very frank conversation about that, and I had a good feeling it'd scare her into surrendering. I certainly was not giving up here.

Though I bloody well wasn't looking forward to that talk. Like every bat-shifter, I had some very real limitations that I was not proud of, and if she'd gotten into the recognition grounds through the line, she'd be aware of them.

With that hanging over my head, I continued my pursuit. Their journey was quieter, and the day progressed with little to note. The Sun God eventually settled to rest, and I climbed the treetops to look for my people. There was no one in sight among the sea of midnight green.

*They're going to hit dragon territory soon,* I said to Iron, hoping he'd have an idea. *What do we do?*

*Who cares?* he replied, sounding bored.

*I need you to step it up a notch, Iron!* I snapped, getting fed up with him. *I need your help!*

*What do you want me to say? You have three choices here. We can go back home, we can grab Keid and hope the witch doesn't destroy us, or we keep following. I mean, you can try to kill the witch, but I'd rather not get stuck in a nightmare loop for the rest of my life. If you could help avoid that, that'd be great.*

I shuddered at his mention of what Queen Hekla had endured and wrapped my arms around myself. The breeze was cold, but I wasn't. I was genuinely scared. The rot-witch terrified me, and just being in the same woods as her was food for nightmares. They didn't destroy in a normal manner. They got creative, and that made my skin crawl. It didn't follow the natural order of things at all.

What was the old woman below me capable of doing? What tortures had she wrought in her long lifetime? No, she couldn't curse me into a nightmare loop, but she could very well do something else. I rubbed my eyes, suffering from exhaustion and hunger, then leaned against a branch to take a steadying breath. This would hopefully be all over soon. I'd be back home, resting in my chamber and gorging on a ration. Then I'd be forced to masturbate before going to sleep. I groaned. The same old life, indeed.

I tried to picture sharing my chambers with a chosen mate, but I couldn't picture anyone but Keid. Why? There were plenty I'd been able to imagine before. I turned my head to look for the Moon Goddess and said, "You're killing me here." I shook my head, yawned, and started crawling slowly down the tree. I was also not adapting well to a daytime schedule either. My whole body was off-kilter.

A scent hit my nose about halfway down the tree, and I groaned. I knocked my skull against the tree several times in frustration before continuing down to where Keid was. That bloody rot-witch…

"—s a lot. I hope you're hungry because I am not helping you with that," Keid's voice was saying, her voice thick with revulsion. I approached as close as I dared and settled on a branch. I no longer bothered with hiding since they were already aware of my presence, so I crankily leaned against the tree and glowered down at the scene.

The rot-witch was bent over a pot of black liquid, and it was obvious to me what the substance was. Somehow, she'd not just found a pig but managed to catch one to bleed out. I'd seen blood prepared this way before, and it was alright, but it was usually fixed for the sick.

That old crone knew, and I hated her even more for it. She knew I was hungry, and she made a vat of blood stew to rub in my face. I waited for it because I knew—I just bloody knew—it was coming.

The rot-witch dunked a wooden cup into the stew and looked straight up at me. Her eyes were red, weeping, and wild, but I saw the glimmer of her lucid tease. She held the cup up and wiggled it a little, like she was calling a puppy to offer a treat.

Keid looked up from something she was working on, threw it aside, and lunged for the cup. When she spotted me reclining on the branch, she hissed under her breath, "Don't feed him, you old fool! Are you crazy?" Keid yanked the cup away from the cackling rot-witch, yelped when she almost spilled the blood on herself, then tossed the cup away from the campsite. In what was becoming an expected gesture, the younger witch shook her finger at the old crone in a flustered rage. "You may think you're being funny, but your jokes have consequences!"

They did indeed. I waited for the old creature to look back up at me, and when she did, she was still laughing mercilessly. I leaned down a little and quietly articulated my deepest desire. "I cannot wait to kill you."

I knew it was stupid to threaten her, but I was so bleedin' cranky. She didn't seem to take it seriously either and just continued gurgling out her horrible laugh. My eyes flickered to Keid, who also didn't appear to enjoy the timbre of her cackles. She grimaced as she pulled her project back onto her lap. Curious and needing a distraction from hunger pains, I moved my vantage to another branch so I could see what she was doing.

By firelight, Keid was weaving together individual barbs plucked from a large grey feather. I blinked in surprise, having no idea how she was doing that. Both human, most fae, and shifter hands were much too big and clumsy to weave something so small. Curious, I wanted to ask about it, but I didn't. I felt like it'd undermine the reason I was still here.

I was fascinated all the same and watched with rapt attention when she'd bend forward to soften some beeswax over a flame. She delicately applied it to specific parts of the braid to keep it from falling apart and occasionally muttered something that might have been a spell. I'd seen very little spellcasting in my life, but it seemed like each barb was receiving some kind of enchantment as she wove. I didn't recognize any of the words. Some of them didn't even sound like words. I'd occasionally catch an odd growl or chirp, like she was speaking with nature's tongue, and it was weirdly beautiful.

I tried not to be impressed, but I was. I didn't think I'd ever seen a beautiful application of witchwork. My memories of witchery were full of blood, gore, screaming, and the smell of rot. This almost had a childlike innocence about it. No, that wasn't right. The motions were purposeful, not fanciful, like she was a tailor simply doing her craft. I was reminded of a leatherworker tooling a fine design into animal skin and thought that seemed about right.

Her face was both relaxed and focused, like this task was something she'd been trained to do and had been doing for years. Now it was all muscle memory. I wondered if she'd be able to do it in the dark by feel alone.

That was the wrong combination of words to be thinking about in regards to Keid. I ignored Iron's laughter for the hundredth time, irritated at how my mind continued to slip. I didn't know what I was expecting from sitting and watching her. Perhaps I'd hoped that her being a witch would continue to put me off... and it was, wasn't it? I placed a hand to my head and shook it, like I was trying to rattle my brain into working correctly again.

*Witches are not sexy*, I reminded myself.

I withered when that thought stoked Iron's mirth. He sounded like he was falling apart in my head, and I simply waited him out in utter defeat. I scrubbed a hand over my tired eyes and bemoaned the struggle of my very existence.

"Of course," Keid said pleasantly, and I glanced down to see her move Vain from her side to her shoulder so the bat could feed. That was my cue to retreat. I'd watched Vain feed before, and the aroma of Keid's blood was far too tempting to be around for long. It was also too much for Iron, who regularly became wild at the sight of Vain lapping at our fated mate's trickle of blood.

A knowing chuckle punctuated my departure, and I didn't need to look back to know that the rot-witch was teasing me. She was turning out to be just as sadistic as one would expect.

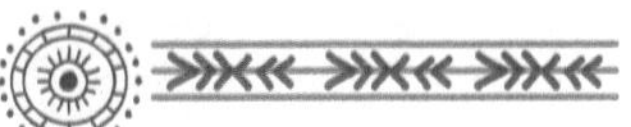
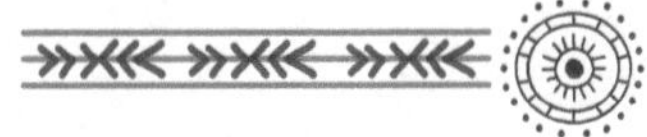

# Chapter 10

## Reid

To say that I was shocked by the witch trying to feed Ferrer was… something. Was I surprised by it in the moment? Yes. Was I surprised by it five minutes later? I wasn't so sure. Did she know about bat-shifters and eating? The bats arrived in our realm during our coven's imprisonment, so I couldn't be sure. Perhaps someone had told her about it on her journey north? Maybe that was who gave her the sack and cooking supplies. I sighed and propped my head up with a palm, staring at Mushy's enjoyment of the blood stew. She'd probably stolen the items. I wouldn't put it past her.

Thoroughly fatigued, I planned on retiring as soon as Vain finished her meal. I reached up with a finger and petted the top of her head as delicately as I could. I was already incredibly fond of her, and for some reason, her partaking of my blood to sustain her made our bond feel that much closer. I wasn't used to it yet, but I also didn't mind, surprisingly. Usually, people did not enjoy being eaten.

Mushy stood and left, probably to clean out her cooking pot. When she returned, the pot was full of water she'd collected from the creek we'd been following. It looked heavy, but I accepted she was more than a mystery at this point. I stared lazily as she started throwing herbs into it. I recognized some of them, but I was no botanist. Potions and medicine from scratch were not my specialty.

"Making some tea, Mushy?" I asked, not particularly curious. The witch didn't laugh this time but stayed focused on what she was doing. It wasn't until she bent over to riffle through the detritus that I noticed the earth we camped on was just as reactive as where I'd summoned Vain. I frowned, twisted my lips in thought, and studied her movements. Did rich soil follow her or did she somehow make rich soil?

Without tilting Vain too much, I nudged some leaves aside to dip my fingertips into the dirt. I felt the gods' essences seep into my skin like water through roots. Yes, this earth was incredibly reactive. I pulled out a clod of dirt and massaged it between my fingers, sighing in pleasure as I quenched my reserves. It felt good. It was like drinking the milk from a well-fed, healthy, and happy animal.

I picked up Vain's collar, which I hadn't finished yet, and idly strengthened the spells that were already in it. However, something different happened. I gasped lightly as the enchantment whisked right out of me and glued itself to the collar without any finessing.

"What in the…" I gasped with wide eyes, furrowed brows, and a mouth that was contorted into what had to be a bizarre shape. I prodded the woven spell, and it was… quite confident. I didn't know how else to describe it. "I don't know what just happened, but I need to check on this tomorrow. I'm going to stop working on this until then, Vain. Let that spell sit and settle."

I picked up a fresh clod of dirt and studied it. It was dark and surprisingly moist for dirt that was a fair distance from the creekside. As it crumbled apart, I noticed little earthworms writhing about, unhappy to be disturbed so. There were also little roly-polies nestled in the soil. I plucked out a morel mushroom and was tempted to take a bite, but I set it aside to wash later. This was very rich soil, probably the richest I'd ever seen. It was teeming with life that fed it generously.

I carefully returned the soil to the ground, apologizing to the little critters I'd disturbed, and glanced back up at the rot-witch. Mushy was tossing little mushrooms and seeds into the pot, occasionally stirring. Whatever she was making appeared to be harmless. Perhaps she was brewing a potion for arthritis or something. Being a rot-witch at the end of life had to be painful. I couldn't imagine. Maybe that was why they seemed to go crazy. I hummed thoughtfully, intrigued by the notion.

She finished making whatever it was and submerged a wooden cup to fill it. She set it aside and waddled off to retrieve the cup I'd thrown. Without bothering to wash it, she dipped the cup into the brew, brought it to her lips, and drank thirstily.

I stared at the second cup and wondered if she was going to offer it to me. Would I accept it? She drained the cup and disposed of it onto the dirt with a satisfied grunt. Reaching behind her, she fumbled for a long stick and tapped the second cup.

I grabbed it and brought it to my nose, sniffing it curiously. I doubted it would hurt me. I'd watched her drink it, and I didn't see why Mushy would poison me. If anything, I was starting to think I was a source of entertainment for her.

"This better not be poison," I said dryly, watching her rock in her seat. She chuckled, and I barely noticed a lateral shake of her head. I imagined that was her denial. She seemed tired. We did move faster today.

"Keid, no!" a voice hissed from above us. I tilted my head up to spy Ferrer on a branch. He swiped his hand and shook his head aggressively. "Do not drink that!"

"She's not going to poison me," I replied, annoyed at his intervention.

"How in the blazing starlight would you know that?"

I set the cup down and dragged my hands through my hair. Vain took one more lick and climbed slowly down my chest to plop onto my lap. I petted her back and tried to contain my irritation. Ferrer was very good at provoking me.

As calmly as possible, I explained, "I don't plan on dying anymore. I have this little one to take care of, but what does it matter to you if I die anyway, Ferrer? If you're so worried about my sister—like you obviously seem to be—just tell her I escaped your valiant clutches." Vain's little thumb hooked onto my finger, and I wiggled it with a smile.

"So what? You're happy to grow a third eyeball or something?" he asked, his wings fluttering in his agitation.

I threw my hands up in the air. "So I'll have three eyes! So what? I'm already hideous!" This whole argument bewildered me.

"Blood clots. You're being reckless."

"Go away."

"Keid…" He flapped again as he adjusted his position in the tree, brushing me again with a slight breeze. If Mushy weren't around, perhaps I would have smelled him. Despite his days in the wild, he still smelled pleasant, gods knew how. He should be reeking. Stars, I probably reeked.

Annoyed by my distraction, I finally snapped. I didn't like how my attraction to him kept disarming me. "Look!" I yelled. "You either apologize and love me and grovel at my feet for the rest of our lives or you get out of our way!" I searched for some kind of insult to end my tirade. "You… Mister…" I fumbled for something and ended on an embarrassingly stupid choice. "M-Mister Flappy Flap!"

His eyes widened, his jaw dropped, and he flapped again, unintentionally punctuating my outburst. In the window of his speechlessness, I grabbed the cup and downed it right before him. The flavor was terrible, but at least it was bland. Setting the cup down, I smacked my lips in distaste.

"Yuck," I muttered.

“Throw that up, Keid!” he said, his pale face blanching more from shock. He white-knuckled the thinner branch that he was using to balance himself, but I doubted he was about to lunge at me.

“Throw… y-yourself!” I shot back pathetically and gestured in a random direction. “Over there, preferably!” I was not an expert at insults during peak agitation.

Ferrer grabbed his head with both his hands, growled an odd panicky sound, and shot up the tree, disappearing from sight. When I noticed Mushy’s quiet giggles, I rolled my head toward her and raised a brow.

“You just love drama, don’t you?” I remarked. She laughed a little louder and smacked a hand on her knee. “Yes, you do, you wretched thing. And that is why you won’t kill me. I’m too much fun.”

I scooped up a tired Vain and moved away from the rot-witch to find a place to sleep. I was feeling pretty good by the time I lay down and curled up under my blanket. Vain hung next to me, wiggling as she cutely wrapped her wings about herself.

I smiled as my belly grew warm, like how it felt after a glass of wine or a flagon of sweet mead. The tea—or whatever you’d call it—had a soothing effect, and I liked how relaxed it made me feel. I squirmed happily and snuggled tighter into a ball, but the sound of rustling leaves startled me out of my bliss. I scowled when I realized who it was. He was ruining my warm fuzzies. The batstard.

“Ferrer,” I growled warningly, drawing out his name. “What are you doing?”

“Go to sleep,” he grumbled from his perch above me. I opened my eyes but couldn’t see anything in the dark. The moon couldn’t reach past the clustered redwood trees and their shielding needles.

“Don’t babysit me,” I complained. “Go sleep elsewhere.”

This time, the words sounded worn out and tired. “Go to sleep.”

I swallowed nervously, not liking the weakness in his tone. I drew the blanket up to my chin and did my best to ignore the bat-shifter roosting above me. I couldn't wait to get to dragon territory and leave him behind for many reasons. It still stung, but I figured it always would.

I was feeling fantastic the next day as I jumped up and out of my blanket. I stood tall and stretched, allowing my spine to crackle delightfully like a popping fire. I hadn't felt this good in a very long time, probably not since I was a kid. A cool breeze ran through my veins, then settled warm and happy in my belly.

Unfortunately, the tea did not cure my vision, and I whimpered as the enchantment that corrected my eyesight finally faded. I hastened to fix my nearsightedness and astigmatism because the reversion always made me claustrophobic. Going from being able to see everything to just being able to focus on my immediate surroundings made me feel like my world had shrunken. I shuddered and hurried to finish the enchantment, not wanting to suffer this affliction a second longer.

I breathed a huge sigh of relief when I finished, able to see fully again. I hadn't realized I'd been holding my breath, and I leaned against a tree while I waited for my lungs to stop burning. Well, the day had started great for a minute. I'd take it.

I went to find Mushy, who was already waiting for me. She definitely wouldn't have been doing that if she'd planned on killing me with poison. I felt my forehead for a third eye and snorted when all I encountered was smooth—perhaps slightly oily—skin. Goodness, I needed a bath. I was going to break out everywhere at this rate. I didn't need to feel uglier than I already was.

Ferrer, of course, continued to follow us at a distance, and by late afternoon, he approached me cautiously. "Keid, we need to talk," he said in a low, serious voice. "We really need to go back."

"Nothing you say can convince me," I replied, stepping over a jutting root as I followed Mushy down a deer trail.

"Well, if you go into dragon territory, nothing will keep me from following you. My people will catch up, and they will pursue extradition with the authorities. This is pointless."

I stopped and turned to face him, nearly making him bump into me. I pushed him away, and he grudgingly retreated a step, looking wary.

"Doing the right thing is never pointless," I asserted, realizing that Mushy was still ambling on merrily. I could hear her gurgling hums as she disappeared from sight.

"What if she's taking advantage of you?" He gestured aggressively with both hands. "Have you not thought about that? Have you not thought about your own safety? What if she's leading you right where she wants you? What if you're some kind of… I don't know… sacrifice?"

I curled my hands in the air and groaned in frustration. "Why do you care? Seriously, Ferrer! This needs to stop!"

"Would you know if you were cursed?" he asked frankly, putting his hands on his hips. "How do you know she hasn't… manipulated you this far?"

I held back a bark of laughter and simply breathed through the impulse. What a ridiculous notion. "It seems to me like you're just arguing to buy time. Well, Mushy is ambling on as ever," I said, pointing to where she'd gone. "We should reach the border today."

He looked away, breathing heavily like he was about to panic. "What about my need to eat?" he asked with urgency. "I won't stop following you until you're both apprehended, but you do not want me getting out of control until then, do you? I certainly don't!"

I scrubbed my fingers over my eyes, completely unshaken by his threat. I snorted, backed up, and threw my hands out wide, like I was encouraging him. "Go on then! I don't care. It'll be the last time any man or male shows interest in me!"

That was not the response he'd expected and it showed. "You cannot be serious," he deadpanned.

"I'm hideous, Ferrer. I won't say no to one last night of sex before I'm a spinster for life! It's not as much of a threat as you think!" I hissed, then turned around to catch up to Mushy, leaving the bat-shifter completely frozen and dumbstruck.

"He is really starting to exhaust me," I mumbled to Vain as we finally crossed over into the dragon kingdom. I knew we'd left his people's territory because I heard him ranting and raving about it from the branches over our heads.

*I hadn't really expected him to give up.* Vain sighed.

"He'll get hungry and leave. He'd do anything to avoid sleeping with a witch," I muttered, "especially an ugly one."

*What makes a human ugly?* she asked curiously. It wasn't the response I'd expected, and I fumbled to come up with an answer.

"Ah… well, I'm not the normal color. You know that," I replied, not sure why I was feeling embarrassed.

*What do you think about white rabbits? Doves?* she inquired even more innocently than before.

"I… think they're pretty… but they're supposed to be that color."

*I don't understand. What does prettiness have to do with that? Something pretty is something pretty. Am I wrong?*

I was a bit confounded by that, I had to admit, and sought an argument. "Well… in nature, abnormality can be a sign of bad health. It's pretty true with me, Vain. I did acquire complications from my albinism. Animals don't want to mate with one who'll give them unhealthy offspring."

*But you're not a rabbit. There are treatments, and your offspring isn't guaranteed to have albinism. I watched you fix your eyes. It doesn't seem like it matters as much with humans.*

Her argument was, admittedly, pretty solid except for one factor. "I'm not able to have children… you know that."

She went silent, and I felt her mortification across our bond. I stroked the top of her head to let her know it was ok, but saying it out loud always depressed me. We didn't talk after that, and I simply followed Mushy deeper into the dragon kingdom. I had a feeling we'd probably turn north soon.

"Any chance of telling me how far we are from your home?" I asked Mushy when she started building a fire for the night. We hadn't been bothered by any dragons, but I figured it was a matter of time. I could only hide so much of the rot-witch's potent scent trail, and someone was bound to notice her campfires.

The witch didn't answer. She just shakily went about boiling water, and I pulled out my last ration. I'd have to start foraging and setting traps soon. It'd been a long time since I'd crafted a snare, but I wasn't particularly worried about it. I remembered enough. Food was not my concern. We still had that bone eater to contend with, wherever it was.

I stared over my shoulder into the dark and shuddered. Campfires always made the black of the night so much more oppressive. The shadows encroached so aggressively at the edge of the light that it was all too easy to imagine shapes in the distance. I turned abruptly to look toward the fire again, not wanting to get too spooked. I still had to sleep out there later.

*Collar,* Vain reminded me, and I nodded with a mouthful of granola. I pulled the little project out of my bag and swept my fingers over the braid.

"Surreal," I murmured. "The enchantment is solid, Vain. It doesn't look like it'll ever decay. I've never seen something like this." I turned the braid around, studying every tight twist. There was a protection spell that would make Vain slippery. If an eagle tried to grab her, she'd be too difficult to grip and she'd slide right out of its talons.

Witchwork was as much of an art as it was a science. Sometimes it seemed like there were no rules, and sometimes it felt incredibly restrictive. Spells were like puzzles, and I supposed that was why I liked enchantment. It kept my mind busy, and the need to innovate was refreshing.

I went back to braiding the delicate thing, excited by how it was developing. I wished I had taken some of that rich soil with me. With the boost I got from Vain and the power of the earth, I could make my familiar a force with which to be reckoned. I didn't have to settle for pure protection. I could probably weave other spells into it.

My mind was so busy thinking of ideas that I didn't notice Mushy slide another cup of tea my way. It wasn't until she rapped my foot with a stick that I jerked my head up, startled. "Oh," I said and accepted the drink. "Thank you."

"Keid…" Ferrer's voice growled from the shadows, but I ignored him. I was focused and didn't want him distracting me. As quickly as possible, I downed the tea.

"Blech…" I shuddered, stuck my tongue out, and licked my lips clear. It didn't taste good, but I definitely loved how it made me feel. I'd sleep well tonight. "Thank you, Mushy," I said idly as I dripped a small bead of wax onto the braid to glue the section together. I held it up and turned it around under the firelight. I was close to finishing it. I could always add certain spells later. Such was the beauty of enchantment.

*Pretty,* Vain remarked, her tone low and sleepy.

I yawned, realizing that I was quite ready to retire as well. I placed the braid in my bag, scooped my familiar up, and said good night to Mushy, who quivered and rocked as usual. She didn't laugh but merely smiled as she stared into the fire with her blushing, wild eyes. Something about her placidity tonight unnerved me, and I quickly left her campsite to find my own space.

When I settled, the same warmth came over me, and I burrowed happily into my blanket. Soon after settling, like last night, I heard Ferrer's telltale sound of roosting, and it sounded significantly closer. I had a feeling that if I reached out, I could maybe poke the top of his head. Why did he have to be so near? Did he think we'd try to sneak off in the middle of the night?

Annoyed, I turned away and closed my eyes to sleep. Out of the blue, a sudden sharp pain hit my lower right abdomen, and I grimaced. "Ah…" I groaned quietly and rubbed at the sore region. The pain faded pretty quickly, so I got comfortable again.

"What's wrong?" Ferrer's voice asked quietly.

"Pulled a muscle," I dismissed, annoyed at his intrusiveness. He needed to stop pretending like he cared. It wasn't going to fool me. "Go to sleep," I added, throwing his old words back at him. He grunted in response but didn't utter a sound after that.

I didn't know how many hours I slept before the pain woke me again. I sat up fast, placed a hand to the same spot on my lower abdomen, and wheezed through the stabbing sensation. Not wanting to wake up Ferrer or Vain, I crept away with my medical kit to find the creek.

We'd slightly deviated from it, but I got there soon enough, fumbling almost blindly in the dark. When I splashed some cold water on my face, I patted my cheeks and frowned. I was a little warm. Was I getting sick?

I shifted my weight as I crouched, and when I noticed a dampness between my legs, I rolled off my leggings and underwear. I couldn't see my undergarment very well, so I gave it a cursory sniff. No, no blood, which was good. The gods knew what that'd do to Ferrer.

They had said that even though I was barren, I'd have occasional spotting, but I never felt it when it occurred. I must have pulled a muscle walking. Maybe I bent over weirdly and strained something. I decided to skip the pain-killing tincture since the stabbing sensation had already faded and focused on cleaning my clothes instead. I methodically scrubbed at my underwear and leggings to clean off whatever mucus had come out of me, then shrugged my tunic off to freshen it up a bit too.

The night air was nice, but it just drew attention to how achy and hot I was feeling. I fanned my face after I wrung the water from my tunic, feeling more flushed by the heartbeat.

"Great goddess," I whispered. As I fumbled around for a branch to hang my clothes from, I noticed some soreness in both my breasts. I palmed them and frowned, then rolled my fingers around to check for any lumps. The last thing I needed was a breast disease.

I didn't notice anything unusual, so I let them be. Maybe I was getting a fever and was developing body aches? My digestion was fine, so I doubted that Mushy's tea had given me food poisoning.

I had no idea what it was, so I shrugged off the sensations until I had more symptoms to help me diagnose. Maybe it was a temporary thing. I leaned against the tree that held my clothes and just kept fanning my face.

A cold, humble breeze would occasionally find its way to me, and I tilted my face into it, sighing with pleasure. I'd normally be freezing, so something was definitely up with my body. I wasn't sure if menopause was even possible for someone like me. Were these hot flashes? Certainly I was too young for that.

I looked down in surprise as more moisture collected between my thighs. "What are you doing?" I quietly asked my body, then groaned when my core began to throb. "Hey now, stop that." I breathed out slowly, unable to recall the last time I'd felt my sex wake like this. "Glittering stars!" I gasped and leaned over to prop my hands on my knees.

Why was I aching so badly? I'd never been this aroused before, even with a partner. I'd just been out here doing laundry. There was nothing alluring about laundry.

"Oh gods," I moaned under my breath, trying to be quiet. "Go away, go away, go away!" I turned to lean against the tree's trunk and rested my forehead against the rough bark in frustration. I hissed, stamped a foot, and agonized over whether I should try masturbating or not. I always had failed orgasms, so I was never inclined to practice self-relief.

I released a startled shriek at the sound of footsteps to my right and ducked to put the tree between me and whatever was on the other side. I could hardly see in the pitch of the forest, so I relied on my hearing for identification.

"Mushy?" I asked quietly, but with how deep the breathing was, I hazarded another guess. "F-Ferrer? Is that you?"

A responding growl alarmed me, and tried as I might to see around the tree, my eyes couldn't make out more than a shadowy silhouette. The growl though… that very much sounded like Ferrer. Was he annoyed that I'd disappeared? That was ridiculous. The babysitting had to stop.

"You could have warned me! I'm naked! Go back to sleep!" I snapped, but my voice wavered from nervousness. He wasn't saying anything. Why wasn't he saying anything?

I became doubly alarmed when there was a flap and his footsteps turned into a run. He was running toward me? I shrieked and started running as well, but it was a complete disaster. Every step in the dark promised to break some bone, and I didn't know if it was worth it. When I ran right into a bush, I knew it definitely hadn't been worth it. I fell into it and became painfully tangled in the branches with the wind knocked out of me.

I was lifted out by large hands, and the tingling sensation between us told me that this definitely was Ferrer. "What is going on?" I gasped, shocked by this behavior. "Ferrer, what are you doing?"

I was hoisted up against his hard chest, and he took me… somewhere. I had no idea how far he'd run before setting me down, but he was either unable or unwilling to answer any of my questions. "Did you eat?" I asked finally, wishing I could see him. "Ah, it's so dark!"

I reached out with a hand and fumbled around, looking for loose soil. I dug my fingers in and did my best to provoke and manipulate the bacteria in the dirt. I'd seen it done before, but I was worried it wouldn't work very well this far from the creek. I must've still had some potent magic left in me because the ground around us started glowing softly where patches of bacteria clustered. I was surprised to see a couple mushrooms with bioluminescence sprout as well.

"Wild." I coughed, then looked up to verify the identity of the mad growler. Ferrer was hastily ripping his clothes off, exposing carved, flexing muscles, and my eyes widened when I saw his mouth. It was stained, but the stain had spread up his face instead of down, like he'd eaten while roosting and had done so messily.

"What…" I murmured, placing a finger to my own lips in confusion. I'd left him sleeping. Had he woken, eaten something upside down, then lost control of his body? That didn't sound right.

I clapped in front of his face, trying to snap him out of it. "Ferrer!" I said loud and clearly. "You're going to be so mad at yourself if you do this!" He ignored me and finished kicking his pants and underclothes off, now gloriously nude.

He looked nothing like my last lover.

*Oh stars above!*

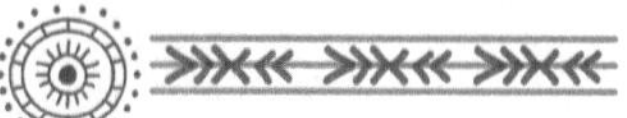
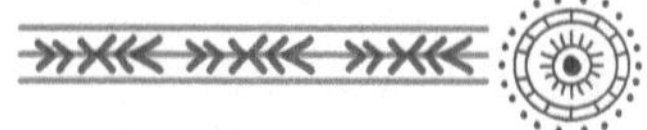

# Chapter 11

Ferrer, aglow from the bed of bioluminescence, was visible now, just barely. The blues and greens of provoked nature should have looked eerie on him, but it only made the shifter more alluring. Though what was happening to him was anything but a secret, the glow brought to light the real mystery behind Ferrer. Who was this person? Was this him or his beast? How did he see me this very second?

I couldn't read him at all, but he was completely fixated on me, staring intently through his tousled locks with pupils blown wide. His fuller lower lip parted, trembling slightly as he crouched. The whites of his teeth were barely showing, but I knew that if he drew his lips farther back, I'd see brutally sharp fangs.

My hand slowly went to my neck, idly thumbing where Vain had fed from earlier. He'd already eaten, right? He wasn't going to bite me, was he? Ferrer's eyes followed my hand, and his gaze slipped over my neck but didn't linger. I shivered and fought an insecure urge to cover my breasts as he studied the rest of my body, moving slowly to climb over me. His eyes flickered about my skin, staring unashamedly from my sex to my chest in full sweeps. I couldn't tell if he was approaching me like something he was about to kill or cherish, and the secret was almost enough to snap my nerves.

I held back a moan as he placed his palms on either side of my shoulders, making the firm, lean muscles of his chest and abdomen flex. Glancing to the side, I could see a vein pulsing in his arm, pushed out by a hard, quivering bicep. I'd never seen a man or male's body in such superior shape before now, and I whimpered when my core clenched in a wave of wanting.

The warmth that radiated from his virile form was enough to make me break into a light sweat, and I was desperate for him to slide his heat into me. I craved to know what the tingling from the mate touch felt like everywhere, and I wanted so badly to lay my fingers on him.

But I couldn't. He had to do it first. I wouldn't take the blame when he came to his senses.

I agonized over a decision as my eyes raked over the fine edge of his jawline and the delicate curve of his flushed cheekbones. Should I push at him? If he managed to remember any of this, would he appreciate it if I'd at least tried to fight him? He was the one who didn't want this.

A plaintive mewl escaped my lips as frustration trickled through my body. After a torturous internal battle, I caved to lust and spread my thighs for him. I couldn't resist, and I couldn't fight it. His show of need was impossible to ignore. Maybe I could've put up a good struggle if my body hadn't already fallen into a state of wanting. As it was now, the momentum was too great.

The spreading of my legs seemed to wake him from his prowling, and he was between them in a heartbeat. He reached hungrily between us to jerk at something, definitely his cock, and bared his teeth to expose his fangs. When I glanced down to study the flesh he was pumping at, I scooted back, startled by what was living between his legs. Everything there was bigger than what I'd seen before!

When Ferrer grabbed my hips and dragged me back to him, I sent a quick prayer to the Sky Gods, hoping that the only man I'd ever been with had been a fluke. Surely, my body could take in more. If not, we'd have a real problem here.

I'd seen plenty of flaccid penises during my time assisting the doctor, but erect ones? I didn't have much to go on other than my last lover, and compared to Ferrer's, well, it hadn't been much to… go on.

The amorous male impatiently positioned his cock to penetrate me, but when there was a prod in an unexpected region, I bucked violently. "Wrong hole! Wrong hole! Wrong hole!" I yelped and slapped his hand away from his erection. Fortunately, Ferrer didn't respond poorly to my emergency deflection but simply groaned appreciatively when I took control of his member.

I swallowed hard when I couldn't completely wrap my fingers around it. He was big… and warm. The flexible skin that sheathed his hardness was soft, silky, and drawn tight from his ardor. A pearl of his precum dripped onto my wrist as I handled him, and my stomach flipped with arousal. I gulped once more as I angled his heavy cock to slide between my folds.

Maybe he sensed my own nervousness because he leaned forward and nuzzled into my neck. I choked on a sob. How sweet that caress was. Why couldn't he be like this normally? Why was his feral mind more affectionate than him?

I turned my thoughts back to the moment and shut everything else out for now. If I had one night left with a man or male, I'd enjoy every second of it. At least I'd get to experience what it was like to make love with a fated mate… despite the lack of love.

With Ferrer's cock notched against my entrance, I slid my hands down his sides to gently pull on him, letting him know that he could move now. He'd obviously never slept with anyone before, and I squeezed his hips with my thighs to further encourage him.

I gasped when he began to push, his head straining my threshold. I gritted my teeth and lightly patted his chest, whispering,

"Go slow, go slow, go slow!" Fortunately, my unusually wet sex was slippery enough to ease some of the tension.

He must have understood through his fog because his upper body started shaking from restrained instinct. His lustful breaths puffed against my ear as I wrapped my legs around him and squeezed to let him know he could push again. His head stretched me farther until it finally slipped wetly into my channel, and we both let out a gasping moan. Ferrer rolled his hips experimentally and pushed again to slide in more.

He seized after that and cried into my shoulder, shaking and jerking uncontrollably. I let my legs fall off him, realizing that he was spending his seed. That had been short… but I'd heard that could happen. I patted his arm consolingly and waited for him to climb off me as he gasped for air. I wondered how many seconds it would take for him to start getting upset about the whole thing. I sighed in dismay and looked away, but Ferrer made no move to leave.

After a minute or two, he released a rumbling, low purr into my neck and rolled his hips again, like he was trying to go deeper. I released another sigh and tried to relax through his last moment of exploration. However, I began to form questions when he showed no sign of losing his erection or his interest in staying inside me. That wasn't normal, was it?

Ferrer grunted and suddenly lurched over me, swinging his hips forward to sink in another inch. I arched and groaned at how intensely he was stretching me. How was he harder than before he came? I breathed into the tense, bunched muscles of his shoulder as he rocked again and again, pushing his cock along my channel until he was buried to his sack and nestled against my cervix.

"Ahhh…" he purred out once more, moaning erotically into my temple. The sound of him continuing to enjoy me was electrifying, and a sizzling bolt of pleasure splintered through my body to settle in my sex, making me buck up into him with a cry. He responded to my movement by jerking his own hips forward, rubbing our groins together.

I tilted my head back and cried again from the resulting pleasure. Everywhere our skin touched generated marrow-deep satisfaction, and the sparks lit up a plethora of nerve endings. Ferrer ground against my clit until I was writhing beneath him from a pleasure I'd never experienced under a man. "More, more!" I begged into his pointed ear, brushing my lower lip against it. I wished I could slide my mouth down to latch onto his, but the blood there kept my sensual gesture at bay.

Ferrer shuddered and raised his hips to slide almost all the way out of my channel. His head stayed buried for just a moment before he swung his abdomen forward, plunging back in between my folds, iron hard and slicked by both my arousal and his seed. I grunted from the impact and groaned through a deep exhale, telling him without words how I loved the way he filled me. I raked my fingers down his back, enjoying the curves of his working muscles. These muscles had only one focus, and it was to fuck his mate.

"More!" I moaned in desperation, clawing at him. "More, Ferrer! Fuck me! Please!" I needed him panting and sweating above me. I needed to feel, just for a moment, like he truly wanted me. I wanted a memory I could relish forever on cold, lonely nights.

I wrapped my legs around him and tugged hard, pressing against his buttocks to urge him again. He cried out through his teeth as he plunged forward once more. Immediately after his thrust, he bit my shoulder lightly and seized. I gasped when I realized he was releasing his seed again, and I wrapped my arms around his sweating, musky torso, enjoying this last moment before it all ended.

I gaped when Ferrer pumped his hips and fell into a regular rhythm. My eyes widened as he continued to show no sign of stopping. How was he still erect? My last lover would fall asleep right after finishing, and Ferrer had finished twice now! I guessed I couldn't call it finishing, could I?

His grunting and panting as he repeatedly buried his cock ignited my libido like a sun flare. My stomach clenched as I was engulfed by a deep yearning to get closer somehow, and I released a drawn-out, keening moan, calling to him to fulfill that. He slapped wetly against me as our sexes drenched in our mixture, and the sound only fueled my desire to melt into him.

"Please, Ferrer! Please!" I begged, sobbing and arching into his rocking form. I dug my fingers into his sweaty back as his chest rubbed against my aching breasts, and I pushed harder against his flexing, taut backside, wanting him closer and closer.

I was drowning euphorically in the pleasurable tingles and sparks of our fated connection, and I was devastated that it'd all be over soon. I screamed in frustration, and he growled in response, nipping at my neck as he accelerated. His movements became feverish as he answered my desperate cry, and a sensation I'd associated all too well with disappointment began to rise between my thighs.

Perhaps he sensed the tension within me because he stopped his penetrations and began grinding his hips into mine, rolling against my swollen clit. I bared my own teeth as my stomach clenched, overwhelmed by the pleasure he was generating. I didn't even flinch when he scraped a fang along my shoulder and started sucking at my flesh. His guttural, sexual groan escalated the rising warmth between my legs, and I was hit by an impossible sensation.

I bucked up against him as I was throttled by a massively tight contraction. Rapture flooded my veins, the hot liquid pleasure bursting, radiating. I screamed through my teeth, arched, and pushed through the merciless pulsing, washed away by a tide of sheer ecstasy.

Ferrer, unable to resist my viselike grip on his cock, ripped his erection back and started fucking wildly with renewed vigor. He gasped frenziedly into my skin and bit hard, spilling his seed as my muscles rubbed his third orgasm free. I barely noticed the pain of his fangs puncturing my skin because my senses spiraled into a second climax. Sobbing and overwhelmed, I succumbed to the paradise we'd formed together. One of his arms slid around my back, jerking me hard up against him as he ejaculated rope by rope. My head lolled back as we pulsed together, unaware of anything but each other.

Tears streamed down my temples as our erotic dance slowed, punctuated by Ferrer's ravenous gulping. He bit harder as he quenched himself, nestling his fangs deeper.

Then, within me, something snapped. I jerked and unexpectedly came one last time, blacking out briefly from the dizzying intensity of this new sensation. There was a tug at my chest, and part of me gave. It wasn't like when I'd summoned Vain. Where our bodies were mashing, our souls had been wrestling, and they finally melted together.

A tether so private, so deep, tied me to the shifter, and we gasped in unison, his sound muffled by flesh. His arms shook violently as he lowered us to the glowing earth, and he lay carefully atop me, still embedded in my shoulder and core. Sweat dripped from him and mingled with mine like the sticky mess between our sexes. I took in a deep, shuddering breath, filling my lungs with the thick aromata of sex and Ferrer. The male above me swallowed a few more times and then his entire body froze.

Tired and drunk from too much pleasure, I turned my face away from his. My head was heavy, but I also didn't want to see the look of horror on his face when he realized he'd taken me in every single way. The realization of what he'd done trickled into my awareness, and I closed my eyes, devastated by the implications. I'd been tied irrevocably to a male who didn't want me—who hated me.

The last tear was dislodged from my eyelash, and it trickled down my cheek like it also wanted to escape the impending misery. I had no words for him. He'd been a falling star, and I'd been the earth. What choice had I but to catch him?

# Ferrer

With body and belly completely sated, it didn't take long for my mind to return from its feral haze. My senses gathered, and I questioned where I was, confused and disoriented. My memories were trickling in too slowly for comfort, and I took a steadying breath. Panicking would only hinder my recollection.

The ground in front of me was glowing in a curious manner, and for a moment, I almost thought I was back in the Night Court. When my sense of touch sharpened, the warm, soft body of a woman beneath me stole my attention. I swallowed hard and when my mouth refilled with a salty, savory, ambrosial blood, I froze.

No… This couldn't be happening. I had my mouth wrapped around Keid's shoulder, and my fangs were embedded into her marking spot.

*What. Have. I. Done?*

The tingling all along my front and around my cock told me that I was lying naked upon her and buried in her sex. I didn't move, and it became harder to not panic. I forced my breathing to stay slow as my mind raced through all the ways I could react to this.

I could get mad. I could get angry at her because I felt violated, and I hated being made vulnerable… but I knew that was misplaced. I couldn't bring myself to lash out at her. She wouldn't have been able to stop me if she'd tried.

I could certainly cry because my dream of being happily mated to anyone but a witch had been completely ruined in the course of a single blurry night. All notions of romance were gone forever, and I'd never have a large family because Keid couldn't produce pups. It was all I ever wanted. I was utterly, unequivocally devastated.

Or… I could shut down completely and accept what had occurred. I didn't think I could do that. I was in too much pain. My eyes grew blurry and moist, but I blinked away the tears, not wanting to slip into despair. Another wave of sadness seeped painfully into me, and I realized with some shock that half of what I felt was coming from Keid.

That was right… I could feel her now. I felt where our souls were joined, and I knew that tugging on that tether wouldn't do a thing. It wouldn't do a gods-forsaken bloody thing.

And Keid? I had no idea how she felt about this other than sa—

That was right… She was human. She was fragile. Was she ok?

My fangs retracted enough to pull from her shoulder, and I swallowed one more time before quietly asking, "Did I hurt you?"

She shook her head and murmured, "No…" Her voice was hoarse, like she'd been screaming. That worried me.

"That's good," I murmured, feeling only a little of my fear lessen. I pulled my now-soft cock from her channel, sat back in a crouch between her shaking legs, and winced at the flood of seed seeping from her core. In that moment, I was painfully conflicted regarding her barrenness. A dull ache formed in my chest, and I resisted the urge to rub at it.

I frowned when marks on her legs caught my attention. Placing a hand on her knee, I tilted her leg inward to find a gash on her outer thigh. There were a number of other scratches and scrapes on her shins as well. "What happened here?" I inquired softly.

"I fell into a bush… It was dark," she answered slowly, sounding tired. I didn't like that. I must have chased her, and I hoped to regain all my memories soon. I'd have to recover from shock first.

"Do you have bandages?" I asked, looking around to see if her bag was here.

"At the creek…"

"Alright…" I responded and stood up slowly. I had an extremely hard time looking her in the eyes, but I reached down all the same to help her stand. She murmured a thank-you, and I turned to look for my pants. I wasn't a fan of getting into them with my sweat-soaked legs, but I'd not risk another visible erection around her.

I politely offered her my shirt, which was torn at the back for obvious reasons. She was naked and shivering, and I didn't need to be a brute... especially right now. I was already infested with loathing, much of it directed at myself.

I began pulling up my pants when I noticed something dark on my cock. It was blood but not a lot of it. "I did hurt you," I said, and she looked over to see what I was studying. She frowned and shook her head.

"No... I can't see very well. Is that blood?" she inquired, stepping closer as she pulled my shirt down to her hips.

"Yes," I replied shortly. "Are you menstruating then?"

"I don't menstruate..." she replied tersely. I felt a jab of her emotional pain, and I clenched my jaw, having an incredibly difficult time being exposed to her emotions right now.

"Then why is there blood on me?" I asked, trying to keep my tone soft so it wouldn't sound like an interrogation. The last thing we needed right now was conflict.

"I don't know... What color is it?" she asked tiredly, wobbling a little.

"This green lighting doesn't help, but it's not as dark as vein blood. I'd guess pink... It's hardly anything, but it's there. Maybe that's just because it's mixed with other... liquids."

She hummed and shook her head, and I noticed that her movements were becoming heavy. I furrowed my brows and stared at the blossoming of crimson on the shirt she was wearing.

"No... no, no, no." I hastily tucked my cock into my pants, reached out, and grabbed Keid as she started to lower herself to the ground. The moment she fell unconscious, panic slammed into me like it'd been driven in by a sledgehammer, and I scooped her up.

I turned in circles to sort out the direction we'd come, but my brain wasn't working. *Iron, Iron, Iron! Help!* I called to him, and he returned lazily from his hibernation.

*Is it over? Did we do it? Thank the go—*

*I can't focus! Help me focus! Which way did we come from?* I asked, frantically interrupting him.

*Hmm? Oh... Wait. What's happening? Turn right. No, more right. There. That way!*

I ran back as fast as I could, keeping my nose alert for any scent I could get of her. Keid reeked of me, and it was hard to scent my way back over our combined smells, but I did the best I could. I heard the creek long before I saw it, and I sprinted, arriving at her bag in seconds.

I laid her down on a flat patch of weeds and rummaged through her bag, looking for anything that could help. I found some cotton and cloth strips along with an assortment of little bottles, but I didn't know what was inside them.

*Shit! I don't know how to take care of a human!* I cried to Iron as I pulled off the shirt that was starting to glue to her, tacky with blood.

*Stop the bleeding first! And don't try to suck out our anti-coagulant; you'll just make it worse,* he ordered, trying to be my rock. I was grateful for him because my mind was spinning. I was barely able to process what I'd done to Keid, and I just couldn't focus.

I groaned in dismay as I propped her up, realizing that bandaging her was going to be tricky. I'd punctured her in five places, looking like I cut into her skin once to suck on her before ultimately biting down with all four canines.

"Shit, shit, shit," I hissed frantically as I placed the cotton and wound the cloth strip around her neck, around her back, under her armpits, and back up to her neck to hold the padding in place. I wanted to secure it with more bandages, but the roll had run out, so I grabbed my shirt and ripped it into long strips. I tied the fabric as tight as I could, then pressed on both sides of her shoulder as more red blossomed through the padding.

I held back tears and gritted my teeth. Humans didn't heal like shifters. That was pretty much all I knew about them because we'd all been warned about it before the event. They had to be handled gently if we chose to mate with them.

Was I about to be the death of my fated mate? My heart pounded and echoed painfully in my head, and I gasped for air, fighting a panic attack that threatened to overcome all my senses.

*I don't think we have a choice, Ferrer,* Iron said quietly, sounding sick.

"Gods no," I croaked out loud, gulping in air like I was about to be drowned.

*Go, Ferrer.*

"No..." I sobbed, pushing harder against Keid's bleeding wounds.

*Go!* he ordered louder, fuming.

"Iron... there has t—"

*Get the shit over there!* he screamed, thrashing violently in my head and making my wings burst painfully from my back. I keeled over, hissed, then gathered Keid and started running again.

Finding her wasn't hard. Even over the heavy scent of blood, I found the rot-witch in minutes. Iron did everything he could to put more strength into my legs, and I bloody near skidded to a stop at the edge of her campsite. My face contorted at the view before me, realizing that the rot-witch had known this was going to happen.

My face was hot, furious, and tearstained as I placed Keid down on the blanket that'd been spread out next to an assortment of herbs. The witch was bent over a pot of boiling water, already dipping in strips of cloth to sterilize them. She quivered in her usual geriatric fashion and wore a rage-inducing expression of idle contentment.

I couldn't bring myself to say anything to her. I couldn't beg for her help. The words just wouldn't come out of my mouth, but fortunately, I didn't have to utter a bleedin' thing. I stepped back, torn about leaving Keid's side, but I didn't want that crone near me. Her very presence prodded at my survival instincts and made my body scream to retreat. I'd back up, but retreat I would not.

*Steady,* Iron warned, trying to lock my legs in place. I didn't fight him, but I was being tortured. I hated that I'd come to her for help, but I had no other option. I wasn't equipped to care for a human. I didn't even know how long their blood took to clot. I should have learned that! Why hadn't I learned that? My anticoagulant could keep her bleeding for hours for all I knew.

I gripped my head with both hands and held back a scream. Shit! Shit! Shit! This was all my fault! I should have given up the chase as soon as my reinforcements had become delayed! If the old hag had ended up bringing more rot-witches to our territory, at least Keid wouldn't have been subjected to my natural impulses.

But what about my people? I had to protect them too. I'd needed answers!

I squeezed my eyes shut, feeling my mind threaten to split in half. I was utterly torn, and everything was falling apart like a brittle wall in a windstorm. I dragged my hands over my face and grimaced at the sticky residue. I spat on my palm and started wiping away the blood, but under the scent of Keid was the smell of pig's blood. I froze, and my eyes centered on the rot-witch, who was applying an unknown brown paste to Keid's wounds.

*She did this,* I said blankly to Iron. *She fed me while I slept.*

Iron was quiet for a long moment. *I'll try to jog our memory,* he murmured. *It's fuzzy.*

A cold settled under my skin as I stared at the witch, who hummed while she worked. It was as if she was completely unconcerned by all of this—like she was knitting a sweater in happy contentment. There was no sense of urgency as Keid was laid out, slowly bleeding to death.

I clenched my fists, wanting nothing more than to rip off the hag's head. It'd pop off so easily in her rotten fragility. She was the reason I'd never get to pick my mate. She was the reason I'd never have pups. She was why Keid's life was at risk this very moment.

"As soon as she's better, and the moment I'm sure of your vulnerability, you're dead," I said slowly, ruthlessly. Of course, the rot-witch merely gurgled a laugh at my warning. I hadn't expected anything less.

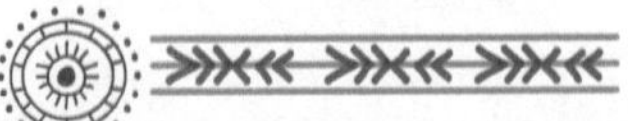
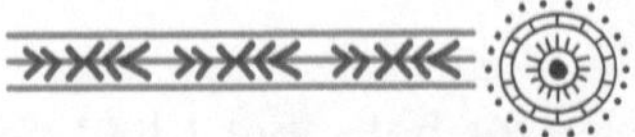

# Chapter 12

## Ferrer

I didn't let Keid out of my sight for longer than it took me to blink. If the rot-witch blocked my view of what she was doing, I moved to another side of her campsite. Nothing would deter me from scrutinizing every movement the crone made in her treatment of the younger witch.

I had two reasons for studying her ministrations. One was that I simply didn't trust the hag. I didn't care if Keid had been traveling with her for days unharmed. Tonight alone was proof that the rot-witch was treacherous. The second reason was if I could learn anything about caring for a human, I could repeat it for Keid. It meant that I had to consider and simultaneously second guess everything I witnessed tonight. It was enough to give a bat a headache.

The rot-witch moved about her campsite, which was littered with small ingredients that had obviously been foraged from the surrounding wilderness. There were piles of fuzzy leaves, mushrooms, and dark balls that I hoped beyond all hope were not dung. I tried to memorize everything I saw and what they were used for, but the hag worked surprisingly fast despite her age and nonchalance. Ultimately, it was too difficult for me to follow everything.

Some of the ingredients she'd made went into creating another batch of brown paste and some went into the boiling water. The second round of paste was being used to treat Keid's leg wounds, which were injuries that made me feel horrifically guilty. I'd scared her so badly that she'd run that recklessly…

I blinked away another wave of tears and quickly rubbed my eyes so as not to miss anything the hag did. When every single one of Keid's cuts, gashes, and punctures were patched, the rot-witch huddled over the boiling water. There truly were moments with this creature where it looked like she knew what she was doing, like how she was particular about measuring ingredients, but then there were moments where it seemed she'd lost her bloody mind. One of those moments was when she crouched, scooped up a handful of dirt, and plopped it into the water—earthworms and all. I could only hope that she wasn't going to make Keid drink any of that. What a nightmarish concoction.

She boiled the mixture until most of the water had evaporated from the pot, leaving behind a dubious, viscous… something. It had the consistency of a grainy, watery pudding, and my fears were realized when she scooped a cupful out and set it to the side. She was going to make her drink that, wasn't she?

When the rot-witch started putting the ingredients back into her bag, it was clear the treatment was done. I bristled and took a step back when the rot-witch approached me, but the only thing she did was set the cup of liquid nonsense at my feet. She didn't even look at me.

I glared down at the drink, then glanced back up to see the rot-witch brushing her hands off, like she thought she'd done a remarkable job. She made a gesture as though she was about to roll the unconscious woman away, and I took that as a message to remove Keid from her campsite.

I released a low warning growl as I cautiously approached Keid and picked her up without letting the hag leave my sight. Backing up, I squatted to pinch the brim of the cup with a couple of free fingers and left the temporary territory of the rot-witch. I didn't let the glow of her campfire out of my sight until it'd disappeared altogether, swallowed by the trees I put between us.

With Keid in my arms, I hiked to where we'd started the night, and I spied the patch of ground where she'd settled. Her blanket was still there, and I looked around for her companion, having completely forgotten about Vain.

"Vain," I called, just above a whisper, but there was no sound of flapping. I focused on my hearing as I lowered Keid to the ground and detected a number of small heartbeats nearby. I angled my head to focus on one that sounded like a blood bat, and found Vain clinging to a thin, twiggy branch near the bottom of the tree where Keid's blanket was.

*She's asleep... How did she sleep through everything?* Iron asked, dismayed.

I crouched to look at her, and sure enough, the bat was out cold. "Vain," I repeated and gently touched the crown of her fuzzy head. There was no response. "Vain," I said louder and with more urgency, but once again, she was unresponsive. This was extremely unusual. It was almost like she was in a coma.

*Did the rot-witch curse her?* Iron asked furiously. *Did she curse my little starshine?*

I ignored the second question and focused on the first. There was a solution for this, but I was incredibly paranoid about executing it. I scrubbed my hands over my face and took a deep breath, then stood up to do an intense scrutiny of my surroundings. I didn't see the rot-witch anywhere, so I closed my eyes and listened for heartbeats once more. There were smaller animals around us, and I couldn't hear anything that would belong to a human or rot-witch. I clicked through my teeth to double check the distance to some of the larger heartbeats, but they weren't within any line of sight. Those probably belonged to deer.

With all that in mind, I decided to risk it. I quickly squatted, pricked the tip of my left pinky finger, and smeared a good amount of blood onto the small bat's mouth. She made no move to lick away the blood, so I fumbled around by the base of the tree, looking for something small I could use to pry open her mouth. I tried a variety of needles and twigs until I got her mouth open, then dripped blood directly into it. All I could do now was wait.

I wiped my finger clean and checked to see if the paste on Keid was dry enough to drape the blanket over her. It'd crusted over and didn't seem like it'd crumble, so I covered her and looked back at Vain. Finally, her heart sped up, and her little eyes blinked.

"Ah... yeah. She was cursed, Iron," I muttered out loud for Vain's benefit. "You must have been knocked out by the rot-witch, Vain," I said, addressing her now. It was unfortunate that I wouldn't be able to h—

*What? What did I miss?* a female's voice chirped in my head, and I started in surprise.

"I can hear you," I blurted.

*How is that possible? You're not my witch,* she asked in alarm. She released the twig and fluttered down to Keid's covered chest. *What... Is she asleep? Is she ok? Why isn't she waking? She doesn't look so good. Why is she lighter than usual? Her heart is faster than normal. Why is that?*

I sighed and settled by Keid's unconscious form, mindful to not knock over the goop-filled cup. "I..." I faltered as I tried to find the words. Saying it out loud was going to be incredibly difficult, especially to someone who obviously cared about Keid. It would also make the results of tonight feel so much more real.

I pinched the bridge of my nose, then slid my fingers up to press into both my tear ducts. I asked them not to weaken. I didn't want to cry again. Despite having fed, I was already so tired.

"I did a bad thing, Vain," I said dully and rubbed my swollen eyes. There really was no good way to go about this. "I mated and marked her. I drank from her and almost killed her. The rot-witch… patched her up, but I've got this… potion or something I have to give her."

*You... bastard,* Vain hissed, her tiny voice overflowing with shock and fury. She didn't move to attack me. I wouldn't hurt her, but it showed her wisdom. I sensed no fear from the small animal, only rage. *Have you not done enough?*

*Vain, you've got to underst—* Iron began to plead.

*Who's that?* she shouted aggressively, interrupting him. Her head turned to locate the speaker.

*It's Ferrer's bat... Iron,* he said lamely in his own introduction.

*And you approve of this?* she questioned him. It was very odd to be interrogated by such a small and—I had to admit—rather cute creature. *You thought you hadn't had enough after breaking her heart?*

It stung to hear it out loud.

"We think the rot-witch fed us in our sleep," I informed her wearily. "There was pig's blood on my face when my feral mind calmed. Do you recall anything at all? Did you see her approach Keid or were you asleep?"

*I don't recall a thing,* she replied primly, crawling closer to Keid's chin. Her thumb claws hooked onto the edge of the blanket, like she was sending a message that she'd let me near the witch over her dead body. I had to admire that. She was brave and loyal—a good companion for Keid.

"Alright, well, I need to retrieve Keid's belongings from the creekside. I don't know why she was out there to begin with, but I need to get them. Please watch over her, and if the rot-witch shows up, get close enough to mind-link me. I don't want to leave her side unattended."

*You need not ask,* she stated coldly, tightening her grip on the cloth. *It's a little late for caring about her well-being though.*

I didn't have a response for that, so I fetched Keid's items as quickly as possible, noting that her clothes were slung over a tree branch. When I returned, I hung the damp clothes on a thin branch, but noticed something interesting. There was a scent that lingered where the clothing hadn't been washed, but I dismissed it because it was impossible.

I yawned and slapped my cheek, wondering if I should try to stay awake or if I should sleep nearby and save my strength for tomorrow. I did not want to get weak again if I was to keep Keid safe. I looked down at her and released a miserable sigh. She looked cold, and she would be after losing blood. The vessels in her extremities would be constricted to compensate for her blood loss.

"I'm going to sleep by her, Vain. Please allow me to keep her warm," I said, not waiting for her permission. I was too tired to argue. I crawled under the blanket and scooted up against the witch, turning on my side so I could cover us all with a wing. It'd help keep her warm and protect from future midnight poisonings. The she-bat crankily moved to a different spot, giving me a bit more space.

I closed my eyes, took a deep calming breath, then froze. I furrowed my brows, propped myself onto an elbow, and leaned over to sniff Keid's neck. I didn't know the details of her medical condition, but she definitely did not smell barren. She smelled fertile to the point of my mouth filling with saliva and my pants growing tight. I kept sniffing until I grew lightheaded, unable to process what I was sensing.

Keid was ovulating. I was certain of it. Could you be barren and ovulate? I didn't know enough about it, but what I did know was that there was an egg available in her, and I'd already flooded her to the point of overflowing with my seed.

I couldn't stop smelling Keid because I couldn't believe what I was scenting. I dipped my nose farther down between her collarbone and the swell of her breasts, taking deeper breaths. Right now, it was easy to forget that Keid was a witch because that information simply wasn't stored in her body. She simply smelled like a fertile woman. Had she smelled like this a day ago? I couldn't recall. My nose had been bombarded so often by the rot-witch's stench, almost everything else seemed bland on occasion… like my nose was recovering from the torture.

I knew I was hypersensitive to Keid's body because we were fated, so I felt like I definitely would have noticed her ovulating yesterday. It must have started tonight. I took another long, slow inhale, torturing myself with the sweetness, then lay back down, holding my breath to keep the aroma in my lungs and mouth. Once I was ready to abandon it, I blew out slowly and accepted the ache in my chest from its absence. I breathed in again, enjoyed it, then released it once more.

My draping wing blocked out all the starlight that filtered through the canopy, so I clicked quietly with my tongue to look at Keid one more time. Her face was relaxed. At least she didn't seem to be in pain. Her pulse was a little faster than normal to maintain her blood pressure, but it was steady, as was her breathing.

I scooted a little closer and draped an arm over her soft belly, knowing I shouldn't but lacked the strength to resist. Though her ovulation continued to sing to me, I wasn't compelled to breed again. Aside from the instinctual satisfaction I got from smelling myself between her thighs, her body was also signaling her weakness, which dampened my own hormones. The erection that'd arrived at my realization of her fertility had already disappeared. It was currently content to wait.

Her sweet aroma slowly began to unlock my memories because I realized it was the first thing I'd noticed when I'd awoken. My instincts had alerted me to the fact that I was fed, primed for breeding, and that my fated mate was currently ovulating. It really had been the perfect disaster. How the rot-witch knew to trigger me this night… I had no idea. Could other humans sense ovulation? They had much weaker senses than bat-shifters. The timing was suspect. The rot-witch had to have known she was ovulating somehow.

Everyone had said she was barren though, even her own sister. Perhaps I didn't know enough about the human body… but my senses couldn't be lying. Could it be that the rot-witch had done something to Keid? Could it have been that drink I warned her not to take? I didn't know what else it could have been. I felt like I'd been pretty vigilant in my watching.

I furrowed my brows as I tried to recall the last handful of hours. I'd woken with the taste of blood on my lips. How much had I been given? It couldn't have been a lot. It was rather hard to force-feed someone who was upside down. No doubt that was why my face had been covered in the stuff.

The blood in my mouth and whatever had made it into my stomach must have metabolized and stimulated my hormones… prodding my feral response. I recalled scenting a ready mate, one that was specifically made for me. The feral instinct that was buried deep between me and Iron had taken control, demanding we find our mate. We were endangered, and our colony needed more pups.

So I followed the scent through the woods, barely able to see and hear through the overwhelming sensory overload her aroma provoked. I adjusted my hips uncomfortably when I recalled what I'd found by the creek. Keid had been mumbling and moaning while she was bent over, bracing herself against a tree trunk. I swallowed hard as I recalled how the starlight illuminated her light skin, cast shadows on her round bottom, and glinted off a smear of moisture on an inner thigh. If she'd been a shifter, she would have been in heat.

I knew I would've had problems with the scene had I not been feral, but that hadn't been the case. I'd already been out of control. I squinted as I tried to pry out the next memory. She'd said something. Had she said my name? I sighed miserably when I remembered that my approach had made her scream before she'd run off into the night. That was when she'd fallen into the bush, and I winced when I recalled untangling her from it. Yes… she'd probably have some bruises come morning as well.

I recalled running with her… then… taking her to a flat spot of woodland that'd be more comfortable for her. My stomach lurched a little when I recalled her lighting up the dirt somehow… Right… That was how it'd gotten like that. It was a visual reminder that she was a witch, and a small piece of me squirmed uncomfortably, like it was berating me for having mated with one. My instincts were both satisfied and deeply traumatized by my actions.

I tried to push that sensation away, wanting to remember more even though I wasn't sure that recalling everything was a good idea. I squeezed my eyes tighter, willing the memories to dislodge. When they did, my eyes relaxed and opened slowly. I clicked again to look at Keid.

She'd clapped and warned me I'd be mad at myself later, but then… after that warning… Simultaneously unsettled and awestruck, I drew in a stuttering breath. Keid had enjoyed it. She'd enjoyed every second of our joining. For some reason, that knowledge almost brought me into a panic, but I stayed where I was, not wanting to let her get cold just because I felt an urge to run or fly out the anxiety.

Blood. Clots. Yesterday, she had said she'd be ok with me going feral on her, but I thought it'd been all false bravado. She'd been angry at the time… I hadn't thought she'd actually meant it. I figured she just wanted to shock me—get me to shut my mouth. Something about being ugly and enjoying a last night of sex. I mean, I thought that what she'd said was extreme and a little surprising, but I hadn't taken it seriously.

Now… I didn't know what to think. Was I slightly relieved that I didn't find memories of her pushing and screaming at me while I took her by force? I was more than slightly relieved. I didn't need to feel like I'd done her more wrong than I already bloody had.

I prodded more gently at my memories, curiously exploring what I could recall, as if finding her enjoyment gave me some odd permission to savor anything good I could find. Turned out there was a lot to savor, but it was unfortunate that I'd lost my virginity this way… in an unromantic haze… and in such strange circumstances.

I could grudgingly admit to myself that Keid was just as beautiful up close as she was from a distance, if not more. Had I wanted this to happen, I would've wanted to spend more time exploring her body before taking her, but my feral mind had been solely focused on producing results. At least Keid had known what to do.

My fingers twitched on her belly as I recalled how her soft hands had felt on my cock. That had been the first time anyone but me had touched it. The corner of my lip pulled back the tiniest bit when I remembered her intimidated face, but she'd put me where I was supposed to go. At the time, my feral mind had picked up on that intimidation, and I winced at how I'd been more affectionate than I would have expected.

I hadn't expected that feral mind to care about her comfort or anxiety, but it had, multiple times. That was surprising to me. It made it seem like there was so much more to myself and intimacy than I knew, but then again, even what I had been aware of was nothing like the actual experience. At the same time, I was uncomfortable knowing that any part of myself had been affectionate with Keid. How much of my feral mind was me? How much of it was ancient instinct… and did that even matter?

Keid had urged me to go slow, and my feral mind had tried once again to accommodate her despite its rush to enter. Gods, I had not expected a woman to be so tight and hot. How was a bat supposed to return to a fist after that? I'd come in less than a minute of pushing into her. I hadn't even been all the way inside yet, and still I was overwhelmed with how good she felt.

The memory of coming into a woman for the first time was powerful. An uncontrollable shudder rocked me for a heartbeat, and I tightened my hold on Keid to steady myself. I relaxed once the sensation passed and released a breath I hadn't realized I was holding. I angled my wing a bit to allow a cold breeze to settle onto my face because my temples had gotten a touch dewy.

Blood clots. That memory was powerful. I swallowed hard to get the extra saliva down my throat.

I turned my face to bury my nose in the back of her star-kissed, pale locks, taking another lungful to calm myself. She was hurt. I didn't want sex right now. I just wanted to remember everything. I exhaled slowly and let my heartbeat relax. That was right… I just needed to stay calm.

Right… I continued after the first round of releasing my seed. She'd seemed to think we were done for some reason, but at least she didn't protest when I continued onto the next round. She must have only been with someone who tired easily. That was not the case with bats. Our bodies were made to make bloody sure our mates got pregnant.

I remember pushing deeper into her, then feeling my head hit a surface. That must have been the barrier of her womb. Another shudder raked over me, and I hissed through my teeth.

*Bloody clots,* I swore to myself, grateful that Iron was resting and not watching me struggle with arousal like this. It was so bloody hard to recall everything without being affected. Still though, holding on to Keid like this made it easier to process the memories.

I cleared my throat as I remembered how her body accepted all of me, how I was pushed in as far as I could go—such snug, wet perfection. Her walls were soft but lined with velvety ridges that stroked my every penetration. Every woman and female had to feel different, but Keid felt like coming home. Aside from the tingling of the mate bond, would it feel that way with anyone else? Something inside me told me that it wouldn't, and I wished that this 'something' was a person so I could deny the claim. As it was, I couldn't argue with myself. I couldn't put on a show if there was no one around to see the performance, the lying. I'd only be trying to fool myself, and since marking Keid, I was quickly tiring of that game.

It was at that point in my memories, when I'd fully buried myself, that Keid had come alive. She'd begged for more, so

I came again for her. At least I'd known what to do when she begged me to 'fuck' her. It wasn't a word I'd known before meeting Queen Hekla and her mate. I'd quickly learned its definition because... well... they'd never been quiet with their own mating sessions, and she often cursed with it.

Keid had been ravenous after my second round, and my feral mind decided to keep going, additionally spurred by her loud enthusiasm. Gods, she'd been so agreeable. She'd pressed up against me when I started a regular, rutting pace. I could almost, in this moment, feel her smooth, sweat-soaked breasts rubbing against my chest, the memory being so vivid. I kept my hand firmly on Keid's belly, not letting it roam while I played out the rest of the night in my head.

When I'd noticed her sex tightening up, I realized that she was headed toward her own orgasm, and my feral mind had gotten excited, desperately wanting to know what it'd feel like when she finished. I'd paused my own search for release in order to give one to Keid, which just seemed so... odd to me. I hadn't expected, once again, for my feral mind to care about that.

Once she got close to finishing... I realized that was where things had gone wrong. Just grinding against her, I'd fixated on her increasing heart rate, and perhaps if I'd eaten more beforehand, I wouldn't have been tempted to take a taste. I'd been tested in that moment, and I'd failed. I'd made a small cut with a fang and started sucking, letting my potent saliva coax her blood out into a steady flow.

She'd been delicious, and I was so deeply ashamed admitting that to myself. It was already shameful enough to be reliant on blood, but to dine so ravenously on a fated mate? That was horrifying to me. I didn't want to take sustenance from Keid ever again.

Tasting her had led me to wanting a mouthful. And I'd gotten so excited when she'd finally orgasmed, I'd lost control and started rutting mindlessly until I just bit her outright. My bite went deeper and deeper until I'd accidentally marked her, not even realizing that I was releasing my venom. It'd been premature… I wished my feral mind hadn't gone that far.

I had the hardest time processing Keid's behavior. Humans didn't go feral. My memories of her weren't of a lust-crazed female in heat. They were of a woman who was still in her own mind and in control of her own decisions, weren't they? She hadn't taken me in grudgingly. She'd allowed herself to go wild with me. She'd made a conscious decision to do that. That was what I didn't understand. Would I ever understand humans? I feared my own loss of control. Control was nigh sacred. Losing it could mean killing someone, which almost happened tonight.

I released an agonized groan and buried my face in her hair. Now that I remembered it all… what now? Could I forget what we'd done? Not the result, but the experience? Could I forget how agonizingly amazing she'd felt wrapped in my arms and around my cock? Could I forget how she screamed my name and begged for more and more? Could I forget how insatiable she'd been?

Having a mate was more than sex though, and I couldn't let this experience be the deciding factor of my entire future… or Keid's. When she woke, and when she was feeling up to talking, I'd ask if her kind could remove my mark from her.

Then I could return her to her sister, and we'd go our separate ways. There's no way she'd continue traveling with the rot-witch after what'd happened.

At this point, it wasn't about waiting to reject her; it was about surviving having marked her. I frowned as my mind focused on a sensation under my palm. I could feel the pulse in Keid's belly from her abdominal aorta. What if, against all odds, there was something forming lower? What if, months later, there was a second pulse? What then?

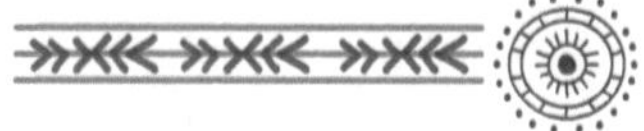

# Chapter 13

## Keid

The first thing I noticed was warmth. The second thing I noticed was a weight. The third thing I noticed was puffs of air. It was enough to pique my curiosity even though I wanted to keep sleeping. Slowly, I opened my dry eyes and blinked rapidly, trying to get some tears going to lubricate my vision.

It was dark, but the bird calls told me it was morning, which added to my disorientation. I smacked my lips and ran my tongue over them, thoroughly parched. I was drier than a piece of driftwood on hot, sunny sand.

A cough escaped my lips, causing the dark ceiling over me to jerk slightly. I narrowed my eyes at it, trying to remember if I'd ever enchanted a tent, and if I did, why would I make it out of leath—

"Wait a minute," I whispered hoarsely and raised a heavy hand to brush my fingers across the surface. A small amount of light was coming through, and I could just barely detect red veins under the dark brown skin. Subtle patches of white, about the size of my hand, were scattered in several places, reminding me of someone I knew.

As I turned my head, I noticed a strong, masculine arm slung over me and a naked shoulder. Then I looked up and found myself staring at Ferrer's chin. I blinked slowly this time as I tried to process this bizarre arrangement.

"Ferrer? Are you awake?" I asked timidly and was only met with a drowsy, noncommittal grunt. Part of me didn't want to disturb him because I was honestly enjoying this. Gods knew why he'd decided to cuddle up with me, but I'd take it.

That was when I recalled last night and realized I was naked. I released an extremely bizarre noise that was something between a wobbly yell and a gasping shriek. Ferrer immediately jolted awake, and I rolled away from him, tugging the blanket with me. Unfortunately, I found myself trapped in the rolled-up cloth and couldn't get away properly.

"Shittin' stars!" Ferrer gasped with wide eyes, holding a hand to his chest. "You scared the bleeding stars out of my sky, Keid!" He raked a hand through his hair, but his face went from shocked to worried. "Please don't... move. You'll dislodge your dressing."

"My dressing appears to have already been dislodged," I gritted out, clutching the blanket to my chest. His nostrils flared, but he didn't seem to have heard what I said.

"No, no, no..." he said hastily, jumping up to his feet and squatting by my side. He fumbled with my hair and blanched, his light skin going a shade lighter, threatening to match my own shade. "Shit, shit, shit!"

I froze when one of his hands came away bloody, and I blanched a bit too. He was patting at something on my neck, like he was smudging some kind of putty across my skin. I kept still and let him continue with whatever he was doing.

"Oh... is my mark still bleeding?" I asked, realizing what was happening.

"Yes," he said tersely, focusing on stopping the bleeding. "It's not as bad as last night. Your movement just messed up the dressing and ripped some kind of scab."

"Ah..." I wasn't sure what else to say.

He gave his emergency patch a cursory look, then sat back and stared down at his bloody fingers. "I'm sorry, Keid," the bat-shifter said brokenly, and I lowered my gaze, not sure if I could meet his eyes if he glanced up again. "It was an accident. I think… Iron and I think someone fed us in the middle of the night. We think it was the…" He gestured lamely in the direction of the rot-witch's campsite.

My brows drew in as I thought back to last night. Honestly, that did explain why the blood had smeared up his face. He had definitely roosted at a height she could've reached.

"Vain!" I gasped and scrambled to unroll myself from the blanket. When I sat up, I immediately blacked out and fell over with an attractive thud.

"She's fine! Gods, Keid! Stop moving! Your blood pressure is low," Ferrer said. I was lifted, moved somewhere, and covered up again. A small furry thing landed on my hand. Vain had found me.

*Keid? He told me the same story last night. I can't verify, but... you have to know that I was cursed asleep,* she said. *Ferrer woke me.*

I frowned and looked up at Ferrer when my vision returned to me. "She said she was lifted from a curse? How did you manage that?"

"Some things don't require magic," he said, purposely vague. I gave him a scrutinizing look, but it really wasn't the pressing matter.

"I wouldn't put it past her," I said, referring to Mushy with a sigh and looked up through the branches. "You have to know what you've done," I added sadly, holding back tears. It was so hard to say my thoughts out loud. "No matter who instigated it, you've done something permanent, Ferrer. What am I to do?"

He didn't answer. He did pass me a cup of disgusting liquid though. "That… thing made it for you," Ferrer said with a trace of heat on the word 'thing.' "She saved you, but I can't tell if that's any good."

I gave the cup a dubious look, then threw it away from me. I didn't want it. Whether she saved me or not, I felt betrayed.

He was silent for a while after that, so I gathered my courage and turned my head. The bat-shifter just sat there, slowly wiping my blood from his fingers with a leaf. To be honest, I was surprised he wasn't licking his hands clean. I snorted out a self-deprecating laugh at that thought. I probably tasted terrible too.

Another thought occurred to me, and my nerves collapsed, allowing me to burst into laughter. My eyes were shut in my mad mirth, but I imagined that Ferrer was looking pretty bewildered right now.

"Keid…" he said slowly, cautiously, which made me laugh harder, gods knew why. "What are you laughing about?"

I placed a hand on my belly, hooting like I just didn't care… and I didn't. At this point, my self-esteem was at an all-time low, and all I could do was laugh. I was too wrung out to cry. My water reserve was low.

Once my chuckling subsided, I took a deep breath before speaking. "The other children used to call me 'bloodless' when I was little," I explained, staring up at the backlit branches and needles of the canopy. "There were many names. Some called me 'ghost,' and some called me 'fallen star,' which was particularly hurtful. Bloodless though… You know how people go pale when the blood drains from their face? From fear? From shock? That's where it's from. I was laughing because I almost bled to death, didn't I?"

My question hung in silence for a minute before Ferrer admitted, "You were… at risk…"

I chuckled once more. "Started this life bloodless and literally almost ended it bloodless. I think it's funny."

"It's not funny, Keid."

I wanted to ask him what he knew about it, but I was becoming too combative and childish. It wasn't like me. I supposed he was right, but laughing was all I could do right now. Everything was absolutely mad. I felt lost.

"What now?" I asked just above a whisper. "What do I do now? Do I keep walking away, knowing we'll always be tethered? Feeling the agonizing pain through our bond every time you have sex with someone else?" He continued to stay quiet, which was starting to frighten me. "You could kill me," I suggested, blinking back tears. "It would hurt you for a while, and you might go crazy, but it's possible to survive and heal from if you're strong. I think you're probably s-s-strong e-enough," I stammered out as tears began to fall.

"You cannot possibly mean that, Keid. That's a terrible thing to say," he admonished, moving to sit closer as I started hiccupping. I kept my gaze on the canopy. I couldn't look at him. I had to push him away first because rejection hurt too much, and I couldn't go through that again.

"What else c-can I do?" I asked through tears. "Honestly, you haven't said anything, and it's scaring m-me."

"You might have to come back to the colony, Keid," he replied nervously.

I frowned. "Why? You hate me, Ferrer. You hate me because I'm a witch. I'm an ugly, barren witch," I accused, rejecting his false sympathy. I bit my lower lip, tasting my salty tears in the corners of my mouth.

"These things you say…" he grunted out. "Not that I've given you reason to think otherwise. Keid, you know what happened last night. What if you get pregnant?"

I snapped my head around to send him my most scathing look. "Do you not understand what barren means?" I snapped, triggered horribly by the sensitive topic. I loathed discussing it.

"Keid… I'm positive you started ovulating last night," he replied with the most miniscule wince.

"How… dare… you," I seethed and propped myself up on an elbow. I raised my hand slightly, desperately wanting to slap him, but I restrained myself. "I don't have any eggs to ovulate, Ferrer!" I yelled, leaning into his face.

He gave me a skeptical look, which enraged me further. "I can smell it, Keid."

"You're smelling wrong then. My doctor told me when I was eighteen that I had no eggs to ovulate!"

He rubbed his brow and sighed. "Is there a way to tell so I can prove it? Can't witches test for pregnancy?"

I shook my head, infuriated and exhausted to have to explain the most basic thing. "Witches can't test themselves, Ferrer. The process requires someone else." I pointed at my stomach. "The other witch targets the reproductive site with her magic, it contrasts with the patient's metabolized magic—because everyone's metabolized magic is different—and returns like an echo so they can visualize it. It's kind of like echolocation, I guess." I gestured at him, thinking he should understand it quite well, being a bat.

"Then come back to the colony so your sister can do it," he countered.

"I. Don't. Want. To," I replied scathingly. "I don't want to go where I'm not wanted. I've lived it my whole life! I can't do that, especially with my twin living out my fantasy right in front of me!"

He released a sharp, exacerbated growl, and I spied his fangs slightly lengthening in his agitation. He scrunched his nose as his lips pressed into a thin line. "What about…" he snarled and pointed to where the rot-witch was. "As much as I'm utterly loath to suggest it!"

I swallowed hard and grimaced, looking over to where he was pointing. "It's just not possible, Ferrer," I replied, feeling more fearful than angry now. I didn't want her sending her magic into me.

He leaned in, stared intensely into my eyes with his red-brown ones, and said very calmly, "And it's just not possible that my nose is wrong. You've got an egg in there, and I might have claimed it. Are you really going to ignore the possibility? What about that drink she gave you? Maybe it… did something!"

I sandwiched my lips between my teeth, not wanting to even consider it. I'd given up that dream. "There's no spell or potion on the planet that could make a woman grow eggs."

"That you know of," he shot back.

That I knew of... Yes, that was always the case with the unknown. Something is always unknown until it is known... It wasn't a new thing. I moved my eyes to the forest floor and grabbed a leaf, picking off the needles one at a time.

*Keid...* Vain piped in nervously, probably scared from our fighting. *You could do it to shut him up. It'd be fast?*

I shook my head and pursed my lips, then looked around for my clothes. Ferrer seemed to be able to read my mind, and he quickly stood to fetch them from a tree branch. Handing them to me, he said, "They're still a little damp... It wasn't a warm night." He sounded apologetic, like it was his fault.

I frowned when I collected the clothes from him, recalling why I'd washed them. Stabbing pain... I ran my hand over my lower abdomen where I'd felt it, where one of my ovaries was. I had the soreness, the libido increase, the spotting—if that was what was on his cock last night, the changes in mucus... It couldn't be possible. I'd treated so many lionesses that I had the ovulation symptoms memorized.

"Fine," I said hoarsely, then cleared my throat and pulled my tunic over my head. "While we're at it, we can ask if she knows how to remove marks." If I hadn't known better, I would have said he looked disappointed at the idea. I continued, "Not that Mushy talks, Ferrer. You know that as well as I do."

I threw my leggings on and dizzily went to find Mushy while Ferrer put a steadying hand on my shoulder. She was going to get a piece of my mind as well. All this accursed torture was her fault. Aside from Ferrer's attempted rejection, I couldn't remember the last time I hurt this much.

I didn't like who I was right now, but the problem was stemming from not knowing what I was. Was I a mother? Was I a mate? Was I an inconvenience?

As angry as I was, I did appreciate Ferrer's dedication in keeping me steady during my march to confront Mushy. Vain was huddled quietly in my palm, but I eventually moved her to my shoulder.

I really wasn't feeling well, and I did regret getting all worked up after suffering serious injuries. I was cold, like there was now ice moving through the veins of my arms and legs. My face was wan and drained, especially now that I was standing.

I blacked out a couple times on the way over, and Ferrer convinced me to sit in between the spells, running back to grab my canteen so I could drink. He even took over carrying Vain. Still, he didn't look happy about my adamance in going to her right now. There really wasn't any way to make him happy, was there?

"I should have made you drink as soon as you woke," Ferrer grumbled, closing my canteen for me. "Replenish that blood volume. I'll bring you some meat after this… but I don't know how to cook."

I twisted my lips at the offer and looked down at the pasty complexion of my hands. Those were very spouse-like things to do, and it stung. He was only doing it out of guilt. It'd all stop as soon as I recovered. I hated this.

"Thank you," I muttered and let him help me to my feet. By the time I arrived at Mushy's foul campsite, my inner fire was more doused than I expected. I wanted to scream at her, but I was already too lethargic.

Mushy was sitting in front of a pot that contained more of the same goop I'd refused earlier, and she didn't appear any different today. Her crusty, liver-spotted hands moved idly over the pot, the long fingers and nails dropping small bits of detritus into the concoction. I frowned when I noticed that a couple of her fingers were missing. When had that happened? I thought back, but I couldn't find the answer to my question. Her finger count had been the last thing on my mind.

The rot-witch glanced up as we approached, and her weepy, wild eyes settled on Ferrer's guiding hand on my arm. She slapped her thigh and started giggling like a child, looking delighted as usual. Her pockmarked, leathery cheeks raised, and her lips pulled back as she laughed, revealing more missing teeth.

I was unaffected by her behavior and just stopped a handful of feet away from her. Ferrer tensed dramatically at our proximity, and he moved slightly behind me, afraid of her per usual. Mushy seemed to find that just as entertaining.

Tilting my head a little, my voice broke on my first question. "Why, Mushy?" I asked sadly. I raised my hands up in a helpless gesture. "Why?"

She just rocked from side to side and sent me a grandmotherly smile. I wanted to slap it off her face, but I was afraid that if I hit her, I'd actually slap the flesh off her bones. Never had I felt such a capacity for violence as I did today. I'd been pushed much too far.

"You won't ever answer, huh?" I inquired and heaved a depressed exhale.

She grinned at that and snickered as she plucked some mushrooms from the soil. That was almost an answer in and of itself. It told me that she was still playing games. I started when Ferrer lightly prodded me, urging me to ask the other questions.

"You know, what you did last night… it felt very much like assault, Mushy," I said tearfully, my voice breaking again. "And I don't feel assaulted by Ferrer; I feel assaulted by you! You're the reason I'm tied to someone who hates me!" I jerked my tunic aside to show her the bites she'd treated. "You've done me such wrong! Can you remove this or not?"

I stood there while I waited, breathing hard and glaring at her while I tugged at the neck of my shirt. The witch leaned back, put her palms up in a gesture of surrender, and pasted a comical grimace on her face that said she couldn't help me. She opened her mouth and pointed at her tongue, then shrugged.

She started laughing again after that, shaking her head and moving to stir the pot's contents. She dipped the other cup into the goop and held it up to me. When I made no move to grab it, she set it down and crossed her arms, still rocking in place and shaking.

"So, it's possible?" I asked incredulously. "Do you know someone else who can remove it?"

She rocked in place, but her head bobbed a little more than usual. I took that as a 'yes.' I exhaled a shaky breath and didn't realize that I was getting weak in the knees until Ferrer gripped my arms from behind to steady me.

"Where you're going, Mushy," I said carefully, trying to word my question in a way that'd be easy for her to answer, "will there be someone there who can help us?"

She repeated the same motion but didn't look very happy about it. She held the cup out for me again, but I declined it with a firm hand. I didn't want her goop!

Ferrer nudged me impatiently again. "The egg," he murmured, reminding me about the question I desperately didn't want to ask. I couldn't handle the crushing ups and downs of dashed hopes. I placed my hand over my stomach, picking idly at the cloth. I'd already suffered the emotional funeral of a million lost chances. My eyes grew wet again and blurred my vision. How could I even word my next question?

"This is really important, Mushy," I started in a tight voice, and my fingers curled around the cloth of my tunic, fisting it at the belly. "I was told I had no eggs in my ovaries. Ferrer says… otherwise. Is he telling the truth? Do I somehow… Am I somehow able to get pregnant now?"

I shouldn't have been surprised when she held the cup out to me again, idly picking a tiny leaf off her lap.

"I'm not drinking that," I snapped. "Answer me, Mushy."

She sighed and leaned back a little, crossing an arm over the one holding the cup like she had all the time in the world. No answers were to be given unless I drank from that cup.

"Please," I begged, desperation crawling in like rotten roots. Ferrer's fingers flexed into my arms. I looked over my shoulder and up at him, hissing, "Be patient. I'm doing my best!"

His eyes widened in surprise, but at least he kept his mouth shut. I sent a pained look over to Mushy, but she wasn't having it. She was looking away, visibly bored now. Her wild grey hair quivered, then swayed when a little breeze passed through the campsite. I glanced up in time to spot a large shadow slide over the treetops. Was that a dragon-shifter? How far up were they patrolling? Could they scent Mushy? The old campfire?

Ferrer seemed to tense further, his grip tightening, but he remained silent. I swallowed past the lump in my throat and reached out to take the cup from the rot-witch.

"Keid…" Ferrer murmured. "Don't… It's not worth the risk."

"You wanted to know, so you get to know," I responded tiredly and studied the muck in the cup. It smelled atrocious. I turned my head to the side and dry-heaved. "Oh Sky Gods, preserve me. Earth Gods, you can come along too."

"Augh…" he growled and reached around to place his wrist under my nose. "If you're going to do this just… hold on to my scent."

I did like how he smelled, but as a human, I couldn't catch all the nuances of a fated mate's scent. I did think he smelled fresher than the lion-shifters, who were a bit on the musky side of the aroma spectrum. I wasn't really sure how much Ferrer's offer was going to help though, to be honest.

I took in a deep breath of his warm, salty skin and knocked the cup back, dumping a good amount of the vile stuff into my throat. I grimaced, having to swallow repeatedly because it was thicker than I'd anticipated. Ferrer handed me the canteen, and I took a sip of water before finishing the rest of the goop.

"Oh gods," I said with a cough, drank more water, then smacked my lips together in disgust. "That was like powdered mushroom dirt." It probably had both of those things in it, but I didn't want verification.

Mushy was already on her feet and waddling over to me. When she bent over to stare at my lower abdomen, Ferrer's hands found their way back to my arms. I held my breath as the rot-witch stood again, then waved at my abdomen like she was greeting someone.

Ferrer caught me before I could hit the ground, and I turned inward, unable to process her response. "No, no, no, no," I moaned, grabbing at my chest as I fought for air.

"Woah, calm down," Ferrer's voice urged from far away, but I slapped my palms over my ears.

I'd already grieved them! I'd spent years grieving them! Learning I was barren was the worst day of my life! It'd ruined everything! How was this possible? How could I accept something I'd long buried with a piece of my own heart?

I opened my eyes and stared wildly at Mushy. "Did they lie to me?" I cried. They couldn't have. My last lover would've gotten me pregnant otherwise.

However, when Mushy rocked a hand in deliberation, I froze. I sat up straighter, barely noticing Ferrer's hand on my elbow again. "What's that gesture, Mushy? What's that mean—what you're doing right there?"

She made a gripping and yanking gesture with her fist, then went back to lazily stirring the concoction.

"Now, what's that mean?" I asked, the pitch of my voice getting higher as I pointed to the hand that had done the yanking gesture.

"They took her eggs," Ferrer said flatly from behind, referring to me, and I stiffened. I stared at Mushy with wide eyes, and she rocked and bobbed her head in an affirmative.

My jaw fell open, and I could taste the stream of tears trickling down my face. My body shivered with throttled nerves. Ferrer's hands tightened on me again.

How? How was that possible? And why?

"And you gave them back?" he inquired slowly, sounding more hesitant with this guess. The rot-witch nodded slower as she rocked, like she had but maybe not in the manner we thought.

A bone-deep sob was wrenched from my throat, and I stood abruptly, yanking myself away from the bat-shifter's grip. I spun on a heel and wobbled, trying to orient myself. Which way was my bag? I needed space. I needed… silence. I… had made a mistake…

Before I could take another step, I continued my tradition of blacking out.

## Ferrer

I caught Keid once more before she hit the ground, feeling almost as stunned as she looked. I glanced up at the rot-witch, aghast. Could she be lying? Would she have reason to lie? She already manipulated us… Had she thought it was to Keid's benefit?

The rot-witch sent me a shooing gesture, seeming done with having us at her campfire. Or perhaps she was just done with me, which was fine. Unless she could do anything else for Keid, I was certainly glad to leave.

When I turned to do so, I received a slap on my buttocks as a send-off. I whirled around, enraged, and bared my fangs at the revolting hag, who was crying in fits of cackling laughter. She picked up a pinecone and tossed it playfully at me. I jumped back, tightened my grip on Keid, and ran like shit.

I hated her.

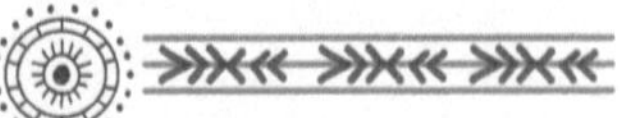
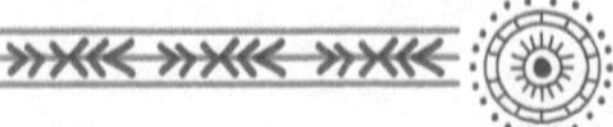

# Chapter 14

## Ferrer

Keid's alertness and vision returned about a minute after I ran from the bloody hag. She moaned miserably and tried to lift her head, but I growled, "Stay flat, Keid. You're simply moving too much right now. Never should've moved you to begin with. This whole thing was a bad idea."

I carefully adjusted her in my arms as I made my way back to her belongings. The state she was in now made me feel even more guilty. My meal had taken a serious toll on her, and I felt like shit.

*Best listen to him,* Vain said in a resigned tone. She'd been pretty quiet today, but I did appreciate her validation. *He is the blood expert, I guess.*

"I worked with a doctor, you know," she said through a sigh.

"Right, so you and I both should have known better," I replied, pushing aside a giant fern before stepping into our temporary campsite. I squatted and placed Keid by her bag, wishing I had a pillow I could offer her. The fact that she could be pregnant made me even more paranoid about her safety. The witch hadn't exactly been clear about whether she was waving to a fertilized egg or an unfertilized one.

*Grab her blanket; she's cold,* Vain commanded, and I did as she asked, snatching it from the ground and dusting it off before covering Keid.

The woman blinked slowly up at me with her periwinkle eyes, then her brows drew up in worry. "Wait... wait..." She placed a palm to her temple and brushed aside a rogue strand of white hair. "You can hear my familiar?"

"I can, Keid," I said, trying to sound calm. I stood and glanced around the woods, trying to find some kind of beast I could kill and bring back for her. She needed meat. She needed iron.

*Yeah, she does,* Iron said with a smirk.

*You're a bloody idiot,* I retorted. My eyes were still terrible during the day, so I focused with my ears and clicked, attempting to see as far as I could with sound alone. There were smaller birds and lizards about, so I'd have to travel a little farther to find a hare or perhaps a fowl. The deer were more aloof.

"But how?" she asked. "I'm not a shifter, and she's not my beast... not like your bat is to you."

I placed my hands on my hips and looked down at her. Her pretty, frosty hair was splayed about her head, and for a moment, I forgot what I was going to say. I frowned and scratched the back of my neck in an attempt to buy time. I made the mistake of looking at her lips when they parted slightly. They looked chapped. She needed more water. Maybe that was what I was going to say.

"I need to get you more water," I said and grabbed the canteen from the ground.

She frowned. "You didn't answer my question..."

*Iron?* I asked, hiding a wince.

*She asked how you could hear her familiar,* he said in a droll voice. He'd spared me additional taunting, and I breathed a sigh of relief.

"You know we're mated, Keid," I said in a low voice, trying to sound casual in my reply. "You're connected to my soul, and I assume Vain's connected to yours. It just goes through the chain."

"But don't I have to be able to mind-link?" she asked, looking confused.

*You can't mind-link me, but Iron and I can mind-link you,* I replied to her through our bond. *I can feel your emotions, but you can't feel mine. We have a one-way connection for the most part since you can't mark me.*

"Of course we do," she muttered, looked away, then whispered, "It was always one-sided." That jabbed at my bloody, sensitive heart, and I had no idea if she had intended me to hear that or not. She was frustrated, and I could understand that. So far, I'd controlled everything that had happened between us, and I still continued to feel the burden of guilt. The only way I could fix this was to get my mark removed.

I cleared my throat and moved Vain from my shoulder to Keid's belly. "Now, I don't know why Vain can mind-link me. Maybe familiar bonds are different, but we can take that as a positive. She'll at least be able to relay your messages to me in an emergency," I said, having no idea if that would offer comfort.

The woman stayed quiet, and I felt a pang of sadness from her. It was mixed with overwhelming anxiety, so I thought it was best to give her some space for a little bit. I needed to find her food anyway.

"I'll be back. I'll bring meat," I told her quietly, then stalked off to hunt the best I could during the daytime.

*I changed my mind,* Iron said as I hopped up into a tree, clicking to verify the distance. My eyesight was trash right now.

*About what?* I asked, keeping my ears open for heartbeats.

*I don't want to remove our mark.*

I nearly lost my handhold when he said that and clawed aggressively into the nearest branch. I had not expected those words.

*Why?* I asked, my palms growing sweaty. Did he know how I felt? I'd tried to keep my own struggles quiet and buried too deep for him to find.

*I just stopped caring about her being a witch,* he replied simply.

*Yeah, alright, but why?* I perched on a branch for a moment while I waited for his answer. I couldn't focus on hunting while we were on this topic.

*Keid's really different from the rot-witch.*

*Yes, so?* I needed a better answer than that.

*And she's different from her sister. The other one too. The one that wanted to steal you.*

My lip curled up at the mention of the blonde. That had been annoying. *And what's your point?*

*The more we meet, the more they seem like us.*

It was another vague reply, but I knew what he meant this time. They'd become less of a label in our mind and more normalized with every encounter. It had been easy to bundle them into one personality. It was easy to say that all witches were the same when you didn't actually know any.

*And what does Keid seem like to you?* I asked, curious about his new assessment.

*She has good mate qualities. She's clearly skilled in witchwork and could help bring income to the colony. She's fertile now, so she could bear us pups. She's a little more analytical than you, so I think she could balance you out a bit. You're kind of emotional.*

*I am not,* I lied shamelessly.

*She's generous, and that kind of mindset fits in very well with bat mentality. She'd do well in the colony, and you know it. Our people would like her. Finally, you're really attracted to her, and by very, I mean veeery.*

*You just want to play around with Vain,* I accused. A drop of salty moisture trickled down my back, and I wiped at the sheen of nervous sweat that'd formed on my brow.

*You're sweating. I've got you on the run!*

*It's daytime,* I countered. *It's warmer.*

*Well, you know my vote,* he replied stubbornly.

*She's the one who brought up removing it. Don't ignore what she wants, Iron. We've already controlled too much.*

*Then change her mind, you clot.*

I sighed and leapt from my perch to go after a pheasant that was bobbing through a thicket, gobbling quietly and obnoxiously. I snapped its neck, the flightless bird dying before it even saw me coming. I felt an urge to bring the bird to my mouth to drain it, but I resisted and ran back to bring Keid her prize. I'd already eaten enough. I wasn't going to feed until I returned to the colony. I didn't want to hurt her ever again.

When I got back, I was upset to see that the woman was busy digging a firepit. "I can do that, Keid. Please, just rest," I said uncomfortably, not sure how she'd respond to my assertion.

"I actually feel a lot better," she replied and looked up at me with a raised brow. Her cheeks were pinker now and looked as rosy as they'd get with her albinism. Surprised, I tossed the bird onto the ground by the firepit and gently claimed one of her hands. I studied the back of it, then turned it around to look at her inner wrist. I hummed, noticing that her veins were a little more inflated. Her blood pressure had increased.

"Too fast of a recovery… Think it was the drink?" I asked grudgingly, letting her hand go.

"It'd have to be." She grabbed the pheasant and began plucking it, to my dismay. She added dryly, "Let me know if I grow a third eye."

"Let me do that," I said, ignoring her statement and reaching for the bird, but she shook her head and moved it out of my immediate reach. I sighed and wandered around the area, collecting firewood so she could cook. I was sick to my stomach about everything. I just didn't know what to do.

A weary sigh escaped me. "I don't hate you, Keid," I said as I placed the wood in the firepit and started collecting kindling.

"And I don't believe you, Ferrer," she said shortly.

I winced at her crisp tone and let my shoulders droop. "It's true," I urged, squatting to face her across the pit. She didn't meet my gaze as she tossed some moss and a handful of decaying detritus into the firepit. I stared as the dry and damp mix started smoking and then burst into flames, consumed completely by tiny licks of orange fire. "That was amazing," I complimented in an attempt to please her. "How did you do that?"

"Decomposition of plant matter can generate heat. I just encouraged the process with magic until spontaneous combustion occurred," she explained, offering nothing more. She dropped some twigs over the little ball of fire, and I adjusted the kindling so it'd catch easier.

"Sounds like rot magic…?" I asked, but I had a feeling it'd come out sounding judgmental.

"I don't know anything about rot-magic," she snapped. "There are many chemical elements involved in spontaneous combustion, Ferrer."

"Sorry… that came out wrong. I was just curious. It was impressive," I said glumly. I studied her pinched face and felt her loathing. As much as my ancient instincts told me to reject the witch because of what she was, I did feel more comfortable around her now. Some of it was due to marking her, but some was just from time spent around her. I just wished I hadn't completely destroyed her trust in me.

"What are you doing, Ferrer?" she asked, plucking aggressively at the dead fowl.

"What do you mean?" I asked nervously.

"Complimenting me. What is your motivation?"

I frowned and hesitated. I didn't know what to say. "I…" I fumbled for words and started to panic. What was my motivation?

*Iron,* I begged, feeling my brain stop working. *Help.*

*Say you want to make amends. You want a fresh start because you realized you massively messed up,* he answered smugly.

I ran a hand through my hair and blew out a puff of breath. Before I could speak, Keid grumbled, "Look, I'm not going to run off with your offspring if I end up getting pregnant because of last night, so you don't need to suck up to me. I don't appreciate lying."

"But I'm not," I protested weakly. "I'm just trying to start fresh here. You've shown me that witches aren't as bad as I thought..."

"Congratulations on achieving the bare minimum." Though she wasn't mollified, her plucking of the bird became slightly less hostile.

"What can I do to make you happy?" I asked and watched as Vain scooted along in the dirt to settle by Keid.

*I'm hungry,* she said, looking up at my mate.

"Come here, Vain. I'll feed you. Let Keid finish her recovery," I offered, patting my knee to call her to me. The little blood bat ran over and jumped onto my leg. I lowered my arm to let her feed from wherever she wanted, not even flinching at her tiny bite. This was nothing compared to feeding another bat-shifter.

"Thank you," Keid said, her tone softening further.

*Taking back what he stole,* Vain reported with a giggle, making an amused smile force its way onto Keid's face. I could tell that she'd fought it, but Vain was a little too cute for her to resist.

"It's only fair," I said playfully, but Keid's smile faded pretty quickly after that.

*Blood clots.*

"Remind me to check your cuts later," I said, gesturing with my other hand to her shoulder. She simply nodded and made no further comment.

I didn't necessarily feel awkward with Keid's unwillingness to chat, but I was getting frustrated. What else could I say? She was as distant as a star.

*Try another compliment,* Iron suggested.

I scrunched my face up, worried about that particular tactic. She wouldn't believe me. I decided to go another route instead and asked, "Why do you think you're ugly, Keid? You keep saying that."

She froze in her movements, and her cheeks flooded with blood. She blinked rapidly before replying, "You know I was teased. I don't need to explain more than that, do I?"

"I don't fully understand. You had a previous lover, did you not? Did he not make you feel desired?" I asked, genuinely wanting to get a better understanding. Maybe I could help?

She snorted angrily and shook her head. "Yes, until he went back to report to his buddies that I was just as white in between my legs," she answered hotly, scowling down at the extra-dead bird as if it was her old lover.

"I like your whiteness..." I mumbled. "My people think it's pretty."

"Wasn't enough to keep you from crushing my heart, was it?" she retorted, her voice quickly growing thick with emotion. "Wasn't enough to keep me from wanting to kill myself—that the only person who should have loved me without reservation was my fated mate! And yet, here we are. This is incredibly fu—"

Her raised voice was interrupted by a near-deafening series of cracks as two dragons broke through the canopy, headed straight for us.

By the time the two dragons landed, they'd shifted back to their human forms, and I had Keid in my arms, who was clutching Vain. My heart pounded with a moment of fear, realizing that I had to explain all of this if these were border scouts. Everything would be easier if these were bandits, but I had a feeling that these two dragons were officials.

"Halt, bat-shifter," one of the dragons said, holding a palm out as the wind of their entrance raked through his choppy red hair. His companion was a muscular woman with thick black hair, and Keid's entire body tensed in my arms, obviously not keen on the casual nudity—just like the fae. "I'm Reinjeri Ellanher. What brings you into the dragon kingdom, and do you have documentation with you?" The male's suspicious eyes swept over the humble campsite, frowning.

I cleared my throat, folded my wings, and stood a little taller. "I am Coronel Ferrer from the bat-shifter colony. We had an emergency situation that led into your territory. I'm very sorry we were not able to alert you in advance."

The female pointed a nail at Keid and growled, "What's wrong with the woman? She was yelling, and I smell blood on her."

"I'm fine," Keid said after clearing her throat. "I was injured, but I'm almost recovered."

The she-dragon glared at me while Keid spoke. She didn't trust me at all. "Women and females often say they're ok when they're not."

"That's none of our business," the redhead said, moving slightly to flank me with an arm out, like I was a horse about to spook. I eyed his movements carefully, not liking the story they told. "Coronel Ferrer, you will have to come with us to the closest outpost. This must be reported." He looked at his companion and pointed at Keid. "Can you take the woman, Brynja?"

"Of course, sir," she said and shifted back into her massive crimson dragon form, knocking a thinner redwood tree over with a hind leg to make more room.

"Reinjeri Brynja will be transporting the lady, Ferrer. Please put her down. No harm will come to either of you if you follow instructions," the dragon-shifter said, waving Keid over to his companion.

"No… I can't go!" Keid protested. "I have an old woman I'm escorting. She's nearby. I can't leave her!" She wrapped her arms around my neck, and I didn't need to feel her through the bond to know that she was utterly terrified. I glanced down at her panicky expression, then up at the officials. A scowl snuck onto my face. I didn't like them scaring her.

"We will send someone back for her," the dragon replied to Keid, getting impatient. A string of white smoke curled from a nostril as he edged closer. "Coronel Ferrer, please put her down and let Brynja escort her."

"No! You can't come back for her! She can't be carried! She's fragile! She'll die!" Keid yelled through fresh tears, her desperation tugging at something in me. I didn't like them making her cry. I detested it. I felt like I couldn't breathe.

"Coronel…" the male said warningly.

Before I could respond and calm the situation, Keid pushed herself out of my arms and ran past the two shifters, heading straight for the rot-witch's camp.

"Keid!" I yelled and darted after her, but Ellanher's hand shot out and snagged my arm in a steel grip.

"Coronel, think carefully about what you're doing here. Do not start an incident with your allies. We're not going to hurt you," he threatened in a low voice. "We're only following our law, something you should have read before stepping foot here."

I was barely paying attention because Brynja's dragon whipped around to block Keid's escape, and I watched in horror as my mate plowed into her lashing tail. Her fragile body flipped over and Keid landed hard on her stomach and face.

I completely lost my mind.

"Keid!" I roared and shoved Ellanher off me, sending him into a redwood. I ran as fast as I could to get to my injured mate, but Brynja's dragon hastily snatched Keid up and launched into the canopy. "Get back here!" I screamed and unfolded my wings to follow her, but I was swallowed by darkness as Ellanher's dragon captured me in his claws.

Several lurches and the sound of cracking branches told me that we'd broken past the canopy, and I fumbled to pry open the dragon's claws. I screamed again in rage and frustration and pulled at the dragon's fingers until a bone dislocated. The dragon shrieked and instinctively released me.

Freed, I spread my wings—only to be slaughtered by the daytime sun. All it took was the slice of a moment for the Sun God to take my vision. I shrieked at the agonizing, white-hot pain of a deity's wrath and clapped my hands over my eyes. Such was my shock that my wings failed, and I fell like a dead star down toward the treetops.

I clicked repeatedly to orient myself, but I was too far from anything that'd return an echo. In my pain and blindness, I had no idea what was up or down. All I could think about was Keid being sent flying, and it burned. It burned so hot that my blood ignited. I'd never felt such fury, and I'd just been smote by a god.

Despite every pain, every inch of me that smoldered, I stabilized myself and spread my blistered wings… only to end up in the dragon's claws again. I roared furiously as I worked to dislocate another finger, but it lifted a claw and flicked it against my head, knocking me out completely.

When I woke, it was to the sensation of a cold stone floor under my face, chest, and hands. I coughed and groaned as I moved to sit up, but my head swam, and I had a hard time maintaining balance.

*Iron,* I called, coughing once more and rubbing my eyes. I slowly opened them to find that I was still blind. *Shit… Iron, are you there?*

*I'm here…* he replied, as shaken as me. *Where are we?*

I clicked and found myself in a cell with one door and no window. All the walls were solid, so there was no shifting to escape here. There were no bars to squeeze through as Iron.

"Shit," I said again and crawled toward a wall to see if I could sit upright. "Shitting stars… Do we have a concussion?" I asked Iron out loud, finding some comfort in my own voice.

*Yes… I'm working on it. It's not that bad, but give me some time. Don't move too much.*

"Thanks," I groaned and eased myself up to lean against the wall. It took me a minute, but I started to recall what had landed us in here. "Shit! Where's Keid?"

My heart pounded at the memory of her falling, and I yelled at the top of my lungs, trying to get someone's attention. I shouted for about five minutes before there were footsteps and the metal creak of the door's slot.

"Are you going to behave now?" a gruff voice said. I didn't recognize this person. It definitely wasn't either of the shifters who took us here.

"Where's my mate? One of your officials hurt her, and it was absolutely unprovoked!" I snarled furiously. "She could be pregnant! Where is she?" I smacked my hand against the wall, feeling very much like not behaving until I got news of her.

"I heard about that. Reinjeri Brynja is facing punishment for not following protocol. Our doctor has already seen your mate. She has some scrapes we've bandaged up but is otherwise fine."

I blew out a long breath and almost collapsed on myself. She was fine. That was all that mattered. "Humans are so fragile," I whispered.

"That they are. Now tell me, what are you doing in dragon territory, Coronel Ferrer? You're speaking to the head of the reinjeri, by the way. I'm Stigandr."

I rubbed my temples, not really sure what to say or how much I wanted him to know. If they went back for the witch and ended up killing her, Keid and I would lose our chance to find someone to remove the mark I gave her. I'd taken all her choices from her, and as much as I was starting to want to keep her, I didn't want to take yet another choice away from her. This was her decision to make.

"This is an incredibly sensitive situation," I admitted with a sigh. "Is there any way I could speak to Spymaster Leofwine? We recently worked together in acquiring permission to hunt those slavers in cat-territory. He's familiar with me, and I thin—"

"He is not here, Coronel," Stigandr drawled patiently. "I'm your date today."

*Blood clots,* I cursed and wiped my sweating palms on my pants. "Alright, you win," I said in a lighter tone. "I met my fated mate at our recognition event, but I stupidly almost rejected her. She ran away, and I pursued her. It wasn't until we got here that I convinced her to forgive me. Look, I'm just a stupid male trying to bring his mate back home. Her sister is worried about her." I didn't know how much they knew about rot-witches, so I didn't want to draw too much attention to that creature. Had they brought her?

I wasn't sure what I was expecting, but I hadn't expected Stigandr's laughter. It instantly got under my skin; I was getting really tired of being laughed it. He slapped his fist on the door when his guffaws subsided to chuckles. "Cute story. Give me the real one tomorrow. I'll send a message to Leofwine for you as a sign of respect for your station. Talk to you soon, Coronel."

"Wait!" I shouted but was met only with the sound of another door clicking shut.

*What now?* Iron asked.

*I'm going to try to reach Keid, but even if she is close enough, she won't be able to reply. I don't know what happened to Vain. Keid fell pretty hard.*

*Vain!* Iron shouted in dismay. *Shit! Shit! Shit! My starshine! We forgot to ask if Keid had her!*

*Keid?* I asked, sending my mind-link out as far as it could go. I knew the general direction she was in, but I wasn't sure if she was too far away to hear. *Keid? I hope you're ok. If Vain is with you, talk through her if you can. I want to know if you're ok. They... they said you were ok... but I'd rather hear it from you...*

I waited. I gave her some time, but she either wasn't close enough or Vain wasn't with her. My heart sank. This was all my fault. If I hadn't driven her away, none of this would have happened.

"Shit..." I hissed and smacked the back of my head against the wall.

*Stop, you clot! I'm trying to fix your bloody concussion!* Iron yelled. *You had one job! Don't bloody move!*

"Sorry," I mumbled, blinking occasionally and still seeing nothing. "Gods, I wished I'd asked what time it was. I'm so disoriented."

*I have no idea,* Iron grumbled.

"Maybe it's best to sleep until they return," I said with a yawn.

*No sleeping until I fix this concussion.*

I groaned and lay down anyway, arching a wing and pretending that Keid was here, curled up under it with me. It was going to be a long day or night. Either way, it was going to be a long one.

I wasn't sure when I'd fallen asleep, or if I'd gotten Iron's permission to do so, but I woke to a harsh rapping on the cell door that startled me upright.

"Hello?" I asked the darkness, then clicked to see if I could sense anything.

"You've got a visitor, Coronel. Shall I send her in?" a voice—probably a warden's—said. "We've searched her, so don't get your hopes up." She didn't sound too good, like she was getting sick.

"A visitor? Yes!" I gasped. Was it Keid? I slowly moved to stand, clicking again.

With the creak of the door came a rush of air. With the air came the scent of rot. I stumbled backward and hit the wall, hissing more from surprise than pain. My next click verified that the rot-witch was waddling in, and I was so terrified to be in such close proximity to her that I thought my heart would fail.

*Ferrer,* Iron squeaked.

I pressed myself as far away as I could get from her. This entire scenario was kindling for night terrors. I was blind and stuck in a small cell with a rot-witch. If I was asked what my biggest nightmare was, this would probably be what I'd describe. I was surprised I wasn't pissing myself. Then again, maybe I was. The gods knew I at least wouldn't smell it over the stench the hag was releasing.

"How did you even ask for me?" I questioned as she slowed her approach. Cold dread pulled at my stomach when the door was locked behind her.

*Heart attack imminent,* Iron whispered.

The witch just giggled at my question, and I shuddered. I still hadn't gotten used to that sound. When I clicked again, I was relieved to find that she hadn't moved. She was scratching at her wrist an awful lot though, and her smell was growing fouler.

"Why are you here? And how?" I asked quietly in a hiss, suddenly paranoid that someone was listening outside the cell. The elements were not in my favor at the moment. "I've been trying not to bring attention to you, and yet you waltz right in! And shouldn't you be checking in on Keid instead? She's the one who was hurt! I'm fine. Please go."

The witch gestured to my eyes, and I shook my head. "They'll heal. It'll just take a while."

She didn't laugh at that. She just nodded and looked around while scratching away at her wrist. It was like she was waiting for something, and that was only kindling for my burning anxiety. I simply stayed still and didn't move, not sure what to make of this entire scenario. What the shit was she doing?

I opened my mouth to address her again, but there was a sudden wet, slopping noise and a grunt, followed by the most terrible stench. I threw my arm over my nose and gagged, but caught the rot-witch throwing something against the back wall of the cell. When she knocked at the door, it opened, and she left.

"Great gods!" the warden cried, making a retching sound. "Get the fuck out of here, you old hag! Sun God's fire! Someone get this lady a bucket!" Her fading ranting was accompanied by the rot-witch's laughter, and I bloody near fainted in relief. My heart had been about to fail.

*WHAT IN THE SHIT WAS THAT?* Iron screamed, his nerves snapping, and I shook my head, still breathing into my arm.

*I don't know,* I lamented, nearly in tears. *I don't, and I never will, understand that wretched creature. For all I know, she came here to stink up my cell and go.*

*She threw something though. What is it? It landed by the far wall.*

I turned my head to where Iron nudged me and clicked again.

*Oh gods, why...*

I took to a knee and nearly threw up at the sight of a recently detached hand—one that had previously belonged to a certain rot-witch.

# Chapter 15

## Ferrer

I moved away from the rot-witch's abandoned hand, beyond revolted. I banged my fist on the door until the warden returned. "What?" she asked tersely, her voice still thick with nausea.

"Can I please, for the love of the Sky Gods, get some fresh air?" I begged. "Or a different cell, I don't care."

"This is our only one, Coronel. Please wait." She left for maybe ten minutes, and when she returned, the door's bottom slot opened. A bucket of water was shoved through with a rag and some soap.

"You cannot be serious," I complained, still covering my nose with my arm.

"Sorry, Coronel. This is the best I can do." The warden departed, leaving me with false hope in the form of soap and water. I wanted to cry.

Instead of wasting the resources on the detached hand and its immediate surroundings, I shucked my clothes and gave myself a quick bath, cursing the entire time. I spot-cleaned my pants, threw them back on, and dumped the rest of the water on the disembodied hand, hoping to… I don't know… hoping for the best, I supposed.

I'd expected the hand to decay relatively fast, as I'd seen a rot-witch dissolve before my very eyes, but the water seemed to expedite the process. I clicked and stared in disturbed fascination as the flesh sank in between the bones. Something unusual was starting to become visible under the rotting flesh, and I crept closer, keeping the bar of soap under my nose.

Another click showed it to be a slip of paper, and I wrinkled my nose as I used the rag to retrieve the curiosity.

*What is this?* I asked, grimacing as I turned it around to examine it.

*It's too bad we don't have our eyes. If there's writing on it… sound won't show it.*

*You're right,* I admitted, not sure what to do with this. *It's clear she smuggled something to us though.*

*With a body part, Ferrer. She smuggled us something in a body part!* Iron bemoaned. *I'll never unsee this.*

*What a sacrifice,* I murmured thoughtfully. *She gave up a hand to give us this, Iron. It's insane.*

*She's not long for death,* he replied darkly. *Maybe it means less to her.*

*I've no idea, but I need to sort out what this is for.*

I backed away from the hand, having gotten all I was going to get out of it… literally. She came in, scratched her hand off, then threw it at the wall. She could have done anything with it, but she chose to throw it at the far wall. Why?

I mulled it over for a while until Stigandr returned to interrogate me again. He did not stay, however. The aroma must have leaked out around the door because he quickly made up an excuse and left in a hurry—something about forgetting to pick up something. I wasn't really paying attention.

*This reminds me of something,* I said to Iron. *This size and shape. You remember those papers that Queen Hekla's friend put some kind of enchantment on? They stuck it on their people and peeled them off to leave a symbol. You remember that?*

*You think this is similar?* Iron asked. *I don't think we should place that on our body. I really... don't want to do that, Ferrer.*

*I don't think it's supposed to go on us,* I replied, clicking and staring at the far wall. I walked toward it and slapped the slip on the wall, then removed it. I waited a couple minutes but nothing happened. *Maybe it's the other side,* I mumbled to myself and turned the paper around to try again.

As soon as the paper touched the wall, a small section of it started to age. The surface became grainier and cracks formed, forking like lightning through the material. Larger chunks fell out, crumbling to the ground until a small hole was fully revealed. It was just big enough for a blood bat to squeeze through.

It was also too small to push my pants through.

I hated her.

I waited nervously outside the hospital wall, waiting to hear from Mushy, who'd wandered off somewhere. When she returned, I nearly fainted. "Where... where's your hand?" I gasped and bent over to stare at her arm. She grinned, looking prouder than the mother of an excelling student.

I gave her a side-eye as I stood up and crossed my arms. She was up to some mischief, and I reminded myself that now, in this very moment, she was at her most dangerous. I supposed that if I was to worry about anyone suddenly losing a hand, it shouldn't be Mushy.

So, previous worries returned to take my attention. I pulled the blanket tighter around me, grateful that the doctor had let me have it. All my possessions, everything that had been in the bag, was now gone. My heart wrenched because Vain's collar had been in there. I was so proud of it, and it'd become priceless. I would never be able to recreate it.

Far more than the bag though, more than anything, I was worried about her. I hoped Vain was with Ferrer because I hadn't seen her since the dragons took us. They'd kept me in a guest room for a day but let me wander freely after that. I was deemed pretty harmless since my story lined up with Ferrer's, albeit rather loosely. Him being kept for further questioning made me anxious though. I didn't know what that meant, and I hoped beyond hopes that they weren't torturing him. He'd done me wrong, but I didn't want him to actually get hurt.

Mushy gestured for me to follow her, and we made the long walk across the creaking wooden bridges to where Ferrer was apparently being held. The dragons hadn't allowed me near, not wanting us to communicate since they noticed I'd been marked. Not knowing how he'd been faring had made the several days and nights we'd been here long indeed. Even now, the third sunrise shone gold beams through the trees, lighting up the grand wooden fort that was built into the canopy of the giant redwoods. It was beautiful... an ideal spot for dragons to land.

It was quiet in this part of the tree fortress, and I had to wonder if Mushy had cleared the area of guards. Perhaps she'd gone around patting butts, forcing the dragons to retire and wash their trousers. It wasn't outside the realm of possibilities.

When I turned a corner, I spied a bat wiggling out of a hole in the wall. My heart leapt for a second, thinking it was Vain, but then I noticed it didn't look like her at all. This one was bigger and had white tips on its wings. Subtle white spots, only a couple of them, dotted said wings. I recognized those wings...

"Ferrer?" I hissed under my breath, then realized I was addressing the wrong person. "I mean... Iron?"

*Yup,* Iron's voice replied, sounding distracted. I reached into the hole and helped pull him out, careful of his tiny thumbs and feet. They looked so fragile. So odd that the tall, muscular bat-shifter was inside this little thing. I could hardly wrap my mind around it.

I put Iron on the ground and stepped back, waiting to see if he'd shift back into Ferrer. He did not.

*Uh... Keid?* Iron asked in hesitation. *You don't happen to have a pair of pants on you, do you?*

My face flushed, burning hotly when I realized what he was implying. I patted myself stupidly, as if I could possibly be carrying such a thing on my person. Then I ripped the blanket off my shoulders and held it out for him. "You can have this!" I offered quietly. "But I didn't think shifters cared about nudity."

*He knows you care,* Iron said dryly. *He doesn't like upsetting you.*

I held back a nasty retort, then took a deep breath and calmed myself. Ferrer was trying. I wanted to respect that. He was trying.

"I can handle it," I said with a sigh. "I've seen a great many naked males at the lions' hospital. I'm just not used to seeing it… outside of an examination room." *Where naked people shouldn't be,* I thought to myself. I hadn't really felt that strongly about it before, but I wondered how much Ferrer had enjoyed looking at that naked she-dragon earlier—the one that sent me head over heels… in a bad way. Gods, that had hurt.

I stomped onto my irrational bout of jealousy and wiggled the blanket, telling Iron to hurry and shift already. Ferrer appeared rather quickly and wrapped the blanket around himself before approaching me with a worried expression.

"Are you badly hurt?" he asked quietly after releasing a frustrated click between his teeth. The bat-shifter reached for my chin, gently tilting my face for his scrutiny. He scowled at the abrasions on my cheek and forehead, looking more enraged than I expected.

"I'll heal…" I murmured, suddenly shy under his seething countenance. "I don't think it'll scar."

Mushy approached and ushered us toward the edge of the platform. She pointed over the railing and moved to poke Ferrer.

"Shit! Witch! I'm going, I'm going!" he whispered hastily, grabbed me, and fell backward off the platform before Mushy could touch him. It took everything in me to hold back a scream as we fell. I had not expected that! Oh, Mushy was going to be in so much trouble! She knew he was scared of her!

Ferrer had to shrug off the blanket to free his wings. Once the fabric was clear, he hoisted me against him and turned our fall into a glide. I hastily wrapped my legs around his hips and shut my eyes tight, too terrified to look at how fast the ground was approaching. A squeal struggled to slip past my lips, but I suppressed it, even though I felt like I was about to burst.

Ferrer flapped quicker, then we landed, though it was a bit of an awkward landing. He laughed quietly and set me down on the pine needles. "I'm not used to flying with someone. The balance is all different."

I pressed my lips into a thin smile and averted my gaze. I'd seen him naked, but he'd been feral at the time, and the situation had been… entirely different. It was especially hard to look at him now after his recent attempts to make amends with me. It didn't mean I trusted him… It just meant that he had a body that'd make any woman melt into a puddle of desire.

I blushed and looked down at my hands as I worried at them. What was I thinking? Focus.

"We need to move—fast, Keid," Ferrer said, running back to me. He'd already fetched the blanket? Gods, he was fast!

"What about Mushy?" I asked, rushing along beside him. "And Vain's not with you? We're not going back for her? You didn't hear about her at all?" My eyes brimmed with tears as my anxiety spiked. No, no, no!

"The witch will find us," he said, looking over his shoulder to scan the treetops. "We'll find Vain. I promise, Keid. I won't fail you again."

"Wh-when did you fail me the first time?" I asked hesitantly, tactfully picking the word 'when' instead of 'which time.' If he was trying, I would try.

"I let that dragon hurt you," he growled, dark brows knotting in anger. "And I let her take you. I tried, Keid. I tried, but I failed."

I didn't know why it took me so long to notice, but he was occasionally clicking through his teeth. I rushed ahead to look at his face, noticing something odd with his eyes. He wasn't really looking where he was going. Not exactly.

"Ferrer," I asked, breathless in my attempt to keep up with him. "What happened to your eyes? You're not… They're not looking like they're focusing right now."

"I'm blind, Keid," he said flatly, his head occasionally turning around like he was scanning the canopy. "I looked at the sun on accident."

I stumbled at those words, shocked, and he reached out to steady me with a hand. Cold horror and dismay dripped into my chest. "Ferrer…" I started saying, but he dismissed my words with a hand.

"It'll heal. I just need to rely on sound for now," he said. "We need to find a place to hide, Keid. After that, we only travel at night. Is that clear?"

Worried, I glanced up at the bat-shifter and whispered, "Like a brook."

I ran alongside Ferrer as long as I could, but I just didn't have his stamina. A sharp stitch in my side finally defeated me, and I gasped through the pain, leaning a little to the right as I stumbled to a stop. I doubled over with my arms wrapped around my waist, gasping for air.

Ferrer stopped and backtracked. "Are you ok, Keid?" he asked in an urgent whisper.

"I can't… I can't run anymore," I said between breaths. The morning air was also cold, and my lungs stung horribly from the chill. "I'm sorry, Ferrer."

"It's ok," he murmured, and I started when he placed a hand on my back, rubbing gently. I swallowed hard and just accepted the comfort. He was trying.

Suddenly, a shadow passed over us, causing Ferrer to scoop me up and slip through the undergrowth to the nearest tree. He crouched under a low-hanging branch and clicked several times.

"You can see that far?" I whispered, curious about his echolocation.

"I mostly felt that shadow. The air was cooler. I'm very sensitive to daylight… even if it's filtered," he replied under his breath. "Otherwise, I noticed the higher branches swaying from that dragon passing overhead."

"Impressive…" I murmured and stared up at the canopy, worried that the dragon would return.

"Keid, I'm going to lure that dragon away. I'm not happy with how close it got to us." He brushed a straight strand of hair from his eyes even though he wasn't using them.

"No," I said, and it came out like a whine. I winced and continued speaking. "Don't! Let's just find a place to hide!"

"I am going to keep you safe," he growled irritably, turning his head to 'look' at me. I bit my lip and drew my brows in worriedly. I didn't want him to go. "Remember too that I may have another life to safeguard," he reminded me, pointing at my abdomen.

My heart plummeted. Of course he was only worried about his potential offspring. How could I keep forgetting that? I looked away, fighting a wretched wave of disappointment. Why did I let myself get so vulnerable agai—

"Keid, stop that," Ferrer said harshly, and my eyes snapped up to him in surprise. "I value you. You. I want to keep you safe, with or without fertility. You."

I blanched at his intensity. Were my emotions that easy for him to read? My stomach churned, not liking that particular disadvantage.

He shook his head. "Clearly, I have a lot of work to do in gaining your trust, and I might never earn it, but I'm going to do what I said I'm going to do. Now wait here, and I'll be back in several hours. I'm going to lead it away to get them searching in a completely different area. I'll keep my senses sharp for signs of Vain. Do that trick where you hide your scent, clever witch."

On that note, Ferrer covered me with the blanket, jumped to his feet, and ran off naked toward where the dragon had disappeared. I scrunched my face, terribly upset. Everything was going so wrong! Vain was missing, my bag was gone, gods knew where Mushy was this very minute, and Ferrer was putting himself in danger. Somehow, I felt even more vulnerable since his attempted rejection. I had more things I cared about now, and I didn't want to lose any of them. I quickly cast the spell to hide my scent and curled up under the tree.

The waiting was intolerable, and it wasn't until sometime after noon that I heard the sound of his return. I peeked around the tree, knowing from the slight pull on my soul that it was his footsteps crunching through the pine needles. I breathed a sigh of relief to see that he was ok, but he looked exhausted. Exhausted and very naked.

I averted my eyes as he approached and collapsed next to me, sweaty and slightly sunburnt. "The good news," he said as he closed his eyes and rubbed tiredly at his temples, "is that I have nothing but good news."

"Oh?" I asked as I studied his burns. I'd had calendula in my bag, but that was gone. Aloe didn't grow in this region, and a beehive might be hard to find. I sighed miserably and started digging at the base of the tree, hoping to get deep enough to find cool, damp soil.

"First of all, I got them all searching in a different area like I said, so we should be safe for quite a while. They'll probably give up in a couple days and report the incident. Secondly, I got far enough away from you to feel the most subtle tug. I think Vain is slightly west of us, so if we head in that direction, we could catch up to her."

A weird, relieved sob burst out of my chest, and I nodded. I didn't start crying, but I was quite frayed at the ends. I was so worried, but if we could find Vain, I'd feel a lot better about the situation in general. Hopefully, Mushy could catch up to us.

Ferrer placed his hand on my back again and rubbed gently. I tensed at the gesture but allowed it. I'd take what I could get right now.

"What are you doing?" he asked as I continued digging.

"Not looking for truffles," I muttered, then snorted at the stupid joke. Oh goodness, the stress was making me lose my mind. "I'm looking for damp soil to put on your burns. I don't know any spells for that."

"Stop." He reached down to pull one of my hands from the dirt. "I'll heal. Shifters heal. I just need a little time." He sat up abruptly and turned to face me. "Shit. When did you last eat? Have you eaten? We should find water… They know we'll be looking for water, but we can be careful enough t—"

I held up a placating hand. "I ate this morning. I'll be fine for a while. I'll forage for food tonight when we get moving again." I looked worriedly at him but kept my eyes at his chest level and above, still acutely aware of his nudity. "When did you eat last?"

"I don't even know how long I was in there, but you were my last mea—" He cleared his throat and pinched the bridge of his nose. "The last time I ate was that night… I-I marked you. I'll be fine for a while."

That'd been about four days ago, and he did not look fine. He'd been running around, caring for me, fighting dragons, getting blinded, interrogated, and only the gods knew what else. I didn't even know how he got that sunburn. Had he ventured from the woods or flown above them?

"Let's find a place to wait out the day," he said with a fatigued groan, then reached down to help me stand. I handed him the blanket to do what he willed with it, but he merely snorted in amusement and wrapped it around his hips. My cheeks burned with embarrassment. Was I being silly?

We traveled northwest as we searched for shelter and discovered a dip in the woods where a tree had fallen against a mossy boulder. A thicket had grown around it, providing a little more cover, so Ferrer crawled in and cleared it of spiders and other undesirables while I worked to remove our scents. I followed him in on my hands and knees, tossing out several pinecones that offended me with their lumpy prickliness.

He collapsed with a wearier groan and lay on his back after retracting his wings. I curled up, joining him on the cool, slightly damp detritus and stared at his profile. There was a lot to discuss going forward, and I thought about our options.

"Assuming Mushy can find us, how long do you think it'd take her to get here?" I asked. I had a hard time picturing the distance we'd actually covered.

"Maybe a day. Her stride is torturously slow," he said, closing his eyes and licking his lips. I hummed in response and stared at the straight slope of his nose. He had a nice nose.

"I… do want to see her home still. She's been a right pain in the ass and did some… horrific things, but… I don't know. I feel like I have to. I'd worry otherwise." I winced and waited for him to fight me on it.

"Then you'll have to tolerate me coming with you," he replied dispassionately. I blinked a couple times, taken aback, then hesitated as I thought about what to say next. Neither of us mentioned getting my mark removed, and the longer I waited, the more it seemed to be a topic neither of us wanted to discuss. Unless it was my imagination, the undiscussed subject hung thick between us.

I tucked my wrist under my chin as I continued to study Ferrer's face. I didn't know what I wanted to do about the mark. All I knew was that I wanted to be loved above all else. I wondered if it was possible to trust him again. I couldn't be sure. My heart still hurt, terribly, so I supposed I'd give it time. We still had some time.

"Are we much farther north than we used to be?" I asked quietly, remembering something.

Ferrer hummed a yes, not bothering to open his eyes.

"Mushy said something was stalking her. Maybe we got far enough away from it?" I said that last part to myself, wondering if the creature would have been able to follow us through the air. It must have lost our tracks, right?

"The bone eater?" Ferrer asked, and I blinked at him again. Right… he'd been following us. He must have heard a lot of one-sided conversations. That was a little embarrassing. "I don't know. I don't know what a bone eater is. My people haven't been in this realm for a very, very long time."

"I've never heard of it either. It's a chilling name though. I don't like it. I hope Vain's ok." I bit my lip nervously. What if she encountered it?

Ferrer reached out with a hand and patted me absently on the arm, completely calm. "I'll kill it if it gets near."

I wondered how he could possibly be that confident if he didn't know a thing about it. Either he was foolish or he was just comforting me. I hoped it was the latter.

"If we're going to be out here a while, you're going to have to eat, Ferrer," I said, addressing the other issue that was weighing on me. "You need to keep your strength up, especially if we encounter anything unsavory. I'm still trying to think of ways to keep Mushy safe from that… creature. I'm not much skilled in anything other than enchanting and some healing."

"I can't eat, Keid," he said shortly. "I can't eat until I return to the colony."

"That's simply not possible, Ferrer," I argued. "You know that as well as I." When he simply sighed and didn't reply, I inquired, "What do we do?"

"Nothing."

"Ferrer!" I snapped, balling my fist and smacking the dirt with it.

"I will not put myself in a position to force myself upon you," he stated, confessing his reason. "If I feed, that's what will happen."

I swallowed and was glad he couldn't see what had to be flaming red on my cheeks. As embarrassing as it was, I experienced an unwanted thrill from those words. Was it unwanted? I cleared my throat. "Like I said before, Ferrer. Go ahead. I'll enjoy what I can get before…" I let my words hang in the air, not sure what else to say. I felt like I'd just talked myself into a corner and promptly snapped my mouth shut.

"Before you make your decision," Ferrer murmured, finishing my sentence with his own twist, "I will neither tell you to remove my mark or force you to keep it. That's your choice. I've taken enough choices from you."

Ferrer continued to shock me, and I swept a hand through my hair, brushing it away from my eyes. What in the gods could I say to that?

"A-anyway," I stammered, thrown from his assertion. "What if you eat little meals more often? Would that help?"

"I don't know, Keid. I've never been stuck in the wilderness with a fated mate before," he replied a little wryly.

"L-look, w-we've got our options here," I stuttered, ridiculously flustered. "You can go eat a full meal out there, then I'll just… accept what happens when you come back. You can fast, get weak, then die a horrible death when the bone eater sneaks up on you. Lastly, you can try to take little meals and maybe it won't be so bad. The longer you wait before eating, the worse it gets, right?"

He was silent for a while, the muscles in his jaw flexing and his nostrils flaring in aggravation. When he didn't reply, I pressed, "Look, let's just test it on me. I'm feeling better, and Mushy can make me that nasty recovery drink when she catches up. Take a little blood, and if you drink for too long, I'll just hit you."

Ferrer covered his mouth to muffle his bark of laughter. He shook his head in disbelief, opened his eyes, and turned his head. When he clicked through his teeth, roguishly baring a singular fang, I knew he was looking right at me. I raised a brow, challenging him.

“No,” he said, fighting a bewildered smile. “I’m not drinking from you ever again. I might as well go catch a squirrel.”

I used my analytical brain to make my last argument. “But the bats at the event said that humans and shifters nourish your kind more than other animals, which is why we were warned so aggressively about it. Look, we’re going to be out here a little while longer, Ferrer. If we don’t find the boundaries, we won’t know how to be effective. Accept the trust I’m finally placing in you because you can trust I’ll punch you in the face if you get out of hand.”

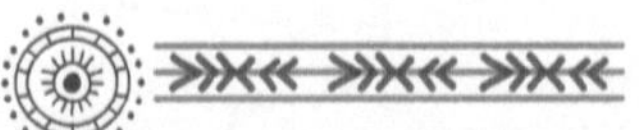

# Chapter 16

## Reid

Ferrer's bewildered half-smile faded, exposing a nervous countenance. I hesitantly placed a cool hand on his forearm to show my earnestness and fought to keep a prickle of arousal at bay. I just discovered that I quite liked how his stone-hard muscles rolled under my fingertips, and the fine brown hairs made his skin feel all the smoother—though it was all a bit sunburnt at the moment.

My stomach cramped from anxiousness and impatience as I lightly patted him. "It's been four days since you ate. Let's get it over with and see, then figure out what to do going forward. Even the field of medicine must take risks before people can benefit." I clung on to the professionalism of the doctor's assistant within me, feeling like I was getting much too stimulated.

Ferrer cleared his throat and nodded slowly. His dark brown lashes fluttered over his red-brown eyes before he replied. "Risky… but I see the wisdom in it." His voice dipped lower than usual in his considering. His gaze drifted past me, focusing on nothing in particular as he gestured for me to turn away from him. "We'll give it a try…"

I tried to hide my excitement from myself as much as I was trying to keep it hidden from him. I didn't know what was wrong with me. Well, that wasn't true at all. I knew very well what was wrong with me. It was the accursed mate bond and how it made me hungry for the accursed log that resided between Ferrer's legs. The back of my mind had turned absolutely filthy, and I was fighting it hard, especially at this very moment. I supposed I also had my hormones to thank for that. However, I shouldn't be ovulating any longer. Right now, I was either carrying a fertilized egg or my body was preparing to reabsorb an unfertilized one.

"The cut will be much smaller this time," Ferrer murmured, his voice growing husky. "I'll go slower. Don't let me feed for more than ten minutes, alright?"

"I'm really bad at judging time, but I'll try," I confessed.

"Well," he replied, clearing his throat yet again, "if I do this right, you won't feel any changes. So obviously, lash out at me if you start to feel any symptoms at all. You'll need to keep pressure on it afterward, but I'm not sure for how long. We'll just keep checking until it stops bleeding."

"Alright." I sighed and did my best to steady my emotions. It was utterly bizarre how much this male made my heart pound without trying, even after he'd broken it.

When his fingers brushed against my neck to gather my hair, I shuddered and goose bumps spread across my skin. I momentarily grew insecure, wondering if he could see my acne scars with his clicks. There were so many things I hated about my body, and that was another one of them. I felt like I'd received all of the bad genetics that my parents had to offer.

"I wish I could cure your insecurity, Keid," Ferrer said gently as he propped himself on an elbow behind me.

Worry twisted my insides. My wish was not being so transparent to him, but I forced it away as fast as possible. Now wasn't the time for that. I had such little to enjoy in my life, and I wanted to enjoy this, as weird as it seemed.

Though I couldn't feel him yet, I absolutely could sense his face's proximity as he drew closer to my neck and shoulder. I fought desperately to withhold another shudder, but all the nerves on my back and between my legs were coming to life. They tickled and tingled, melting into the hot anticipation buzzing through my muscles.

"Just a little puncture, then I'll suck and lick. I won't keep any teeth in there, I promise. That'd been the wrong way to do it." He placed a hand on my shoulder to position me, then tugged a little at my collar and said, "I'll try to keep blood away from your tunic."

"D-do you want me to remove it?" I asked, unable to believe my gall. A mad giggle nearly escaped, fed by the threat of a total nervous collapse.

"That is a terrible idea," he murmured as he lowered his lips to my neck. I nearly squealed from the shooting sensations created by his warm, soft flesh. When a sharp edge of his fang grazed my skin, the tingling that splintered down my body spiked. It took all my self-control to stay silent, but I feared it was only a matter of time before I'd break. Already my stomach was tied into knots, and my jealous clit had started to pulse. My sex clenched, as if asking for something to come and fill it… double meaning intended.

He took several subtle but ragged breaths before pressing that sharp fang into my skin. It pushed slowly, dimpling my skin until it broke through the thin layer of tissue. My flesh sprang back up and swelled against his accessory to feeding. I winced at the sting, but it wasn't intolerable, and I suspected the mate touch had something to do with the pain relief.

He slowly slid his fang back out, and something warm, smooth, and wet eased onto my neck. The tiniest whimper escaped through my mouth, and my face lit on fire. I held my breath after that, not trusting any traitorous air to escape and form a sound.

His tongue dragged lazily up my neck, leaving behind a cool sensation as his saliva mingled with the shaded forest air. Another whimper escaped me, and I gave up entirely. I breathed out and tried to relax through every exhale, but my entire body threatened to cramp up with tension. My toes curled as he dragged his tongue up again, then pressed it against the puncture, letting his saliva sink in to instigate a heavier bleed.

Fortunately, none of this continued to hurt, but even if it did, I wouldn't be able to pay attention. The tingles from the mate bond spread and rippled from every lave of his tongue and brush of his lips. I'd occasionally feel a fang scrape past, dragging across my skin. I held on to a squeal as another fang grazed me but didn't break the surface. It never did. Ferrer was being incredibly careful.

I grunted embarrassingly through an exhale when he planted his lips around the puncture and started taking draws, forming a suction to direct his small meal. I scrunched up my face and gripped at the bottom of my tunic, white-knuckling so hard that my finger joints and palms burned.

Perhaps he sensed the pain because he groped blindly for one of my hands and laid it flat on the dirt, lacing his rough fingers through mine to keep me from doing it again.

"Try to relax," he murmured in a rush, then hastily ducked his head to lick up a trail of blood before it could soak into my tunic. His tongue traveled up the length of my neck, causing me to press my thighs together and rub them anxiously against each other. If he noticed the squirming, he didn't say anything, and I agonized over whether that was good or bad.

The noises of the occasional swallow had me flaring with arousal, but the worst part was when something poked against my bottom. I knew that was his erection, and I nearly opened my mouth to beg for it. The only thing that kept me from doing it was my self-esteem and his prior attempt to reject me. I was afraid of another rejection, especially because he didn't seem to be going feral. The accursed male was staying in control like he'd promised.

He shifted his hips back after the accidental prod and raised his lips long enough to issue an apology. "Sorry, Keid. You know how it is." He grunted like he was holding a breath or clenching, then licked up another busy trail of blood. “I’m sorry. I have to do this. Don’t be offended.”

I was about to ask what he meant, but I very quickly found out when he moved the blanket and start jerking at something. Another whimper managed to sneak out from between my lips, and he released a deeper, breathier noise, like he was replying in kind. I scrunched my face up tighter and tried to pace my lungs, but exhales were coming out fast in between desperate holds. My core screamed at me, furious that what he was fervently pumping at wasn’t being shoved into it.

My clit pulsed just as vehemently. I reached down now that Ferrer was no longer able to pin my hand and pressed desperately down on my sex, trying to get it to hang in there. I was pretty certain that with my racing heart, my heaving lungs, the seizing of muscles, and the tingling of every nerve ending, I was about to die.

Ferrer lifted his lips once more and breathed out an order. “Keid, you gotta tuck your knees up or I’m going to come on the back of your legs.”

*Oh my fuck!* my brain screamed, and I drew my knees to my chest as Ferrer’s jerking turned feverish. He groaned loudly into my neck while he fed, vibrating my sensitive skin, and I started patting the ground in front of me with mad impatience. I’d broken into a sweat without doing an accursed thing. I couldn’t handle this anymore. I was going to lose my blessed mind!

“Almost done,” he choked out and returned to my neck, his voice trembling with each accelerating pump.

“Ferrer,” I croaked out, hardly able to form words, “pl—”

He moaned loudly, interrupting my begging, and seized up behind me. My eyes widened as I watched ropes of his pale seed shoot from behind my tucked feet, splattering on the dirt just past me to form a puddle. I shut my eyes again, unable to watch the erotic scene play out in its entirety. It would be my undoing.

He grunted several more times into my neck, muffled as he spent the rest of himself. He scrambled to his feet after that and hurriedly brought my palm to my neck to stem the flow.

"I… I have to get some space. I'm s-sorry. Need fresh air." He gasped and crawled past me to leave the den. His sweaty, lithe, now-winged form raced into the woods, then I waited exactly one heartbeat before shoving my other hand into my leggings to search for the end of my torture.

I swallowed a frustrated scream and turned my head into the dirt, not caring about the leaf litter or the needles. I tried to approach my clit from different angles, but orgasms always fucking eluded me when I sought relief. I tried stroking down my folds, curling a finger into my sex, but nothing ever worked well enough to satisfy me.

I tried to think about how arousing Ferrer was, and it helped a little bit, but I kept getting distracted about how he hadn't ended up fucking me. I'd wanted him to, but I also hadn't, and I couldn't for the life of me figure out why! Wouldn't it make sense to jump at every opportunity for intimacy before I got the mark removed?

But my mind kept going back to Ferrer saying he wanted a fresh start. He'd been trying to make amends, and it had me wondering if he was starting to change his mind. If he did, would I forgive him? Would I accept him back into my hesitant heart? I had no idea.

It was at that point that the peak I was slowly building simply fizzled out into a disappointing throb. My muscles contracted a couple times in a faint release, and a pathetic sob escaped my lips. What did I want?

I wanted more than an orgasm, that was for sure, though a decent one sure would've been nice. My mind was in turmoil, and it was clearly affecting my body. Another sob escaped my lips, wishing I knew if I still wanted him and if I did, was able to make him want me.

If I was pregnant, I'd definitely be tied to him, with or without his mark. I'd move to the colony, not wanting to leave my child or keep him from his offspring. It'd also be the best place to raise a bat-shifter, among their own kind and in the shaded protection of their territory.

Did I want to be pregnant? Yes, I did. I honestly did. I'd always wanted a child, and it became more precious as soon as I discovered I wouldn't be able to have one. I frowned and stared blankly into the dirt. I had to amend that thought. It became more precious after they'd stolen my eggs from me. They'd stolen my dream.

I owed Mushy everything if I was able to conceive again. Escorting her home to pass away no longer felt like enough, but it'd have to be.

As if the wretched thing had heard my thoughts, the old lady squeezed between two large ferns to approach my hiding place. She looked straight at me and grinned, giggling in her slow amble. She was the same as the first day I met her, shaking, wild-eyed, and as crazed as an angry goose. Well, she was the same minus a hand, a tongue, and likely several more teeth since then.

Her gaze moved to my leggings, and I gasped, slipping my hand out from them while blushing furiously. I opened my mouth to say something, anything, to move on from what she'd caught me doing. "H-how did you get here so fast?" I asked in a hushed yell, my boiling cheeks radiating embarrassment.

She just cackled in her normal fashion and settled clumsily by a tree to rock and stare up at the sky. I fumbled out of the little den and ran to find some privacy to pee before I developed an infection on top of everything else. Oh gods, that'd been mortifying.

## Ferrer

I'd starved with my people in the Night Court, and I'd battled with my people in the Summer Court, but it wasn't until today that I discovered a new kind of suffering. It pulled at something deeper than the accursed craving for lifeblood, and it was more uncontrollable than the cycle of the Sun God.

Days and days ago, I thought that the ordeal with my fated mate was decided. I'd already set my mind upon rejecting her, but it turned out that the night of our recognition was only the first of my trials, and I'd failed it. I'd failed miserably, and now my torment was incalculable. My mind was changing, and the transition from one belief to another tested my sense of reality. It meant complete acceptance of my misjudgment before I could see the new path my choices had created.

It was, however, a little hard to see any paths at all when one was blind. I clicked regularly to hear my surroundings but struggled to concentrate when my body was one step closer to going feral. I'd already physically slipped on the ground several times during my rush to put some distance between Keid and me, something that would've never happened normally.

Leaving her lying there in a state of wanting had been the hardest thing I'd ever done. It'd never been my intention to arouse her, at least not to that intensity. The more I thought about it, the more I realized that feeding from an erogenous zone had simply added to Keid's and my perfect disaster. I thought that maybe I'd have an easier time controlling my desire with her facing away from me, but I hadn't taken into consideration how it'd stimulate her, and in turn, stimulate me.

I hoped the next time would be easier since I wouldn't have to wait as long for a small meal. I hated the idea of feeding on Keid, and I hated that I loved doing it. I hated that I loved how she fought against her body's urge to sing. I'd practically felt her cries and moans vibrating under her skin, desperate to be set free through her shy lips. She'd eventually crumbled, and it'd been a euphoric thrill to hear her raging desire leak through her serious mask.

I knew she fought it because she was mad at me. I felt her rage and sadness often, and it was starting to crush me. At this point, any glimmer of her enjoying something from me, anything, was just enough to keep me going. She'd wanted me to try to feed from her, so I did. I did it carefully because I wanted her to sense my thoughtfulness. I needed her to see that I could be attentive. Attentive…

I came to a stop and dug my claws into the nearest tree, finding realization hidden away in a memory. I finally made the connection. Blood clots… I had already known all this!

When I took her days ago and marked her as mine… my feral mind had already known. None of this was new and yet I was just seeing it now. I'd been desperate for forgiveness back then, and I hadn't even been aware of it. My feral mind had sought her forgiveness through attentiveness that night. I felt like such a blind fool… and right now, I truly was both.

I turned and buried my face in my arm, leaning into the tree while I continued to pump at my stubborn erection. I gasped and bit at my lower lip, wanting nothing more than to run back and plunge my cock into Keid's wanting.

Maybe if I tried to return the favor and give her pleasure, I could soften the hard edge I'd created from breaking her heart. If I proved to her that I could keep her safe, keep her fed, keep her satisfied, and nurture her heart, maybe she wouldn't want to remove my mark after all. I still had time, and I had to hang on to that.

I swallowed, still tasting traces of Keid's savory flavor in my mouth, and pictured her for my pleasure. My erection and sack still had one or two more rounds to go before they'd calm. The cocky bastards knew that my fated mate was near and was stubbornly refilling loads. I was not going back until I was calm. I wanted to be able to completely focus on her.

I rapidly fisted my erection, reminiscing about how I'd stealthily adjusted the bottom of Keid's tunic after freeing my cock from the blanket. In between licks and sucks, I'd glanced down to look at the beautiful curves of her rump. The cotton leggings hugged her cheeks nicely, not that I'd needed further stimulation at the time. Still, it'd helped me finish faster then, and it'd help me finish now.

I groaned like I had then, spasming tightly while releasing for the second time today. I hastily massaged out my seed, urging it to get out of me so I could return to Keid's side. The ropes splashed messily onto the ferns by my feet, weighing down the fronds.

Still hard, I scrunched my face up and thought about what I wished I'd done to Keid. I imagined myself sliding my hands up under her tunic to follow the slope of her soft white waist to her ribs. Then…

I came again before my brain could even get to the good part, and I grunted in pleasure, relief, and irritation. Even imaginings of her were potent—almost as potent as her being right next to me. I chuckled tiredly into the flaky redwood bark, then wobbled a couple steps backward before straightening myself.

I cracked my neck, shifted away my wings, and strolled back to where I'd left Keid. Upon approaching the den, I was massively disappointed when I smelled someone I hadn't expected yet. She'd caught up to us already?

*There goes my plan to pleasure Keid.*

Fortunately, the old crone had been wise enough to not start a campfire. I gave her a begrudging nod and grunted a very reluctant hello. It was like pulling teeth, but I felt like I owed her a modicum of decency for helping me escape. She'd sacrificed a body part to do it. I still loathed that she was here.

The hag sent me a crazed but enthusiastic grin and lifted her arms to start applauding my return. She clapped silently since the other hand was no longer around to assist her cheering. I couldn't tell if it was a sick joke or the result of some odd dementia.

"It's time to sleep," I said as I turned to face Keid, who sat just outside the den. I tried very hard to not sound as cranky as I felt. "When night falls, you need to eat, then we'll start moving."

Before Keid could say anything, I was pelted in the face by a black cloth. I snarled as I ripped the item off my head and surveyed it. It was a pair of pants.

"Oh…" Keid said quietly, looking between me and the rot-witch with pursed lips. "She brought you pants. Let me… um"—she hesitantly plucked the clothing from my hands—"remove the… aroma." Keid wrinkled her nose and focused on the pants, performing some kind of magic I couldn't see while she kept a finger on the puncture mark I'd made.

I heaved a sigh and swung my head to stare at the crone, who was cackling in delight at having gotten me with a surprise attack. I hated her. Still, I made an effort. It took everything in me to do what I did next.

Forcing bile down my protesting throat and ignoring my shrieking instincts, I grumbled, "Thank you." I couldn't keep the bitterness off my face as I said it, and for some reason, that only made her laugh harder. The sight of her laughter-induced spittle forced me to close my eyes and pray to the gods for resilience. I supposed it'd been too much to ask for another day without her.

Keid handed the pants back to me, and I donned them, surprised that they fit well enough. I was warmer in my gratitude to my fated mate, giving her a small smile. "Appreciate it… Get some rest soon, Keid. Maybe ask for that… mucky stuff." I jerked my head toward the rot-witch, and the younger woman nodded thoughtfully. "I… am moving my sleeping spot for… obvious reasons," I added hesitantly. Maybe Keid could tolerate it, but I certainly couldn't. "Stay in the den. Stay hidden. Please."

I felt awkward standing there, wanting to thank Keid for the meal and apologize for leaving in a rush, but I just couldn't do it in front of the hag. The young woman also seemed a little lost in her thoughts, so I lumbered off to find a place to roost. I wanted to ask her to come sleep with me, but I couldn't gather the courage, and the den truly was a safer location.

I roosted on a low branch and released my wings, wrapping them differently to keep my face completely blocked. There was no way I was risking another forced feeding. The hag was not going to surprise me again.

I watched Ferrer depart with mixed feelings, then glanced down at Mushy, pursing my lips in thought. "I'm glad you got here safely," I said and checked to see if my neck still bled. I withdrew my fingers and sighed at the red smear on them. "Can we make that recovery potion later, Mushy?" I asked, pressing my finger to my neck again. The old witch nodded subtly as she rocked, not making eye contact. Her wild, bloodshot gaze just roved about the canopy, and I couldn't tell if she was looking for a dragon, daydreaming, or just high. There really was no telling with Mushy.

I crawled into the den and used a large piece of bark to scrape away Ferrer's… puddle. I shivered and curled up into a ball to sleep, trying to forget about what we'd done in here not that long ago. It was too bad that Mushy had decided to camp here. The forest was cold, and I really could have used Ferrer's body heat.

My rest was disturbed as I tried to nap away the day. Forcing myself into a nocturnal schedule was going to be difficult, but if Ferrer had managed a day cycle all this time, I could make the effort to switch to a night one. Upon my fifth awakening, the sky had fallen into a quiet shade of indigo, and I breathed a sigh of relief. I could allow myself to get up now. There was no way I could squeeze in another blink of sleep.

Mushy was bent over another pot of blood stew, which was immensely suspicious. I narrowed my eyes to tell her I was keeping an eye on her, but she just beamed at me and groped for a cup she'd set on the dirt. When I grabbed it and looked inside, I noticed it was the same goop she'd made me drink before, so I emptied it in one go to cope with the flavor. I soon realized my mistake. I didn't have my canteen of water.

With the potent taste of Mushy's dreadful brew stuck in my mouth, I rushed off in search of water while there was still a sliver of purple light. Using hints given to me by the wildlife, plant life, and terrain, I found a small stream and hurriedly rinsed out my mouth. I drank my fill after that, shuddering from finally purging that terrible flavor. I crouched for one last moment on the mossy soil and thought briefly about Vain, hoping we'd find her tonight. I was terribly worried, and I hoped she wasn't thinking I'd forgotten about her.

I trudged slowly back, but when I returned and didn't see Mushy or the blood stew, I felt a flare of alarm. "Mushy?" I hissed and ran in the direction that Ferrer had gone, having a bad feeling that the hag was about to create chaos.

The woods had darkened so much that I almost passed Mushy outright without noticing. She giggled quietly, toddling back through the shrubs to return to her campfire. She did not have her stew with her.

"No, no, no, no," I moaned and ran ahead, worrying that whatever she'd done was going to enrage Ferrer—if not now, then much later.

I had to run past another giant redwood before I saw it. Mushy had placed the pot of stew right under where Ferrer roosted. The steam was rising up, its pale tendrils sneaking through the gaps that his wings couldn't completely seal. The rot-witch had set some kind of trap for him.

I held my breath and inched forward as quietly as possible, listening and squinting for any sign of him waking. My feet searched blindly for the flattest, most compact patches of leaf litter as I approached. All I needed to do was grab the pot and leave before he woke.

It wasn't until Ferrer's wings snapped open and I was yanked forward that I'd realized something. The bait hadn't been set for him. It'd been set for me, and I'd fallen for Mushy's trap.

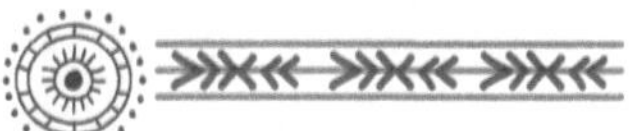

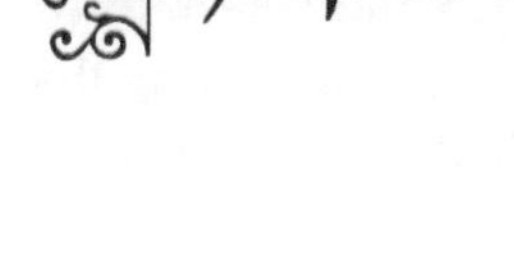

# Chapter 17

## Ferrer

At first something smelled terrible. A stench crept into my dreams but faded as quickly as it'd arrived, replaced by the aroma of food. The rich, salty smell dissolved seamlessly into me as I became comfortable again. Whatever had reeked had disappeared, and I was happy with its replacement.

Slowly, though, something else arrived. It approached cautiously but was much more interesting than the scent of food. This perfume came with a heartbeat, and it tugged at my drowsy one. I was too tired to move, but I grew impatient with this sluggish curiosity. What was just outside my reach that smelled so irresistible?

Whatever it was had to be caught as soon as it drew near. I wanted it. I wanted so badly to bury myself in it, wrap it around me, and sleep forever. I desired it, so I waited, all the while drifting through a dream.

As soon as it came close enough, I reached for it and ripped it into my arms, then I locked my wings back in place to keep it from escaping. The perfume and heartbeat emitted a sound.

It was soft and urgent, but I didn't see any problem to fix. I had what I wanted, and I buried my face into it like it was the finest pillow stuffed with the freshest herbs.

The perfume, heartbeat, and sound started to develop emotions, and I lazily allowed them to caress my mind while I nuzzled the delectable source of my desire. I was distantly aware of my cock reacting to all of these external forces and dismissed it as being from an erotic dream. What was happening now, with my half-asleep mind, was far more interesting than any sex dream.

"Ferrer!" the voice called quietly. "Ferrer, oh my gods..."

I liked the smooth voice. It complemented the softness pressed against my face. I let my hands slide around the softness as my wings kept it locked in place, and they settled onto warm hills that were a pleasure to squeeze.

"Ferrer, wake u—aaahhh," the voice sang quietly. I liked that. I wanted it to sing more for me.

There was pressure against my cock, which ignited a wave of heat in my groin, and an aroused groan grated out of my throat. Something nudged against it and continued to do so while I rubbed the softness. I gripped it and angled my mouth to take a taste but was disappointed to find only cloth. Perhaps the cloth hid something like how a beehive guarded honey.

As I searched for the edge of the cloth, the delicate moans found their way to my cock. I found the bottom of the first layer and pushed it up, continuing my search. My fingertips caught on another lip, but this one had to be pulled down, and that was exactly what I did.

"Ferrer, Ferrer, Ferrer, no.... Oh my gods... Ahhh..." The voice hummed, simultaneously frantic and pleased. It was so deliciously tormented.

It wasn't until I slid the fabric down over the soft hills that I felt something different. A quiet squeal accompanied the sensation of soft, damp curls brushing my face. The moisture against my nose and upper lips tugged me from my dreamlike world.

I came to the realization that I was still hanging upside down with my face buried between Keid's thighs. She was still standing on the ground, though I'd drawn her up onto her toes with my tugging. Apparently, I was hanging with my head at the perfect crotch height.

Perhaps it was due to this all starting in a drowsy state, but when the reality made itself known, I didn't panic. Instead, I let a languid smile sneak onto my face, and I squeezed Keid's butt cheeks, making her squeal one more time. It was so quiet but oh so satisfying.

What I decided to do from here on out was to continue my mac-tallan act of playing dead and do what I'd planned on doing earlier—pleasure her. I curled my fingers inward, let them sink into her plush flesh, then rubbed in circles. I massaged her butt cheeks and drew in a deep breath, letting the perfume of her sex seep into my lungs. From there, I could swear it settled into my soul as proof of her need for me.

I let my palms cup her lovely bottom one more time before I dragged my fingers down, slowly latching onto the edge of her leggings and underwear. I pulled them down to her thighs, wanting to make more room to bury my face. When I lazily spread one of her legs to nuzzle deeper, she protested. "No, no, no, you're going to rip my leggings! Ah…"

She fumbled to remove her shoes with her feet so she could wiggle her leggings off, struggling because she couldn't bend over to do it. I suffered greatly holding back laughter when she ended up having to hop on one foot. In her wiggling, her foot kicked something away that seemed to spill, but I paid it no mind. Keid had my full attention.

When she freed herself of her clingy garment, I reached between her legs with an arm and lifted one of them to hook her knee over my armpit, keeping that leg raised high for me. She yelped quietly when I grabbed her other leg firmly and hoisted her whole body up, hooking the next leg over my other armpit. Now I was holding her off the ground as she sat on my arms like a swing, her core still displayed before my lips, and I was quite pleased with my creativity. Keid squeaked, hesitated, then wrapped her arms around my hips, not trusting my wings to hold her upright. I held back a shiver as the warm puffs of her breath sank into the crotch of my pants.

Keeping my palms on her bottom, I let my thumbs reach inward to spread the folds of her sex. Looking at her for the first time was a euphoric experience. She looked so pretty there, her blushing entrance hidden by the soft white curls. My pants became unbearably tight, and I believed Keid noticed too because she moaned against the strained bulge, nuzzling into the fabric like I'd done to her.

I wanted so badly to go back to the ground that was only several feet away and slide my sex into hers, but I resisted. I wanted to be attentive, and I hoped that if I did well enough, she'd allow it to become a regular occurrence. I hoped she'd allow me to stay a thoughtful mate. Maybe I'd have a chance if I passed this test. We'd see soon enough because I had no bloody idea what I was doing.

I smiled as I drew my nose along one of her swollen folds. I could smell the blood just beneath the skin as it swelled the tissue of her sex, priming her for breeding. I was tempted to make the tiniest prick with a fang so I could taste her arousal and blood at the same time, but I resisted that too. I didn't want to give her a single second of pain.

When a line of arousal dripped down a fold, I tilted my chin and dipped my tongue into it, tasting her for the first time. I closed my eyes, and a hum of pleasure purred from my throat. It was shortly echoed by a thrilled moan from Keid. I wasn't sure if it was from her own carnal hunger or a sense of reciprocation, but she gently mouthed the bulge in my pants, dragging her lower lip along it. It was like she wanted it but didn't have the courage to uncover me.

I decided to let her do whatever she wanted and simply paid attention to giving whatever bliss I could. I dipped my tongue again, catching another drip of her arousal before it was wasted on the forest floor. She was a combination of sweet and savory, and it mixed so well with her alluring beech fragrance.

I felt the moment that Keid let down her guard, and it was the most erotic thing I'd ever experienced in my life. Her weight settled into my broad palms along with her trust, and I held her confidently up with her knees kept hooked over my armpits. I groaned and my abdomen clench with scorching gratification, pleased beyond words.

Keid moaned into my cock again, and her fingernails shyly tucked under the edge of my pants. They stayed there for a handful of moments while I brought my lips to my handful of Keid. I wrapped them around what I knew to be the clit, one of the centers of a woman's delight, and gave it a gentle, experimental suck.

She responded quite well to that. She gasped and arched timidly but leaned forward so as not to detach my lips from her flesh. Her pulse throbbed under my suction, and I flicked the tip of my tongue across it, squeezing a plaintive mewl from the beautiful human nuzzling my erection. I released her from the suction and drew my tongue along the length of her folds, pressing in to elicit more noises. My licks turned into wet laps as her arousal increased, and my abdomen contracted again with lust. I nuzzled as close as I could and slipped my tongue through her opening, burying it as far as it could go.

She bucked, and I grinned, then began pulsing my tongue in and out of her, feverishly sending the muscle where I wanted to bury my erection. This seemed to send her past the point of propriety because her hands deftly opened my pants, and she slid her palms up my waist, catching the edge of the fabric with her thumbs to release my cock. It fell heavily out, and the long, deep, ravenous groan that was dragged from her throat nearly made me come from excitement alone. A fire hotter than the Sun God razed my nerves from groin to chest, nearly knocking the wind out of me.

I echoed her groan into her sex and retracted my tongue, fervently kissing, licking, and sucking at her folds. She gasped and wrapped her slender fingers around my cock, lifting it to meet the softness of her lips. I tightened my fingers on her cheeks when her mouth took in my head, and for a second, I was worried I'd come instantly. The tingling of the mate bond along such sensitive skin nearly had me bucking in pleasure.

I tilted my head back and gritted out an agonized groan as she buried me halfway into her mouth. Her hands squeezed me as her warm, wet, and tight mouth formed a suction. I choked back a long string of curses and did the only thing I could, return to her pleasure.

With renewed determination, I lapped rhythmically up her clit, paying fierce attention to her emotions through the bond. I listened to whatever I could sense and moved my mouth to the areas that seemed to stimulate her more. It wasn't long before she was squirming against my mouth and tongue, moaning into my erection.

My cock fell from her lips, slathered in spit and precum as she gasped. "Oh gods. Oh gods, Ferrer!"

Hearing my name on her lips like that spread the flames and set my bloody soul on fire, and I redoubled my efforts, spurred and inspired by her blissful reaction. My heart raced as her core clenched through the surface of her sex, and I imagined those muscles gripping my cock, which wasn't hard because Keid had slipped me into her mouth once more.

Her panting breath blew down my throbbing length, and at the first sign of sweat trickling down her legs and bottom, I briefly opened my wings for her. I flapped a couple times to swaddle her skin in cool air, and once I felt like she was doing better, I rewrapped us. I wanted a space where the only things that existed was her and me. No searching dragons, no other witches, no problems of any kind—just her and me.

As if she was thanking me for cooling her, she bobbed her mouth along my cock while stroking the rest of me with her hands.

I quivered under her assault, nearly yelling into her sex. My lust soared skyward from this new act, and out of nowhere, my sack tightened and released, filling Keid's mouth with my seed.

I gripped her viciously as I came, holding back a great number of noises as my hips pulsed. Through my euphoria, I worried I'd disgusted her with my sudden ejaculation, but shockingly, she only gave a sensual, guttural moan. The sound of her thick swallowing, each spurt followed by the flexing of her neck and tongue, threatened to make me come a second time. My body trembled with hot, tingling pleasure, every single thing about her flooding me with passionate heat and starlight.

I feverishly worked on Keid, not giving up on her release, which made me realize that I didn't want to give up on her in any way—ever. I wanted her. I wanted her more fiercely than I had ever wanted anything.

I would prove it to her if it was the last thing I did.

Keid's hands continued to pump, knowing by now that she could expect more. I tried to ignore the pleasure of her voracious mouth and lapped at her until her muscles started to clench differently. Elated and hoping to push an orgasm out of her, I moved my tongue around, chasing the cues I got from her, and it wasn't long before she started pushing down against my mouth.

Realizing we'd found something, I sucked and lapped until her back slowly curled into a deeper arch. Her thighs flexed into my ribs, and her body began shaking like mine. I grunted excitedly as she built up to it, then moaned loudly when she bucked. Keid released my cock from her mouth and screamed through her teeth.

I brought my lips back to her to lap along with her contractions and there was a rush of her arousal. I was surprised by the sudden gush of fluid and became so turned on that I came with her. I had no idea where in the bloody stars I was ejaculating, but it was going to go where it was going to go. I didn't care. All I could think about was having brought my fated mate to her completion. I heard it, I saw it, I tasted it, I felt it, I sensed it across the tether I had on her—euphoria.

And I reveled.

We were a writhing tangle, so wrapped in pulsing, hot bliss that I barely heard the bloody tree branch creak. Distantly concerned, I unlocked the tendons in my legs, lifted Keid's panting body, and flapped wildly enough to make sure I fell onto my back instead of my skull. Then I landed painfully on the forest floor.

When I looked up to make sure the branch wasn't about to break and fall on us, I let my head plop back onto the leaf litter in exhaustion. Keid and I were slathered in cooling sweat, and I let my eyes drift over her beautiful, starlit silhouette. I barely had enough energy to grin at her naked rump, which was only inches away from me, so I did. I grinned happily.

She was draped diagonally across me, her blushing face resting against my thigh. After a settling breath, I waited for her to speak.

"You're awake, aren't you?" Despite everything she'd done to me with gusto, I felt her mild embarrassment mixed in with her soul-deep satisfaction.

I couldn't stop grinning when I gave her my reply. "Caught me."

I held on to all of them, wanting to engrave every sensation into my memories. I carved along my thoughts, replaying the softness of Ferrer's tongue, the warmth of his breath, the excited draws of his lungs, the way his hands spanned my butt cheeks… I wanted to be able to recall everything for the many lonely years to come.

I knew he'd awoken at some point; I just didn't know when. Did it matter? He was awake now, and he certainly was aware of what we'd done. I could have sworn I'd heard a smile in his answer. The words had certainly been playful.

My brain ran through things to say, but I struggled to pick. I decided that it was probably best that I crawled off of him first, so I cautiously removed myself. I blinked rapidly as I raised my head. It was pitch-black now, and I couldn't see a blessed thing.

I sat back, but when I placed my hand in something warm and wet, I let out a dismayed moan. "Ewww… Ah, curses, Mushy," I swore and lifted my hand out of the spilled pig's blood stew. I'd tried to kick it away from us earlier, but I supposed it hadn't gone very far.

"Why's there stew here?" Ferrer inquired and sat upright. I jumped when he wiped at my hand with a leaf to get the blood off me.

"Mushy set a trap," I mumbled, trying to be unaffected by his thoughtful tending. I was so confused right now.

"How so?" He took a fresh leaf to my hand to finish cleaning it the best he could.

"I found her bringing the stew to you and set it beneath your head while you were asleep. When I tried to sneak up and remove it, you… grabbed me." I sniffed from the cold air and turned my head away from him.

"I don't know what her game is," Ferrer said quietly. "I can't wrap my head around her… nature. Perhaps it's just her way to pass the time."

I thought he'd be angrier about it, and I was even more surprised that he seemed to be letting Mushy off the hook… at least a little. Perhaps she'd made an impression, helping him escape his cell. Either way, I was relieved that the night wasn't about to begin with bloodshed. I grimaced at the smell of the stew. Well, some blood had been shed… Poor pig.

"This still hurt?" Ferrer's voice was as gentle as his fingers when they brushed the abrasion on my cheek. I started in surprise, having not seen that touch coming either.

"It's not so bad," I murmured, but then a thought occurred to me. "Wait, has your vision returned? You're not clicking."

"While I was sleeping, yes. Told you I would heal," he said, his tone returning to mildly playful.

I swallowed hard at that, finding my saliva thicker for some reason. "That's good… because I can't see a thing." I laughed nervously and raised my gaze, but the canopy was so thick that I could only make out a couple of stars. The ones I could see were pretty though.

"I'm glad you were the first thing I saw," he confessed as his thumb stroked down my cheek.

My heart jolted with a spark, everything did actually, and my face heated terribly from those words. Since I didn't know whether to be pleased or angry, I turned into a flustered mess. I couldn't even speak; such was my discombobulation. Why did he have to say that?

"What?" he pressed, now concerned.

"I wish you couldn't read my emotions like that," I said, not wanting to address my dilemma.

"Blame the Moon Goddess," he replied as he adjusted and retied his pants. "What's wrong?"

"You're still being… not mean, and it's still confusing me," I admitted. I realized then it was easier to speak my feelings when I couldn't see him. "It felt like yesterday that you were looking at me like I was the most disgusting thing in the world."

He heaved a colossal sigh, and I heard the scraping of stubble as he scrubbed his hands over his face. "I made multiple mistakes that night… and yes, I was blinded by prejudice. I thought you were a rot-witch."

"What?" I asked, my brow shooting up in surprise.

"Your dress, it had a strand of that rot-witch's hair on it."

I leaned toward him as if to plead my case. "That's not possible. I hadn't seen her since acquiring that dress… And before that, I was so careful to remove any evidence of my interactions with her."

His tone turned uncertain. "Are you sure…? Her scent was at the campsite you shared with your sister…"

Suddenly, the night air became a lot colder, and as goose bumps spread across my skin, I looked over in her camp's direction. "No, Ferrer," I whispered, now thoroughly spooked. Had she followed me? Had she planted a hair on me? She couldn't have known what that would do. She hadn't orchestrated this whole thing… had she?

I then went from being spooked to frightened. Ferrer must have sensed it because he grabbed me and dragged me into his lap. My mind reeled from what I'd just learned.

I tried to find some sense in it. "Maybe she wanted me to get kicked out so she'd have someone to walk her home? I don't understand."

"She's a stranger, Keid," Ferrer replied. "No matter what you think you know, you don't know her."

He was right. She'd always seemed a bit harmlessly deceitful, but everything she'd done had ended up being a benefit… I thought? Another notion occurred to me.

"Ferrer?" I asked quietly, and he hummed a response. "Would you have still tried to reject me if you'd known I was just a witch, not a rot-witch?"

From his hesitation alone, I knew I wouldn't like the answer. He was quiet for far too long, but when tears stung my eyes, he rushed out his answer. "Probably, Keid. My people… most of us…" He fumbled as he tried to explain. "You have to understand that the only witches we'd ever encountered were rot-witches, and they were responsible for banishing us to the Night Court in the fae realm. They took everything from us, even our original forms. It was the deepest violation, all because our gods offended them by removing them from the Night Court and the fae realm entirely."

"Original forms?" I frowned. I didn't know about this part.

"We were sky-shifters. Birds and insects among other odd things, all made to fly—to celebrate our Sky Gods. These were ancient times, Keid. The rot-witches cursed us—replaced our unique beasts with blood bats. These new enemies took us from our ancestral lands in this realm and trapped us in the Night Court in hopes we'd drink each other to extinction. We survived on game for a while, but… Keid, there used to be hundreds of thousands of us." Ferrer sounded like he'd told this story a million times, and he probably had. "If Queen Hekla had not liberated us… Well, we were already starving to death. You would not have recognized me."

I was crying by the time he was done talking. I hadn't known it was that bad. They hadn't exactly given us their entire history at the door.

"Oh gods, don't," Ferrer lamented, fussing away at my tears with his thumbs. "No, no, shush. Please."

"I'd hate me too," I sobbed out childishly. "And I already do!"

"Oh no, Keid, come on. Stop that," he chided and gently shook my shoulder. "I told you already. I don't hate you. You just don't believe me." I let my head thud against his chest as I wept like a silly girl. "I had no excuse for what I did. We just… it's hard to separate witches from rot-witches. For us, they're too similar. We're so little in number that we're on the defensive right now. I did act far too hostile with you, even after I learned the truth." He sighed when I continued to sniffle. "If it makes you feel any better, your sister got her mate to slap me silly."

A laugh burst from my lips, and I immediately apologized, but he just chuckled with me. When I calmed and worried over my next question. Should I go that far? What if…

"And what if I'd just been a normal woman?" I asked in the quietest voice. If he hadn't been a shifter, I would have worried that my inquiry was inaudible.

"Keid, I would've accepted you easily. I told you I was blinded by prejudice," he answered. "And I know why you're asking. You're not ugly. I wish you could see yourself better."

The words were kind, but my heart still carried too much doubt. He could be lying. It could be that as soon as I gave him offspring, he'd never look at me again.

Dryly, as if his point was flawless, he added, "I would not have chosen to pleasure you if I thought you were unattractive."

"It's dark out," I grumbled.

"Not for me." He snorted. "Granted I had no idea what I was doing until I woke up a bit. I was thrown by the scent of blood and my mate."

I didn't know how my mind felt about him calling me that, but my heart reluctantly enjoyed it. I hid my face in my palms, stuck in turmoil. I wanted to stay mad at Ferrer, but he was making it difficult. He'd changed his mind so fast. What if he changed it again? I wouldn't be able to take it.

"I'm not giving up." He squeezed my arm to punctuate his assertion.

"I'm not telling you to give up on anything," I mumbled into my hands. I didn't want to hear his clarification. I was starting to feel too vulnerable.

"I'm going to prove that I can be a good m—"

"What now?" I blurted, getting too nervous about the current topic.

"What do you mean?"

"Well, we just… W-well, I just discovered that Mushy sabotaged my recognition night at the colony," I said through wound nerves. "What now?"

"That's your decision, Keid. Do you still wish to see her home? If that's where she's going."

"I don't know anymore. So far, she almost got me rejected and forced a mating on me."

Ferrer tensed at those words, and I felt a little bad about the way I worded it. It was true though. Mushy practically drugged someone into mating and marking me.

"She also returned your fertility…"

I dropped my hands from my face and stared blankly into the darkness. "Yes… I think she might have. I feel like I won't believe it until I see it… but I can't ignore the symptoms I experienced… She also helped me get Vain; I'm certain of that."

"Seems like everything she does is extreme, doesn't it?" Ferrer asked thoughtfully, then wrapped his arms around me and squeezed. I both tolerated and savored it simultaneously.

"We've already come this far." I sighed and came to a decision. "May as well see it through to the end. We just need to keep an eye on her. Plus, there's someone who can remove the mark apparently."

"Keid… I don't w—"

An absurd whimper squeezed from my throat, interrupting him. I didn't have any tools for this topic. My heart still worried over rejection, and I didn't know how to cope with it. Just thinking about it made me short of breath, panicky.

"I'll prove it then," Ferrer said, moving to stand while helping me get to my feet. He repeated himself as I dressed. "I'll prove it, Keid. You won't doubt it by the time we arrive."

I nodded and rubbed my chest, nursing my bruised heart. When my fingers hit something sticky, I held my fingers up to my nose and withered. Oh, Ferrer… I supposed that was actually my fault.

"What? Oh… That's where it went. Let's find some water and get you cleaned up." He grabbed my hand and strode off through the dark while I stumbled after him, as blind as a bat.

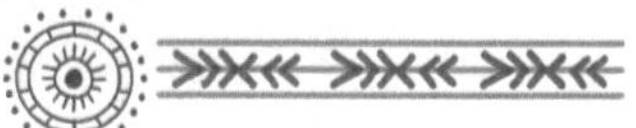
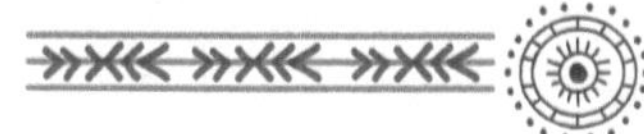

# Chapter 18

## Ferrer

By the time Keid and I returned from the stream she'd told me about, the rot-witch was already ambling on north. Keid seemed surprised that she hadn't waited for us, but I wasn't. This creature had made it clear she was always going to do what she wanted to do.

"We're going this way, Mushy," the younger witch said, pointing where she thought westward was, then looked in my direction for confirmation.

"More like this." I grabbed her hand and made it actually point west, then crossed my arms. The creature paid her no mind and continued her shambling journey north, trembling and occasionally slipping on leaf litter.

"Mushy?" Keid asked after her falteringly. "Ferrer, is she walking away from us? Mushy, we need to get Vain…"

"I don't think she cares," I said, tilting my head as the rot-witch slowly left my line of sight. "Either that or she expects us to catch up with her."

I felt my mate's frustration through our bond, but I was pleased to note that she never once felt torn over the decision. "We have to go find Vain," she stated flatly. "I'm not going to waste energy worrying over Mushy if she's going to run off like that."

"I think 'running' might be a bit generous," I commented, not bothering to hide my wry smile. She couldn't see me.

"Indeed…" She snorted and gestured for us to start our search. "Lead the way."

Curious to see what she'd do and wanting to watch, I started walking like she asked but did so backward. She pressed her lips together, her little nostrils flaring as her eyes searched the darkness. They followed the sound of my footsteps, and to her credit, she did try to take several steps before tripping on a rogue root.

She clapped a hand over her mouth to muffle her surprise, obviously not wanting to alert me to her struggle. I grinned and wondered when she'd cave. Keid, I was learning, valued logic to a pretty good extent, and I wouldn't expect her to be one to sacrifice goal over pride.

"Ferrer, can you pause for a moment?" she asked, stopping all attempts to walk in her absolute blindness. I kept smiling and crossed my arms, waiting for her to ask me to hold her hand or carry her. I watched in curiosity as she crouched to do neither of those things.

Keid sorted through the leaf litter and dug past detritus into the soil. She examined the dirt in her hands and frowned in annoyance. "Not enough bacteria. None of the right spores…" She sighed and turned her face toward me. "Can we go back to the water? If I can get a good sample, I could maybe make a light source for myself. I can't see a blessed thing out here."

"That's in the opposite direction, mate," I reminded, smirking at her grimace. I was going to get her used to hearing that word whether she liked it or not. "I thought we were in a hurry."

"I am…" She bit at her lower lip. "But I can't see…"

"What do you want me to do about that?" I mirrored her mouth movements but only to taste what remained of her on my lips.

"I…" She scrunched her nose, balled her fists, and, almost in a pout, said, "Maybe I should hold your hand again."

"You might still trip," I warned and reached down to grab her hand. She jerked nervously and moved forward to close the distance between us.

"I might… I did fine on the way to the water though," she mumbled and pushed against my hand, urging me onward.

"Yes, you did admirably," I replied and strolled westward. Keid followed behind me, occasionally tugging whenever she slowed.

I wasn't purposely taking her near roots and rocks, but I didn't necessarily warn her every time she got close to something. Perhaps I was playing a bit unfairly. The truth was twofold; I wanted to carry her, I wanted her to ask me to carry her, and we really were making terrible time with her stumbling along like this. Wait, that was three things. The truth was threefold.

Keid caved when her boot hit a root, and I caught her before she could twist her ankle, completely prepared for it. "Do you think," she inquired grudgingly, "you could carry me on your back, Ferrer? My sister and I used to give each other rides all the time when we were kids."

"You want to ride me?" I asked, doing my best to keep my grin out of my voice.

Her face pinched and pinkened in embarrassment. "I… You know what I'm… Ferrer…"

I rescued her and said, "I'd love for you to ride me, but if I need my wings, you'd be in the way." Alright, that wasn't much of a rescue because my words had her looking even more appalled.

"Would it be an inconvenience to carry me… in… f-front?" she asked. If her lips pressed any tighter, I was afraid her face would cramp up like that.

"What, like this?" I asked, picking her up and bringing her torso to mine. She instinctively latched on, wrapping her arms and legs around me while protesting the option. The complaints loudened when I moved my hands to the backs of her thighs to keep her elevated. It all very much threatened to make me burst into laughter.

"You kn-know that's not what I meant!" she argued, keeping her head turned away from me.

"Look, I'm just trying to get us to Vain," I said in a serious tone. She was so pretty when she was flustered, bright eyed and blushing. It was much better this way than her being depressed or angry.

I started walking with her, and she was so embarrassed that she just thudded her face into my shoulder and stayed quiet. I grinned and waited for it, but she never spoke up, not once. I knew how she wanted to be carried, but she just couldn't bring herself to be straight with me. Truly, that was her fault.

I liked it like this anyway, her embracing me. I liked the feel of her clothed breasts pressed against my chest and the warmth of her inner thighs around my waist. I would have liked it much better had we nothing to do and we were both horizontal, but I'd accept what came my way.

We traveled westward like this for about an hour, and her embarrassment slowly trickled away until it disappeared entirely. I could hear her blinking as she tried to see, but from her sighing, she was obviously at a loss.

"You shifters are so lucky," she said a touch jealously. "I'd love to be able to see in the dark. There's only so much my eyes can adjust to. I already have to enchant them to see straight."

The last thing she'd grumbled out surprised me. "You enchant your eyes?"

"My far vision is poor, and I have astigmatism…" she mumbled into my shoulder, her embarrassment returning.

"What's that?"

"The clear part on the front of my eye isn't shaped right… as if having everything else wasn't enough."

"And you fixed your vision with magic? That's remarkable," I complimented, then beamed when she momentarily swelled with pleasure.

"Took me years to get the spell right… Enchanting isn't just about magic. You have to truly understand anatomy and biology to make it work. I had to consult with our doctors to further finesse it."

"That's brilliant. I'm really impressed," I said honestly, hoping she believed me, hoping she could hear it in my voice this time.

"Not that you shifters need such things," she added thoughtfully, if a bit gloomily.

"Not so. Some of us are born differently. It's rare, but we have had our own star-kissed," I informed, and her body tensed up around me.

"Star-kissed?"

"Like you," I said casually. "Born lighter."

Her reaction was bittersweet. "Not that I like being called anything other than a person, but I like that better than being called an albino…" I felt a small swell of melancholy over our bond. Shit. I hadn't intended to make her sad.

"I've told you that my people think it's pretty."

"Even though it can come with health problems?" she added dryly.

"Someone can only be so perfect." I shrugged and she clapped me lightly on the chest. "Ow," I said clearly and dryly.

"That's more than a little over-the-top," she reprimanded. "That's deeply offensive."

I didn't see how, but I supposed it was yet another cultural difference or maybe I was more ignorant than I thought. "I'm just saying that we think it's very pretty and that the Sky Gods had to take something back in return for such beauty. That's why star-kissed occasionally have complications."

"Don't say that to anyone else with albinism," she growled. "I'd much rather be like everyone else—and in perfect health—than have this. My people don't seem to find it pretty either."

"Look," I argued, hoisting her up to get a better hold on her. "Forget all that, and you certainly can't speak for anyone else other than yourself, Keid. You are who you are, and if you're to stay that way, you will be happier if you embrace yourself. I can—as you can see—only embrace you so much." I squeezed her thighs playfully to make my point. She squeaked and jerked a little, then deflated against me.

"Until you love yourself, I'll keep reminding you of how beautiful you are. Not just your color, but the shape of your body, your nose, your chin, your eyes, your legs… all of it. Your clever brain too, but that's a different kind of beauty."

I felt her swirl of complex emotions as she simply relaxed her head against me. I stroked her thigh a little with a thumb, wishing I could comfort her better. I could only give her so many compliments. She had to go the rest of the way herself.

*I like you just the way you are,* I expressed, mind-linking her for my last thought, wanting to keep the moment quiet. *I wouldn't change a thing about you.*

She didn't reply as expected, and I simply continued our trek west, keeping my senses alert for what I'd felt last time. I'd gotten far enough from Keid to feel something similar to our bond. It was smaller, but it had definitely tugged on my soul. I wondered if Vain had felt it too and if she was working her way toward us.

I was concerned about one thing though; if she knew where we were, why wasn't she here yet? Certainly, she could fly, and I'd seen it. She hadn't seemed so far that it'd take her over a day to reach us.

*Keep your senses alert for her,* I told Keid. *Wait for a pull on your soul. You'll notice it when we get close enough. Well, I think you should. I could find you anywhere in the world, but it seems like familiars are a little tricky over long distance.*

"Could be that it's hard to feel her over your soul," she murmured thoughtfully. "I feel you strongly."

I held back a wry comment out of respect for her sanity and simply nodded. "The fated mate connection is more potent, it seems."

As the next hour passed, I smiled when her head bobbed with drowsiness. Her sleepiness meant that she was feeling more secure with me, and that was comforting. I didn't think I had much time left to prove myself to her, and us meeting that goal gave me some relief. I resisted nuzzling against her head and stayed focused.

About twenty minutes later, we both stiffened. Something tugged on my soul, and I asked Keid, "Did you feel her?"

"Yes, yes, yes! Hurry!" she said excitedly, trying to look over her shoulder. I lifted her up into a cradle and started running in the direction I'd felt Vain. Keid yelped and wrapped her arms around my neck. She wasn't going anywhere. I wouldn't drop her in a million years.

"Call to her," I said, then tried to mind-link Vain. *Vain, can you hear me?*

*Starshine, talk to us!* Iron called, and Keid snorted in bewilderment.

"Starshine?"

*You've been quiet,* I said privately to Iron.

*I'm worried about Starshine... Also, you seem to be doing much better without any advice. I'm just sitting back and enjoying the show. Creative swingwork, I must say.*

I held back a bark of laughter as I zeroed in on Vain's location, sprinting as fast as I could while carrying a person. It took another hour, but I finally spotted something large and awkward flapping about in the distance.

"What the shit?" I mumbled, slightly out of breath. "Keid, I think I see her, but something is... Hang on."

The blood bat seemed to notice us as well and came straight for me.

*Help,* Vain sobbed, and I saw what the problem was. I slid to a stop, put Keid down, and rushed up to a struggling Vain, grabbing the backpack that she was tied to and somehow carrying. *They're behind me...*

*What?*

"Keid," I said hastily and brought her arms up to place her backpack in them. With a claw, I quickly cut away the thin rope binding Vain's ankle—the knot was too tight to waste time with—and the tiny bat crawled tiredly to Keid's neck where she huddled for protection. "She was tied to the bag and carrying it somehow, but I think someone's coming. Stay here."

"V-Vain. You poor thing! I've got you… You're safe now," Keid sobbed quietly as I jogged ahead, then climbed the next tree to get a better advantage. Two cat-shifters and a wolf were apparently in pursuit, and I had a feeling that they were bandits trying to steal Keid's bag. Vain didn't make a particularly terrifying protector of private property.

I had to admit that this was a very bizarre string of encounters.

Making sure I wouldn't dislodge my sweet Vain, I shrugged my bag on so that I could run hands free at a moment's notice. Where I would run and if I would trip were two entirely different concerns. I placed a gentle hand on Vain's fuzzy body to soothe her, stroking her tiny head with a thumb.

My eyes did a pointless search of the nighttime void around me. All I could see was black, black, and more black. The darkness was so encroaching that it almost felt like someone had draped a thick, suffocating blanket over my head. The worst part was when my eyes played tricks on me, making me think something was there when it was simply my brain interpreting the darkness the best it could. Oh, to be a shifter…

"What happened?" I asked Vain in a hushed whisper, nearly too scared to talk.

*I was left behind,* Vain cried. *Then that wretched Mushy tied me to your bag!*

"What?" I hissed. I was shocked and then I was angry at myself for being shocked. I shouldn't be surprised! I fumed over yet another one of Mushy's betrayals but then paused when I noticed something on Vain's neck. As quickly as it'd arrived, my rage dissipated and was replaced by confusion.

*Yes! She tied my leg to the strap of your bag and then abandoned me! I was so scared! When I tried flying, I ended up dragging your bag along. It was lucky you emptied it because I never would've been able to leave! I can't believe I carried it at all!*

I couldn't speak as I felt around Vain's neck. I was simply too distracted by what I'd found.

*And even worse,* she continued, prattling along nervously, *I passed by a band of nasty shifters who started running after me! They wanted your bag or wanted to eat me or I don't know! I tried going up through the canopy, but the cats climbed, and I just kept getting snagged on branches with the bag, so I just kept flying to where I felt you and Ferrer! I'm so tired, Keid! I'm so tired!*

"My gods," I commented under my breath as I continued tracing with my fingers. "And they're still following?"

*Yes, but Ferrer looks like he's going to stop them.*

"Wait a minute." I gasped and dropped my hand from her neck. "How many did you say?"

*Uh... there were three the last time I looked back,* she answered promptly.

"Three against one!" I hissed and fumbled around in the dark for an anchoring tree. "I have to help h—!"

*He said to stay here,* Vain interrupted stubbornly. *Don't go. Let the shifter take care of it.*

I couldn't accept that at all. I whined quietly through my teeth and squatted, then started searching for stones in the dirt. There was no way I could handle waiting without helping in some manner. It would stress me out far too much.

*What are you doing?* Vain asked.

"Helping from a distance," I whispered nervously. I grabbed three small pebbles and then promptly forgot every spell I'd ever learned. "Oh gods, what did you suggest last time? I can't remember. Help, Vain!"

*When did I suggest what?* she chirped tiredly.

"Remember when you first discovered that Ferrer was stalking us, but we didn't know what he w—"

*Oh! Numbness! We discussed numbness. Does that help?*

"Right…" I murmured and fingered the tiny pebbles in my hand. I sat by the base of the tree and focused on a pebble.

I needed to put a transferal attribute on it because I didn't want to make the stone itself numb. Stones didn't have nerves to numb anyway. I started layering several enchantments onto the pebble, making sure to include immunity for myself and Vain, since we'd both be touching the pebbles. Also, if the pebble didn't touch skin, I'd need the transferred curse to slip through whatever it touched and ricochet into adjacent flesh. This would let the curse travel through clothes. It needed to touch skin to work.

My temples throbbed as I quickly crafted the little curse bombs. I was stressed, and rushing under these conditions had me worried that I was going to make a mistake. I quickly wrapped up the curse enchantments, then placed the small pebbles in my open palm for Vain to grab.

"I know you're tired, but after this, I'll let you eat and rest, alright?" I whispered out in a rush, frightened because there was some shouting. "Oh gods, is he fighting them?" I stared into the darkness, wishing I could see something… anything!

*What are these?* Vain asked, and she fluttered over to my open palm. I almost didn't hear her question because someone simultaneously yelled, but I couldn't tell if it was in pain or anger.

"Drop one on anyone attacking Ferrer, and they'll go numb. Just don't hit Ferrer!" I ordered anxiously.

*I'll have to do multiple trips,* Vain said nervously after biting one. *I'll be back.*

"Be safe! Stay high!" I hissed as she launched from my hand. I stared into the black void, barely able to hear the skirmish over the pumping of my heart. It throbbed obnoxiously loud in my ears when all I wanted to do was identify who was saying what.

I shrank back when a bloodcurdling scream pierced the night, thinking it was Ferrer's for just a moment. I didn't know what his scream sounded like, but I ultimately didn't think it was him. I would have felt something, right? Or did one need to mark their partner to feel their pain. I didn't know! Still, it terrified me. I'd almost swallowed my heart!

*Not me,* Ferrer said in a mind-link. I melted against the tree trunk. He sounded ok. It wasn't him.

*How nice he thought to check in,* I thought gratefully to myself while placing a hand over my thumping chest. I wasn't being sarcastic either. I genuinely appreciated it! I only wished I could mind-link him directly.

I muffled a shriek when Vain landed back on my palm. I wished she'd warned me! She was a very quiet flapper. *One down, but I think Ferrer's got it under contro—*

"Go, go, go!" I urged, desperately worried. "Please!" That scream had utterly shattered my nerves.

Vain flew off with the second pebble but returned several minutes later with it. *Not needed,* she informed and dropped the pebble back into my waiting palm. She landed on my chest and crawled up to hide on my shoulder and under my hair.

Casual footsteps in the darkness made their way over to me, and I breathed out a shaky breath. Ferrer had returned, thank the Sky Gods.

"All done," he said calmly from the blackness.

I stood unsteadily, having a very poor sense of balance at the moment, and groped in the dark for Ferrer. He came closer, and he grabbed my hand to let me know I'd found him. A pathetic, frazzled moan left my mouth, and I felt my way forward to wrap my arms around the bat-shifter.

"Are you hurt?" I asked breathlessly, burying my face in his sweaty chest.

"Nothing that won't heal," he said and slid his arms around me to accept my hug. "What's Vain doing dropping stones though? She conked me right in the head."

"What?" I gasped and turned my head just a little in Vain's direction. "You said 'one down!'"

*I... didn't specify whether that was a body or a rock...* she said uncomfortably, trying to weasel out of her lie. *I tried, Keid... I really did.*

I pulled back from Ferrer, then reached up to grab his skull. "Come down here, you giant," I ordered, trying to feel around for where he may have gotten hit. I didn't notice any bumps, but then again, the pebbles were tiny. It wouldn't have given him a bump. "Where did it hit you? It was cursed, Ferrer! Are you experiencing any numbness? Oh, I don't know what it'd do to your brain! Can you feel this?" I poked his forehead, and he jerked his head away with a wary chuckle.

"Uh… maybe it didn't after all. I must have imagined it," he said, clearing his throat. "I feel fine…"

*I could have sworn I hit him...* Vain said with an audible flinch. *On accident!* she amended.

"I'm fine, I'm fine," Ferrer said, grabbing my hands to stop my poking.

"What happened to the… whoever was chasing Vain?" I asked.

Ferrer hesitated for a moment. "I tried to warn them away, but I figured they took me for easy pickings since they only scented me, you, and a small bat. After I killed the first one, they attacked. I let the last one go when she tried to run. Maybe she'll change careers…"

"Or she'll just kill the next vulnerable person she comes across," I seethed and tried to reclaim my hands, but Ferrer wouldn't let go of them.

"Hard to kill without drawing blood when you're hungry," he said with a sigh, and then I realized why he was acting odd.

"Oh…" I said softly. Him walking away from those bodies was like me walking away from a hearty four-course meal. I hadn't eaten in a while either. I hadn't even thought about foraging because I couldn't see a blessed thing…

Now that I was thinking about it, I was famished. My stomach growled silently, but somehow Ferrer still heard it.

"Shit, you didn't eat," he said, sounding more alarmed than warranted.

I wasn't going to fight him on it. I did need to find food. "Can we settle somewhere for a little bit? I need to forage or something, but I can't see."

"Here," Ferrer grunted, lifting me up into a less embarrassing cradle this time. He walked for about twenty minutes before setting me down, and there was the telltale trickling of a tiny stream. "Fill your canteen while we're here. I'll be back."

"Oh, he's a genius," I whispered, walking in tiny, paranoid steps toward the sound of water. I didn't know how he found it, but I was glad he had. I supposed his ears were as good as his eyes.

*Fill the canteen? Your bag's empty...* Vain squeaked in confusion.

I opened my bag and felt around inside it. "No, Vain. Everything's in here. Somehow you carried all this. I think I know how, but I need to see it to believe it."

After filling my canteen, I set down the bag and crouched by the water so I could find a nice clump of mud to light. When my fingers landed on a particularly reactive part of the bank, I smiled in victory. I thought it had exactly what I needed. I scooped out a large chunk and manipulated the right bacteria inside it to create bioluminescence.

"My new favorite trick," I said with a grin, holding the faintly glowing mudball like a torch. It wasn't nearly as bright as fire, but that was my next project. I found a decent place to build one and set the ball down so I could see what I was doing. "Come eat, Vain," I said softly, patting my shoulder. "You didn't want to partake of Ferrer's victims?"

I could admit that it was a pretty dark joke.

*Ferrer told me not to eat trash,* she replied, and I nearly choked on the water I was taking from the canteen.

After coughing and sputtering for a good minute with Vain panicking over my state, I cleared my throat and croaked, "Oh, did he now?"

Vain complained that I was moving too much while I dug a pit for the fire, so I moved her to the ground and shucked a boot. She'd have to settle for an ankle, but she seemed content with it. I built my fire and waited for the blood bat to eat before I'd look for food. I wasn't a botanist, but I knew of a couple plants that grew among redwoods. I'd just have to do the best I could.

Ferrer returned before Vain finished her meal and sat down next to me. I blinked at the pheasant that he started plucking furiously. My goodness, I'd hate to be his enemy if that was what he did to food. Well, I supposed he didn't see it as food.

"Wow… that's a beautiful pheasant. Is that for me?" It was a stupid question, and I winced as I said it.

"You need to keep your belly filled if your belly's to fill," he responded as he defeathered the pheasant faster than I'd seen anyone pluck a bird. My face ignited at his words. His casual reference to my potential pregnancy was surprisingly erotic to me, but I had no idea why. Either way, it made me press my thighs together, and I fought for something to say. I'd gone a bit dumbstruck.

"Y-you and Vain didn't find the shifters to be good… to eat?" I asked, scratching nervously behind an ear. Ferrer shook his head and heaved a sigh that was surprisingly sad.

"Blood wasn't safe to drink. They were high on some kind of drug. It was still in their bloodstream," he answered, drawing his brows in as he worked. "I'm thinking they might not've attacked if they hadn't been on what they'd taken." He cleared his throat before saying, "I just… took it as an opportunity to teach Vain what bad blood smelled like…"

Oh. The bandits' poor, drug-induced decision was actually rather sad. I could see why killing two bothered him. I stared thoughtfully at Ferrer. He was much more sensitive than I'd thought. If it was anything but rot-witches, he seemed very reasonable. It was surprisingly arousing at the same time. He'd protected my Vain too and nurtured her education. That was even more appealing.

Goodness, I needed a distraction. I remembered something and focused once again on Vain. I parted her soft fur as she ate and spied the collar I'd been working on for her.

"Oh dear," I murmured, quite concerned about this development.

"What's wrong?" Ferrer asked.

I traced my finger over it. "Ferrer… she's wearing the collar I'd been enchanting…"

"Is that a bad thing?"

"I never finished it…" I answered, licking my lips nervously. "I'm quite concerned that Mushy put it on her. She could have easily tampered with it."

"Oh shitting stars," he cursed, tossing feathers angrily into my little fire. "I swear I don't bloody know what to do with that creature!"

"She…" I frowned and looked down at Vain. "Vain carried more weight than she'd ever be able to lift. I don't know if an entire colony could have absconded with my bag. Mushy had to have added extra strength to the collar… How though? I could have sworn you needed specific vocalizations for that one, and I can't imagine her reproducing some of them without a tongue…"

"She's a mystery to us all," Ferrer grouched and then handed me the dead, plucked bird. "I'm truly concerned about what might be in that collar. You might want to remove it."

I frowned, feeling terribly torn over it. "I couldn't imagine her hurting Vain… but she did allow some rather unspeakable things to occur," I replied, resisting the urge to touch the mark Ferrer had given me. "And I still can't fathom why she'd plant a hair on me. Your colony could have even executed me."

I cringed as I stroked the collar. It still had several remarkable enchantments I feared I'd never be able to reproduce. The thought of snipping it off… It'd destroy the protective loop of magic. It'd be utterly useless.

"It's your choice," Ferrer said with a sigh, watching me gut the bird. "Vain's too, actually."

I sighed miserably. "Vain, what do you want to do? You want me to remove it?"

*I… don't know. How long would it take to make another one?*

"It wouldn't be the same, but something close would take a couple of days."

*Maybe make another one, then take it off when you're ready to replace it. I like the thought of being hard to grab. Birds are scary.*

I cringed and shook my head with indecision. When a thought occurred to me, I gasped, appalled. "That accursed Mushy," I hissed. "She used my sweet Vain as a courier service!"

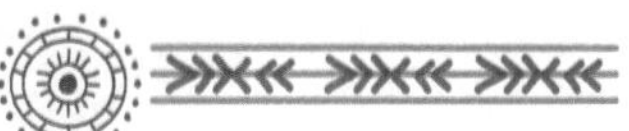

# Chapter 19

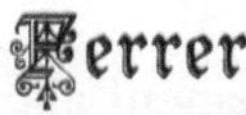

## Ferrer

I studied how Keid was preparing the bird for cooking while she fumed over the rot-witch's newest misbehavior. I needed to learn. I wanted to provide for her, and I needed her to see my dedication. I was going to do all of this for her the next time she needed to eat. She'd have to fight me over gutting the bird, and I was going to win because I'd just fly up into the tree to do it. My plan was solid. It looked easy enough; she just slit open the bottom part and dragged everything out of the lower cavity in almost one piece.

"Can't believe it. No, I can. I can definitely believe it. Still, though… can't believe it!" she muttered angrily as she sterilized her knife with the fire. She slid the now wingless, legless, headless, and gutless animal onto a pole, a long, sturdy sharpened branch that was propped up over the fire. She then stuck a sharpened stick through the bird, through a hole in the pole, and out the other side of the bird so that it'd turn with it. The process of cooking was disgusting in the most fascinating way. It was now that I wished I'd watched Queen Hekla and her mate whenever they settled down to cook over a campfire. Perhaps I could have shared a different method to impress her.

*Done feeding. Roosting,* Vain muttered tiredly and flapped up into a tree. *Bravely sleeping here because I'm invincible now!*

"Euh…" Keid vocalized warily. "Careful with that attitude, Vain. You're not exactly invincible."

*Proud of you, Starshine,* Iron complimented smugly, and Vain just giggled in response, sounding loopy from exhaustion. I felt bad that she'd been through some serious trials over the last handful of days. I wished we'd found her sooner, and I bet Keid felt the same way. I definitely sensed her looming guilt over the bond.

"If you want me to try to kill Mushy, tell me, but I think I know your answer," I offered, trying to make her smile or laugh. It worked.

"I might surprise you." She snorted in dry amusement and rotated the carcass over the fire. She did this to keep it from turning black. Burned meat was not good, apparently.

I smiled at her reaction, feeling my soul glow with how she was warming up to me. She'd been concerned about me fighting off the shifters. Worrying meant caring, and I felt some relief that we'd met that goal. Keid cared about me now… I was pretty sure. At least, that hug had felt like caring. She'd also sent Vain to help me. Well… she'd tried.

*Thank the Sky Gods we were immune to that flub,* Iron remarked.

After about an hour and a half, Keid pulled the bird off the flames and cut into the chest meat. I leaned over to watch, taking note of the muscle's color. The skin was a dark, crispy brown, and the inside was steamy, white, and moist. The fluids were clear. I needed to recreate this preference.

Keid rummaged through her bag and pulled out a little bottle. She turned it upside down over the exposed meat and shook it, letting fine white grains sprinkle onto the dead bird. I'd seen other mates do this to their food, but I never thought to ask why.

"What is that?" I inquired curiously. I scented it and realized it was salt. I did like its presence in human and shifter bodies. Wildlife didn't taste as salty as people. "Oh, that's good for managing blood pressure," I said, recalling a distant memory.

"Exactly," Keid said. "Makes meat taste good too. I don't really like it unflavored."

I nodded. "I'll remember that. Anything else you like on your meat?"

I withheld a grin as she blushed furiously. She was so much fun to fluster, and it was far too easy. "Y-yes. There are other herbs, but I don't have any."

"You can show me later then," I replied, casually tossing another feather into the fire. If I could get her to return to the colony with me, I'd bring her all the herbs we had. I recalled seeing decorations called 'bouquets' at Queen Hekla's wedding. Perhaps I could arrange the herbs in an attractive manner before giving them to her. Flowers were not something we had a lot of in the Night Court.

"Forgive me," Keid said as she brought some white meat to her soft, light lips. It wasn't that long ago that those lips had been wrapped around my cock. Arousal slipped into my abdomen, and I heaved a sigh as I watched.

"What for?" I asked lazily as she cut out another piece of cooked pheasant muscle.

"For eating in front of you. I know you're hungry. I'll… f-feed you when I'm done," she explained, and her cheeks ruddied when she stumbled over the last part. Her heart sped up just a touch, and I was intrigued by how she shifted in her seated position.

"There's no rush," I said, trying to put her first for a little while. "I could go another day."

"No, we're doing small, regular meals like we agreed." She then dragged her tongue up a juice-slicked thumb. Oh gods, that'd been unconsciously seductive of her. My cock swelled slightly, additionally excited by the prospect of feeding. I scrubbed a hand over my lower face, hiding how I wiped saliva from the corners of my mouth with a thumb and forefinger. She was making me salivate, making me hungry in far too many ways.

She never looked at me while she ate, likely because she felt rude or guilty. All I could really read was a sense of anticipation from her. There was also a little nervousness but a little excitement too. Was she looking forward to feeding me? That was intriguing. Last time, I'd left her in a state of wanting. That couldn't have been enjoyable, so why was she looking forward to it? Well, if I could tolerate it and she'd let me, I'd satisfy her so she wouldn't have to suffer.

I would not have expected a partner to get aroused from a feeding. That was supposed to be our reaction as bat-shifters. It was as bizarre as the time Keid allowed herself to go wild with me—the night I lost control. She gave in while I struggled to manage myself. We had a curious nature together and completely different relationships with our own instincts.

As much as I wished I could embrace my instincts and tackle Keid out of lust right now, I had a lot to prove first. I dragged my eyes from the swells of my mate's breasts and glanced up at the sky. Once again, several stars twinkled at me. Only the Sky Gods knew what they were saying.

"I'm ready," Keid said in an oddly professional tone, licking her fingers clean before rinsing them with water. "Where do you want me to be?"

I ran a hand through my hair, then simply gestured for her to stand. I did not want to do it lying down again, I would not have her sit on my lap, and it would be awkward to have her sit in front of me. Standing would give me the option to run if I felt my control waver. I would not let anything get in the way of wooing Keid.

I turned her toward a tree and said, "Lean against it, and let me know if you get dizzy. I'll stop if that occurs. Is that clear?"

"Very," she acknowledged and placed a palm on the tree to steady herself.

I brushed her beautiful, gleaming hair aside and leaned over to pick the spot I wanted. I frowned at the fresh scab from yesterday's feeding, and my heart clenched in a moment of unhappiness. That made six bite injuries so far that I'd caused. If she were a shifter, she'd be healed already. It made me feel terrible. Why was I partaking from my mate, a human? I should be drinking from something I didn't care about, like a wild animal.

"Come on," Keid urged, shuffling impatiently in front of me.

"I don't think I want to…" I confessed miserably, making her emotions waver. "It's not the taste!" I almost shouted in an attempt to keep her from going there. "I just feel bad… You still have scabs… I'm ruining your skin."

"My skin is already ruined," she snapped. "Feed already, Ferrer. Follow our plan."

"It's not already ruined," I grumbled, almost in a pout. "You have lovely skin." I scowled and traced a thumb over her old scars. They were so faded and did nothing to mar her perfection.

Keid shuddered under my caress, and I sighed, caving to her want. I placed my hands gently on her shoulders and leaned down to graze her skin with an elongated fang, opening a tiny slit in her neck. I pressed the tip of my tongue against it and waited a moment for the anticoagulant to start working. The woman beneath my mouth shivered, and she moved her other hand to the tree, steadying herself.

I withdrew my tongue and wrapped my lips around the blossoming bleed, letting my mouth fill a little before taking my first swallow of her savory essence. Like clockwork, my cock worked, swelling and pressing uncomfortably against my pants. My mouth tingled pleasurably with the taking of her fluid, and it was so fine that it was difficult to savor. I wanted to binge on it.

There was something far too erotic about drinking from Keid, my fated mate. My body was taking her in, and it wanted to give something back out of gratitude. It was working to turn a part of her into me, and in return, wanted to grow a part of me within her. It didn't matter that she could already be pregnant.

My instincts pressed me to take her over and over again until my seed flowed from her as readily as blood.

Already, the muscles in my abdomen and groin were throbbing, threatening to close the distance between Keid and me without my permission. I shifted uncomfortably, moving my weight from one foot to the other to remind my body that I was in control. I was going to feed, then I was going to stop. That was the plan. That was what Keid wanted.

She wasn't making it easy though. I knew she didn't like being easy to read over the bond, and sometimes, like now, I wasn't a fan of it either. The woman was, simply put, aroused.

I'd tried. I'd really tried to not stimulate her, but it seemed to be impossible. I'd been careful with the incision so I wouldn't have to lick her neck, but just having my lips on her was making her crumble.

I detected the slightest trembling under my hands, and I squeezed her shoulders to remind her to relax. Instead, the gesture wrung a long, desirous groan from her, one that sounded like she'd been trying to keep it imprisoned.

"Keid," I murmured quickly before having to catch her blood again, "the calmer you are, the calmer I can stay." I was trying to warn her that I only had so much control. She needed to behave.

"I'm quite calm," she said primly. It was a bold-faced lie, so bad that I nearly barked out a laugh. I sorely wished I could tease her for that, but I was pretty busy. No, no, her emotions were anything but calm, and it was only getting worse.

I released my own groan when my next swallow made her whimper. I glanced over to her fingers, which were starting to flex into the redwood bark. Her nails subtly clawed at the wood, scraping off red flakes in a nervous tic. The savageness of the motion was an aphrodisiac to my feral mind, like she was calling to that side of me, trying to encourage it to play.

I didn't want it to go play. I wanted to retain my mind. The next time—if ever—I joined with Keid, I wanted to properly, bloody well remember it!

Maybe a release would help me through this. It barely got me through last time. I removed my right hand from Keid and fumbled with the front of my pants to remove my cock, this time taking great care to not brush it against her.

It didn't seem to matter though, because once I yanked it from its confines, she released a long, low moan and tried to lean into the tree. Her excitement spiked dramatically, and her heart started pounding. This was bad.

"No, no, no," I said through her skin, muffled, as I pulled her back upright. "Dom move!"

She gasped timidly and tried to stay still, but I could tell that her body was fighting her mind.

*Keid,* I mind-linked her, *spread your legs a little. I need room for... some toleration.*

It might have been a bad idea. Not only did my words act as an unintentional tease for her, I could smell her desire now, and it was bloody ambrosial. My guts cramped so tight from desire that I nearly screamed into her flesh out of sexual frustration. I had to handle this right now.

I moved my left hand to the tree, propping myself up while I continued to slowly drink. I wrapped my right fingers around my cock and started pumping feverishly, needing to find release to get to the end of this feeding without forcing myself on her. I angled my erection down, pointing between her legs so I'd spend onto the dirt when I reached climax.

I huffed through her skin as I slid my grip up and down, trying to massage out the aching desire I had for this woman. My fist had nothing on her sweet, clenching core, and I shut my eyes tight, trying to focus on that sensation so I could come. It was at this point that I didn't even know why we were doing this. It was at this point that hunger and sexual desire started muddying into a form of madness that made me wonder if the torture was even worth it.

Keid was whimpering at this point. Her heart and lungs were racing, and I could tell that her core was weeping. She smelled so good. She tasted so good. Everything about her was a bloody delicacy that I wished I had the sanity to savor. Worse than that, I was kept from it all by a desire for her to truly want me. I didn't want to be her last 'good time' before she disappeared on me. The lust I was feeling from her was a new kind of miserable curse. I could let it stroke my cock, but if I did, it'd rip my heart to shreds within the next heartbeat.

I broke into an anxious sweat, and imagining Keid's warm lips around my cock one more time made my hips lurch into my grip. I came hard with a grunt, shaking and moaning into her skin as I spent my seed on the tree's roots between her feet. I massaged out as much of my desire as I could, cursing the very existence of my cock and the madness it wrought.

When I spent it all, I continued rubbing it, trying to get through the last minute of feeding. Something suddenly changed in Keid's emotions. It was some kind of calm acceptance that made me concerned. I huffed out a breath in between swallows, trying to keep my own sounds of pleasure to a minimum, but whatever had inspired her wasn't conceding.

Panting slightly, Keid moved her hands to her tunic, and my eyes shot wide open at the sound of her leggings being pulled downward.

*Keid? What are you doing?* I asked her nervously, trying to wrap up my tiny meal. I slowed the pumping of my unrelenting erection as my worry increased.

She released a frustrated sob that was so subtle I almost didn't notice it. "Please, Ferrer," she breathed out, emotions cringing around her confession. "Please… Please, please, please…"

Keid was begging me for something, and for a moment, I couldn't move. I slowly removed my hand from my cock, took one last swallow of her blood, and stoppered the bleeding with my left thumb. Her pulse was loud and vibrant in its call to me, as loud as the pleads that came through her lips. It was as if I could follow that pulse anywhere in her body and find nothing but my name being cried.

I spoke softly to her. I was worried and nervous, but mostly, I just wanted to make her happy—at least happy enough to stay with me. I'd found some relief. Maybe I could stay in control.

"What is it, Keid?" I looked down as I spoke to her, swallowing hard at the sight of her trembling hands beneath her tunic, gripping the lowered band of her leggings. She'd moved it just past her bottom and was fidgeting with it there.

"Please," she whispered quieter and leaned forward to pull her tunic up, knotting it at the waist to keep it elevated. My breath caught, and I stared unashamedly at her rump, the rump that she was putting on display for me. "Please, Ferrer..."

"Please what?" I murmured, no longer capable of keeping myself from her skin. My right thumb and fingertips landed shakily on her bottom as I fought a losing battle against lust. Her pale skin, not so different from mine, was pliant under my touch, so I stroked her. I let my fingers graze across her skin, noting the pleasant sparks from the mate touch, but paid so much more attention to how she actually felt.

"P-please... d-don't make me say it," she begged, dipping her head as I caressed her. I tilted my head as I struggled to keep my feral instincts at bay. I so badly wanted to study her, memorize her, and never forget her. The loss of control meant hazy memories... and Keid was worth so much more than hazy memories. If she decided she didn't want me, this would be all I'd have.

"You don't have to say anything," I replied, "but I can't make you happy if I don't know what you want..." I swallowed hard as she arched her back, tilting her pelvis more for me. Did she want my finger? My mouth? What did she want? Perhaps she wanted me to leave so she could pleasure herself? Based on her pose, I doubted it, but still, I didn't know.

She whimpered and pushed against the tree to nudge herself against my erect cock, which was swelling excessively. I didn't know how I was keeping myself from plunging into her. I supposed that my fear was overriding everything. I was terrified of losing her if I made a mistake here. I'd already made so many, and somehow, I felt like we were at a crossroads.

"Please," she groaned, pushing and rubbing. "Come closer," she added under her breath, like she hadn't intended it for my ears. I took a step forward, cupping her bottom while she shivered in delight. I felt her unbelievable carnal lust over our bond, and I truly had to wonder if humans had a feral side after all.

I enjoyed my palmful of Keid's bottom for one more moment, squeezing dimples into it before letting go. She had a lovely rump; I'd never seen finer. I moved my hand to my cock again, which was swollen more than I'd ever seen it. I gritted my teeth, feeling an agonizing flare of arousal drip into me like liquid fire. I let my thumb drag over the tight, shiny, near-purple tip of my crown. It slavered for Keid, and I wiped away a line of cum. Already my seed was trying to get into her sex.

I leaned forward to check on her cut, wanting to free my hand but not wanting to let her bleed freely. Keid pushed back again and raised herself onto tiptoes to get above my erection, then came back down to tuck my cock between her thighs. We both released moans simultaneously, mine more from surprise than anything else. Hers was less from pleasure and more from arousal. She wasn't satisfied yet.

I released a strangled grunt when she rubbed her thighs together. Those legs were so soft, so plush even with her slenderness, and I slid my grip to the base of my cock because she was slowly making my length disappear.

"Keid," I repeated in a lower voice, more commanding as I tried to get an answer from her. "Tell me what you want." I peeked at her cut again, but it was still bleeding.

I groaned with both pleasure and frustration as she pulled away, then pushed back, sliding my length between her legs. When I noticed her warm slick, I couldn't keep my hips from bucking, using the slippery substance to thrust into her softness.

I tilted my head back and hissed, baring my fangs to the bloody, twinkling stars. I could barely see them through the haze of pleasure. My intimate, taut skin was alive as the mate bond embraced it, sending prickles of ecstasy along all my nerve endings. Everything she did made me swell, becoming stone-hard between her softness. It was such a stark difference, and only the gods knew why it was so arousing.

I pumped my hips several more times, unable to resist my demanding muscles. I took another step toward Keid, pressing her bottom tight against my groin. I leaned my forehead into the back of her bowed neck and brushed her trembling spine with my lips. "Keid… Let me make you happy. I'm begging you," I whispered, my voice getting husky from the driving need to mate. "Tell me what you need."

I didn't know what to do in her silence, and I needed release or I was going to take her right now. I bit onto her other shoulder to keep her steady while I grabbed her hip with my right hand. I drew my hips back and drove between her thighs. I yanked backward, then drove forward again, grunting in pleasure. I felt myself start to lose my mind, and I grieved its slow departure. I didn't want this. I wanted to stay present. I wanted to stay here for Keid.

I growled into her neck, making her jerk in surprise, then she melted under me. She moaned as I thrust between her thighs again, and I echoed her as her flesh massaged my sensitive, rigid length.

*Gods, I've never been so hard in my life,* I confessed to Keid through a mind-link, too muffled in her shoulder to speak. The bond flared with her yearning, and I squeezed my eyes shut as I drove forward again and again. *If this isn't proof of your beauty, I don't know what is,* I added, almost delirious with ardor.

I bit a little harder and dug my fingers into the softness of her hips, then accelerated until I was panting into her skin. After one last pull back and thrust, I came again, ejaculating against the tree that she was holding on to with a blanched grip.

"No, no, no," she moaned, shaking her dipped head. She was trembling now as she finally made her confession. "I wanted that inside me," she whispered.

"That can easily be fixed, Keid," I murmured, releasing her skin to speak into her ear. I thumbed the hem of my pants and made them slip off my hips so they'd drop to my ankles. I stepped out of them and tilted her hips more, drawing her onto her toes. "Why didn't you tell me? You've shared your acceptance before."

She shook her head, seemingly unable to answer. I didn't understand it at all. I took a step back from Keid to grip my erection and search for her opening. I'd only done this once before, and she'd guided me in my feral haze, which I was fighting now. It gripped my skull and threatened to take over, finding my approach to breeding far too slow for its liking. Fortunately, I'd studied her already when I'd gorged on her sex. I knew where to go.

"Lower one, lower one, lower one," she said through gritted teeth, anticipating a mistake. Oh, now she was talking? I prodded the upper one momentarily to startle her. "Lower one!" she cried, the bond flooding with panic now.

I grinned for just a heartbeat, then lowered the crown of my erection to her swollen mound, which was wreathed in delicate white curls. I nuzzled the slick folds aside and pressed against her threshold, notched in place.

"What do you want, Keid?" I asked into her neck, mouthing a bump in her spine. A shudder raked down her torso, and she released a quiet, keening sound. "Do you want me? I'm trying to stay in control for you."

She tried to push back, to force me into her without having to answer, but I pulled back, too fast and far too agile for her to outmaneuver. I remained notched against her, teasing her with the prodding head of my erection. She slapped the poor redwood tree that was suffering her abuse and sobbed.

"I want it," she gasped out, caving completely. "I know you already spent it. I know you don't need it anymore, but I wanted you to lose control!" She raked her fingers down the tree, and I made a mental note to check her for splinters after this. "I just wanted to feel beautiful. I just wanted to be desired. I know it's only out of your need, but I also don't want it to be done out of need!"

I felt her confusion, her turmoil, and it bruised my heart. She didn't know what she wanted, and though it stung, it simultaneously gave me hope. Until she found her true desire, she still wanted me, if only to fill an emotional void. I'd take that for now. I'd show her I could be as good of a lover as an attentive mate. I'd show it all, whatever she needed—whatever she demanded. If I wanted to win her back, I'd have to put in my all.

And so I did. I thrust forward with a determined growl, squeezing through her entrance to tuck my length inside her, wrapped tight by her heat and aided by her slick. I shoved one more time, spurred by her lengthy, guttural groan. She rocked forward from my thrust, but I jerked her back into me, finding purchase on the bone of her hip. I mashed us together, bottom to groin, and my head kissed the back of her sex.

Keid screamed through her teeth, and I was so overly stimulated that I came immediately. I threw my head back and moaned with her, pulsing my hips with my spurting. I released against her womb, pressing my head against it, desperate for closeness in all ways.

Gasping for air, I forced myself to pull back out and push back inside her. I could still go, and I would. She'd not received her pleasure yet, and I'd continue until she did, even if it took hours.

Keeping my left hand on her neck with my thumb over the cut, I wrapped my right arm around her chest, just below her breasts, to keep her more evenly in place. Moving more from just my lower abdomen and hips now, I started rocking into Keid's sex, sliding back and forth along her channel.

I moaned into her neck as she remained bent before me, panting and hanging on to the tree. "I wish…" I said between gasping breaths, "you could see… how sexy… you are now."

My groin tightened when I sensed a flush of pleasure from her. She hadn't rejected my compliment, and I smiled briefly in gratification. It felt so good to fulfill the void in her heart, to tell her the things she should have heard her entire adult life.

"Oh gods," I whispered into her neck, feeding her thrills with a quick, regular pace. "It was so worth it, Keid. Waiting to have sex with you… my whole life… so worth it."

I was surprised to feel her hot core tensing already, which nearly excited me into another release. I could tell that she was nigh intoxicated with lust and pleasure. It was almost enough to send me into a feral frenzy, but somehow, I hung in there. The gods only knew how.

Her moaning was languid and continuous as I hammered into her. I bit into her shoulder again and squeezed my eyes tight.

*Come for me, you incredibly sexy creature,* I pleaded over a mind-link. *Come for me, and I'll fill you with all the offspring you desire. Let me give you my gift, woman.*

Keid rocked under my penetrations, panting louder by the heartbeat. "Ha… ha… ha…!" she vocalized, trying to push back and keep up with my pummeling. The pleading seemed to spike her excitement, so I continued to charm her.

*Come on, I can feel you. You're so close. You're gripping me like a goddess. Come on, Keid. Gods, you feel so good.*

My thrusts grew wetter as she arched deeper, and the sound drew me over the edge. I gritted my teeth and hissed as I came again, but I didn't stop. I growled furiously into Keid's shoulder and finally slid my hand down to see if I could reach her clit. Tucking my hand between her thighs, I dug around until I found it.

Astonishingly, it only took a couple of rubs for her to bring her mouth to her arm and scream into it. Her body seized up and shook as her core contracted, sucking on the erection that'd just finished spending itself. I groaned in amazement and euphoria as I was enveloped by her pleasure over our bond. Her legs buckled in their shaking, but I held her up against me as she continued contracting, receiving wave after wave of delight.

I could feel it over our connection, the way she was wrapped in ecstasy. It was the most beautiful thing I'd ever experienced, and I nuzzled into her neck as her climax faded. I pulled my cock from her and lifted her, smiling through my light pants at the way her head lolled back in supreme fulfillment.

I settled by the fire, keeping her cradled against my chest. She was limp and utterly relaxed as she caught her breath. Her brow was soft, and her eyes were closed, her long frosty lashes brushing against her blushing cheeks. She looked good satisfied.

"You've never looked sexier," I confessed quietly and brushed a strand of snowy hair from her face. I took a moment to stare at her, then picked up her hand to start looking for splinters.

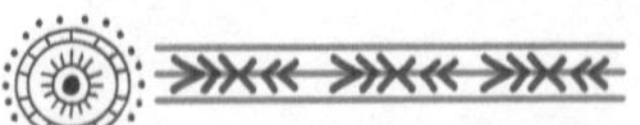 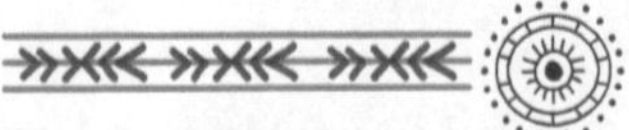

# Chapter 20

## Keid

Ferrer held me to him as I slowly recovered from our activity and my resulting orgasm. I put a heavy hand to my chest, feeling it rise and fall at a much slower rate than the one my heart was using. My heart was nearly thrumming as I came down from… which one was it now?

"Three," I mumbled under my breath as Ferrer prodded at my other hand.

"Three what, Keid?" he asked gently. I was so tired I didn't even flinch when his claws dug out what was probably a redwood splinter.

"That was my third… good orgasm… ever," I answered with the smallest slurring. I was so relaxed, I almost felt drunk. It'd been a long time since I'd partaken, but I liked this feeling much better.

"Oh?" he asked, and I detected a smile in his voice. I was certain he was smirking. "When were the other two?"

"You know when. Don't act coy," I reprimanded sluggishly, jabbing a finger weakly into his pec.

"I'm just trying to figure out how I can make it better than 'good' next time," he replied innocently. It'd been more than good, but his statement jarred me.

I opened my eyes slowly. 'Next time' was sobering. Would there be a next time? Did I want a next time? I didn't have the courage to follow up with any questions, so I just stayed quiet.

I stared at Ferrer's firm, pale chest, studying the curve of his pectorals and the way they met in the middle, creasing along his sternum. He was fascinating to study. Paleness and developed musculature didn't make sense to my brain, but it was right in front of me. The strongest men we had were muscular from doing manual labor outside in the sunlight, so they were fairly bronzed.

It was a reminder that he was from a different realm. My hand slid to my lower abdomen. I could be carrying a bat-shifter inside me right now. It would be just as pale as its father, and it would be about as pale as me. It was an odd comfort. The only thing that would make me look different in a family portrait would be the white hair. It wouldn't be nearly as stark as the difference between my sister and me, and we were twins. What a strange thought.

"I should be able to tell soon," Ferrer said in a voice that carried a touch of reassurance. I needed him to clarify, but his sensitive tone continued to take me by surprise. I wished I knew if this was who he truly was or if it was an act to retain the mother of his potential offspring.

"About what?" I inquired, untying the knot that was holding up my tunic. I was starting to feel shy with my exposure. My leggings were still pulled down, so I pressed my legs together and tried to angle my hips so he couldn't really look at me.

"We can scent pregnancy as hormones develop. They say it smells different for the parents though—well, shifter parents. You'd carry my scent along with yours."

My heart did a little flip, and my belly followed suit. Though we'd just had sex, those words somehow affected me like an aphrodisiac. I was fatigued though, and I merely sighed through the stimulation, letting it go with an exhale.

"When do you think you'll notice?" I asked, trying not to get nervous about it. Whatever would be would be. It'd be days still before I could detect implantation.

"How long has it been?" he asked, and we both simultaneously started counting with our fingers. I couldn't resist the tired giggle that burst through my lips, and Ferrer smiled at the sound. "I don't know what human pregnancies are like, but with a shifter or fae mate… I've heard it could possibly be as soon as tomorrow or the following night. It's been five days now."

"And if I'm not?" I asked, the question leaving my lips before I could reexamine it. It was just at nightfall that he'd asserted he'd strive to become a good mate for me. I hadn't wanted to hear it. This was simply bringing up the same issue from a different angle. Why was I doing this to myself? Why was I doing this to him?

Ferrer moved his gaze from mine, choosing to stare at the hand he was checking for splinters. "Nothing would change," he answered quietly, his tone thick with sincerity. "I'd bring you home, still marked, and we'd start a family whenever you wanted—a mini colony with lots of pups."

I was too tired to cry, but by the gods I wished he'd said that when we first met. It almost seemed fake now—too good to be true. The only thing I hung on to was the yearning in his voice.

Before I could reply, he shook his head and added, "I almost hope you aren't pregnant." I blinked in surprise, and he sighed. "That way, you'd know for sure that I wanted you. I suppose that would be the silver lining if I hadn't managed to claim your egg." I had to admit that his admission was compelling. Also, how did he manage to make everything sound so erotic to me?

Ferrer released my hand and started searching the other one for splinters. I wondered if he'd even think to do this if he didn't actually care about me. The splinters definitely wouldn't impact a pregnancy. No… this did seem genuine. I couldn't imagine many males or men noticing anything like that while fucking, but Ferrer had seen to it as soon as he carried me to the fire.

Perhaps he did care.

"What do you want to do now, Keid?" he asked, prying out a particularly long splinter. I winced, and he mouthed an apology. "Do you need to rest or do you wish to try to catch up to your charge? I can't promise we'd be able to find her by sunrise. In fact, I doubt we will."

I glanced over to my ball of mud, noticing the bacteria tiring and fading. I could find a fresh clod to excite, then Ferrer wouldn't be forced to carry me. I was tired after two intimate sessions tonight plus a feeding, and I wished I could just rest here, especially now that we'd found Vain.

"Let's walk a little more, then settle before the Sun God wakes," I said reluctantly, and Ferrer frowned. It seemed like he wanted to stay. "I think we should put some distance between us and this campfire. The smoke might attract nearby dragons. It's best we don't sleep by one."

"Clever witch," the bat-shifter said, looking resigned.

"I'm just a person," I said, feeling a sudden need to remind him. "A witch, sure. Albinism? Yes, I have that, but at the end of the day, I'm a woman."

"I definitely don't need a reminder of you being a woman," he said, his smile turning lopsided as he moved a hand to stroke my naked hip. Speaking of reminders, I climbed carefully off his naked lap and pulled up my leggings.

"I'm going to relieve myself," I murmured, then went to do that. Upon my return, Ferrer helped me retrieve a sleepy Vain from her roosting, and we left to travel northeast for the remainder of the night. The bat-shifter also seemed disappointed that I'd found a light source for myself. Surely, he couldn't have wanted to carry me the entire way. That sounded exhausting.

As Ferrer predicted, we weren't able to catch up to Mushy by sunrise, but at least he'd found her potent scent trail. We also weren't able to find another nice little den like we had before, so

Ferrer scooped me up and jumped into one of the giant redwoods. Until he found a spot he liked, he climbed without using the arms that held me, using instead the thumbs of his colossal bat wings; they hooked over branches as well as any hand. It was surprisingly impressive, and therefore somewhat arousing. I couldn't say that I knew any man who could climb with a woman in his arms.

Instead of roosting upside down in his usual fashion, Ferrer sat on a broad branch and reclined against the tree trunk, keeping me cradled against him. I made a strict effort to not look down because I very much didn't want to know how high we were.

"You won't be dropped," he said with a grunt, hooking the thumbs of his wings into the branch above us to secure his position like a mooring line. "I can lock special tendons in my body. Apparently, we're the only ones who can do that."

"Humans definitely can't," I said warily, then relaxed when I realized that his wings blocked my view of the woods. I rested my head against his chest as his arm muscles flexed against me. Yes, I definitely felt secure… and I had to admit that I felt very safe. A satisfied sigh slinked out of me, and Ferrer echoed it in turn. Swaddled with the calming tingles of the mate bond, I slowly fell asleep, lulled by the sound of his steady heartbeat.

Waking up in Ferrer's arms was pleasant, but I discovered that sleeping without being able to shift about had put a kink in my neck. When we returned to the forest floor, I had to stretch and pop my sleepy bones. I'd decided that when I was done escorting Mushy home, I was going to enchant the softest bed in the world and just sleep for a week. My muscles were already threatening to cramp up on me, and the soles of both feet and shoes were definitely complaining about the abuse. I'd never walked so much in my life.

Ferrer did end up having to carry me because my ball of bacteria had tired, and I couldn't make a replacement. If I had some cloth and time to draw sap, I could've technically made a torch, but I was never comfortable with the thought of carrying fire through woodland. It just seemed to be asking for a forest fire. It was unfortunate I'd never studied elemental arts. Conjuring fire seemed pretty useful now.

"I don't think she's moved today," Ferrer murmured to me. "We're almost upon her, Keid."

I frowned and turned my head, noticing a campfire crackling in the distance. "I supposed she decided to wait for us after all."

"Maybe because the forest ends ahead," he added.

"It does?" I asked, feeling a little excited. Perhaps we were close to her town!

Ferrer put me down as soon as I was able to see properly, and I jogged up to Mushy's little campsite. When I laid eyes upon the witch, the blood drained from my face. She wasn't looking good. She was also short one leg, and the rest of her handless arm was gone, leaving only a limp sleeve to dangle from her shoulder.

Mushy looked up slowly from her fire and smiled. Technically, it was the same smile, but her eyes seemed more tired. They weren't as wild as they used to be, and that scared me. Vain scratched gently at my neck in comfort, probably noticing how fast my heart was accelerating.

"Mushy?" I asked warily, moving slowly toward her and looking about the area. "Where did your leg go?"

The ancient rot-witch chuckled lethargically, slowly bobbing in a muted version of her normal rocking. I spied her leg off to the side, already rotting, and I turned around to dry-heave. Ferrer hastily dragged me away from it, moving me to the other end of the campfire in a rock-solid grip. I couldn't imagine how the dead flesh smelled to him. The fact that he was still here was beyond impressive.

"Have you eaten, Mushy?" I asked worriedly, noticing that her bag was off to the side, seemingly untouched. I opened my own pack to rummage for the pheasant leftovers. When I offered her a piece of meat, she raised her remaining palm in rejection.

She then pointed to the bag, like she wanted something else inside of it.

I offered her everything, focusing first on my medical kit, but I couldn't figure out what she wanted. Finally, scraping the bottom of the bag, I pulled out my two numbing pebbles. I looked up at her with worried, drawn brows. Did she want one of these? How she'd known I'd made them was beyond my realm of understanding.

I held my palm out, offering a single pebble to her. "Is this what you want Mushy? Whatever for…?"

She reached out with a cloth to take the cursed stone, and I yelled in dismay when she tilted her head back and swallowed it. Ferrer pulled me back against him when I'd jerked forward to stop her. He was right. It was too late.

"Mushy… that was cursed," I lamented, not wanting to accept why she'd done it.

The old witch closed her eyes as the curse took effect, and she sighed in relief.

"She must be in a great deal of pain, Keid," Ferrer said quietly, rubbing my arms comfortingly.

Mushy stared off through the trees, looking at what was past the woodland. "What's out there, Ferrer?" I whispered, feeling a bit sick from stress plus Mushy's worsening stench.

"Nothing, it seems," he replied tersely. "I'm not scenting much. Lots of dirt… dead, dry plants. Whatever it is, Keid, it's unnatural."

I looked over to Mushy's complacent expression and worried at my lower lip with my teeth. "How many days, Mushy? How many days left to walk?" I asked, terrified of the answer. Was she going to make it? I'd have to carry her somehow. Ferrer definitely wouldn't, and I couldn't ask him to do such a thing.

Mushy gave me a rare answer this time. She opened and closed her palm two times.

"Two days?" I asked with a grimace, and she simply nodded, trembling a little more violently. "Can you… If I carry you, will you make it?" Tears sprang into my eyes as I tried to judge her weight. She didn't seem to have much on her at all. In fact, she seemed thinner than the last time I saw her, and I'd considered her emaciated then.

"If I fly you," Ferrer said out of the blue, "will you make it?"

I was too stunned already to process his unbelievable offer. To both our questions, Mushy simply shook her head, blinking slowly, like she was sleepy. I covered my face with my hands, realizing that I'd failed the one thing I'd set out to do. She was finally dying, and I wasn't going to get her home in time.

## errer

I didn't need our mate bond to know that Keid was feeling crushed. I also didn't restrain her this time when she fell to the rot-witch's feet. If the old creature was indeed dying, I'd let the woman get her closure.

"I'm sorry!" Keid croaked in a voice so thick, so broken, that it nearly dragged tears from my eyes. "I'm sorry, Mushy! I should have tried harder. I should've..." The young witch shook her head, sending her alabaster hair flying. Vain had been momentarily forgotten, and the blood bat escaped her quaking companion, flying straight to me for safety.

*Don't take it personally,* Iron said to Vain in consolation.

*She's not thinking straight. Let's let her have a moment,* I added and stroked the little blood bat's quivering head. The she-bat didn't say anything, but I could feel her deep sadness.

"—orses!" Keid was saying. "Why didn't I divert to get horses? I know that could have been risky for you, but we would've made better time, and... maybe I could have done a couple quick jobs to afford a cart? Maybe we could've put you in a cart?"

I stayed quiet, knowing that the slowdown had been my fault. I would accept Keid's wrath when she turned it to me. Had we not been sighted by the dragon-shifters, the witches wouldn't have needed to wait while I was stuck in confinement. I'd made it worse just by tagging along with them. This entire outcome was born from both my ignorance and prejudice.

I scrubbed a hand over my face, feeling extremely weary from all of this. Why was it so bloody hard to figure out the right course of action? I thought I'd been doing everything correct at the time. How could I trust my judgment after something like this?

*I should give up my coronel title when we return,* I said blankly to Iron.

*Don't make decisions when you're emotional,* he scolded. I knew he was right, but my head was a mess. Why was I so torn up over this? I should be celebrating the demise of my natural enemy, but it just felt wrong. My instincts were furious with my growing compassion, but how could I spit upon a creature who'd returned my mate's fertility to her? I truly wondered if being human was easier in some regards. Keid did not seem to be a slave to her instincts, and I dearly admired her clear, sharp mind.

The rot-witch patted Keid's head through the cloth she was holding, like she didn't want to get any of her smell on the young woman. It was surprisingly thoughtful and gentle—not like how she'd once sent me off with a smack on the butt. No, the creature looked saner than she ever had, and I had to admit that it was intimidating. Intelligence was far more frightening than madness in any enemy. I'd much rather deal with a rabid cù-sìth than a sadistic, conniving mac-talla.

When the dying creature gestured for her bag, Keid brought it promptly to her, only for the hag to start emptying it. She piled random items in the old cooking pot she'd set aside, then opened the sack wide. I furrowed my brows as I watched her sit in the bag and pull it up as much as she could around her shrunken, emaciated form… like a sleeping bag. It looked a little ridiculous because she was not going to completely fit in there. Did she want to be carried like that? What was she doing?

The hag finally brushed a crying Keid to the side and gestured for me to approach her. I leaned back warily, barely able to hear anything over my instincts. My feral mind was telling me to run, and if I wouldn't, it'd take over and do it for me. I felt my claws elongate, and I dug them into the dirt, needing to find some stability.

*She wants us,* Iron squeaked, terrified. *What do we do?*

*I don't know,* I replied, unable to rip my gaze from the rot-witch's weeping, bloodshot eyes. Her look was far too calm, and it had me on high alert. Keid scooted back and put a hand on my arm, noticing that I'd been frozen by the hag's invitation. My mate's touch was calming, and it freed me enough to take a settling breath.

"You don't have to," she whispered to me. "I think she'd understand if you didn't."

I was finally able to tear myself from the hag's stare and brought my gaze to Keid. Her white brows were drawn up over worried eyes that now looked more like lavender than periwinkle. It was the firelight's warm caress that was responsible. In the daytime, the blues were much more apparent. The color change was so seamless that it reminded me of how Keid adapted so easily to the flow of her instincts. She went wild when she needed to and called upon calm for all other times.

I reached up to wipe at the glossy skin under Keid's swollen, devastated eyes. I didn't like seeing her cry. I wanted to make her happy. Would going to the witch make her happy? Could I draw upon that same calm?

Closing my eyes, I took three long, self-soothing breaths before I stood and moved to crouch before the dying creature. Every muscle, bone, nerve, and wrinkle in my bloody brain was screaming at me to retreat, but retreat I would not. In fact, I locked my leg tendons in place to get through whatever this was.

The witch chuckled lowly at my obvious struggle, then turned her head to spit out another tooth. It seemed like she was breaking with the smallest movements. This was not a graceful way to die, and I was glad that Keid wouldn't suffer such a departure.

I stared into the ancient eyes of my mortal enemy and saw the depth I knew to be there. This was no doddering old fool. Like I'd known from the beginning, this body hosted a potent mind. This mind wanted something from me, and I waited restlessly for it. My nose told me there was not much time left. The decay was worsening, and my eyes were watering from the torture.

"What is it, Mushy?" I asked, trying to keep my tone dry in my urgency. I was barely holding on to my courage and stomach as it was, so I prodded her with the nickname given by my mate.

The rot-witch was greatly amused by it and laughed for a moment before falling into a coughing fit. They were wretched, wet coughs, and I unwillingly pictured the damage it was doing to her insides. At least she could rely on the cursed stone for numbness… however long that would last.

"Goo goy," she gagged out and reached up to pat my cheek.

I flinched dramatically, but after my nerves stopped ricocheting lightning and terror through my body, I let her touch me. If I had to explain her touch to anyone, I'd say that it felt like the opposite of being touched by a mate. Her touch was of death, of dread, and it was the most taxing contact I'd ever endured in my life.

All I could do was repeat a chant in my head. Every movement I made or didn't make, I did it for Keid. I was accepting the touch of my natural enemy for Keid. I wanted my mate to see that I'd do anything for her, and it included facing my worst nightmares. This was definitely one of them. The hag's touch was everything I'd expected, but I forced myself not to regret it if I survived this.

"Oo oy, goo oy," she repeated.

I felt it coming from all directions. I felt it from her palm, under my feet, and in the redwood dust that drifted onto my skin from the calm woodland air. I also felt it within me. Her wild grey hair shivered one last time with her final, deep, gurgling breath.

Something was revealed within me, and in return, the witch crumbled in on herself. In a predetermined move, her remains landed almost perfectly into the bag. All that was left of the hag was a pile of rotten flesh.

Keid shrieked and lunged forward to panic over the remains, but my entire world pitched to the side. I lost my balance as my head spun, and my tendons unlocked on their own, making me fall backward. Something was wrong.

I dug my claws into the dirt and gritted my teeth through a scream. I'd only felt this sensation once before, and I was terrified. I was scared because this was not something any shifter could experience twice in a lifetime. It was impossible!

I couldn't hear anything anymore, and my vision blurred. Soothing hands on me suggested that Keid was by my side now, but there was no way to communicate with her. I didn't even think I could mind-link at the moment because my brain was shrieking. Was that Iron screaming or was that me?

My body writhed in the dirt under Keid's fumbling grip, and I was finally able to free a yell when my first bone dislocated. The pain was not only intolerable, it was horrifyingly familiar, and I screamed through the next series of dislocations, breaks, and fusions that were forced upon me. This was a dance I'd done before, but somehow all of the steps were new.

How could I go through this again? I already had Iron. Why would I ever have another forced shift? How could the witch force me back into my beast's form? Had she intended to trap me like this? Was this one last joke to make sure Keid and I could never be?

I couldn't ask any more questions because the pain became all-consuming and my mind stopped working. My screams turned into horrible, shrill whistles, making me think that my throat had been torn open in some kind of nightmarish shifting accident. My arms were gone now, having merged into the wings I'd already had out during my stressful encounter with the rot-witch. I still couldn't maintain my balance, and Keid's hands continued to hold me, trying to steady me in my panicking.

As my skeleton rearranged, my guts followed suit, and it was pure, white-hot agony. Familiarity faded away, and that was what terrified me the most. I was left alone in a strange darkness. Had I been able to, I'd be sobbing in utter terror, but I couldn't do anything but emit shrill cries.

"Oh no, oh no, oh no," Keid was saying as my ears regained their sharpness. "Ferrer, what is happening to you?" I looked up at her as she was crying, and the fear on her face made everything so much worse.

After several more adjustments, my body stopped shifting, and I went limp. I had no idea what I was because I was not Iron. I was too big to be a blood bat, but I still had wings. I tried flapping them, but Keid wrestled me to pin my wings down along my body, seeming to think I was panicking. Well… I was. I was very much still panicking.

*Ferrer!* Iron's voice called out to me.

*Iron!* I cried, utterly relieved to hear him. *What happened to us?*

*I don't know, but we're not alone in here.*

*What?* I was alarmed, and a chill swept over me. That was not the answer I'd wanted to hear. I turned my head to stare up at my mate, hoping she could help me understand what was happening. What had the rot-witch done to me?

*Vain!* Iron called in a mind-link, and I felt a swell of gratitude toward my bat for still being able to function. Even parts of my mind felt different.

*Iron!* Vain replied, sounding stricken. *What happened to you and Ferrer?*

*We're both here,* I said to her and pulled Keid into the mind-link so she could hear. *We're still in here, but we don't know what we are. We don't know what happened. Keid…* I didn't want to say it, but for the first time, I really felt like I needed help. I really… really needed her. *Keid, I'm scared,* I said, deflating.

Keid's face, wrinkled from worry and desperation, released a heavy sob when she finally heard me speak. I was so glad she hadn't run away in terror. She could have abandoned me when the rot-witch died, but she didn't. I would have felt so lost witho—

*Hello.*

I froze, and so did Keid. That was not Iron. That was not Vain.

That was a new voice.

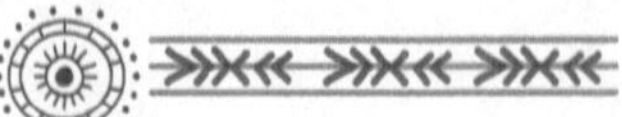
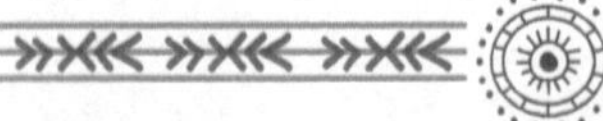

# Chapter 21

## Reid

It was brutal. Watching Mushy dissolve instantly was one of the most traumatizing things I'd ever witnessed in my life. She just… crumbled. I knew in that moment that I'd never be able to escape the image of her face caving inward. She'd touched Ferrer's face, garbled out some tongueless words, then… then she became nothing but a pile of rot. Mushy finally became what she'd been promising to turn into her entire life.

It shattered me. I'd failed her. I'd looked to give my life some meaning to get me by, and I'd failed to take an old woman home so she could die in peace. Instead, she died out in the wilderness, staring into the eyes of a male who hated her. I couldn't fathom it, but all I needed to do was wait. The answer, it seemed, was thrown at me in mere minutes.

When Ferrer collapsed into his own pile of misery, I realized that she'd used the last of her reserves on him. She hadn't planned on living another day or two, clinging pointlessly to a body desperate for sleep. No… in her usual fashion, she'd chosen the most extreme route out of her life. After gods knew how many centuries she'd lived, in the most powerful moment of her existence, and on the precipice of death, she'd done something to him.

The fear was like a lightning strike. It scared me out of my gods-forsaken mind, and I completely stopped caring about what'd just happened to Mushy. What had she done to Ferrer?

I spun and dove for the male, trying to hold on to him as he writhed. I held back a scream when he yelled, but I couldn't keep my tears from falling. Panic gripped me at the telltale sounds of a first shift.

"Vain!" I shouted through tears. "Vain, what did she do to Ferrer?"

*I don't know! I don't know!* the blood bat wailed, landing on my upper arm and crawling to my shoulder. I released Ferrer for a moment to make sure she was safely latched on to my tunic before trying to grab him again.

"He's having a first shift, but isn't that impossible?" I gasped, trying to keep him from hurting himself as he thrashed. "I've helped countless cubs through their first shift at the castle, but I don't know what to do here! I can't predict what'll break or dislocate! I don't know! I don't know!" My voice became shriller as my mind fought to work. "Is he becoming a bat? Why… would…"

*Keid!* Vain urged in a stronger tone. *We have to be strong for him! Try a general numbing curse! We can't predict what'll shift next, and the injuries heal immediately. Let's try a proactive treatment! And get those pants off in case he gets bigger and rips them!*

"Ok, ok!" I choked through tears. I fumbled for his pants, gritting my teeth through his screams of agony. Each one wrenched at my heart, and I swore my body ached in a dull echo of his pain. As I yanked his pants off, I noticed that he wasn't getting larger. He was getting smaller. "Bat or something else," I noted hastily and winced as his arms and legs dislocated quite visibly.

I moved my hands over him, trying to apply the curse, but it didn't seem to get absorbed.

*It's not working, Keid,* Vain replied, sounding a bit panicky now. *That's not possible. Did she prevent him getting help?*

"Oh gods," I moaned, fumbling at his body as I tried to offer whatever relief I could. Nothing seemed to be helping, and I racked my brain for any solution. If Vain was panicking, that wasn't a good sign. I took a deep breath and accepted that I could only control so much of this. What could I control?

As Ferrer got smaller, I noticed that he was very much not changing into a blood bat. I knew I couldn't use magic because nothing was working, so I saved my energy for helping his body adjust as quickly and painlessly as possible. If I noticed a dislocation or break, I turned his body to keep any pressure away from that bone so it could reposition properly. Whatever I couldn't help with, like the rearrangement of his internal organs, absolutely killed me.

He was in so much pain, I could barely stand it. I wanted to be strong for him, but there was something about him hurting this much that almost broke me. I shouldn't have let him near Mushy. We knew she was capable of anything, and I'd let her fool me again. Whatever she'd done this time might have permanent repercussions.

When he'd lost about a foot of his height, feathers blossomed out of his skin. They rippled down his body in black and white, dressing him anew.

*Avian!* Vain shrieked, simultaneously shocked and terrified.

"Oh no, oh no, oh no," I moaned. "Ferrer, what is happening to you?" At the sound of his name, his head turned to face me, and somehow I could see deep fear in his bird eyes. They'd become striking—pale gold irises surrounded by blood-red sclera. I bit my lip and summoned all my courage to be strong for him; it was a brutal testing of my will.

Ferrer's body had stopped shrinking and finally settled into the form of a very large black-and-white bird of prey. Had I seen this species? What was he? It was hard to get a good look at him with how he squirmed against me. I was particularly afraid of his talons. I needed to figure out the species so I could better help. Oh gods, what if he was stuck like this?

Comparing his new form to my body, I'd have to guess that he was between four and five feet long, and the powerful wings that'd startled me with their violent flapping were individually roughly around the length of my body—and I was tall for a woman.

The size was not going to help me identify him. Whatever this avian was, he was definitely larger than normal. Shifters tended to be bigger than their wild counterparts. It was the only reason why Iron was bigger than Vain.

I folded his wings to his body to the best of my ability, not wanting him to move until he calmed. If he went feral and panicked, Ferrer could easily be whisked away, and I'd lose him. Unless Vain could keep up with him, he could end up miles upon miles away from me.

*Iron mind-linked me!* Vain chirped. I breathed a sigh of relief, and Ferrer's body seemed to calm under me.

Finally, Ferrer mind-linked me, and when he said he was scared, it absolutely gutted me. I didn't know how to help him! I had to figure out how to help him!

I tried to calm myself, but it was an uphill battle. First, I needed information. I had so many questions, but before I could say anything, a new voice popped into my head.

*Hello.*

I froze and Ferrer's goliath bird body stiffened under me. Both our hearts were racing as we tried to process what we'd heard.

"Hello?" I croaked out, not sure where the voice was coming from. It felt like it was coming from Ferrer, but that didn't make sense. I cautiously turned Ferrer's avian form toward the ground, releasing him to his feet. He backed away from me slowly, obviously still distressed.

*Who's that?* Iron barked, sounding very defensive. The poor bat had to be just as rattled.

*I've found you, my human,* the voice said, which simultaneously confused and spooked me. I looked over my shoulder, but I didn't see anyone or anything. I was the only human here.

*What?* Ferrer's voice asked, sounding breathless through his open mind-link.

*I'm your beast... but you seem to already have one,* the smooth, almost commanding voice said, and the bird's head quirked, like the new voice was controlling it now.

*I do...* Ferrer replied warily. *I... am confused.*

"Oh," I murmured aloud. "Ferrer is the human here. I get it." I nodded thoughtfully. Ferrer was the human side of the shifter body. Their beasts saw them as the human half. That made sense.

*I'm his beast,* Iron stammered, suddenly very insecure. *I-I was here first...*

I closed my eyes and lowered my face into my palms, thinking hard. "Hold a moment," I said to everyone, slightly muffled. "Ferrer, when she touched you, what did you feel?"

He took a moment to reply, but when he did, he sounded strained. *I... It's hard to remember over the pain. It happened so fast.*

*It was like something heavy was taken off our body... maybe the brain? I don't know,* Iron added very quietly. I tried not to get too distracted by it because I needed to focus, but I was deeply worried for him. He seemed to be handling the sudden change the worst.

"Something taken off," I murmured and went through all the possibilities in my mind. That was not what it felt like to be cursed. Rather, that was usually how it was described when curses were lifted—enchantments too, actually. "Did she lift the curse…?" I mumbled as I mulled it over in my head. Surely, if anyone could undo something as powerful as a lasting, species-wide curse, it'd be the same kind of person who placed it. A powerful rot-witch would be the only one who'd even have a chance at removing something like that. How many rot-witches had placed the curse anyway? It had to have been more than one…

*We don't have enough information,* Vain concluded with a deep sigh.

"We don't need a whole lot of information if that's what was done," I said, continuing to mumble into my hands. "We just need to test it to see if that theory is correct. New voice," I asked, "identify yourself and your nature." Clean questions provoked clean answers.

*Should I answer her?* the new voice asked.

*Euh...* Ferrer blurted, taken by surprise. *Yes. That's... Keid. She's... Uh... I marked her.*

*I noticed that... but we're yet to be marked. Is she our mate? She's our fated mate, you know. I'm confused. I recognize her, but we seem to have an incompl—*

*Please, just answer her question.* Ferrer sighed.

*My human, Keid, and... the other beast that seems to be here, I'm Marrow. I'm Ferrer's beast... or... one of. I'm his sky counterpart.* The bird's head moved along with the words on occasion, so he was definitely the one in control of the body. The bird before me was Marrow. *I've always been here, but... I was asleep, I suppose. We're not eighteen. I'm confused... and late... apparently.*

*We're all confused,* Iron bemoaned timidly.

"I'm not," I said, pulling my hands away from my face. I looked into the bird's eyes and added, "Ferrer, I think you're not confused either—or at least you shouldn't be. This is the soul the Sky Gods gave you. It was suppressed because of the rot-witch's curse. The curse never got rid of the sky souls; it just suppressed them. The rot-witch's curse suppressed it while adding a blood bat soul upon birth. It was never replaced or mutated. I'm concluding this because it reminds me of how mating marks can be suppressed, which involves two souls. I know—I've suppressed a mark before... under duress."

*Oh...* was all Ferrer uttered for a second. *That's... a lot. Having two beasts... that's a lot. That's a lot to accept. This sounds... very permanent.*

I couldn't blame him. Being tied to one soul with a different personality seemed like a lot on its own. Would he be able to manage having two? That was a lot of voices to have in one head.

I took a deep breath and tried to find balance within myself. Ferrer might have two other minds to assist him now, but he needed me. He needed me to stay calm and help him through this. No doubt Iron and Marrow were uncomfortable as well.

"Vain," I said to the blood bat on my shoulder, and she hummed a reply. "We're going to be very methodical in our treatment here. Are you listening carefully?"

*Yes!* she chirped, sounding all business now.

"You're in charge of Iron. Can you talk to him privately? Mind-links can be private, yes?"

*I don't need anyone to be in charge of m—* Iron began complaining, but I shushed him with an aggressive finger jab. I pointed the digit right at Marrow's black-bearded beak, having no doubt that Iron saw the gesture.

*I can,* Vain answered sternly.

"Ok, good. You're going to be his emotional support, so I need you all in." I scratched the back of my neck and addressed the next item. "We're going one step at a time here, you three. We're going to be calm and methodical about this. We need to understand what we're working with now to give everyone some peace of mind. Is that understood?" I raised my hands as I waited for acknowledgement.

It was bizarre to see the bird nod, but nevertheless, it wasn't enough.

"Words," I prompted, and Ferrer, Iron, and Marrow all mumbled their reply over our mind-link. Ferrer sounded a little lighter in his response, like he was relieved to have firm direction now. Good.

I clapped. "Now, we're going to need to see if Ferrer can return to his body. I don't think we need to panic, alright? Let's all stay calm. We'll test Ferrer, then see if Iron can still come out. I suspect that you'll be able to, Iron. If your soul is here, I don't see why you'd be unable to come out. Marrow, what is this species? What bird are you?"

*Ossifrage,* Marrow replied. *I'm a vulture.*

"You have a beautiful head of feathers for a vulture," I commented wryly and twiddled the white feathers atop his crown with a couple fingers. If he was a vulture, he was the most beautiful one I'd ever seen. I held back a laugh as Marrow raised his head, pleased by the compliment.

*I am only as handsome as my human,* he replied humbly.

*What a suck-up,* Iron grumbled irritably.

*And of course, my bat would be an equally attractive bat,* Marrow added seriously.

*Welcome!*

A laugh burst from my lips, and Ferrer's chuckles came across the link. I felt a little more relaxed, and I think he did too. This was good. We could get through this. We just needed to take one step at a time.

*Also... I smell food,* Marrow noted and started bobbing past me.

"No, no, no, no!" I gasped, turning to intercept him. "That's Mushy; don't eat her remains!"

*Oh Sky Gods, no. Never.* Marrow gagged and moved around me to dig through the pile of items she'd set aside from her bag.

I frowned, watching curiously as he rummaged about her belongings. He pulled out a cloth sack and started tearing it open to get at its contents.

"Maybe you shouldn't touch anything that belongs to her, Marrow," I suggested anxiously, then froze at what tumbled out of the small package.

Bones. All that was in there were bones. I slowly picked up the abandoned cloth, barely paying attention to how Marrow swallowed the small pieces whole. Written roughly on the fabric in charcoal, though smeared, was Ferrer's name.

I stared at the fabric for a minute, trying to process something new now. "How did she know?" I asked no one. I reached down and picked up one of the small bones before Marrow could eat it. It was a piece of a larger animal, perhaps a fragment from a goat's or pig's leg bone? I had no idea. The marrow in the middle was plentiful; no doubt it was a very nutritious snack for an ossifrage.

"Is this all you eat?" I asked Marrow vacantly, moving closer to the campfire to study the bone fragment in more detail. I didn't detect any curse or enchantment, and it didn't smell like it had any chemicals or herbs on it. I held it to Vain, who was still perched on my shoulder, and murmured a separate question, "Does this smell safe to you?"

*Bone is my preference, yes*, Marrow answered while Vain was busy sniffing the shard. *I'm not a fan of flesh, but I'll eat it if forced to.*

*Yes,* Vain said, supplying the answer to my second question, *but I don't know everything. All I smell is bone, and the middle stuff seems safe. It's kinda dry, but it actually smells a little like blood.*

"That's because bone marrow helps make blood for the body. It makes most of the ingredients for it..." I informed, grateful in this moment for having studied medicine with the doctor. I chuckled quietly at the irony. "One of the things it makes helps with blood clotting. Platelets..."

*Baby plates,* Vain said solemnly. *Cute.*

"Hardly. We need to get you caught up," I replied wryly, snorting in amusement. I turned the bone over once more, then offered it to Marrow, who took it gingerly from my fingers. "And you can digest this stuff?" I asked him in disbelief.

*Within a day,* he replied, swallowing the offering whole. *Bone keeps well too once it dries.*

"No doubt," I said, placing a hand to my forehead. "Go ahead and let Ferrer shift back when you're done."

*Bone eater*... Mushy's warning, one that'd terrorized me for days, had been nothing but a joke. I slid my hand down to cover my face and muttered, "And she made him a packed lunch."

It seemed like Marrow was done, because Ferrer quickly returned to his body, grunting slightly in discomfort when he finished the transformation. It wasn't as quick as the time he shifted back from Iron, but the first time back from a new shift never was. Something in Ferrer's pose drew my eyes to his, and my lips parted in surprise.

His eyes momentarily flickered red and gold before he strode up to me. I blinked several times, thinking I was seeing things, but then I realized that Marrow had peeked through for half a heartbeat. That eye change usually happened with stimulation in shifters, but I brushed it aside because I was so happy to see Ferrer. He hadn't gotten stuck after all!

I rushed to meet him and pulled him into a relieved hug, but his response became incredibly aggressive. A low, masculine growl rumbled from his chest as he swung an arm to jerk me into him.

His left hand slid between us and landed on my right breast. I gasped as he held it through my tunic, squeezing and lifting while burying his face in my temple. He took a deep, ragged breath before pressing his hips into me.

My eyes flew wide open at the feeling of his erection against my abdomen. No pants! The log was back! A thrill shot up my spine like a spark of electricity.

"Oh gods," I exclaimed quietly in realization, pulling my hands back to palm his ribs. "You ate… and rather quickly too. I didn't even think about it!"

"Blood and bones," Ferrer growled into the side of my head like it was a curse.

Instead of thinking about his new diet, all I could think about was how those words very much described his cock. Blood was what engorged it, making it fiery hot, and bones like… well… he certainly was as hard as one. Blood and bones indeed!

His hand tightened around my breast, and I bit back an aroused moan. He'd never touched me like this before… and I… liked it.

"Marrow is apologetic. He's holding me back like I asked him to," he panted softly, puffing his lustful words into the shell of my ear. "He's keeping me from mounting you, Keid. He's keeping me from splitting your beautiful body open with my dick. He's keeping me from making my seed gush from between your sweet, blood-filled folds."

*Oh my fuck!* my brain screamed. *What filth!*

He nuzzled affectionately as his palm raised my breast higher, then slipped off it to glide up my chest and around my throat. He traced my jaw until he cupped my face, holding my head to his. After stroking my blushing cheek with a rough thumb, he pushed himself away from me, panting heavily.

*No...* my brain lamented pathetically.

"Sorry," he grunted, backing away quickly. His eyes were averted, and his face was blushing. Was he embarrassed or just stimulated? I couldn't tell. "I should see if Iron can come out… then go for a fly… to calm down."

The poor, aroused male shifted in a heartbeat, bringing out the blood bat who swooped up and into the night. I was relieved that Iron could still come out of Ferrer! Perhaps it was good for him to get a little time. Iron was probably at risk of feeling like the oldest or middle child of neglectful parents—forgotten because of the shiny new baby.

"Maybe you should go follow him, Vain," I said, feeling a little anxious. I knew they needed space, but I couldn't help worrying.

*Uh...* Vain replied, delaying an answer as I turned to stare sadly at Mushy's remains. What should I do here?

"What is it?" I asked, distracted.

*Ferrer is aroused.*

"Yes, that's probably why he left," I agreed and started placing Mushy's belongings back into the cooking pot. I didn't want to go through her things. Part of me was scared to see what she'd collected throughout her short-lived journey.

*And Iron is out,* Vain added.

"So he'd be easy to follow, wouldn't he?" I asked and moved to grab a strip of cloth from my bag. My bandages had all been used up, but I needed to cover my nose and mouth with something to deal with her remains. I was not leaving her leg out either. Gods knew where her arm went. I sighed and ran a hand through my hair.

*I'm a female bat,* she said, and I finally got what she was inferring.

"Oh! Ohhh…" I gasped. "Oh, then definitely not! Good call, Vain. That was a very good call. You… That could have been bad."

*Or good,* she replied, a shrug in her voice.

I furrowed my brows in thought. I wasn't sure how I felt about that. Was that cheating? I'd certainly never have sex with a bat, and Vain was kind of like my beast. I supposed Iron having sex with Vain would be acceptable. Ferrer would have to be ok with it though. It was also his body… I think?

I slapped myself in the face—hard. What in the name of the gods was I thinking? Cheating? Bat sex?

*What'd you do that for?* Vain squeaked.

"Mosquito," I lied outrageously. She hummed a disbelieving note but didn't challenge me. She knew there was no mosquito, but I'd stick to that story until the day I died.

I sighed heavily and moved to perform my morbid task. I didn't want to just leave Mushy's body out in the open like this. She'd tried to… I choked on a sob when I stared at the sack holding most of her remains. She'd planned it. She'd freed Ferrer's trapped beast knowing it would kill her.

My nose flared and started stinging along with my eyes. I sniffed wetly and looked around for something to scoop up the rest of her. She'd tried to get her whole body into that sack, and I was going to finish the job. I grabbed a smaller branch and a strip of bark, then scooped what had fallen out back into the bag. She looked less like human remains now and more like compost. I released a sobbing laugh when I spied a little earthworm slinking along beneath the surface.

"How'd you get in there so fast?" I asked it, wiping my tears away with a wrist. "Maybe you're her reincarnation. That would be appropriate, wouldn't it?"

It definitely wasn't her, but it was helpful for my heart to pretend. I lifted the sack and waddled over to where her leg was to add it to the bag. It was disgusting, but it had to be done. I gagged and kept my head turned throughout the majority of the process. I could only pray that I'd never have to do anything this nightmarish ever again.

Vain helped me find some water about a mile away, and I wished I'd waited for Ferrer. Bumping around in the pitch-black woods made it feel like a three-mile hike. I ended up giggling a lot with Vain because it got a little ridiculous with her calling out warnings left and right, usually too late. The laughter came easily because my nerves were absolutely shot. My body didn't know what to feel so my remaining energy came out a little crazed. I was happy for Ferrer, worried for Ferrer, and simultaneously heartbroken over Mushy's death. It'd all happened so fast that I felt like I needed a month to process everything.

I was going to just wash my hands, but ended up washing my entire body. Cleaning up human remains made me feel dirty all over, even if I hadn't really touched anything. I wanted it gone from my skin.

"I wish I could clean my memories too," I said sadly to Vain. "What a horrid way to die."

*Quick though,* she replied.

"Is it though?" I asked with a wince. "Wasn't she already rotting for months… or even years? I have no idea. We know so little about their kind."

*At least she had that cursed stone.* Vain sighed.

"She knew too much, Vain," I said as I rinsed the soap from my body. "Bone eater… She knew what he was before anyone else did. She knew about my eggs… She knew Ferrer was my fated mate…" I mulled it over in my head, trying to make sense of it. Why did she do all of this? I felt like it was all leading up to something, but what? "Oh Mushy, what was your game?"

*Maybe she could sense what the curse was hiding, since she was a rot-witch?* Vain guessed.

"Or…" I said, throwing up my hands with my own theory, "maybe she was a coven mother at some point. Who knows if rot-witches even have them? Coven mothers are the only ones allowed to scry. Maybe she looked ahead?"

*That's. Utterly. Terrifying,* Vain sputtered. *If Mushy knew the future, could she have changed anything?*

I swallowed hard. That was a good question. How much did rot-witches comply with Fate? Fate was… bigger than any god and not one to be disrespected. Not even coven mothers were allowed to interfere. They could watch some of what's meant to come, but they couldn't share it. They only used the ability to inform smaller decisions, things Fate wouldn't care about in the long run.

"That's a good point, Vain," I replied, trying to wipe the water from my skin before donning my tunic. I put my underwear back on but forwent the leggings, needing my legs to dry off a bit more before I attempted that hurdle. "They seem so wild. It's hard to imagine any hierarchy in a rot-witch coven. I don't even know if they have covens. We've certainly never encountered any in our recorded history." I stopped in my tracks and looked up at the stars through the canopy's black silhouette.

The cluster of stars in our galaxy was spread out over our heads. What must it be like to be one of the Sky Gods? They could see all so easily. I bet They knew where the rot hid… unless it was underground. A chill swept through me. If that was the case, I supposed the Earth Gods would know the answer to that question.

I shuddered again, but this time it was because I was actually freezing. "Cold, cold, cold," I muttered and started fumbling around in the dark with Vain's assistance.

"What are you doing? You're shivering and your hair's all wet," Ferrer's voice growled from behind me. It was the one warning I had before getting swept off my feet. A yelp flew from my lips, and I gripped at his arm and shoulder to steady myself.

"You scared me!" I gasped and held a hand to my chest. My heart was positively protesting the surprise.

"And why are you not wearing your pants?" he added with a frown. "You're going to get sick."

I didn't bother arguing with him. I just let my head thunk against his shoulder while he walked us back to Mushy's old campsite. There would be no complaints about the source of heat carrying me.

"How did the flight go?" I asked when he put me down and looked around the campsite.

"Calming," he said distractedly. "Where's her remains?"

"I put the rest of her in the bag… I couldn't find her arm, but I got her leg in there. Oh, you just had to remind me," I said, my voice trickling into a mumble. I pointed off to the right and added, "I moved the bag out a ways. It actually stinks a little less now, but it still needed to go."

Ferrer nodded slowly, then sighed and went to my bag. He yanked my blanket out and wrapped it around my shoulders. "You need to keep warm," he chastised with pressed lips, then started grabbing more wood for the fire. I kept my eyes averted from his own… branch, very much aware of his continued nudity.

I turned my back to him and sat by the fire to just feel my emotions. I could relax now, if only for a night. I wasn't sure if I could grieve yet. There was too much to sort out first.

"I'm sorry about earlier," Ferrer said flatly. "I didn't mean to do it. Touch you. It was…"

"It's… forget it," I replied before he could struggle further, and I waved a hand in dismissal. Now was not the time to talk about how much I'd liked it.

"Your feelings are complicated," he said, his voice much louder now as he sat behind me. I let him pull me back against his chest, and I clutched my blanket tighter, appreciating the warmth. I could see my breath puff in the frosty air and realized it was actually getting quite cold. Were we at a higher elevation?

"They are," I replied as he wrapped his arms under mine. "I'm sure yours are too, but I lack the advantage of being able to read them."

"Like I said… blame the Moon Goddess for that one," he replied dryly. "And yes… I am distracted." After sighing, he took a moment, then asked, "What now, Keid? Bury her? Do… you want to come back with me?"

I could tell he was nervous; I didn't need the mate bond in order to know that. He was very still as I thought out my answer. It didn't feel right to just bury her.

I shook my head. "No, I'm not done. I'm taking Mushy home. I said I was going to take her home, and I will. Maybe I didn't make it in time, but at least she'll be home. I can't just stop when I'm so close. It's just two more days. I can do that. There's got to be a town or house ahead."

"You think she has family?" he asked nervously, but I knew the real question he wanted to ask. I didn't know if he was too afraid to touch it, but I definitely knew that I was too afraid to answer it.

"It's possible. If so, they'd probably appreciate getting her back…" I answered quietly.

"Alright, well…" he murmured, resting his chin on top of my head, "let's get some rest and see what the path ahead looks like later."

"You're coming?" I asked, tilting my head up, not that I could see him.

"Of course. The remains will be heavy anyway. I'll carry them for you."

I let my head drift back down and stared blankly at the wavering dance in the firepit, mulling over his generous offer. Ferrer continued to surprise me.

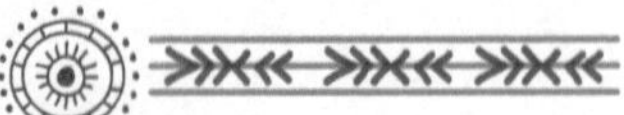 

# Chapter 22

## Ferrer

*Look, she didn't bring it up either,* Marrow argued calmly, which I did appreciate. Iron had enough energy for all of us.

*Maybe she doesn't want to hurt us until we get there! We really need to step up the courtship,* Iron said stubbornly.

*And I said I'd help with that. My breed is mostly monogamous. We know how to keep our breeding partners happy,* the ossifrage responded to my blood bat… with incredible patience.

*Yeah, well, it takes a skillful breed to keep an entire harem happy,* Iron defended.

*Keid's not a blood bat,* I pointed out, glancing down her damp, alabaster hair to her shoulder. *Nor is she a vulture.* I could just barely see part of my mark peeking out from underneath her tunic. My stomach twisted at the thought of her even considering its removal. Not knowing how she saw it was killing me. She had two more days to make up her mind. If I couldn't win her over by then…

I had to admit that worrying over Keid keeping my mark was helping to muffle my new, near-crippling identity crisis. Now was not the time to stress over what the shit I was. Was I a bat-shifter or a sky-shifter? Who the bloody shit knew? All I knew was that I could lose the most precious thing a shifter could be gifted. My meltdown could bloody well wait.

*We're losing him, Iron,* Marrow murmured.

*Ferrer, keep it together,* Iron snapped. *Don't think about meltdowns! We have a mate to woo, so woo her!*

*She's still cold. Whose wings are warmer?*

I hadn't even thought to bring Marrow's wings out, and I was worried they might not come out of my back like Iron's could. Would my arms shift instead? Bat-shifter or not, I had the same amount of fae in my blood as yesterday. I could push them out through my back… right?

*You know yours are,* Iron huffed.

*Not necessarily. Feathers are great for keeping in heat,* Marrow replied. *Flesh is also warm to the touch. Your wings are full of warm veins.*

*Not yet,* Iron muttered, disgruntled.

*Huh?* Marrow seemed to miss the wordplay entirely.

"Are you tired?" I asked Keid while trying to ignore the arguing in my head. I squeezed her with my arms as I asked, wanting her to sense my attentiveness. "Can I get you anything?"

"I'm… not so much tired as… It's hard to put into words," she answered quietly.

"Depressed? Anxious? Happy? Overwhelmed?" I supplied, reading her emotions as they tumbled through her body. It was like I could pluck a different one out at any moment, like her body was a tide pool and each wave brought something new.

Her head shook just the tiniest bit. "It's not fair…" she murmured.

"I'm sorry," I apologized and bit my lip with a fang in regret. I knew she disliked being on display like that. Keid didn't like being vulnerable, but I wished she didn't mind it with me. "Is it really so terrible for someone to know what you're feeling so they can better help?"

She didn't respond to my question. Instead, she replied with her own. "Would you answer any question truthfully, Ferrer? Would you do that no matter what?"

"I will," I said firmly, "except for one exception."

"What sort of instance would that be?"

"If your life's in danger, or more seriously, if I have a surprise for you, and I don't want it spoiled."

Keid burst into bewildered laughter at my odd joke, and I smiled when a flurry of positive emotions swelled in her. She was pleasantly surprised and amused, but my heart bloody flipped when I felt something else. The emotion grew stronger as she stopped chuckling and became pensive. It was the first time I'd noticed strong affection coming from her, and I tried to contain my excitement.

"So, what are you feeling now?" she asked, and though it sounded timid, I could hear the smallest smile in her voice.

My excitement turned into fear, and the smile dropped from my face. Ahhh… how could I explain this?

*Honesty,* Marrow said. *It's what she wants.*

*No, no, no, no, no…* Iron moaned.

I cringed and hung my head, staring at the mark on her shoulder. "I… am scared," I admitted reluctantly. Oh gods, what was I doing?

"Why?" The smile had faded from her voice as well.

Oh gods, oh gods, oh gods, she hated when I read her emotions! I nearly panicked and couldn't hear any of the advice that Marrow and Iron were throwing at me. There was no helping it. I was wingless and miles from the ground.

Since my brain stopped working, I just blurted out the truth. "I got excited because I thought you were growing fond of me just now, but I know you hate it when I read your emotions. I'm afraid that you'll now feel like you can't grow your emotions in private… and the truth is… you can't," I said in a rush. "N-not with me."

When she moved from me to stand, I covered my face and cringed. I did everything I could to keep from feeling her emotions, but there was no stopping it. There they were, right before me—embarrassment, horror, violation. The worst was the feeling of violation.

They abated when she turned in my direction. Now I just felt her frustration, then resignment, followed by a touch of pity. At the quiet sound of her knee popping, a small exhale, and a change in the air flow, I knew she was squatting facing me.

"Ferrer, look at me," she said through a world-weary sigh. I peeked through my fingers to find her giving me an odd look. After shaking her head, she briefly looked away and licked her lips. "Do I have to talk about them?"

"What do you mean?" I asked, drawing my brows in worry as I dropped my hands from my face. Her expression was grim, and her periwinkle eyes were pleading. She looked so bloody sad.

"Do I have to discuss everything I feel? Can we only talk about what I choose to share?" she clarified, looking more tired by the word. "I know you can't help it."

"Absolutely," I replied faster than a star's wink. "That is not a problem. I can definitely do that."

"And you have to share your feelings honestly if I ever ask. It's only fair," she asserted, eyes growing misty. "I cannot be hurt again. I would not survive it, Ferrer. You have to understand that. You have to."

"Completely," I breathed, waving my hands back in forth in complete surrender.

"Good." Keid stood and looked around the campsite. "I'm tired now. I'm going to sleep, and we can see what lies north when day hits." She began clearing a space by the campfire, making sure to pick a spot the farthest from where the rot-witch had died… the spot where she lifted my curse. I still had a hard time believing it. Perhaps it would sink in more after a night's sleep.

I watched her chuck away pinecones before settling, and I wasn't sure if I should ask my pressing question. I licked my lips and went for it anyway. "Do you want me to… keep you warm tonight?"

"Only if you want to," she answered shyly as she drew the blanket up to her chin. "It's cold…"

"Oh, I want to," I replied and jumped to my feet, likely sounding much too eager. I felt like I was constantly on the cusp of losing her, but that was the penalty for treating her like I had.

Noticing her averted eyes, I swiped my pants from the ground and slipped into them, realizing I hadn't dressed for her like a forgetful idiot. I needed to try something new as well to keep her warm.

Focusing on my back muscles, scapula, and spine, I called to Marrow for a little assistance. He helped me ease his wings out of my back for the first time, and I grunted, uncomfortable with how my human bones and muscles moved to accommodate them. The feathery appendages spread from my back, feeling heavier than Iron's wings. It was also unsettling to be without Iron's extra fingers and thumbs, and I made a mental note to make sure it was my bat who was out when I was climbing trees.

*Let me get fully settled—one second,* Marrow said, helping with the last adjustments. *This'll be easier next time…*

The wings were lighter now, like Marrow was carrying some of the weight, or maybe just having him made me stronger now. We'd have to do some testing later. The more I thought about it, the more exciting it was to have a new form to explore.

I cracked my neck and back, tested how the wings folded and approached Keid's sleeping spot. She was staring with wide eyes now, her gaze glued to Marrow's wings. Her soft lips then parted in awe, like she was searching for the right words.

"They're h-huge," she said, gaping.

I looked over my shoulder and stretched one so I could see it better. Yeah, they were definitely larger than Iron's… and made for gliding.

"Bulkier too, but not heavy—not anymore," I said and crawled to lay down next to her. "I think Marrow made me stronger. We'll have to do some exploration." I lay on my side and watched her stare at the wing I draped over us to keep in the heat. Some firelight flickered through the feathers, casting a weak orange glow across Keid. Her skin and hair caught the color so well. I wanted to tell her she was beautiful, but a movement interrupted me.

Keid reached up to stroke a tan feather, and I knew I had a struggle coming. Her eyes could have simply been dilated from the darkness, but as she lay on her back, there was no mistaking how the peaks under her tunic looked stiffer than normal. There was no mistaking the blood rushing to her cheeks, the thudding of her heart, or the shortness of her breath.

I could feel it across our bond, I could see it, I could hear it, and I could smell it. Keid was aroused, and there was nothing to be done. She lowered her hand from the feather and draped it across her chest, self-consciously hiding her breasts as subtly as she could. Staring at her profile, I saw the very moment she realized that I could tell without any visual cues. Her embarrassment trickled across, but I didn't say a word like I promised. If she didn't want to talk about it, we wouldn't. If she didn't want to act on it, I wouldn't prompt her. I'd keep her secrets from us both.

The only thing I could do was make her comfortable, so I acted like I didn't know. There was so much trust left to build, not that I didn't want to reach under her tunic and grope her. I still had not been able to explore her, and it was painful. I couldn't though. I couldn't pressure her if I wanted to keep her.

I could see Keid's eyes struggle along with her emotions. She was looking for a distraction but ultimately stumbled into the wrong memory. Her despair swelled, and all I could do was wait calmly for it.

"Mushy's dead," she blurted out in a sob.

"I know..." I said quietly and rested a hand on her arm. She immediately turned into me and started bawling, crying from the deepest part within her. I wrapped an arm around her and pulled, bringing her flush against me.

"She saved my life, you know," she moaned after a stuttering inhalation. As much as that piqued my curiosity, I just let the woman spill her tears on me. Her body convulsed with her gasping, racking sobs, and I tightened my grip, wanting her to feel safe.

Then… I listened. After a bout of crying, Keid started recounting her time in the lions' dungeon and castle, sharing through sobs how the rot-witch got her transferred when the guards began plotting the young woman's death. She described her years in the hospital with her wrist constantly being held over the chopping block. It was sickening to know that'd been the safer option.

It explained why she fought so hard to see the old woman home. Her adamance made more sense now. It was like our life debt to Queen Hekla. I understood it quite well, but our Queen Hekla was no rot-witch. The dubiousness was never there. Still though, Keid was working with whatever the gods happened to throw at her. Unfortunately, she'd gotten me thrown at her at the worst possible time.

At some point, Keid ran out of energy, and her body fell limp. As I slid a hand up to cup the back of her head, she leaned into me. She was looking for comfort, and I'd provide. I tucked her head under my chin and tightened my wing around us, keeping the chill at bay while we fell asleep.

I just hoped I could pass whatever tests were thrown at me over the next couple of days. I just wanted to bring her home. She'd been through enough.

I was tired. I was so wretchedly tired, and it felt like I had anchors tied to every single limb. Someone had been occasionally attempting to wake me, but all I could do was grunt and slip back into sleep. Anytime my brain got close to rising, it balked at the negative emotions waiting outside of rest. I didn't want to deal with them. Sleep was safe, and I hadn't had any nightmares throughout the night. Ferrer had been warm and welcoming, and as much as I might try to deny it, I was certain he'd chased away the bad dreams.

My stomach, however, was not on the same page as my brain. Something faintly sweet passed by my nose, and my nostrils perked up in curiosity. I could also smell the hand holding the food, and my brain sluggishly dragged itself towards the day.

"Flappy… flap…" I grumbled groggily when there was a cool breeze and the sound of light flapping. The flapping was then accompanied by a low chuckle. I was tempted to roll over and go back to sleep, but the smell made my stomach growl, and I forced open a dry eye.

Ferrer was kneeling at my side and holding a palmful of berries under my nose, a slight smirk tugging delicately at one of his cheeks. I sat up slowly, feeling incredibly parched, and rubbed my eyes to get some moisture flowing.

"Are these edible?" Ferrer asked me, glancing from my face to his palm. I held my hands out sleepily to receive the offering, and he filled them. "There's not much around here. All the berry bushes look spent."

"It's late in the season for them," I said, trying not to yawn. I was quite certain my breath was atrocious. "I'm surprised you found any at all." I picked through the berries, discarding any that I didn't recognize. "These are good, but I forgot what they're called," I mumbled at my palmful of little midnight-blue berries with small hairs. They might not look the most appealing, but they were sweet, nutritious little treats.

"Vain helped," Ferrer said simply. The berries were already rinsed too, and affection swelled in my heart for the bat-shifter. It was unfortunate that I couldn't keep such feelings to myself. I wished I could process them before he learned of them. I could only wonder why the goddess chose to keep humans from feeling their shifter mates' emotions… or perhaps the Earth Gods simply didn't want it for Their children. Who was to say?

Ferrer's words sunk in, and I looked back up at him. "Oh goodness, is it late?"

"The Sun God hasn't passed us by yet, but He's been up for a little while," Ferrer answered, his smile slowly fading as he looked at me. Oh, shit! I didn't thank him! My accursed brain was half asleep!

I pushed my blanket away, placed the edible berries in one hand and held out the other, showing trust in him to help me stand. When he pulled me up to my feet, I used the momentum to step closer and wrap my arms around his chest. I hugged him tightly, fearfully. I was scared, but his gesture made me want to go out on a limb even though the branch looked a little too young, too small to carry me.

I tightened my hold and squeezed my eyes tight, fighting through the fear that came with any form of initiation. I knew I'd hugged him before, but the hugs weren't exactly planned... not really. Fortunately, Ferrer responded quickly and wrapped his arms around me in turn. I breathed a sigh of relief. I knew he'd felt my fear... and in a way, I was grateful for the bond this time. I'd been too afraid, too shy to ask.

"Thank you," I said into his warm, hard chest. It was what I'd burrowed into last night and was starting to associate with safety. All of this was a risk, and I prayed that my branch would hold for a minute more.

"Of course," he replied and tightened his arms before releasing me. I was disappointed, but hugs could only last so long, I supposed. "Grab your bag. I want you to come with me," he said, staring intently at my face. He lifted Mushy's bag, and I noticed that he'd packaged the rest of her belongings and tied it to the sack.

I picked up my bag, bundled my blanket under an arm, and moved to follow him. He grabbed my hand and walked me north but was acting very odd. After every couple of steps, Ferrer would turn his head to stare at my face. I didn't have a free hand, but I was very tempted to search my face for leaves, mud, or twigs. What was he looking at?

"What?" I asked him after the fifth time, but he just shook his head.

"Just a minute, Keid," he said.

The area grew brighter, and I saw what Ferrer had been talking about last night. The woodland stopped, and there was a completely different wilderness ahead of us. There were hardly any trees, and whatever trees were visible had been dead for quite some time. The earth was dry too, and I hesitated when Ferrer tried to pull me past the border of the two environments.

He tugged on my arm, unaware that I'd stopped, and turned to face me with a surprised expression. I didn't want to go out into the new terrain, but I forced myself to, knowing that Mushy's home was this way. I let him lead me until we cleared the woodland's shadows and stepped right into sunlight. I turned my face toward the sun for a moment, enjoying a little warmth before I needed to figure out how to cover myself. The Sun God was not kind to my skin.

"Shitting. Stars," Ferrer cursed slowly, and I glanced back over to see what he was admiring. I started in surprise when I found him staring straight at me. He was looking at me like... well, like something that was pretty. My face flushed in embarrassment, not used to anyone staring at me like that. I dropped my bag onto the packed dirt and scrubbed a hand over my face.

"What's on my face, Ferrer? You keep star— Wait." I stopped talking when I realized that he was out in the sunlight and not squinting. I lamented in worry, "Oh, Ferrer, did you go blind again? Did you look at the sun?"

He shook his head, and his slow smile stretched into a grin. I shifted uncomfortably under his blazing red-brown gaze. His eyes were going to burn a hole in me if he didn't stop!

"What's on your face is your face, Keid, and that's what I'm looking at," he began, taking a step closer and placing both hands on my shoulders. I tilted my head back, shying from his intensity. "Keid, you were beautiful in the starlight, but, woman, you're an absolute star goddess under the sunlight. Look at you shine!"

It dawned on me what was happening, and I gaped. "You can see! You can see in the day because of Marrow!" I shouted in excitement. I was addressing my realization because his compliment was far too grand to accept. I was no goddess, not even in the darkest of rooms. Still, his words made my cheeks burn, and I felt an urge to cover them with my cold hands.

Ferrer just nodded absently at my words and continued to stare in wonder at me. Whatever he was seeing was certainly making him happy, but it was a little overwhelming for me.

"So many colors. I've never seen such… light," he murmured and reached to cup my face, but he hesitated when he realized he might be doing something unwanted. I nodded that he could continue, knowing that this was just a novelty. Ferrer then cupped my face and seemed to immerse himself in my features. He was so enthralled that I didn't even think he was aware of the roguish grin he was sporting.

I could only imagine how mind-blowing it must be for him to see in daylight now. I stared back into his excited eyes and noticed that his pupils did seem smaller. I'd occasionally catch a glint of pale gold and realized that Marrow was just underneath, helping him see.

Ferrer's features paused momentarily, like he was fighting an internal battle. After closing his eyes and exhaling, he looked at me in earnest.

"I hope, someday, that you'll let me kiss you," he murmured, then pressed his lips together, like he was worried he'd said too much.

I went rigid under his hands because his confession had struck me senseless. My stomach flipped at his words, and I was quite sure that stomachs were not supposed to be able to do that. Pancakes flipped, coins flipped, flippers… flipped.

*Ah, goodbye brain,* I grieved.

My mouth went dry, which was unfortunate because I needed to make some words. I opened my mouth to try to respond, but I had no idea what to say. I swallowed, licked my lips, and did the best I could, given the circumstances. "You've never been kissed?" I asked hoarsely. It was somewhat on topic.

His grin faded to a gentle smile, and he shook his head, then released my face. He looked almost sheepish, like he thought he'd made progress but not as much as he'd liked. I wished I could read him, but he did give me permission to ask, so m—

A throat clearing had us both starting, and Ferrer whirled around to see who'd arrived. His wings shot out to form a wall between me and the stranger… but it was Marrow's wings this time. I stepped back, worried I'd get slapped on accident by one of the big, feathery flappers.

"I… was not expecting… that…" a smooth voice stated, and it was one I immediately recognized. I peeked around a black-and-tan wing to verify.

"Bloody stars, Leofwine, you scared the bloody stars out of my bloody, shitty sky," Ferrer cursed, dragging his claws through his hair in relief. His posture relaxed, and he folded his wings, turning to look apologetically at me.

"You must have terrible weather," the dragon replied with a grin, not missing a beat.

"Dragon-shifter," I acknowledged nervously. This lithe, muscular male was both physically and politically powerful. That was all I really knew about him. He'd been the one trying to get permission to hunt slavers that crossed over into cat territory.

"Adelais, a pleasure," Ferrer said politely, his voice carrying a professional tone now. A female with blackberry curls was standing by the naked dragon-shifter, apparently unbothered by his nudity. I kept my gaze locked desperately on Leofwine's face, feeling like it'd be rude to look away from him in embarrassment. Also, I was pretty sure that the female was his mate, and I didn't want to receive a claw to the face if my eyes accidentally drifted in any direction.

"You know, Ferrer," the dragon said, looking shaken, "I had questions coming out here, but now I've got a whole new set of them."

"Yeah," Ferrer replied on a breath and strolled up to greet him. They clasped each other's forearms, and Leofwine spread his own dragon wings.

"Most importantly…" the male said, placing a finger to his lips, "whose wings are bigger now?"

The female, Adelais, scoffed and sent a look my way that said a great number of things. This dragon-shifter was the kingdom's spymaster, and I supposed he had no problem being this casual around another leader.

"At least they're not comparing something else," Adelais remarked dryly to me, then grabbed a pair of pants from her rucksack. She handed it to Leofwine, who looked at her in confusion. "Please, mate, the sweet one is human."

"Oh," he said and flashed a grin my way. "I don't think she has eyes for me anyway. Look at her neck, sex kitty."

"You know that's not what I meant." Adelais turned to address Ferrer. "Keyon's convinced he's not a full dragon-shifter. He may be half dragon, half windbag," she retorted with a laugh and bumped her hip against her mate's leg.

Despite everyone's relaxed attitude, I was getting extremely nervous, and Ferrer turned to look worriedly at me. "We should probably get to business. It's been a trying week," he said and gestured for everyone to take a seat in the shade. I breathed a sigh of relief, glad to be out of the sun's wrath. I'd been a minute away from hiding under my blanket.

"Last time I saw you, Ferrer, you were a bat-shifter," Leofwine said, crossing his arms. Adelais pulled out a ration similar to the ones that the castle had and offered it to me. I accepted it gratefully, finally getting an opportunity to eat the berries as well. I was famished.

"Rot-witch," Ferrer said flatly and patted the bag he'd been carrying. Fortunately, the scent-remover spell I'd placed on it was still holding.

"Are you fucking kidding?" Leofwine asked, his face dropping all gaiety. He looked very much like a spymaster now. His brows were drawn flat over his sharp, black eyes, and a white fang glinted smartly off his lower lip. Adelais glanced nervously at me, then back at Ferrer.

"To summarize," Ferrer said, holding his palms up, "I discovered that Keid was escorting this rot-witch home, which is how we got dragged into dragon territory, but she passed away last night. You know the witches were all just liberated, Leof?" The dragon nodded, his eyes flickering to me before going back to Ferrer, just like Adelais had done. "Keid had a life debt to repay, so even though the rot-witch never made it home, we're bringing the remains back. There was just no time to contact authorities. The entire situation just kept escalating unintentionally."

"So, wait," Leofwine said, momentarily closing his eyes in confusion, "the rot-witch gave you wings?"

"She undid part of the curse on me. It's the same curse that's on all bat-shifters," Ferrer reminded him impatiently.

"Right, right… Sky-shifters. I remember," Leofwine said and scratched at his clean-shaven chin.

"I still have Iron, so I'm still a bat-shifter, but I have Marrow now. A vulture." Ferrer shrugged and let his hands drop.

"It's got to be busy in there…" Leofwine sympathized with a raised brow. He frowned and tilted his head, asking, "She was captured in cat territory, but she said her home was… north?"

"She just… suggested her home was north. She never spoke—not really. She was voluntarily mute until she lost her… tongue," I supplied and finished my last berry. That was a memory I'd love to forget.

"Eugh…" Adelais gagged, and a shudder raked over her, prompting her mate to drag her to him.

"Keyon, Adelais, and I sorta ran into a rot-witch northeast of here. Well, we mostly missed each other, and she disappeared. Are you sure she wasn't taking you back to a coven?" the dragon asked.

"Wouldn't you know if there was a coven on your lands?" Ferrer inquired curiously.

"To be honest, we don't go that far north. Our people don't settle here, so we don't use resources on it. What you see here goes on for days and days, my friend," Leofwine replied. "Dry, useless land."

It was both those things and more. I held a grimace back as I looked at the dirt beneath me. It made me feel like I was sitting on glass, perched above absolute nothingness. The sensation almost gave me vertigo.

"What's wrong?" Ferrer asked, turning to me. I jerked a little bit, startled, then worried at my hands. There weren't any witches here to back up my claim, and I didn't want to sound silly.

"You said it felt unnatural," I reminded him. He nodded and prompted me to say more. "It's not natural. The earth here is… empty. I don't like it." Vain clawed gently at my neck, silently echoing my sentiment.

"Empty?"

I didn't reply. What I thought had been a slow drain from standing in the sun was actually the sensation of my eye enchantment finally fading. I whimpered under my breath as my vision blurred, and I once again suffered the shrinking of my immediate world.

"Keid? What's wrong?"

I felt around in the dirt, but there was nothing there. I couldn't feel my gods, and I couldn't fuel my magic. This land was dead, which was absolutely impossible. What was going on here?

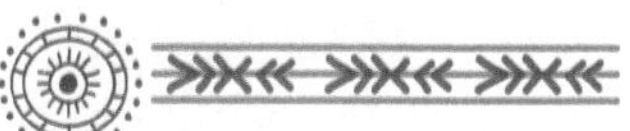
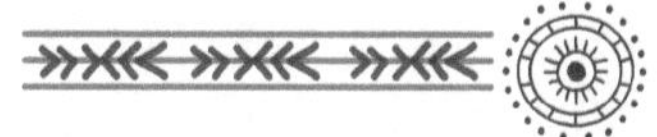

# Chapter 23

## Keid

I grew a little panicky as I raked across the hard, parched ground, scraping away sunbaked roots and chunks of rock. Nothing. There was nothing here but silence. I'd never encountered or heard of anything like this in my life.

Fear trickled down my spine, making the hairs on the back of my neck stand on end. The fear turned into panic, and I gripped my chest. In the corner of my eye, I could see the others getting to their feet to surround me, but that only made me feel like I couldn't draw in enough air.

"Keid. Something's wrong with her," Ferrer faintly said, sounding alarmed.

I jumped to my feet and ran back to the woods as fast as I could, leaving my belongings behind because they'd only hinder me. I slid to a stop and fell to my knees as soon as I crossed the threshold. The gods came back, so I pressed my cheek against the ground and dug in my fingers to absorb what I could. Vain finally caught up to me, spooked by my sudden fleeing.

I wanted to rip my clothes off to drink with as much of my skin as possible, but knowing that there were people around kept me from doing it. I wouldn't die with empty reserves, regular humans survived just fine, but not feeling the presence that'd been there my whole life was traumatizing. Even when I wasn't on soil, anything from the earth gave me a sense of the Earth Gods. The castle stone had been just fine, and I'd been allowed into the gardens to absorb whatever I needed to do my witchwork.

"Keid, please talk to me. You're scaring me," Ferrer's voice said. He sounded closer this time, and a broad hand eased onto my back. It caressed downward as the male stroked me, and it helped calm. He hiked my tunic up to place his hand on my lower back, rubbing and offering the soothing sensation of the mate bond. A huge breath escaped through my lips as I stabilized, and I blinked my eyes open for the second time today.

"Sorry," I whispered, and he slid his hand from my tunic to place it over mine.

"What happened?" he asked, tucking a rogue strand of hair behind his pointed ear so he could see better.

"I couldn't... feel anything out there. There was no magic in the ground. The Earth Gods were just... gone. That place is a void, Ferrer," I said and slowly got up from the ground.

Ferrer's nose flared, and he looked down with a pained expression. "Ah, Keid..." He squatted and brushed dirt from my knees. I winced at a sting and discovered a torn legging over a skinned knee. The area was a mess of dirt and blood.

"Shit," I breathed, then looked out into the dead lands. My bag was out there, but so was Mushy's home. I'd found myself in quite the conundrum. "What am I to do?"

"How do I take care of this?" Ferrer asked, looking up at me in worry.

"I'll be fine. I just need to clean it and put on a topical."

"I'll get your bag."

"No, no, Ferrer. Let's... go back. I just need a minute," I said, placing a hand to my forehead. Once I felt that I was completely steady, I renewed the enchantment on my eyes. Oh, to see clearly was a blessing. Thank the gods for magic.

"I…" Ferrer looked torn, like he was keeping something from me.

"What?" I asked, frowning. "Tell me what you're feeling."

"I'm feeling frustration, Keid," he snapped, then scrubbed his hands over his face. "I… don't want you going any farther out there."

I had to give him credit for being honest. "I want to take her home, Ferrer, like I said I would," I asserted. "I just need to get used to… whatever that is out there." I pointed to the withered landscape. "I won't die without access to magic. It's just… anxiety inducing. I was surprised and taken off guard. I won't panic again."

Ferrer paced a couple times, his glossy ossifrage wings twitching with his anxiousness. He turned to face me, stared at me for a long moment, then dropped his shoulders in defeat. "And I'm going with you, Keid, like I said I would." He stood straight again and crossed his arms, like he was challenging any argument.

To be honest, I was fucking relieved to hear that. I turned to face the deadlands and reminded myself that I had considerable restraint. Maybe I couldn't fool Ferrer into thinking I was alright, but I knew I could keep myself from fleeing. I just had to consider this a test of endurance. In all things but love, I believed my mind was strong.

"I can persevere," I stated, not really speaking to myself or Ferrer. Perhaps I was warning the deadlands or telling the Earth Gods I'd return safely. I stepped up to the threshold and crossed it, wincing at the sensation of nothing beneath my landing foot. It was almost like stepping off a cliff, but there was dirt, and it caught me nonetheless.

I took a second step, then another until I was walking at a steady pace toward the dragon, his mate, Mushy's remains, and our belongings. Our visitors perked up at my approach, and I held my hands up in supplication.

"I'm sorry for the alarm," I stated, projecting confidence though it was false. "There is something blocking the Earth Gods in this area, and I was taken by surprise over the loss of Their presence. I think that's why everything is dead. I had to replenish my reserves."

"Should we visit the Solar Coven?" Adelais asked, turning to Leofwine.

"It seems too big for them to not have known about it, especially considering the vantage they have, but we should definitely get that answer for ourselves. I can't recall a time where this area hasn't been like this. I always assumed it was natural, especially with so much fog and cloud cover," the dragon-shifter said thoughtfully. "It extends past our territory. We have everything we need with the land we have, so we never explored past here. If we have, it's not in any records I've seen. We could interview the castle scholars. We have some historians."

"Seems like a good lead," Adelais murmured, and Leofwine grinned at her.

"Sounding like a true spy, sex kitty." He grinned and slapped her on the bottom. I raised a brow at this, and the dragon just laughed at my expression, which was possibly a little judgmental. "Oh, you don't even know, woman. She's much more violent than me in the bedroom."

Adelais gasped and smacked him on the arm, forcing him to feign some deep injury. He gathered himself just as quickly and pointed to Ferrer, turning serious. "I've dismissed that incident you had with our reinjeri, but I'm going to need the full story later. I'm trusting you to cooperate with us in good faith for traveling through our territory without communication."

"That is something I am happy to give. I was not pleased with how this played out," Ferrer replied in an equally professional tone, and I knew I shouldn't feel guilty, but I did feel a tiny bit sorry for the trouble that came out of walking Mushy home. It was kind of his fault though… No, it was definitely his fault. I doubted they would have batted an eye at Mushy and me… unless those border guards knew what a rot-witch was. I supposed there could have been trouble…

"That being said," Leofwine added, softening as he looked at me. "I'm sorry to hear about your injury. Our reinjeri acted with unnecessary violence. I know you've been told, but she is facing consequences."

"Thank you," I replied politely. Perhaps that tail swing wouldn't have been a big threat to a shifter, but I sure as shit could've broken something. I ran my fingers over the abrasions on my face. They'd scabbed and were healing. Now I just had to treat my bloody knee.

"We'll have to pass this way on our return. Should I report to someone or send word once I return to the colony?" Ferrer asked.

I noticed he said 'I' instead of 'we,' and I could only criticize myself if that made me feel a little bad. I was becoming less torn, but the hurt was hanging in there… if just by a thread. The fear was diminishing too, which was a relief. It'd been a colossal burden.

"I'm going to station two dragons here to receive your report and take you home, for multiple reasons," he informed, ending on a dry note. "Any idea when your return will be?"

"She seemed to suggest it was two days…" I replied, putting my fingers to my lips as I planned it. "Drop off her remains, maybe a night spent in the area to rest, then a two-day walk back here…"

"I'll have them here in five days, and they'll wait for two. If you don't return, they'll report it to me, and we'll assume something went wrong. We'll alert your colony and go from there," Leofwine formulated with a nod.

"If you could also please send word to the other coronels today…" Ferrer requested hesitantly, and Leofwine grinned.

"Of course!" he said and gripped forearms with Ferrer. He nodded politely to me and led his mate away with a hand on her lower back. "Let's go, sex kitty."

He tossed her up surprisingly high into the air, shifted, and caught her with his svelte black dragon before she landed. I couldn't for the life of me tell if she'd shrieked in delight or horror, but I had a feeling he'd pay for that later. Leofwine's dragon launched into the air, blowing only a touch of dirt and dust our way, and the last thing I heard was Adelais's screaming giggles.

I stared up at them as they slowly gained altitude, and all I could say was, "Wow."

"She's a tough female," Ferrer said from behind me. "Don't worry about her. She's not human."

I knew he didn't mean it like that, but it still cut. I looked down at my bloody knee and suddenly felt incredibly worthless. I turned, but I couldn't meet Ferrer's eyes. He knew what I was feeling, and like he promised, he didn't say anything. In the corner of my eye, however, I did notice his wince.

I grabbed my bag and licked my lips as I glanced at the sunny deadlands. There was some fog on the horizon like Leofwine had mentioned, but there wasn't really any cover from the Sun God. Ferrer looked where I was staring and scratched his jaw.

"Perhaps nighttime would be better for traveling," he stated. "I may have better eyesight, but my skin is still… sensitive. Marrow can't give me different skin." He looked at me with a grim smile. "I imagine it's not much better for you."

I shook my head and gave a bitter laugh. "Assuredly not."

"Do you want to go back to the woods until the stars come out?" he asked, gesturing back the way we'd come. I eyed the tree line nervously, knowing that crossing that threshold a third time would be just as difficult. I already wanted to go back, but I didn't want to fall to temptation. I also really wanted to complete this errand and move on with my life.

I tried to glance at Vain to see what she thought, but she was dead to the world again, hidden under my hair. I could sympathize. Our sleep schedule had been all over the place, and she was exhausted from her own adventure.

I leaned out from the shade of the shallow outcrop and stared into the distance again. There were a couple places that looked like halfway decent areas to stop, so we could get in a little walking today. I could use my blanket like a shawl, but Ferrer was shirtless. I cleared my throat, not really minding that… personally.

"If you're worried about me, Keid, I can fly a bit as Marrow. It'd give me an opportunity to see what's ahead. His eyes are good," Ferrer said with a casual shrug. I was also wide awake and didn't really want to sleep yet.

"Alright," I answered, making a judgment call. "Let's go as soon as I get my knee cleaned." I hated bringing attention to my human weaknesses now, but it was what it was. I sat down with my bag and pulled out my little medical kit. The bandages and cotton were gone, but I could make do without them.

"Can you show me?" Ferrer asked, squatting in front of me. "I need to learn."

"Shifters still get injuries, don't they?" I asked, feeling like this shouldn't be completely alien to him.

"Yes, but I want to make sure," he replied firmly. Ah, that was accursedly sweet, and it really pleased the shit out of me.

"Alright," I agreed, letting my guard down a little more. I handed him my canteen and said, "Rinse first. There's dirt, and that means germs. Get as much off that way, then we can clean with soap."

Ferrer followed my instructions, his brows furrowed in concentration as he poured the water over my knee. I held the split in my legging open so he could wipe away as much dirt as he could, then handed him the soap. After washing and rinsing it one more time, the skinned section started oozing more blood. Instead of looking tempted, Ferrer just looked bitter.

"What are you feeling?" I asked curiously as I searched for my purifying topical. I pulled out the little tin and handed it to him.

"I'm angry."

"Why?" I tilted my head and studied his expression as he brushed aside a strand of his hair, then opened the tin.

"Because you look and smell delicious, and I hate that. I don't want to hurt you again. I don't want to feed on you. It makes me furious with myself." His tone was clipped. It was obvious he hadn't liked sharing that.

"Thank you for being honest. It means a lot," I said and placed a hand on his to show my genuine appreciation. He just swallowed hard and gestured to the cream.

"What is this? Do you eat it?"

I laughed and shook my head. "Definitely not. That goes on the injury. It helps prevent infections. I assume you know what an infection is."

"I knew someone who was like one," he muttered under his breath as he applied the cream. Another laugh burst from my chest, and I jabbed a finger at him.

"Don't speak ill of the dead," I warned, but he just let a tiny grin slip onto his face and closed the tin.

"You know she would have laughed at that," he growled playfully, looking through a couple loose strands of hair at me.

I looked over at the sack that held her remains and sighed. Yes, I believed she would've.

When I helped Keid back to her feet, she gave me yet another hug in thanks. I was elated with how she slid her arms around my chest and pulled herself to me. It was given freely, and I basked in the novel affection I felt coming from her. It seeped straight from her soul to mine, like how the Sky Gods quenched the Earth Gods. I could only hope it'd become just as regular.

I was no longer in a rush to let her go. When she'd hugged me earlier, I was anxious to see how she'd look in the sunlight. Dawn had brought a glorious surprise when Marrow's eyes settled in properly, and I was speechless because it felt like we'd entered a new realm. I knew that some light changed the colors of things, like how torchlight bathed a room in orange, but the sun… It was a true testament to the power of the Sun God that He could amplify every color I'd ever known into something new, special, and powerful.

So, I'd nearly dragged Keid out of the shadows and into the sun. I couldn't wait to see her as the gods, shifters, and humans did, bathed in the light of day. I looked down and tentatively raised a palm to stroke the back of her head, mindful of her shoulder where Vain was resting. Her hair caught the light and filtered it so finely that a variety of the subtlest hues danced in the sea of white. Such small clusters of colors… They were beautiful.

Little did she know that she was the brightest, most colorful thing I'd ever seen in my life. I'd wanted to share that, but Leofwine's arrival had not been ideal in its timing. I supposed it was just as well; my confession about wanting to kiss her had sent her into a fluster. There'd been no helping it. Both Marrow and Iron had been pressing me to share my desire, such was its strength.

Keid tightened her embrace, and I felt her not wanting to let go, but she was also feeling embarrassed about it. It was like she was hiding herself against me. I had to admit that it was a little cute.

I decided to do it for her and pulled away with a smile. "I'm going to take Marrow up now, and we'll meet by the farthest hill? I won't stray far, I promise."

She swallowed and nodded with a serious look on her face. I didn't like the fear I felt from Keid, but if she wanted to walk a little, I couldn't be out here with her. I had to fly away, and it made me sorry in so many ways.

I grabbed her face one more time, got my fill of all the blues and purples her eyes had to give, and backed up to shift, leaving her to blush furiously over how I'd stared. Kicking my pants off made her even more flustered, and I loved it.

Turning into Marrow was faster this time, and since Iron had his own energy to offer, the transformation was brutally swift. It'd almost given me a head rush! I shook it off and reached with

Marrow's claws to grab the sack of Mushy's remains. There was no doubt that he could carry it.

I relaxed and let him take over his body. He turned to look at Keid, said, *Meet you soon, pretty mate,* then launched into the sky. His wings pumped to elevate us, and I enjoyed the peaceful experience until something hit us—a force that took both Iron and me by surprise.

*Shitting staaaaaaars!* Iron screamed as hot air caught under our feathers and shot us up into the blue wilderness. If I'd been in my human body, it was possible I would've had a small heart attack, but Marrow was full of joy. He entered this space, the highest of mortal highs, like he was coming home—a true master of the daylight.

*Blood clots, blood clots, blood clots,* I cursed nonstop, seeing how high we were from the ground. Iron and I had never flown this high, and I'd no idea that we could've ever been intimidated by something like this. It was surreal.

We were bathed in light, color, and heat, and I could only wonder if this was a small fraction of how the Sun God felt. He'd been terrifying since we met Him, and He still was, but now we found ourselves in a space where we could safely admire Him and the many-colored facets of the Sky Gods.

*You are both me,* Marrow reminded us. *You'll get used to it.*

*Ahhhhhh...* was all Iron could contribute.

*We do need to find a source of food for Keid,* Marrow stated, able to think while Iron and I fumbled to function.

*I'd not forgotten. I'd considered quickly returning to the woods to grab several birds...* I informed, forcing myself to get used to what I was seeing. Part of me wanted to turn away from his vision, feeling overwhelmed by the alien scenery.

*We need water too though...* Iron reminded, and Marrow hummed in acknowledgment. He banked toward the right, gliding east in search of something that could sustain us. The heat carried us higher, and we spied a canyon farther east, but it was inconveniently far for water trips. I had to conserve my energy too.

*Maybe there's a split,* I murmured, trying to see where it ran north. Turned out, it did feed a small river that ran northwest, and it was a good sign that there were people living north from Keid's location.

*Where there's water, there's life,* Marrow commented.

*Usually,* Iron muttered. *This land looks as lifeless as our mate describes. Look at all that dirt and dead wood.*

The scenery was barren as far as Marrow's eyes could see, which was bloody far. The beige wasteland stretched to the horizon, but at least there was water.

*Water fowl,* Iron reported. *Get some for our mate. She'll need... four maybe?*

*I don't hunt...* Marrow replied anxiously. *I prefer to clean up other predator's messes.*

*You still have talons,* Iron said.

*Can you dive and grab one?* I inquired. *Then I can shift and make the kill if you're unsure. If not, I can shift back now.*

*I'll... learn how to.* Stubbornness flared in him for the first time.

*For Keid,* I said, finishing his thought. We seemed to all be on the same page.

*Yes.*

We settled on the canyon cliff to drop off the sack before attempting our first hunt. The birds were oblivious so far, bathing and grooming as they bobbed along the lazy current. This was going to be a whole new test of our skills.

*Alright! Let's go, go, go!* Iron shouted, wanting to get this over with so we could bring our prizes back to Keid. His enthusiasm was short-lived when Marrow dropped off the cliff and fell into a dive. The regret was instantaneous.

I tried to block out Iron's aggravating hollering and focused on the small flock of waterfowl that was scattered across the surface of the canyon river. The birds were alerted to his descent, and though they were startled, they didn't seem to scatter far. Perhaps they weren't afraid of vultures? That was convenient.

I shifted back into my human form, keeping Marrow's wings to aid in my pursuit… and not dying. The birds now seemed to take me very seriously, and I couldn't hold back a thrilled bark of laughter. My ossifrage had gotten me close to one fowl, which I snatched and killed in a snap. Iron boosted my speed as the birds dispersed, and I was able to snag two more before the rest had successfully escaped me.

I landed on the river bank and plopped down to catch my breath, laughing heartily at the rush of the hunt. It'd been an entirely new experience under the light of day, a completely different challenge, and I reveled in the resulting rush. I felt profoundly alive, refreshed, and it was bloody amazing.

Even the blue of the sky seemed to celebrate our big step. What a miracle color was to be able to make me feel… more. The only thing missing was Keid sharing this moment with me. I couldn't wait to go back and tell her all about our first hunt under the Sun God. I thought it was impressive!

After a couple minutes of tolerating the light on my pale skin, I shifted back into Marrow, who didn't immediately grab the fowl we'd caught. Instead, he prowled around the riverbed, searching for something. I grew suspicious when he wandered toward some red soil that was being lapped at by the water's edge. What was he doing?

*So many factors in wooing a female,* he said, then flopped over to roll in the stained water. *I will help with our mate.*

*What the shit are you doing?* I complained, absolutely appalled. *You're getting us filthy, Marrow!*

*Oh no, Ferrer, iron makes us look nice.*

*I do, don't I?* my bat agreed.

*What?* I shouted in bewilderment and tried to yank control back from Marrow, but he was holding me off just as stubbornly.

*Look, this shows that we have great sense, alright? The ladies approve, just trust me on this,* he argued, splashing around to get as much of the red-stained water on him as possible. *The stain will look quite good. She'll love it. She'll love the way it looks. I promise.*

*I don't think it'll have the same effect on me! And Keid isn't a bloody vulture!* I growled as he ducked under one last time. I finally wrested back control of our body and floundered from the river as an extremely pissed-off bird. Waddling back to land, I shook out Marrow's feathers and groaned at the red stain on them. *This shit better not transfer onto my human body, Marrow!* I snapped, furious.

*I don't know... could be nice,* Iron mused, always ready to try anything for a chance at sex.

*Don't you bloody start with me, Iron,* I snarled, ambling back to retrieve the fowl. The day was completely ruined. Sure, I'd have some fine fare for Keid, but there was no way she'd give me a second look if I returned orange. *Shit! I'm so pissed!*

The walk should have been easy, but it was anything but a stroll. Though the path was straightforward, and there wasn't any undergrowth to trip me like there had been in the redwood forest, it was incredibly stressful. I'd also become ridiculously sweaty from the combination of anxiety and being huddled under the blanket. I hadn't even traveled halfway to my destination when I accepted that this had been an extraordinarily bad idea.

It was late in the afternoon when I'd arrived at the place where Ferrer said to meet, a very small outcrop at the base of a rolling hill. The shade was a little more generous with the sun dipping down on the other side, and I immediately threw my blanket onto the ground so I could huddle on it.

I hugged my knees and tried to catch my emotional breath. My mental stamina had been severely tested, and I'd fought the impulse to run the entire time. I really wished Ferrer could've been able to walk with me, and I kicked myself for not waiting until dark. Rushing had not been wise.

Rubbing my eyes, I scanned the skies for a while until I spied a large bird. I frowned when it looked blurrier than it should, and I rubbed my eyes once more. Oh gods, was my enchantment wearing out already? Was this land sapping my reserves? That was not good…

I pushed that worry aside when Marrow landed because something looked… very off about him. Even while I was digging in my bag for Ferrer's pants, I couldn't keep my eyes off his stained feathers. Was that blood? Why were all of Marrow's white feathers that color? It looked like he'd bathed in either blood or rust!

"Did you get hurt? Are you alright?" I asked, alarmed. It didn't really look like blood, and it was too uniform to be from an injury, but I didn't know what else it could be. "What happened out there?"

Ferrer shifted back in a severe manner, forgoing keeping any wings, and my alarm turned into shock. The male looked furious, scowling as he dropped three waterfowl at my feet. He set aside Mushy's sack and waved away the proffered pants.

"You're orange!" I gasped, dropping the clothes onto my backpack and standing to go to him.

*Surprise…* Iron said weakly.

*Don't you l—* Marrow began and Ferrer growled an interruption.

"You don't get to talk, Marrow!" he snapped, and I stared at several veins that were bulging in his neck from his anger.

"What…" I began, tilting my head as he stomped away from me, stark naked.

"My skin got stained," he growled. "I don't want to explain it. I went to try to wash it off but couldn't get it completely off."

I caught up to him and grabbed his hand to stop his grumpy departure. "Let's try my soap," I offered, keeping my voice gentle even though all I wanted to do was cackle at the top of my lungs. He was so angry over such a small thing, my goodness.

His shoulders dropped, and I took that as a sign that he'd follow. I pulled him to where I'd set up camp and sat us down on the blanket. Looking for my soap and canteen, I glanced at the birds he'd brought once more.

"Thank you for the game, Ferrer. They will make delicious meals," I stated with a warm smile, trying to cheer him up. "You might even like the bones. Between you and me, nothing will go to waste," I added with a laugh.

The large male was very nearly pouting now, and when he reached for the soap in my hands, I fended him off. "You can't even see. I'll try," I asserted and lathered a small cloth to scrub at a shoulder. I hoped this would work or I'd have an extremely disgruntled shifter to contend with for the rest of the trip.

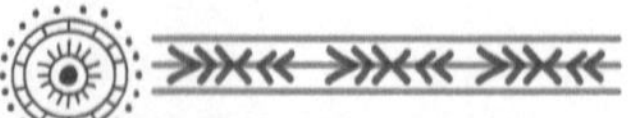 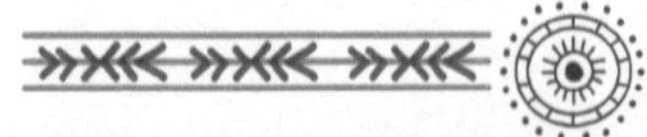

# Chapter 24

## Keid

"Going to need to fill the canteen soon," I said quietly, just to have something to say as I scrubbed a damp, soapy cloth against the back of Ferrer's shoulder. His torso and arms had received the worst of the rust-colored stain, and I hoped I had enough water for it all. I needed to keep some for drinking. "Getting a little low."

"I can refill it," he answered flatly. "We'll also hit a river tomorrow that we should be able to follow. I have no doubt that wherever Mushy lived, it relied on that source of water."

"You'll have to thank Marrow for me," I said, scrubbing at his prominent back muscles. I ran the cloth around his shoulder blade, pressing in with a single finger to swipe down a sharp groove. Oh gods, why was I doing this? Could I explain this to myself? This was far too arousing. I had to focus or he'd notice. Oh gods, maybe he already had. Curses!

"Marrow deserves nothing," Ferrer growled under his breath. Hmm. Maybe he was responsible for the orange-tinting fiasco. I wanted to ask what happened, but I decided to wait until he was in a better mood. Perhaps he'd be able to laugh about it then.

The male reached for one of the birds and began plucking it violently. I grimaced at his hostile preparing but deeply struggled to contain my amusement. Even though I was behind him, I was too self-conscious of my lips trying to twitch into a smile. It very much looked like he was pretending that bird was his ossifrage. Feathers were getting everywhere. Everything but the bird was flying.

"You need to eat, Keid," he grumbled. "I'll do this."

"That's fair," I replied with a wince, hoping he wasn't paying attention to my new struggle—the one where I was trying not to laugh. I couldn't help it. His grumpiness was hilarious to me for some reason. "Why are you so mad?" I asked, about to lose it. "This isn't that bad of a stain."

I mean, it was pretty bad.

"It looks stupid," he grunted so lowly that I almost missed it. I scrunched up my nose, desperately holding back a snorty, raucous laugh. My stomach clenched, and I was forced to release my next breath through my mouth as slowly as possible. I had to contain myself!

"If I have to be 'white' my entire life, you can handle being orange for a day," I replied with an accursed waver in my tone, feeling like I was about to die if I didn't laugh.

"You're exactly the color you're supposed to be." His response was slightly less cranky. "Done."

"Hmm?" I asked and looked at what he was holding. The bird was already plucked and gutted, but the skin was horribly ripped. That meant a dry meal.

Still though, the sight of the abused corpse did it. My scrunched-up, tear-soaked, and likely red face gave as I collapsed into high-pitched, uncontrollable, breathy giggles. I fanned my face as I cried, unable to control literally anything. Ferrer stood abruptly, and I felt terrible, but I continued to lose my mind.

"I'll get more water… you should cook it…" he mumbled and gestured in a random direction. "Plenty of dead wood and grass." He wasn't addressing my laughter, and it was probably the most gracious thing he'd ever done. That thought sent me into a new bout.

I tried not to stare at his butt as he stood, unable to get flustered through my mirth. Even though I was cackling, I could still appreciate a nice butt. Without another word, Ferrer shifted into his ossifrage, grabbed the canteen, and took off to refill it.

"Phwooo..." I breathed out and held my breath, but then burst into a new set of giggles. Oh, poor Ferrer. I felt so bad. It took me a minute, but I finally giggled out the last one. The giggles. The giggles! Once they started...

Goodness, I didn't recall the last time I'd smiled and laughed this much. I stared at his blurry form in the sky and sighed. My defenses were crumbling.

I took the opportunity to quickly wash some critical areas on my body, feeling a bit in need myself. I left my leggings off, leaving my tunic to act as a short dress while I set up a fire for our delicious, very dry meal. I'd agonized over it, but I also forwent my underwear. Part of me was hoping he'd lose control after eating, and I was a little sickened by that thought. It was the quickest I'd ever sobered after laughing.

Why couldn't I just ask for what I wanted? After how he'd changed his behavior and started treating me like royalty, I should feel comfortable enough to at least... urge him. I didn't quite believe that I was beautiful, but I was starting to believe that he saw me that way. Still, I was restrained by fear.

Ferrer returned and eyed my legging-less legs but didn't say anything. I was relieved to have him back for another reason. The ground continued to unnerve me, and his presence helped. He handed me a full canteen with a weary smile, and I returned it in gratitude. When he sat down, I continued with my ministrations on his back, scrubbing the stain away the best I could.

"I'm sorry for laughing," I apologized, trying to sound as regretful as I felt.

He just grunted and pointed at the bird. "Is that done yet?"

"The legs might be..." I replied, uncertain.

"I'll check. Clean please," he ordered, holding his hands out for me. After washing, he used a claw to swipe a line down the meat and nodded. "Done."

I glanced over and was suitably impressed. Looked like he remembered. That moved me quite a bit, actually, and I knew my affection for him was deepening. My fear of him reverting into a cold person was dissolving faster and faster.

"I'll feed you while you work. You need to eat." His tone was gentle now, likely having felt the change in me. He sure was adamant about me eating as well. I wondered how much longer it'd take for him to be able to sense a pregnancy.

Feeling mostly satisfied with his back, I moved to take care of his chest. He could absolutely do this himself, but it was too hard to resist the temptation of my plan. I knew it was silly. If I asked, he'd probably have me on my back in less than a heartbeat, but I didn't want to ask! If he lost control, it'd make me feel beautiful again.

Gods, I was pathetic, and my head was a complete mess. I was simply not good at this. I'd been fooled before… and my self-esteem had just reverted to what it'd been before my first lover.

When I moved to Ferrer's front, he crossed his legs and tucked them closer to let me sit before him, but when he noticed I planned to straddle his lap, he straightened them again. I couldn't read his accursed face; his expression was inscrutable. Curses!

I sat unnecessarily on his naked lap. It was obvious that he hadn't put his pants on because he didn't want them stained. Or maybe it was just an excuse to be naked. I wasn't going to complain about it anymore. I was getting used to it with him, and it only made my goal easier to achieve.

When I started scrubbing his hard pec, he leaned over to tear a leg off the roasted fowl. He hissed, probably not expecting it to be as hot as it was and blew on his fingers before attempting again. He moved to palm my hip so he could steady himself while leaning over, and I was pretty sure it was just an excuse to feel for any underwear. I tried to hide my satisfaction at that, but I had a feeling that I was an open book to him.

He held the cooked leg up to my mouth as he maintained his neutral expression. I wished I knew what he was thinking! I supposed I could ask. Maybe in a minute… I couldn't deny that the mystery was a little exciting to me.

"Can you take the skin off?" I asked as I moved my cloth to his other pectoral. "I'm not fond of it."

"I'll remember that," he said gently, almost affectionately. Gods, that was arousing too. He peeled the skin off and hesitated before bringing it to my mouth. "This work?"

I nodded and opened my mouth to take a bite. I wanted to salt it, but I didn't want the interruption. The flavor of this moment was much more delicious than what any seasoning could accomplish.

I hid a smile and chewed on the dry meat before he offered another bite, gazing a little more intently at my face. In the corner of my vision, I could see the way he stared at me, and it pleased me a great deal. After a couple more bites, his cock brushed the inside of my thigh. He likely noticed the sudden spike in my arousal from that, and I quickly moved on to scrub his tense abdomen.

When I finished eating the roasted meat from the fowl, he picked idly at the remaining bone, staring almost as intensely at the food as he'd stared at me. "What do you want, Keid?" he asked, and the directness startled me. I hadn't really expected him to ask about my intentions.

"To get you clean," I replied, sounding a little terser than I'd liked. My stomach clenched from nerves, and I was suddenly uncertain about this strategy.

"Without underwear?"

I swallowed heavily and licked my lips anxiously. "I was cleaning them. Why? Is that a problem?"

He shifted uncomfortably under me, and his erection slid up my thigh to press against my sex. My face flushed as I tried to pretend that I didn't know I was straddling the hard, hot length of his wicked log. Oh my gods, what was I doing? This must look so fucking stupid! This was backfiring, and I was facing humiliation.

"Clots, Keid," he swore and looked dubiously at the bone in his hand. My plan was obviously… obvious at this point. I swallowed again, ignoring how his breath began to accelerate. His chest and the packed muscles of his abdomen rose and fell under my tending hand. "What do you want?" he repeated.

My plan was exposed. "To feel beautiful," I whispered, on the verge of tears. I couldn't even enjoy how his arms started trembling and how he white-knuckled his fist.

"And how will feeding me do that? It's a loss of control. Wouldn't you rather a lover choose to mount you instead of being forced to?" he asked, demanding a direct answer.

He wasn't wrong. I searched for the right words, trying to sort out what I wanted. "Yes… but also… I suppose the intensity helps me feel even more s—"

"I can be just as intense by choice with you," he interrupted, his voice hardening as much as his cock. "Very easily, Keid. I want you. I want to bring you home. I'd—what's that word—fuck you nonstop if I could. I'm just trying to win your heart as well. I hurt you, and I don't want to risk losing you."

*Great gods! Curse me to the moon and back!* my brain screamed nonsensically.

When I glanced up at his face, his eyes had turned black and crimson, like both his beasts were showing. He was intensely aroused, and my entire body was racked by a flood of desire. My hands trembled as my scrubbing faltered, and I was about to assert my wants, but he made the first move.

"Fine," he replied flatly and brought the bone to his mouth. I nearly gaped when he cracked off a bite with his teeth, but then he froze. "How the shit do I swallow solid food? Oh gods," he said through the food in his mouth. "Oh gods, what do I do?"

"M-Marrow did it before," I stammered, thrown by this interruption.

"Well, I haven't!"

"Your body will know what to do," I said, placing a soothing hand on his chest. "If you choke, I'll unblock it. I was a doctor's assistant for years, Ferrer. Trust me."

His eyes snapped to mine. "I do." He took a moment to gather himself, and I could see the way he was trying to work more saliva into his mouth. I tried to not be nervous because people accidentally choked on bones all the time, but I chose not to say that. He was meant to eat this food by the very gods who made him. He'd be fine.

He closed his eyes like he was saying a prayer and swallowed. It seemed to go well because he didn't start dying on me. His eyes snapped open, and he took another bite, finishing the leg bone rather quickly.

"Good job," I praised, but it came out a little breathy. Perhaps it was his vulnerability that stirred me past the point of fear because I moved to a crouch, placed my hands on his shoulders, and raised my hips until the head of his cock was brushing along my core. I sent him a pleading look. "Please," I whispered. "I want you to want me..."

"I do. I always do," he growled. "But Keid, don't you want me too?" He was frowning, but the subtle way his dark brows drew up in the middle belied his own worry.

I hadn't expected that either, and I was so nervous that a droplet of sweat rolled down my temple. He knew the answer, but he wanted to hear it. Was he truly just as afraid of rejection as me? Was it real? That seemed to be the biggest sign yet that he'd changed, and that did something to me. The last line of my defenses dissolved.

"I do..." I murmured fearfully. "Please, Ferrer... I want you. Please take me. Please."

Ferrer's scowl deepened, but somehow, I knew it wasn't directed at me. It wasn't the mate bond that told me, because our emotional connection was one-way. I supposed it was intuition. Though he looked furious, I felt neither scared nor attacked.

His upper lip curled to show an elongated fang as he slid his hand up my neck to palm the back of my head. His chest was rising and falling, pushing breaths past his bared teeth. Black irises with red sclera stared up at me as I hovered over his erection, and in the slanted, late-afternoon light, I could make out my own silhouette in his eyes.

His hand gripped the hair at the back of my head, fisting it to bring me closer to his face. "I can't force you to into feeling beautiful, Keid," he said shortly, his words laced with frustration. "You cannot sense its proof through our bond either." Ferrer's jaw clenched, and his left hand pulled at my tunic. "Get this off."

I dropped my hands from his shoulders and yanked the tunic up and over my head. Nervously covering my exposed breasts with an arm, I placed my other hand back on his shoulder to steady myself. He glared at my offending limb and shot an angry look up at me.

"Why? Why cover what I obviously like?" he asked, shaking his head and narrowing his eyes.

"I… don't like them…" I mumbled shyly and looked away from his piercing stare.

"Why?" he repeated heatedly, sliding a finger under my arm to expose my breasts. My face heated up in embarrassment as they dangled freely, but I resisted the urge to cover them again.

"Think my… um…" I struggled to say it, speaking as quietly as I could. "Nipples are too long."

His eyes narrowed more. "I've seen much longer," he snapped. "And I don't know why you think it's a bad thing. Working with a doctor, you must have seen many females, Keid. Is it not true that every female—every woman—is different?"

"Yes," I replied a little defensively, "I have… It's just, among my people… small and tight ones are ideal…"

"You know, I… ah…" Ferrer began but lost his train of thought once his hand closed around my naked breast for the first time. "Clots," he cursed through his bared teeth. "Just touching you makes me want to come." His hands were shaking, and he leaned forward to rest his head against my chest. His erection lurched, and the suddenness of his response sent heat through me.

Glancing between my legs, I stared at his jutting, slavering length. His flesh was stretched tight over his wide shaft, the skin shiny and red under a swell of blood. His crown, almost purple, was glazed in precum, and my stomach clenched at the sight. A rivulet down his veiny length showed that he'd been dripping for some time. My breathing accelerated the more I stared at it. I wanted that inside me. "Blood and bones," I breathed mindlessly.

"Blood and bones," he repeated, like it was a curse. "I need none to feel lust for you," he said into my chest, massaging with the hand that held my breast. The mindful way he kneaded it squeezed a moan through my lips. He dug into the softer, fatty tissue, but his caresses gentled whenever his touch found something firmer.

I started when he angled his head to kiss the swell of my other breast. He placed his next kiss just below it, and I bit my quivering lip, silently willing him to go lower despite my insecurities. His lips pulled from my skin, leaving moisture behind that cooled from the air. Another kiss was placed lower… then another.

My core clenched as I stared down, watching his lips hover over my nipple. My skin was writhing with electricity as all my nerves anticipated his warm, wet embrace. Ferrer muttered something under his breath, and his free hand went to his cock.

"What was that?" I breathed as he made a pained expression.

"I asked myself why I was bothering to hold back," he growled. "If you want to know how I find you, Keid, then you need to expect a bloody mess."

He didn't give me a lot of time to decipher that before he leaned forward and began devouring a breast. His mouth opened as far as it could go, and he scraped his fangs across my sensitive, intimate skin before clamping his lips down on a nipple. I shrieked through my teeth as cold lightning forked deep into my breast and trickled down to my sex.

My legs almost buckled from their crouch. Oh gods, his lips were ravenous, but they gave as delightfully as they took. The intense, shooting pleasure had me torn; I didn't know if I wanted to push him away or yank him closer. Each pull he took assaulted me with sharp, exquisite sensations, ignited by the mate touch. I nearly screamed when his tongue slid across the tip he was suckling. My hands went to the sides of his head and became tangled in his brown and now-red hair.

His long groan turned into a drawn-out growl. In moments, he bucked beneath me, crying passionately into my flesh. My core was immediately soaked by bursts of warm fluid. After a moment of receiving his climax, Ferrer removed his guiding hand from his cock to press my fingers to my core. His seed was spent all over it and had soaked the surrounding white curls.

"Do you see… that?" he said forcefully through heaving breaths. "Do you feel that?" I nodded hastily, and he moved my hand to his unrelenting erection, unhumbled by one climax. "That part of your body—the part you dislike—aroused me so much that I came on your body, Keid! These nipples… I bleedin' prefer them! Clots, it's more to bloody play with! I prefer breasts exactly like y— Ahhh…"

Since he'd brought my hand to his cock, I decided to squeeze it, and his head fell back with a moan. Maybe it was because I felt emboldened or maybe it was because I didn't want to talk about nipples anymore, but I used the inertia of his aggressive complimenting to assert my needs. I lined him up against my seed-covered sex, notched him in place, and pushed down to try to get him inside me.

"Hsss… Clots!" Ferrer hissed with bared fangs, clamping down on my hips to help pull me down his erection. "Do you not see how bloody hard you make me?" he groaned, digging in his fingers. I spread the folds of my sex until he was sliding in properly and braced my knees into the blanket beneath us to get leverage. I pushed down, breathing hard and trying to ignore the jostling of my breasts as I did so.

A long, grating groan curled from my throat as I slid down his length. "Pull me," I gasped, and Ferrer yanked hard to seat me flush against his groin, impaling me with his length. I screamed into my teeth and leaned against his shoulder, overwhelmed by the stretching. "Fuck!" I dragged my fingers down his chest, nearly lost to sensation. He was hot inside me—hot, hard, and slathering. I couldn't take it.

"Shit, Keid," he croaked and slid his hands around my hips to dig them into my butt cheeks. He massaged them downward to rub me into his lap. "You're sounding a little feral yourself."

Being completely naked with a sober Ferrer… I couldn't explain it, but a wildness was encroaching on my mind. It was asking if I wanted to hide behind it, and I wasn't sure. I drew my brows in worry and focused on the skin in front of me. I nuzzled into his neck, wishing I hadn't washed him so he could smell more like himself. Ferrer had the best musk of any man or male I knew.

I wiggled my hips into his lap, drawing a rumbling groan from his chest. He took a deep breath and lifted me up to massage himself with my sex. I whimpered and nipped at his neck, feeling my core throb in delight as he traveled along its shape. His head was gradually dragged out until it rested just inside my folds, and I scratched at Ferrer's chest once more, desperate to have him back inside me.

"Look at it, Keid," he commanded, nodding to his cock. I turned my head to stare at the lewd sight. It was glossy, covered in both our desire and his seed. I wiggled my hips again with impatience. Just looking at it was making me want it more.

"Please," I complained into his ear, stroking his other ear with an idle finger. "Please. I miss you. Go back in."

"Shit," he snarled and jerked me back to his lap, kissing my cervix aggressively with the head of his cock. I bit his shoulder out of a sheer ravenous, lustful need and was surprised by Ferrer's euphoric cry. He palmed the back of my head, keeping it locked to his shoulder as he spent his seed. “Ahh! Yes! Shit!” he shouted and fell back with me atop him. “Bite, woman! Bite! Harder!”

I bit harder like he asked, making him writhe and moan beneath me, filling my channel with his seed. The marking spot on either shoulder was incredibly sensitive on shifters, and I was glad I could at least use it to bring him more pleasure. The amount of power was arousing, and the fact that I alone could stimulate him this much made me see myself a little differently. For the first time ever, I felt… sexy.

I cursed into his hot, sweaty flesh and licked up his neck, moaning at how his chest muscles flexed under my breasts. When my body lurched forward, propelled by a hard thrust of his hips, I scrabbled to find purchase on his shoulders.

When I nipped at his earlobe, he cried out in bliss and slapped his hips up into me, then held it there, shaking. I gaped into his neck at the sheer erotic pleasure of knowing he was spending his seed again. “Oh gods!” I breathed and pushed back down against his groin, wanting every drop of it. “More,” I moaned into his jaw and licked a line up the rim of his pointed ear. “More, Ferrer!”

“I could die happily doing this,” he said breathlessly and returned to thrusting. I propped my torso up and began rocking into his hips, meeting each penetration in a hard, wet slap. I was so lost to the moment, so drowned in our erotic rhythm that parts of my body just didn’t know what to do. Sometimes my head would roll back as I rode the bat-shifter, but sometimes it would hang limply. Nothing else mattered so long as I was here, soaking him with my desire.

“Clots, look at you,” Ferrer said, and I rolled my head down to stare at him through a feverish haze. He slid his hands up my hips to cup my breasts, letting them bob around into his palms from my rocking. He swallowed heavily and accelerated, causing a fresh sheen of sweat to break out at his temples. “You’re so…” He gasped and slammed up into me, holding himself there as he came again, “bloody… perfectly… ravishing! Shit!”

He rolled his hips up into me as he unloaded, causing me to sob in marrow-deep satisfaction. I ground back into him, wanting his cum. I wanted all of it. I'd ride his hips all through the accursed day and night to empty him.

"What else?" he rasped, then dug his thumbs into my nipples, rubbing them in gentle circles. I shrieked and leaned into his touch, grinding harder against his groin. I shook my head, sending my hair flying everywhere as I fought through the sparks of pleasure. They stole my breath, and I arched back, gasping loudly. Arousal had my sex wrapped in heat, and Ferrer's touch scattered lightning through my body. It was so captivating that I could barely make out his words. "What else don't you like?"

It was easy now. "I'm too tall," I bemoaned, undulating my hips around on his lap while arching and lolling my head.

"You mean the right height to bend over for mounting?" Ferrer retorted, a glimmer of playfulness in his tone. "The next time we're out in public, I'll show you my ideas for broom closets."

I brought my hands to my face and raked my fingers over my scalp and through my hair. Ferrer was breaking apart every excuse I had for feeling ugly. It was simultaneously freeing and irritating. The anger, I knew, was from how vulnerable it made me. The skin I had under the old grimy shell was tender—fragile. It'd tear easily. My old shell had been comfortable. If anything happened, I'd have to grow a whole new layer.

"Stop that," Ferrer growled and pulled me down onto him. He tightened an arm around my torso and slid a hand between us to play with my aching clit. I exhaled a stuttering breath into his throat, a little emotional from how he always knew to yank me from my fears. "Be here with me. Please. I miss you."

The way he turned my words back onto me with a new twist was stunning. Tears streamed down my face, and his pace slowed. One hand stroked the back of my head while the other rubbed my clit lazily.

"You're so beautiful, Keid," he murmured, nuzzling my temple. "Everything about you is my ideal. The Moon Goddess knew what I liked." His hand slid down my back and rubbed my shoulder blades as his long cock slid easily along my channel, now excessively lubricated and sopping from his climaxes. "The only issue I had was my prejudice, alright? Had that not been there, I would have absconded with you into the woods and marked you senseless."

The thought was arousing, but if he had done that, I never would have gotten my eggs back… I wouldn't have been able to give my fated mate any of the pups that his colony so desperately needed.

"Be here with me," he whispered again and kissed the temple he'd nuzzled. I nodded and tried to focus on his attentive fingers between our bodies. "I'm trying to tell you that you're perfect to me. Line up all the females and women in the world, and you'd stand out every single time. I'd pick you every single time."

I swallowed and raised my hips to give him a little more room to work. "I could never masturbate properly myself," I confessed, changing the subject entirely because his fingers were distracting me. "If I go back with you…" Also, Ferrer's confessions made me nervous about my own feelings.

"You come to me every time," he said into my ear, brushing it with his lips, "and I'll take care of you straightaway."

My heart throbbed, and my core clenched at those words. That'd been worth the risk of asking. Maybe I'd be less scared next time. Gods, no one could turn me on like Ferrer. I licked idly at his neck as he massaged with more purpose, bringing a deeper heat to my sex. I wished I could just melt into him right now.

Languid sounds of pleasure drawled from my lips. I rocked my breasts against Ferrer's chest as he took care of me. The swell was building with every stroke, and he always seemed to move to the right place at the right time. Ferrer was keen to give the mate touch. From how he responded to my noises, I was becoming convinced that I could ask for it anytime.

"Does that feel good, woman?" he asked in a low voice, massaging a little faster when my breathing accelerated into panting.

I whimpered, whined, and made all sorts of bizarre noises as he rubbed pleasure into me.

When his finger found the right place at the right time, I froze and held my breath, feeling the climax approaching. My legs and arms shook as I hung on to the precipice of ecstasy. It was there.

The wave of euphoria shattered me. Pleasure rippled up my body, forcing me to contract tightly around Ferrer's cock. I gaped, then hissed, squealing through my teeth as I clutched at his arms. Each shock wave pulsed through me, pushing blinding pleasure into every nerve. My toes curled so tightly that they risked cramping as much as my core.

I moaned as Ferrer dug his finger in deeper, prolonging my climax like only he could. Not wanting to orgasm alone, I licked along his shoulder and bit his marking spot hard, hoping I could get a last one out of him. He shouted and bucked up into me. I pushed back onto his cock, moaning around my fading climax until he came one last time, then I returned to his embrace to enjoy the glow of carnal satisfaction.

We were a shaking, shivering tangle of limbs and soft voices. I was lost in his scent and sounds. My heart flushed as hotly as my body, and for the first time in a long time, something felt right. Something felt right, and it made me want more.

Wrapped in Ferrer's muscles, we caught our breaths and calmed our hearts. He pulled my sweaty, sticky body up higher to properly hug me and took a deep breath of my neck. His gratified noise pulled a tired smile from my lips. When he kept sniffing, however, I held back an uncharacteristic giggle. I hadn't realized I was kind of ticklish there.

"Keid," Ferrer began hesitantly, then forced both of us into a seated position. He pressed his nose to my neck and sniffed down my chest. I frowned and watched him obsess over my skin. He abruptly stood us up and worked his nose down my body.

"What is it…?" I asked. I couldn't bring myself to ask the real question.

He was silent for a long moment before answering, and his voice was thick with emotion. “You’re staying with me,” he whispered into my abdomen as he knelt. The bat-shifter wrapped his arms around my hips and buried his face in my stomach. Something warm and wet began dripping down my skin—Ferrer’s tears.

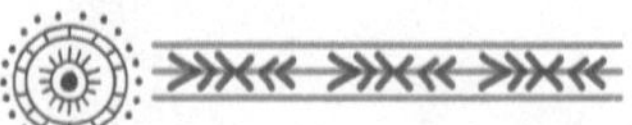
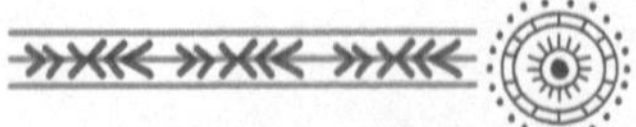

# Chapter 25

## Ferrer

I kept my face buried in Keid's abdomen. My whole world was right here now, wrapped in my arms. This woman, the one I'd spurned, was not only softening, she was coming back with me. What she might not immediately know was why.

I drew in a deep breath, expanding my overheated, dripping chest to fill my lungs with her sweat's aroma. If I hadn't worked the perspiration out of her, I probably wouldn't have noticed until tomorrow. As it was, the moisture from her body pushed out her glands' message, and the news was potent. I inhaled again and held back a sob. I'd spent my seed so many times, and yet I was being swept into a new climax—an emotional one.

After several more breaths, my system took in the chemicals she'd unknowingly sent, and a calm came upon me. I no longer felt the extreme compulsion to breed. Like a new form, I was shifting into a different role. My body was informed of a new duty, and it wouldn't be long before my hormones responded.

Fingers timidly brushed my shoulders, and her anticipation bubbled over into concern. "Ferrer? What do you mean?" Keid asked. Though she was obviously fatigued, her voice was alert and laced with uncertainty.

"All those days ago," I managed to say through my tears, "I did claim your egg. You're with pup, Keid. My pup."

Her sharp intake of breath was a prelude to the most beautiful flurry of emotions. Excitement and hope blossomed from her heart, feeding my own in the process. "Ferrer! You're sure? You..."

I nodded into her belly, nuzzling the softness that formed the wall between me and my offspring. I didn't want to ever move from this position, but I knew I had to at some point. Her scent was pleasing but in a different way now. Instead of making me hungry, it was satisfying. I'd never experienced such deep satiation in my entire life... and never from an aroma, not even blood.

"I can smell your hormonal change. You sweated so much, it's like your body is singing your state." My murmurs grew lower as I spoke, and as my lips brushed her skin, I felt an urge to kiss her salty sweetness. If only she wanted me to claim her lips.

"Oh my gods," she uttered in a breathy voice. "Oh my gods!" That time, the words sounded much happier, and I figured that she was finally absorbing the news. She bobbed up and down on her toes, like she wanted to jump but was anchored by me. I released her reluctantly and stood to regard her countenance.

She was also crying, and her hands were cupped over her mouth, illustrating her speechlessness quite well. Keid hopped in excitement. I openly admired her beautiful breasts as she did this, envisioning them months from now. They'd be heavier with milk, and I couldn't wait to taste her gift. If it was as nectarous as her blood, my offspring would be well nourished.

Her movements dislodged more of my seed from between her legs, and it slid down a thigh, but she seemed too distracted to notice or perhaps care. With my slight shift in mood, the evidence of our joining was still arousing, but the escape of my fluid no longer bothered me. It was as if my seed had noticed that the job had already been done and had simply chosen to depart.

My cock swelled from the alluring display before me, but I could easily ignore it now. I wanted to fully enjoy Keid's bubbling happiness. Though I wasn't positive she was happy that her breeding had occurred with me in particular, I knew she was overjoyed with the prospect of having her own young. It wouldn't have been possible without the rot-witch, but I felt a muddy sense of pride in being the one to give Keid her long-abandoned dream.

The woman rubbed her tearful eyes, then strode forward to wrap me in an impulsive hug. There was no fear this time, just gratitude, joy, and relief. I wiped at my own wet face and returned her embrace, feeling positively euphoric by her more confident display of affection. Perhaps there was hope she could love me someday.

"Do you need to eat more?" I asked gently, stroking the back of her head. The calmness in the air about us was refreshing, and I was at peace. She turned her head and looked down at the roast, then burst into uncharacteristic giggles. I followed her gaze and noticed that the bird had blackened over the fire. That probably wasn't appealing to her, and I tried to frown in disappointment, but her perky laughter was making it difficult.

"Worth it," she expressed between breaths and buried her face in my chest once more. "I'll be fine. I'm sure there's something salvageable in there."

I hummed a disbelieving note but dropped it. Humans were fragile, but I didn't know better than Keid on caring for one. That being said, we had a whole new challenge ahead of us, and the more I thought about it, the more nervous it made me.

After wiping her down a little and cleaning her knee, which had gotten dirty during our joining, I shook the dirt from her blanket so I could flip it. It was a little sweaty and seed soaked, and I growled in annoyance. I didn't want Keid sleeping on a damp blanket, but I spread it out all the same. She immediately hopped onto it but still appeared anxious. Her expression was mildly sour now, and I recalled her aversion to the ground here.

"Is it noticeable through the blanket?" I asked, laying down so we could rest before traveling again.

She frowned and nodded, so I opened my arms, albeit hesitantly. I'd understand if she said no, but it'd still hurt. Fortunately, Keid didn't seem to think it was a hard decision and immediately climbed over me. A pleased groan snuck out of my chest as I pulled her up my body so she could sleep. I was worried she'd take my sound the wrong way, but all I sensed out of her was deep contentment.

It took some finagling, but we managed to get her comfortable on my chest. I was intrigued that she'd chosen to lie naked on me but dismissed it as her not wanting to get her clothes sweaty. It was still blissful to feel her face, breasts, and belly pressing into my skin with her legs slightly entangled in mine. I rocked from side to side to release Marrow's wings and wrapped them around us to cover her. Though we were in a small sliver of shade, I still wanted to protect her from the Sun God's fire.

"I can't believe I'm pregnant. I had lost all hope of it," she whispered into my chest, her warm breath puffing pleasantly across my skin.

"And what you said still goes, yes?" I asked just as quietly, trying not to sound as anxious as I was. "You're coming back to the colony?"

"I won't separate you from your pup, no. I'm coming back." There was some sadness, but I was mildly soothed by a small amount of her hope and sense of comfort.

"I will give you everything you need and want," I murmured, then added reluctantly, "even if you choose not to be my mate…" Swallowing hard, I said something that was probably risky and more than a little stupid. "I'd still… offer to sate you… like I said… if you ever get lonely, that is."

Somehow, she was not offended. Her emotions flooded with pleasure, and her self-esteem seemed to mature a touch more. It was taken as a compliment, thank the gods above and below us.

"Thank you..." she whispered in a vague reply. I got no hints as to the status of her decision, and I tried not to become crestfallen. I'd barely given her time to change her mind. "I... don't think..." she continued unexpectedly, but her statement faltered. She was full of conflicting emotions now, warring with insecurity, fear, hope, and longing. I held on to the last one as I waited for her to speak, but the silence was too agonizing.

"What don't you think?" I pressed when my own worry became too great. She didn't think she'd choose to be my mate or keep my mark? Was that what she was about to say?

"I..." Keid seemed terrified to finish her thought, and my nose stung with unshed tears. If she rejected me now, it'd kill my soul. Iron and Marrow wouldn't survive it either, not at this point. Perhaps I could convince her to spend more time thinking about it.

"Y-you don't have to decide now," I blurted, my ragged inhalation and stutter sabotaging my attempted stoicism.

Alarm sparked within her, and she rushed out what she'd been meaning to say. "I don't think I'll... remove the mark. I... If that's alright. I..."

"Shitting stars," I cursed, yanking her up a little to cover her cheeks and forehead in feverish kisses. I had no idea if she was ready to receive such attention to her face, but I was so relieved and overjoyed that I couldn't resist. Not only was I infatuated with the taste of her skin, she was giving me an opportunity to enjoy her forever—all of her.

I placed one last kiss on her forehead and pressed it to mine. Closing my eyes, I whispered, "Thank you. You won't regret it. I'll make you happy. I'll provide. I'll be a good mate. Our pups will have everything they need to thrive." Was I getting too ahead of myself? Yes, but I didn't care. She was giving me a chance, and I was not going to squander it. My heart wasn't just glowing, it was burning with euphoric heat.

Keid swallowed heavily and nodded against my forehead. The woman's relief was nigh palpable, matching mine in its intensity. It was obvious the confession had taken a great deal of effort. With shaking arms, she pushed herself up to press a soft, brief kiss on my forehead and moved down to rest on my chest. I was stunned by the unexpected gesture and brought a hand to my forehead in awe. Such was my stupefaction that it took me a moment to remember the last thing I needed to discuss.

"I have… one more thing to say before we sleep." I was very nervous to share it, but honesty was important to her, and she'd find out soon anyway. When she hummed her question, I informed her of our next challenge. "So… you've been told about and… unfortunately experienced our mating impulse firsthand." I swallowed heavily and licked my lips before continuing. "When our mates are pregnant, that drive moves from sex to… um…" I started over because I was fumbling excessively. "Since we were going extinct, the drive to protect becomes… rather intense. I apologize in advance if I do or say anything unreasonable. The hormones are difficult to fight, or so I've heard from our eldest. I just hope it's not worse with an extra soul."

"Oof…" she muttered under her breath. After a long inhale and a thorough exhale, she said, "Thank you for being straightforward. I'll keep it in mind. Just… don't be an ass to me. I'm warning you. I don't tolerate unkindness anymore."

"No, no, no," I blurted, frightened. "Not to you. Never to you… Not again." I tightened my arms around her for a brief moment before relaxing and locking my tendons. The adrenaline from the turn of events was wearing off, and I was growing tired. After a trying day, the mating had been a drain. Keid was an unknowing expert at making me come. I explained further, "I may slaughter the smallest creature for even getting close to you."

"Please don't." Her chuckle was sleepy, but she quickly sobered and inquired, "Wait… so you don't want to have sex anymore?" Her head lifted off my chest with her query.

"Shit, no! That's not what I meant!" I answered hastily, my eyes snapping wide open to stare down at her. "I'll always crave you, but I'll just have greater control. I should be able to eat without going feral now… that's all. The energy is just being diverted into… protectiveness. Your hormones affect mine…"

"Oh," she muttered, and her surge of disappointment was absolutely confounding to me. She rested her head again and yawned.

It triggered a yawn in me as well, and I murmured, "Time for sleep, mate." I took a chance asserting it and was rewarded by her not correcting me. Oh, thank the gods. I was taking more risks than my heart could handle. I really needed to spread this shit out better.

We shared an exhausted, contented sigh, and I began to drift off into sleep.

Marrow decided to briefly come out of hibernation to ask something before I succumbed to exhaustion. *So… am I no longer grounded?*

The night had come much too soon. I'd woken several times before and after sunset but just didn't have it in me to wake Keid, who was still sound asleep. Allowing her only four or five hours of rest was unacceptable, so I decided that I'd let her sleep a little more before rousing her.

Speaking of rousing… I was amazed that I was tolerating our sleeping arrangement so well. Granted, I was at least half erect most of the time, but due to the slow adjustment of my hormones, I was able to maintain control.

It was strange to be able to unknot the tie between my body and mind regarding sex. I could feel her soft weight, smell her provocative scent, and see her nudity; those observations should've been partnered with going at least a little feral, but I maintained a novel kind of clarity. The severance was strange to me, but I was pleased by the calm it rendered. It allowed me to enjoy and appreciate her more.

I smiled and tested my newfound restraint with some fantasizing. Closing my eyes again, I pictured Keid getting mischievous. Thinking I was asleep, she'd slide just a little down my body to cup the head of my cock in her sex, wiggling to nuzzle me in between her folds. She wouldn't move past that, not wanting to wake me, but I'd surprise her by letting her know I wasn't asleep. I'd tilt my hips up slowly t—

An involuntary, pleased groan left my throat as I fantasized, and it startled me. My body jerked slightly, jolting Keid awake. Ah, clots!

I peeked with one eye to find her yawning and rubbing at her pretty, sleepy face. Perhaps I didn't have as much control as I thought. Needless to say, I was more than a little embarrassed.

Her arms shook as she stretched them out, and she propped her head up to see if I was awake. I opened my other eye uneasily, feeling a little guilty.

"Do you feel rested?" I asked in a low voice and unlocked my tendons to let her move if she wished. Keid sat up slowly as I folded Marrow's wings, and I tried not to think about how she was straddling me. I needed to master my voice now, apparently.

"I do," she murmured sleepily.

"Because you can sleep longer if you need to…" I offered, propping myself up on my elbows. "If not, we should start moving. We'll reach the river tonight, so if you wish to get clean, that'd be the easiest way to do it."

She nodded and stood up slowly, then went through her waking tradition of cracking her back and stretching her legs. I admired her form, and though she caught me staring multiple times, I wasn't ashamed.

"You're beautiful," I said with a shrug after she pulled on her tunic and noticed that I was still watching. "I won't apologize." I stood abruptly and looked around for my own pants, acting like I didn't know how much she was starting to enjoy my compliments. Her fear had been blocking her ability to appreciate attention, and I was happy to watch that darkness dissipate over time.

I found my pants, but my skin was covered in sweat and a mix of both our arousals, so I definitely wasn't wanting to wear them. Perhaps she'd allow me to travel naked until we got to the river. I hated dirtying clothes.

When Keid had her belongings properly packed, she walked away from our campsite, and I felt a moment of panic. "Where are you going?" I blurted to my pregnant woman.

She stopped and frowned over her shoulder at me. "I'm just going to relieve myself. I'll be back."

"You can do it here," I affirmed, then turned my back to her. "I won't watch. Don't go wandering."

"Uh… no. I'll be back. Just wait here." I bristled at her defiance but just fisted my hands and kept my mouth shut. It was just my hormones making me paranoid. Listening to my surroundings, I detected no other heartbeats. We were alone, and she was safe.

*So… a couple of things,* Iron said, coming out of hibernation.

*Yes?* I asked, distracted. I was on higher alert than I wanted to be. It meant burning more energy, so I'd have to stay well fed. Fortunately, I wasn't worried about finding food now that I could eat bones. There were plenty that Keid wouldn't be able to eat in those fowl I brought her.

*First of all, you're welcome. I'm saying it for Marrow because he's too polite to rub it in,* Iron remarked.

*For what?* I growled back, staring unwaveringly at where Keid had disappeared.

*The fake tan worked,* he clarified smugly, like it'd been his idea.

*I mean, in a way…* Marrow piped in cautiously.

*It got you some amazing sex, Ferrer, which won over our mate. I just want to lay that fact out there,* Iron added, his tone becoming way too arrogant and obnoxiously benevolent for my current mood. *I mean, you should really thank our vulture. He fixed everything, really.*

*Red is hardly what you'd call a tan. Marrow made me look like an idiot,* I replied flatly. I was not going to thank him for turning me red.

*It got her eyes on you!* Iron argued. *And I mean, they were all over you. The rest of her too.*

*It was just intended to fancy him up a bit...* Marrow protested.

*A suit is fancy, Marrow,* I snapped, shifting my weight from foot to foot now. I perked up when Keid appeared again, looking refreshed and ready to travel. Relief rolled a heavy weight off my shoulders, and I turned to join her when she passed me. It looked like we were headed out now.

Keid appeared on edge herself, and I noticed that she was making an effort to keep her eyes off the ground. I couldn't imagine her discomfort, but I slid my hand into hers to hold it and waited to see what she'd do. Her posture softened, and she exhaled a small noise of reprieve. I squeezed her hand, trying to offer comfort, and though she didn't look at me, she returned the gesture very subtly. I took that as a victory and enjoyed the tingling and comfort that our mate touch provided.

She seemed a little more reserved tonight—probably lost in thought. It was obvious that her mind was somewhere else as she tried not to look at her surroundings. Also, though we were out from the trees and had the starlight to navigate by, she'd occasionally stumble on something.

"Want me to carry you?" I asked hopefully. I was quickly beginning to understand why shifters practically carried their females and women everywhere. It wasn't that they thought the females were weak—the urge to be close to a fated mate was simply too hard to resist.

"I'm alright, thank you. I'm just a little sore and stiff," she murmured.

"Oh... was it how you slept?" I asked, pulling Keid gently toward me before she tripped on a jutting stone. She simply shook her head in response. She didn't seem to want to talk about it, so I dropped it. I thought about something else to fill the silence.

"What would you like to name our offspring?" I asked and was rewarded with a blossoming of joy from her.

"I hadn't thought about it… Assuming I don't miscarry, it's a long way from delivery," she remarked thoughtfully. Her eyes fell upon the moon, which was making Her appearance over the horizon. The goddess's light would aid Keid's stride. "I'd like something meaningful," she added softly.

"Speaking of meanings," I said, "what does your name mean? It's unusual." I didn't mention that it sounded like a male's name; it didn't really matter.

"It's the name of a white star," she answered and looked up at the night sky. "It's getting hazy," she added in a low voice. "The star's not visible."

We did seem to be approaching the layer of fog that hung over the deadlands, and I wondered if that would make flying a challenge for Marrow. I'd find out soon enough. I turned my attention back to our conversation.

"White star?" I inquired and frowned up at the sky. "Are they not all white?"

Keid laughed, delivering a beautiful noise that I wished I could hear more often. "Not at all. There are many colors; you just cannot really see them well this far away."

"How do you know then?" I was very curious now. This was something I didn't know about my own gods. How had I not known that the Sky Gods had more variety in Their stars?

"You do not live in the Stellar Coven and worship the Sky Gods without learning such things," she answered with a smile. "Our own sun is a star, but it's a yellow one."

I nearly stopped in my tracks. "No, that is not possible!" I protested. The Sun God was too large, too powerful, too fierce to be a star. He traveled separately from them as well.

Keid chuckled quietly as she picked her way up a rocky incline with me. I held her hand in a tighter grip so I'd catch her if she slipped.

"He is so," she responded confidently. "The stars are suns in their own right. Some have their own planets. In fact, some stars are actually planets." She pointed at a particularly bright one. "There is one right there."

"Your brain must be clotted!" I blurted, baffled by her claim, but she just fell deeper into mirth. My face twitched as I fought a smile. I was so very confused.

"Anyway." She chuckled once more, waving a hand in dismissal. "The stars come in many colors—red, orange, yellow, white… some are green and some are blue."

I sputtered and held up my other hand in disbelief. "I see no green! I think you are taking me for a fool, little star." I didn't necessarily disbelieve her, but I was enjoying making her laugh, so I was turning playful.

She snorted at the nickname. "Hardly little," she muttered, but her words weren't bereft of amusement. "If I ever get my hands on a stellar lens, I will show you. They are hard to come by. I suppose I could try to enchant my own… but it is quite difficult…" She continued muttering to herself, but I couldn't follow it; I was too distracted by what she'd said.

Her reference to time spent in the future together sent my soul aglow. I would remember those words for a long time to come. Any instance of her warming up to me was worth more than blood and bones. It kept me going.

"I look forward to that," I replied, feeling embarrassingly shy for some strange reason. I shook my head and tried to unclot my brain. "Perhaps we will name our offspring after another star. I think I would like that. Let's pick a blue star; you will have to tell me the names. I like blue. It reminds me of the night… like the Night Court."

"Do you ever miss it?" she asked hesitantly, looking up at me for the first time in a while.

"The Night Court… it was like an abusive mother. Aside from what the witches did, it made us what we are, but it was killing us. No, I only miss its eternal night, but it was a prison nonetheless. A prison could never be a home," I answered sadly. "At least there is night here half the time… for the most part. We are lucky the Earth Gods saved land for us and that the fae are helping to build our home."

She nodded in understanding and squeezed my hand. She was returning the comfort back to me. I was such a fool to have attempted rejection. Keid was wonderful, and I was developing very strong feelings for her.

*No*, I thought, staring at her for a moment while we walked. *It's more than that.*

I was definitely falling in love with her.

"Meissa," Keid said promptly. It shook me from my awakening, and I furrowed my brows in confusion.

"What was that?" I asked, not sure I heard her correctly. My heart was beating too loudly.

"There's Meissa, Cygni, Lacertae, Alcyone, Naos… I like Naos," she said in a far-off voice, like she was daydreaming. Keid blinked and looked up at me. "Blue stars. I'm trying to remember their names…"

"Strange names, but I like them." I nodded in consideration. "I like Meissa for a female and Naos for a male."

"Good choices…" she praised with a grunt as I helped her climb around a steep outcrop. I was growing more paranoid about her safety by the hour, and even the thought of her tripping put me on edge. The eldest of the colony had not been joking about the hormonal reaction. "There might be others, but I cannot recall them. We have time…"

*We have time,* I repeated to myself, savoring her words about our future together. It nearly gave me chills. I was becoming quite happy with how we were developing. Perhaps only fated mates could've survived what we'd been through together.

We talked less as the terrain became more uneven, and I had to make several trips up some cliffs to carry the bag of remains before returning to lift Keid. I'd just brought Iron's wings out, deciding to save time by flying us up when climbing was too slow or too dangerous. However, at this point, everything seemed too dangerous when it came to Keid's safety. She'd reprimanded me quite harshly when I threw a scorpion as far away from us as I could, which was quite far. To be honest, it was all I could do to not kill it outright.

The sound of the river eventually reached my ears, and I grinned at the prospect of a proper wash. I didn't mind Keid's smell on me, but hygiene was important, and I didn't want to displease my mate. She'd fortunately not made any remarks on me traveling naked, and I wondered if that would explain why she'd barely looked at me throughout the night. Humans were so strange about that sort of thing.

When we reached the canyon that hosted the river, I grabbed Keid and flew her down, grinning at her excited gasping. She didn't seem to be afraid of heights, which pleased me. I'd make sure to request a family chamber with a good view.

I ordered Keid to bathe first, staying near in case anything happened. In my survey of the immediate area, all I found were fish, roosted birds, and the occasional insect. There was life in the deadlands, but it was minimal and relied heavily upon the river for nourishment.

When the wind shifted in the canyon, a new smell reached my nose that made the hairs on the back of my neck stand on end. I wanted to fly out to verify the origin, but I couldn't pry myself from Keid's side. I glanced over at my woman, who had finished bathing and was returning from the bank with the soap for me. She was glorious, even in the shade of the canyon. The starlight did her justice.

She handed the soap over when she reached me, and I'd forgotten what I was about to say. I already wanted to mount her quite badly, but I resisted, and my mind accepted it.

She didn't look at me while she dressed, but she knew I was watching. I could feel her pleasure from it, and it was satisfying. Her growing confidence spread warmth into me and made her even more alluring.

When she finished dressing, she gestured to the water, prompting me out of my stupor. It made me recall what I was going to say, and I cleared my throat. "Mate… I scented smoke when the wind pushed into the canyon. I had not noticed anyone near the river during the day, so…"

Keid seemed to understand my train of thought, and she continued for me. "There's nothing here to burn but dead trees, and I can't imagine one spontaneously combusting. It must be a campfire."

"And we're not near a town…" I added.

"Do you want to go check?" she asked, tilting her head as she refilled her canteen.

"I do, but I am not leaving your side. It might not be safe," I answered flatly. It was not negotiable.

"Those people might not be safe," she warned, twisting her lips and raising a brow as she made her point.

Alright, maybe it was somewhat negotiable. Still though, it made me run my hands through my hair in agitation, torn on what to do. I didn't think it was actually possible to leave her side. Even the thought of her out of my sight tied my guts into knots. I stepped into the river and washed as quickly as possible while I considered.

*Don't you dare go,* Iron snarled. *If it comes to us, we'll meet it and kill it. Don't leave her side!*

*You can be fast,* Marrow argued. *It's best to plan for future problems.*

I groaned as I listened to my beasts' debate. They were not helping. The only thing I did know was that we weren't alone in the deadlands, and what I hadn't shared with Keid yet was the scent of rot.

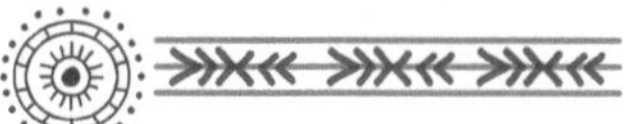

# Chapter 26

## Keid

*Pup, pup, pup, pup, pup, pup, pup!* Vain was singing cutely as Ferrer rushed to bathe in the river. I wished I could watch him, but my eyesight had reverted back into its pathetic, nearsighted state. Between not being able to see well and feeling emptiness under my feet, I was struggling. Fortunately, there were monumental positives that aided in that struggle, so I found myself feeling fairly neutral at the moment. I tried to focus on my life after this last task to keep my spirits up, and Vain was helping with that more than she knew.

I smiled and gently petted her head as she sang obsessively about my pregnancy. *I can't wait to see what she looks like!* Vain chirped happily. *I'm going to spoil her! She gets to have all the regurgitated blood. I won't share my meals with anyone else!*

"Euh…" I blurted, tongue-tied. What could I say to that? Was that normal among bat-shifters? Even blood bat pups drank their mother's milk until they got older. I decided to table that question for a much, much later time. "She?" I inquired instead.

*Definitely,* she answered knowingly. I snorted in response.

"How is Iron doing anyway?" I asked, keeping my eyes on the small bat on my lap since I was struggling to look at anything else. It was just a stroke of luck earlier that I'd been able to find a planet in the sky because all I could really pick out were the brightest lights. I supposed I should tell Ferrer, but it was embarrassing. I was also embarrassed about how sore I was from so much intimate activity. A shifter female could last longer, and I supposed it was another insecurity I never knew I had. It hadn't mattered until now. It was obvious that Ferrer could go for hours.

I quickly tabled that thought because I didn't want the bat-shifter to pick up on my emotions if he hadn't already. It was hard to feel like I had no privacy, which was something I'd always relied on to feel safe. At least he did make me feel safe… now. I'd have to come to terms with it soon if I was to live with him.

*Keid?* Vain said. *Are you listening?*

I snapped out of my thoughts, startled, then shook my head. "I'm sorry. What was that?"

*I said he's doing much better. The dynamic is starting to feel more natural to him because Marrow is so different.*

"He does seem more reserved and polite," I said quietly but suffered no illusion that Ferrer couldn't hear what I was saying. I imagined his ears were peerless.

*Exactly. He sees Marrow as...* Vain faltered like she was about to accidentally divulge something, and I arched a brow.

"As what?" I inquired curiously.

Vain was quiet for a moment, like she was kicking herself for speaking. *Er... well... considering what happened earlier, he sees Marrow as being all the more help to get Ferrer some... er...*

"Ah…" I replied, understanding well enough so she didn't need to say it. If she was a person, the poor thing would be blushing from head to toe. I supposed that Marrow had been responsible for the skin-tinting debacle. If my senses weren't being strained, I'd probably be chuckling.

I touched my face, noticing some soreness in my cheeks too. I'd been laughing and smiling so much lately, even through moments of despair. It was strange, but Ferrer was making something that used to be so alien into something commonplace. I glanced at his blurry form and sighed. There was much to get used to, but I was looking forward to it.

"Are you feeling well, Vain?" I asked as I stroked her. "Hungry yet?"

*I am well, and no, I will eat from Ferrer later. I won't take from you when you are with pup. It feels wrong.*

"I see. Do you feel like doing a little reconnaissance then? I think it'd be nice to save Ferrer from his own hormones right now," I inquired.

*He is already overreacting. I agree. Shall I fly by the source of the smoke?*

"Only if you want to and if you can stay safe," I asserted, thumbing her collar. I needed to get started on a new one. Perhaps the collar was irreplaceable, but I couldn't keep something on Vain that had unknowns. She meant too much to me.

*I do. I've been feeling useless lately. I can't even help you with magic now,* she complained, then fluttered into the air to investigate the smoke. *I'll be back soon!*

I smiled in the direction that my familiar had gone, loving her from the bottom of my heart. Without Mushy, I never would have acquired her. This journey had been worth the suffering.

Ferrer came back rather quickly after Vain had departed, ruffling his hair to dry it quicker. "Where'd she go?" he asked directly, looking both stern and concerned as he donned his pants.

"She's investigating the origin of the smoke. Don't worry, she'll stay out of sight. The fog will help," I explained, and his face grew stormy.

*She what?* Iron shouted over the bond Ferrer shared with me.

"She'll be back soon. This will keep you from agonizing over your decision," I said firmly, anticipating a fight here.

Ferrer growled and scrubbed his hands angrily over his face. "I smelled rot, Keid! I didn't tell you right away because I wanted to make sure first!"

The blood drained from my face. "You didn't say that..." I whispered, horror-struck.

"I'm no happier letting her go than letting you go! She means too much to you!" he snarled and started pacing restlessly. "Shit!"

*Let me out, let me out, let me out!* Iron cried, his screams becoming progressively more violent. His agitation startled me and Ferrer doubled over like someone had kicked him in the stomach.

"Calm the shit down!" he hissed through his teeth and stumbled back a step. Faster than I'd ever seen him shift, Iron forced his way out of Ferrer. The bat-shifter turned into a seething bat so quickly that his pants fell from midair. I would have laughed had Iron's reaction not been so frightening.

Iron had barely flown away before Vain returned with him hovering close. She landed on my knee and stared at the other blood bat... looking... well, I couldn't really read her expression.

*What got into you?* she snapped at him in irritation. Turning her attention to me, she didn't seem any calmer. *Keid, it's scary over there. I didn't go close.*

"What?" I asked, squinting as I centered all my attention to her. Ferrer shifted back, cursing angrily under his breath as he shook the dirt from his pants.

*Old women creatures... rotty like what Ferrer smelled. Also... humans with large bags,* she reported, *but the humans also look unhappy. Lots are shackled.*

"Oh my gods!" I gasped, jerking my head back in alarm. I glanced up at Ferrer's slightly blurry face, and he looked paler than normal.

"How many?" he inquired hoarsely. "Iron didn't get that far out before you returned."

*I don't know. Maybe over a hundred?* she guessed. *I left promptly.*

"But how many rot-witches... if that's what they are," he asked, desperate for some idea.

*Um... maybe three or four? It could be more. I really don't know, Ferrer.*

"We need to go. Now," he said, picking up both my bag and Mushy's. "We need to get away from them. Were they east, Vain? Northeast? Southeast?"

*East,* she answered nervously, crawling back to my shoulder to hide under my hair. *Seems like they came from the east too.*

"They had to've," Ferrer growled and swung me up into his arms, carrying everything now. I held back a surprised cry as Ferrer launched us off the ground, using Iron's wings to propel up the cliffside. He was terrifyingly strong, and his countenance right now was harsh. Ferrer wasn't joking around here.

He touched down a ways from the edge of the cliff and put me down but didn't give me a breather before grabbing my hand, urging me to follow him. I tried to claim my bag from his back, but he swatted my hand away without actually touching me. "No," was his simple assertion.

"What are we doing?" I asked breathlessly, almost having to jog to keep pace with him.

"We're still heading north," he replied tersely, and I could just make out the tension in his face. A muscle in his jaw was twitching restlessly.

"We are?" I asked, surprised. I half expected him to drag me straight back to the colony after seeing several rot-witches.

"Look ahead, Keid. There may be caves north so that means more places to hide. If there's a village, then perhaps they can offer some form of safety, I don't know. I'll not chance turning back now with such little coverage."

The terrain at our high altitude was becoming more mountainous, so he was likely correct about there being caves. My stomach soured from the stress, and I bit my lower lip. I could tell he also didn't want to mention his daytime vulnerability. Even with the benefits he got from Marrow, he could still function better in the shade.

A thought occurred to me and I asked, "Vain, how were the old creatures faring? Did they seem like they were managing? I can't imagine them not suffering in these deadlands. I'm struggling myself, and I'm young and… well, relatively healthy. Did you notice anything at all?"

*Um…* she pondered for a minute before speaking up again. *I vaguely recall that the ground under them was loose. It looked odd, but I was hardly concerned about the state of the ground.*

I frowned and considered the implications. "Was the dirt the same color?"

*Ah… I don't see like you do. Um, I recall it was darker?* she answered hesitantly.

"Soil," I said between breaths and Ferrer glanced down at me. He slowed when he realized I'd started jogging and looked somewhere between apologetic and impatient. "The bags are filled with soil," I clarified my realization, catching my breath as I fell back into a walk. "They're making a living bridge, Ferrer. Temporary, but… enough to pass over without weakening."

His eyes widened. "A bridge to where?" he inquired warily.

*I don't know…* Vain said quietly. *Do you want me to go back and verify the direction they came from?*

"No," he snapped heatedly, rejecting her idea completely. "Iron will force his way out if you do." The warning seemed potent enough to silence Vain.

"How would Mushy have crossed this?" I asked myself, rubbing my temple with a free hand. Had she expected to die before getting here? No, that was absurd. Maybe she expected to be carried? Maybe that's why she let me come along? Augh! I needed more information!

"Do you truly think it would have affected her? Aren't they at their strongest near death?" Ferrer asked, sounding confused.

"Magically," I explained, trying to ignore my sore muscles. It'd been nice to bathe, but I wished I could have rested longer. "What do you think keeps them alive while they rot away?"

"Fair point," he murmured, then frowned. "Keid, what about your eyes?"

"Enchantment faded," I answered flatly, not wanting to talk about it. I hated feeling so vulnerable; no magic, no farsight.

"Shit," he cursed and tightened his grip on my hand. I sighed, and we both continued north in silence. We had much on our minds and new worries to consider.

Ferrer seemed to be getting more agitated and paranoid by the hour, especially when Vain volunteered to fly ahead to start looking for caves. The sun would be rising, and we'd have to find cover. Even if Ferrer could keep walking, I couldn't. My skinned knee was throbbing, and I'd developed a stitch in my side.

*Found something,* Vain said after returning from her foray. Ferrer hadn't been happy with her flying off, but Iron had grudgingly allowed it since the sky was paling. The Sun God would be greeting us soon.

"Thank the gods." I gasped, holding my cramping side. Vain led us to a gap in a cliff's rock face. It opened into a small cave that was just big enough to huddle in and perhaps start a small fire. Ferrer didn't like creating any amount of smoke, but I had to eat and raw fowl was out of the question. It was simply a risk we had to take.

"Well done, Vain," Ferrer said vacantly as he stared out the opening of the cave, watching anxiously for any signs of life. "We'll stay here until the Sun God retires."

I frowned worriedly as I started roasting our dinner. All I could do was hope that the witches were headed south. Still... that meant trouble for the dragons. The ones Leofwine were sending wouldn't arrive in time to see them enter the redwoods. Would their scouts be able to spot them? It made me horribly nervous.

When we finished returning her remains, we'd have to go straight to someone to warn them. Unlike Mushy, I feared that these creatures were from the dark side of her ilk.

Between Ferrer and me, all that remained of the roasted fowl were the guts. I smiled half-heartedly at the spit where the bird had been and said, "And he was never seen again…"

I looked over to the bat-shifter, who was currently gnawing on a thin bone with an irritated look on his face. "What's wrong?" I asked, resting my chin on a palm.

"Something is wedged between my teeth," he growled. "It's bloody awful! How do you manage this clottin' solid food?"

I pressed my lips together, fighting a horrid wave of amusement. He simply scowled, and I winced. There really was no hiding anything from him.

"I'm sorry," I said with a laugh, surrendering. "Here, you can fix that with some string." I opened my medical kit and removed a small section of thread that I saved for sutures. I demonstrated the process of flossing before handing it over to the cranky shifter. It took him a moment to search around for the right tooth, but he eventually dislodged the food and collapsed against the wall of the cave in relief.

"Great Sky Gods," he grumbled. "I was a second away from just ripping my tooth out!"

"Please don't," I cautioned wryly and put away my medical kit.

"Thank you…" He crawled over and sat behind me. I wasn't sure what he was planning, but I found out quickly enough when he started feeling around my ribs and waist. "You've been nursing something here. Are you hurt?"

"No." I sighed, my mood plummeting. "It was just a stitch in my side. It's kind of like a cramp, I guess."

"Oh," he said quietly and continued to massage around the affected area.

"I'm sorry I'm not an extremely fit shifter female," I muttered bitterly, feeling yet another swell of insecurity. I was tired, in pain, and afraid; those things weren't helping my mood.

Expecting him to snap at me, I was surprised when he simply laid a soft kiss on my neck. I grimaced, hating and loving that he did that. "Need I remind you I don't want anyone else?" he rumbled into my ear.

"I'm too sore for sex," I lamented, worried about where this was going. "I'm human. My clit can only take so much."

"I wasn't going to ask for it," he replied casually, sounding unsurprised… surprisingly. He kept massaging my ribs and nuzzled into the side of my head, making my pulse quicken. I was not expecting this. "Do men only care for their women when they want something?" he inquired.

I wanted to say yes, but I knew that wouldn't be fair. Trying to keep up with an attractive, muscular male was scary. I was so used to being paranoid that I wouldn't be enough to keep anyone's interest for long. Ferrer was different. I had to stop being this way.

"I'm sorry," I apologized and leaned back into him. "I'm just worn out. I didn't mean those things."

"Maybe I don't show it, but I am tired too, Keid. Let's put out this fire and sleep while we can. I want to hurry tomorrow," he said gently, rubbing my shoulders before helping me cover the pit with dirt. I grimaced as I touched the ground with my bare hands. It was almost like grabbing spiderwebs; it felt like something and nothing at the same time.

Ferrer moved my hands from the dirt and finished the chore himself. I sighed and watched him, feeling bad for my behavior. He was trying so hard. What was I contributing aside from cooking the blasted bird?

He yanked me from my thoughts by grabbing me and settling me on top of him. When he closed his eyes, I realized that he did intend to sleep. I glanced behind, noticing the bulge in his pants and was indecisive. Should I offer?

"Sleep, Keid," he murmured, palming the back of my head to press it down to his chest.

"But you're…" I whispered, embarrassed. "If you want, I could…"

He laughed suddenly, startling me a little. "Do human men die if their erections remain unattended?"

"Er… no…"

"Does it make them sick? Can they not tend to themselves?"

"Just uncomfortable, I guess?"

"I'm used to discomfort, Keid." He chuckled, his laughs rumbling attractively through his chest. "If you haven't noticed that I'm in this state often around you, then we need to adjust that eye enchantment the next time you can cast it."

I snorted a laugh into his chest and nodded, yawning. He wrapped his arms around me and relaxed, not bothering to bring his wings out this time. I glanced up and smiled to see Vain hanging from the roof of the cave, looking like a proper bat. She really was too precious to describe.

"Sleep now, mate. Know that there's more to enjoy about you than mating. I do care. I… care… a lot. I care a lot about you," Ferrer said quietly, sounding more unsteady as he spoke. He cleared his throat and said once more, "Sleep."

We woke just before nightfall and rushed to prepare our food for the day because we wouldn't be stopping, not out in the open. The fowl meat was separated from the bones, and we packed it for later, then left to keep traveling north.

Vain would occasionally fly ahead to scout, which made Iron cranky and anxious. He really was acting like she was his mate, and the behavior was curious to me. I wished I could talk to the Moon Goddess about it. I had a plethora of questions for Her in general.

Like the previous night, we kept from speaking, trying to conserve our energy while we hurried to… wherever we were supposed to go. Fortunately, our route north kept us by the river, so we always had a supply of water and food. I didn't know how to fish, but at least it was an option.

On her sixth flight, Vain returned, vibrating with excitement. *Lights,* she yapped. *Lights ahead!*

"We might be there," Ferrer said in a quiet voice, cracking his neck and releasing his wings. He was looking on edge again, and I prayed for all the scorpions in the area to run while they could. His grip on my hand tightened, and when we climbed over the last cliff, we were faced with a much thicker fog that blocked our view of the sky and ground.

"It's so dense," I whispered, trying to peer down into the darkness. "Do you see anything?"

"No…" he answered, then clicked with his teeth. "Too far…"

"Let's climb down slowly then… Vain, how far is it to the bottom?" I asked, and she fluttered off to check.

*Ah… perhaps a five-minute climb down for you? It's flat down here… not a lot of buildings. Watch out for holes in the ground… there's a good number of them.*

"Holes?" Ferrer frowned as he secured everything to him, including me, and started climbing down the cliffside with his feet and Iron's wings.

"I can't believe everything you're carrying," I whispered as he descended. He shrugged in response, focusing intently on his footing. I decided to stop distracting him but marveled at his prowess. Marrow must have made him stronger because this feat was almost absurd.

There was very little to see on our way down, but I was finally able to spy dim lantern light when Ferrer touched the ground. It was blurry, but at least I had a direction to pursue. I took an excited step forward, but Vain nipped my neck in a panic.

*Stop! Hole!* she warned, and I looked down to find one several steps away from me. I shuddered, goose bumps crawling up my body and making my hairs stand on end. It was bad enough that the ground felt dead. The holes made it even worse.

"You don't need to look down," Ferrer whispered and reached for my hand. "Just follow me." He clicked and navigated us through the dense fog toward the first source of light.

A domed structure made of mud bricks waited for us. It wasn't very tall, probably as big as any single home we had at the coven, and there were only a couple round windows. Nobody seemed to be there despite the lantern hanging by the entrance.

"Do you see anything else? Anyone?" I whispered, gazing from one blurry, distant light to another. Vain jumped from my shoulder and flew off, causing me to hiss at her in panic. "Come back here this instant!"

*I'll look around. I promise I'll be right back,* she squeaked, ignoring my command. Was she allowed to do that?

*Vain!* Iron growled furiously, but it did no good. She'd wandered off recklessly.

*Vain, you better get back here in five seconds,* Ferrer mind-linked her in a severe tone. *Do not disobey. Do not test me right now.*

She squeaked in fright over the link, and I glanced up at him with an arched brow. Oh, she took him seriously? Vain and I would have to have a little chat.

*Ahh! Someone has me!* Vain's voice shrieked, and it struck my soul like cold lightning. The terror froze me but not Ferrer. He grabbed my hand and tugged me in the direction she was in, but a voice called out a warning through the fog.

"Don't move! I have your familiar! Who are you? You're trespassing!" It sounded like a woman, but I could hardly pay attention to the words. A cold sweat broke out of me, and my head spun like I was about to faint, like my heart was in her clutch instead. I couldn't lose Vain!

"Let her go!" I screamed as the blood pounded painfully hard in my ears. Tears streamed down my face as I tried to stumble forward, but Ferrer tightened his grip on my hand.

"You heard her! Release her or you'll be dead in seconds," he growled. "I promise you that. You hurt that bat, and your throat will be ripped out before you hit the ground."

"This bat," the woman's voice returned, her voice full of seething anger, "is wearing something made by a missing person! You came onto private property, so don't you dare threaten me!

You're asking for a curse, shifter… or whatever the fuck you are! What the shit do you want?"

Ferrer didn't look threatened, which made me nervous. Then I realized something through my muggy haze of terror. "Wait, you're a witch? How…" How could she threaten with a curse? "You can't curse us… there's no magic…" My voice was weak. "Ferrer, she's bluffing," I rasped as quietly as possible through my stream of tears.

"Doesn't matter," he said dismissively.

"You're a witch?" the woman's voice blurted, echoing my question. "Why are you here, but more importantly, what do you know about Cordycaris? I won't ask again!"

"I don't know that name," I cried, desperately trying to pull away from Ferrer's grip so I could run to Vain. "I was trying to escort an old… witch home after we were freed because she was dying. She didn't make it, so I brought her remains… out of respect…" My voice grew ragged as I tried to explain. "Please, let her go! Please! Please! Please! Oh Sky Gods, please!"

I must have convinced her because Vain shot toward me out of the fog, and I fumbled to catch her. I sobbed as I held her to my chest, trying to comfort both of us and slow our racing hearts. My legs weakened, and I collapsed to the ground, shaking from shattered nerves. I turned Vain over in my hands, checking her tiny, fragile body for injuries, but I didn't see anything. The collar was gone though…

"Where are the remains you speak of?" the woman's voice asked harshly, sounding closer this time. Her footsteps became audible as she approached, and I spied a dark silhouette in the lantern-lit fog. The figure marched cautiously toward us and stopped just as we became visible to each other.

Ferrer didn't hesitate. He swung the bag containing Mushy's remains off his shoulder and placed it on the dirt. The woman was cowled, so I couldn't get a good look at her. Curses, not that I could anyway because my vision was so bad right now.

The woman tilted her head and stared down at the sack, seeming lost in thought. Her pose became less rigid by the heartbeat, and she eventually crouched to open it. Reluctant hands pulled at the ties, like she knew what she was going to find but was forcing herself to check.

"Best not to loo—" I began saying, but I stopped, noticing no aroma coming from the bag. In fact, it should have started smelling when the enchantment faded, but it never did. I gasped when the woman dipped her hand in the sack and raised it, holding what appeared to be a clod of dark soil in her hand.

"That was her!" I protested, not understanding how she'd turned into earth so fast.

"It is her," the woman agreed, but she did so softly. She stared at the dirt in her hands, stroking the clumps with a thumb. "You brought Cordycaris home… but your story concerns me," she said, her tone growing hard. "You must come with me and speak to our elders."

"We must do nothing. Our obligation to her and only her is complete," Ferrer replied flatly and pulled me up off the ground.

I huddled next to him but was starting to feel hot, cold, and disoriented. Something was unusual here, and my body was reacting to the anomaly. I ended up dry heaving, and Ferrer's gaze shot down to look at me in alarm. "Keid?"

"If she's a witch, she'll do better underground where our reserves are. I'm surprised she made it this far. She must have significant restraint. Let me rephrase my request. If you have no ill will, you will be treated as a guest until you're ready to leave. Please consider sharing your story with our elders. It would be a last favor to Cordycaris. She was well loved."

"Reserves?" I croaked out as I squatted, my feverish face planted in my cold hands. The longer I sat here, the more I was able to discern what was happening to my body. If there was a source nearby, my body was trying to absorb it, but it kept getting expelled as fast as it'd get absorbed. It was wreaking havoc on my magic digestion.

"Yes," the woman said and quickly closed the sack, sounding a little ill herself. "It is your choice. It's not worth fighting a witch's shifter mate to get closure."

I looked up at Ferrer, who held his hands out for me. I grabbed them and let him lift me to my feet. Feeling a little better, I swiped a hand across my brow to wipe away the cold sweat. "Ferrer, what should we do?" I asked, certain that he was thinking what I was thinking. It could be a good place to seek refuge for a day or so.

"What is this place?" he asked the woman, drawing me closer to him. "Your people live underground?"

"It's a last bastion of sorts," she replied, tight-lipped.

"It sounds like a coven," Ferrer retorted.

"I have people to protect," she hissed. "You either come or go! Make up your mind!"

Those words seemed to strike a chord with Ferrer, and he looked down at me. *Your call, but anyone who touches you is dead, Keid, keep that in mind. I can only control so much.*

That was a bit frightening but so was the prospect of being out in the barren deadlands with rot-witches. I decided that going into the unknown with a stranger was less terrifying than staying out here.

"No one is to touch us," I whispered, and the woman nodded.

"I'll take you to our elders and then find you a guest room. You'll feel better underground," she said, her tone softening into resignation as she spun on a heel. Ferrer and I followed her cautiously as she brought us into the mud-brick dome. A door inside led to a stone staircase, but I couldn't immediately tell how far down it went. Natural torches were used to light the descent, which I thought was curious. If there was magic here, why weren't they using it?

"How shall I introduce you to our elders?" the woman asked in a clipped tone as she gently cradled the bag of remains.

"I am Ferrer and this is Keid," the bat-shifter said, holding my hand in an iron grip. The poor male seemed so much more anxious here than me. Perhaps this had been a mistake.

"And what are you?" she asked him, catching onto his vagueness.

"That's not important," he snapped. "Don't harm us, and I won't kill you. It's simple."

"Quite," she replied tersely as she led us into the depths of the bastion.

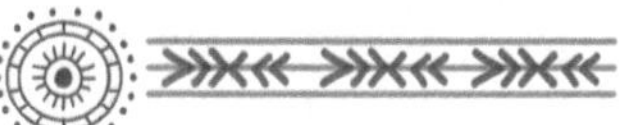

# Chapter 27

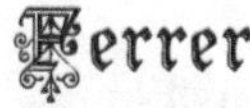

## Ferrer

I wasn't sure what I was expecting, but I hadn't anticipated the underground space looking so decrepit. The stone stairs ended in a large room that branched off into a number of torch-lit halls, each looking as worn down as the first room. Two chairs and a table were tucked into a corner, like guards were posted there on occasion. The wooden floor was uneven, as though roughly hewn from the surrounding dead trees, and the mud-bricked walls were cracked, exposing in places the oppressive presence of the surrounding earth. The support beams, also unevenly cut, framed the corners of the room but were occasionally used to brace weaker-looking walls. All in all, the place was in sad shape.

The witch led us down several halls, passing rooms that were occasionally lacking a door. Peering inside, they appeared to be sleeping chambers, and I was accosted by a number of surprising scents. There were shifters here as well as humans. I smelled cats, wolves, lycans, dragons…

"What is this place?" I asked once more in a low voice, but the woman didn't respond. I growled impatiently, and Keid squeezed my hand in reassurance. I didn't like bringing my mate into unknowns. It infuriated me! Already my back was itching to release my wings, and my claws simply refused to retract.

I looked down at my woman, and she seemed to be feeling better. Whatever ailment she'd suffered had been left at the surface. I'd still feel better once they sorted out a bed for her. She needed rest.

"I do not know if they are awake, but they do not sleep well, so it's possible they are," the woman said, pulling on a larger chamber door to let us pass. When the door creaked open, I was slammed with the scent of rot and stumbled back in shock, fear, and rage. My wings erupted from my back, and I growled furiously at the betrayal.

"We're l-leaving," Keid said falteringly, backing up with a hand against the wall.

The woman frowned at our reactions and looked at us like we were the threat. A voice came from inside, but it was so garbled that I couldn't make out the words.

"Al... right..." the other witch said, looking dubiously at me. "Go then."

"Really...?" Keid asked breathlessly, stunned. Neither of us had expected that. This had very much felt like a trap, and they were just letting us go?

"Yes, you shits. Here I am, offering a place to rest, and you both are acting like animals—a rabid one and a skittish one," she chastised, pointing a finger to each of us in turn.

"There are rot-witches in there!" I hissed, showing my fangs. "And don't call my mate a shit if you value your ability to speak!"

"I won't tolerate your tongue either," she retorted, then pointed back the way we'd come. "Go!"

The voice once again spoke from the room, and the woman's shoulders sagged at whatever had been said. Her expression turned bitter as she looked at us and said, "I apologize." It was the least genuine apology I'd ever received, and I was dumbstruck.

"Could they be like Mushy?" Keid asked, tugging at my arm. "Do you think they're safe? She did live here. She said she was loved."

I didn't like it. I didn't like it one bit. "I don't know," I replied flatly. The woman spoke to the elders inside, explaining who we were while Keid and I were whispering to each other.

"Maybe we could talk to them?" Keid asked, stepping closer to me and wrapping her arms around one of mine. I clenched my jaw, feeling extremely agitated, but her touch was soothing enough for me to keep my mind intact. I was on the verge of turning feral, and I needed to keep my wits about me if there was danger.

"It's the last thing I want to do," I replied.

"Alright, then let's go."

"But it might be your only chance to get answers," I added tersely, not really finished with what I had been saying before her reply.

Keid sighed and chewed on a nail, something I'd never seen her do. She looked incredibly stressed, maybe almost as much as I felt. "Perhaps… It might be worth it to find out why there are rot-witches out there laying down soil…"

"What did you say?" the woman who'd escorted us hissed. I bristled at her tone, and several voices called out to her from within the chamber now. The woman did not look well, and the witches inside sounded alarmed.

"Did you… not know?" Keid asked her, visibly confused.

"How far away are they?" the woman asked, her eyes watering with extreme fear, which shocked me a great deal.

"We've traveled a little over a day since then, but we were moving fast to put distance between us…" I disclosed, realizing that they were not connected to that activity. Her body language held no attempt at deception.

The woman's face contorted as she tried not to cry, and she pointed to the inside of the chamber. "Can you p-please… please… share that with the elders? Whatever you saw?"

I looked down at Keid, who seemed extremely taken aback. "I... um..." she began, flustered. "I guess we could..." She looked up at me. "Yes?"

"We can," I answered tightly and moved into the chamber, keeping my mate behind me as I did so. It took all my effort not to run. Even though I had experience tolerating Mushy—or Cordycaris, I supposed—my instincts tolerated these creatures no better. My skin was alive with fear, flecked with goose bumps and taut hairs.

Three sunken creatures sat in rickety, old wooden chairs with blankets over their laps. Though their skins were of different shades, they all had wiry grey hair and milky eyes. The women looked almost as old as Cordycaris had, and I had to wonder if any of them could actually talk. The garbled voice had not given me confidence.

"Welcome," the one on the left rasped as she sat by a lit stone fireplace. Where did the smoke vent? I hadn't noticed the smell aboveground. "Thank you for bringing Cordycaris home... Before we talk about the ones laying dirt, please explain where you found her."

"Found her?" Keid asked, puzzled by the wording. "Well, she was rounded up with all the other witches in the cat territory... The lions' occupation spread six years ago, and they threw most of the Stellar Coven into a dungeon. I imagine that Mush—I mean, Cordycaris—got mixed in with us."

The rot-witch's face contorted as Keid spoke, giving my mate a long, hard look. The other two glanced at their companion, seemingly asking silent questions.

"Our connection to the outside world is nonexistent right now. We sent people out to collect her body seven years ago, but they never returned." The woman coughed but did not spit out a tooth. She seemed to have more time left in her than Mushy had.

"Who-whose body?" Keid stammered, biting her nail again.

"Cordycaris died seven years ago," she replied and bent over to open the sack the younger witch placed at her feet. Keid glanced up at me, lips parted in her bafflement.

"That couldn't have been her," I said. "That rot-witch was alive mere days ago."

The ancient woman placed her long, clawed hand into the bag and released a sigh, like she'd been holding her breath. "She was always reliable," she whispered, pulling out a handful of rich soil like the other woman had done earlier. I curled a lip in revulsion at this. What was with these people and touching remains?

A witch on the right gurgled a question, and the other nodded. I had no idea how they could understand each other, but somehow, they did.

"You weren't dealing with Cordycaris," the one in the middle wheezed so quietly that I could barely hear it. I repeated the words to Keid, who'd missed them with her human ears. When the words sunk in the second time, a chill dropped into my belly like a giant chunk of ice. What had she said?

"That's... I don't understand," Keid stammered with wide eyes.

"I can't believe she did it," the younger witch said, rubbing her tearstained face. The one on the right garbled something, and it seemed to somewhat calm the woman.

"Apparently, she was right on time. Reliable but never one to follow the rules," the one on the left said with another cough. "I wonder if Fate will punish us for her actions. Non-mothers aren't allowed to scry."

"If it... saves lives... so be it..." the one in the middle replied in a strangled voice.

I grew furious because their discussion among themselves was distressing my mate. Her fear and confusion were spiking, and I growled sharply to get everyone's attention. "Explain what you're talking about!"

The three rot-witches looked weary from my demand, like they hadn't slept in days and were lacking the energy.

"Can it wait until tomorrow?" the younger witch asked, straightening her spine again. "You've come at a late hour, and they are fragile."

I didn't need to know what they meant by fragile. Mushy had disintegrated right before my bloody eyes. I'd never forget that nightmare.

"The others... above..." the one in the middle prompted with a rasp.

"A day's travel south of us, but like I said, we moved in a hurry. They might have come from the east—about a hundred humans with bags, some shackled. There were a handful of rot-witches, but we didn't stick around long enough to count," I reported in a rush, wanting to get Keid to a bed if they weren't going to talk to us.

"They're going to finish the job," the one on the left murmured, looking resigned, but the speechless one on the right snarled at her, prompting a stream of drool to slide down her chin. The young woman moved forward to clean her face up, then stepped out of the way.

"We have... chance now..." the one in the middle argued in a louder voice, but started hacking wetly from the effort.

"Agabius, please... don't strain your voice," the younger witch pleaded. Agabius simply waved her away in dismissal, grunting in annoyance.

"Finish what job?" I asked harshly, getting a bad feeling about coming here. "Are we not safe here?"

"Two days," the one on the left said, staring vacantly into the fireplace. "If they're laying down soil to reach us, they'll be moving much slower. You can rest here, but I suggest you leave before they arrive."

"What... What happens when they arrive?" Keid asked, squeezing up against me.

The witches sighed, obviously tiring, and the one on the left gestured to the younger witch. "Eriu, please..."

Eriu frowned, wiped mucus from her nose, and said, "They are coming to recruit. Whoever doesn't join will be executed. We've run from this countless times over thousands of years, and it seems like our safeguards are no longer strong enough."

The witch shook her head, getting angry once more. "They're the ones who killed the Earth Coven! They're the ones who drove us out! They're the ones who spit upon our gods!"

"Wait, so this is a coven?" Keid asked, rubbing her temples.

"Perhaps the tattered remains of several," Eriu answered bitterly. "We take in strays too. Most here are not witches, and they're all going to have to leave to find a new home before they're killed." She looked at the rot-witches. "We will make the announcement in the morning for the evacuation..."

"There's not enough time to get back to the dragons to get help... is there?" Keid asked, looking up at me with tears in her eyes. Oh gods, I couldn't handle seeing her cry over this, but I didn't know who to kill for it. I scrubbed my palms over my face and growled.

"No," I said gruffly. "Not even if I flew. Not even if I didn't sleep. If I did get to the meeting spot, we'd still have to fly back here, and we'd only have two extra dragons. It'd take more time to get reinforcements, an—"

"I get it, I get it," Keid said quietly, interrupting my frustrated tirade.

The witch on the right gargled something, and Eriu translated but did so while giving me a curious look. "Morchenta said she's sorry for what her sisters did to your kind..." Eriu frowned at the old woman. "What are you talking about?"

My eyes locked onto Morchenta, who was looking more exhausted by the second. Her cataract-ridden eyes were bloodshot and watery, leaking tears as she blinked, but I couldn't tell why those tears were there. Did she feel remorse? I didn't understand.

"Sorry isn't enough," I snapped, my throat trying to lock up out of fear and rage. "It will never be enough."

"Cantharius?" Eriu appealed to the witch on the left. "What is she talking about?" Cantharius waved her off as well and yawned. The younger witch wrinkled her nose, then snorted in irritation. "Tomorrow then," she said through her teeth and looked back at Keid and me. "After the announcement, I will gather you both, and we will discuss this further. I'm sure they'll be in better shape to answer my questions as well as yours."

The younger witch opened the chamber door for us, and I took a long look at Morchenta before leaving. She'd better be alive tomorrow for those answers.

Eriu brought us to an empty chamber and showed us where the essentials were. "We have basic plumbing, so you do have a toilet and a sink," she explained and marched back to the door as briskly as she'd entered the room. "I'm assigning a guard for outside your room," she added, turning on a heel to address us before leaving, "for everyone's safety. There is clearly distrust remaining."

"It's my job to distrust," Ferrer growled aggressively, enunciating each word in that sentence, and I placed a hand on his arm in an attempt to calm him. I couldn't blame him for getting worked up because this was probably the worst place for him to be in his state. He was extremely territorial now and had found himself in what he'd normally consider to be enemy territory with a pregnant mate.

Eriu glanced at me and connected the dots rather quickly. "I see now," she said in a softer tone. "I will have Akira look at you tomorrow. How far along?"

Ferrer and I—once again—simultaneously started counting on our fingers, and I burst into laughter. The bat-shifter seemed to calm from the sound, and I regained my focus enough to answer her question. "If it's after midnight, that makes it... about ten days." I blinked up at Ferrer. "Wow. Ten days already?" He put his hands down and nodded thoughtfully.

"I see... So, recent. That makes even more sense. Good night," Eriu murmured from beneath her cowl and left us alone.

I went through my bag to find our packed food while Ferrer refilled my canteen at the sink. "Here," he said, handing the water to me after taking a sip, "it seems safe."

"Thank you," I said, passing him his meal so we could eat before resting. I guessed we'd be switching to a daytime schedule now for at least a day? It was utterly exhausting to keep switching back and forth. I didn't care what my schedule ended up being at the colony; so long as it was consistent, I'd be overjoyed.

I crawled onto the bed with my food and ate in silence, trying to process what little we'd learned. It was all a horrid tease. We'd been exposed to a great number of half-truths, but the one that bothered me the most was Mushy being dead before she'd died. Certainly, they had the wrong person… right? How could someone die twice?

I shuddered and finished my meal while Ferrer climbed onto the bed. I wasn't surprised that he'd practically inhaled his food. He must have burned half of today's calories from stress alone. I washed up at the sink, feeling incredibly eager to sleep in a bed again. Aside from its own, my bottom had forgotten what cushions felt like.

Ferrer had already crawled into the small bed but had saved room for me. He lay on his side as he watched me climb under the sheet and start plucking at one of the feathers I'd saved from the waterfowl. If the rot-witches were nearby, I'd not leave Vain without protection. She desperately needed another collar. I glanced over at her roosting spot just under a support beam and was uneasy. I'd gotten a taste of what it'd feel like to almost lose her, and I never wanted to experience that again. I'd never been so scared in my life. I didn't know how Eriu managed to grab her, but I needed to make the next collar a much smarter one.

"What are you doing?" Ferrer asked in a quiet voice as he stared at my plucking.

"Vain needs a new collar. I'm tired, but I'm not quite sleepy yet, and my mind is buzzing…" I sighed as I started to form a pile of barbs to weave together later. "Feathers work the best for cramming more enchantments into smaller projects," I explained and held a barb up for him to see. "There's tiny little barbs on each barb called barbules, and each barbule has many hooklets. There are so many parts to weave enchantments into. Sturdy and flexible… Feathers truly are a marvel of nature."

Ferrer was silent for a minute as he watched me work. "You're so clever," he remarked. "I recall watching you enchant before. You make witchwork beautiful."

Oh gods, that was extremely flattering. My cheeks grew hot from the compliment, and as much as I wanted to deny it, I knew better than to try that with him at this point. I bit my lip, then whispered, "Thank you." He must've been expecting me to fight him on that because he relaxed after I expressed my gratitude.

In my peripheral vision, Ferrer let out one of Marrow's wings and held it over him. "Cold?" I asked, then noticed that I had goose bumps myself. It was very chilly underground, and I was fortunate that Ferrer was here to keep me warm.

"Not really," he responded thoughtfully. His hand jerked at something, and when I looked at what he was holding out for me, my lips parted in surprise.

"Ferrer?" I asked hesitantly, staring at the large brown-and-white feather.

"I want you to use mine instead," he said softly, his warm eyes staring up at me, waiting for my reaction.

"Ferrer…" I repeated, speechless for a good, long moment. "Do you understand what I could do with that? Do you understand the dangers of giving a piece of yourself to a witch? This has a part of you in it. I could use it against you."

"I had a feeling, and yes, I've considered it," he said calmly, but his hand never wavered as he continued to hold it out for me. "Let me help protect her."

I couldn't believe he was doing this—trusting me with a piece of himself. I could hurt him in so many ways, but all he wanted to do was to help protect Vain? I raised my hand slowly and closed my fingers around the delicate offering. Tears brimmed in my eyes, and my breath stuttered. Did he not understand? Did he not know what this meant?

This gesture was the greatest show of trust he could ever place in me, and it utterly shattered the last of my defenses. Every piece of my wall disintegrated. In deep shock, I placed the feathers and the pile of barbs on the small table by the bed and turned to face Ferrer. His expression was enigmatic as he waited for me, but it didn't bother me this time because his feather had spoken the truth. I saw him so clearly now.

He loved me.

A momentum built within me that accelerated with each heartbeat—faster and fiercer than a meteor shower. Perhaps what had shattered was my own horizon, for I was no longer able to hide behind it. I was exposed and so were my feelings to myself. I could see them just as clearly now.

"I love you," I breathed, unable to suppress the confession. The words beat their way out of me like they had their own accursed wings. What else could I do but let them go?

I didn't wait for him to say anything. He might have awakened me, but my feelings were not reliant on his, and I wanted him to know that. I palmed his gaping, blushing face and gave him his first kiss.

Sensations erupted where our lips met, and I couldn't tell which of the soft, muffled groans in the air was mine. I threaded my fingers through his hair, cupping the back of his head to crush our lips together. Ferrer's hand mirrored mine, gripping possessively while the other slid beneath me to pull me to his chest.

I massaged his lips with mine, somewhat embarrassed about the tears streaming down my cheeks, but he simply wiped them away with a thumb. A soft growl purred from his throat, and for some reason, I was comforted by the noise. Like how I knew he loved me, I knew that noise was meant to soothe. With a glowing heart and growing confidence, I prodded between his lips with my tongue, wanting to show him the pleasures of a deeper kiss.

When he opened his mouth, I slipped my tongue inside, making him growl loudly and roll on top of me. His reaction reinforced my self-esteem, and my face grew wet again. Ferrer made me feel so beautiful, and I was overwhelmed. It was like my body couldn't contain the experience, and my emotions had to leak out in the form of tears. They just wouldn't fit.

I explored his groaning mouth until I noticed his fangs elongating. Perhaps I should have been worried about them cutting me, but for some reason, flirting about them with my tongue was exciting. Those fangs had been in my neck. Those were what he'd used to claim me for himself when he didn't even know he wanted me. In all honesty, they probably aroused me as much as his cock.

And speaking of the accursed log, I could feel its heat through his pants as he lay on top of me, gently grinding between my legs. I was still sore, but I wanted him. Could I bring myself to…?

"Ferrer." I gasped softly, moving my lips away from his, which I realized I hated doing. "Please… I…"

The male propped himself up over me and gave me a calm, patient look despite his heaving chest and thrumming pulse. I swallowed hard, staring at his rouged, swollen lips. The evidence of our kissing, and how he'd embraced it, emboldened me.

Placing a hand on his chest, I whispered, "Make love to me? Gently?"

If he didn't know what that phrase meant, he figured it out quickly enough. He shucked his pants off faster than I could blink and began helping me undress, breathing heavily in anticipation. I couldn't believe the effect I had on him. Had my eyes been closed this entire time?

Feeling less shy now, I opened my arms for him as I lay back on the bed, and he was in them in half a heartbeat. This time, he initiated the kiss, but it was different from mine. Taking the word 'gently' to heart, he eased his lips onto mine and slowly slid his tongue between them, prying my mouth open to deliver a deep, long, and languid kiss.

I shivered and wrapped my arms around his neck to pull him closer. The skin of his chest pressed into my stomach and breasts while his cock lay hard and heavy between us. He barely moved at first as he focused on delivering the most sensual kiss I'd ever received in my life. I was certain that I had melted like butter by the time he released my lips and moved down to let his cock fall between my thighs.

"Oh gods, Ferrer," I moaned, staring down at him and feeling so very thankful for my nearsight. He was beautiful—made to be looked at, so I did. My eyes roved over a body I couldn't believe was mine. For once, I saw how it mirrored his inner self. Brutally strong but capable of so much sweetness.

"Look at what you do to me, Keid," Ferrer said, thumbing a stream of precum that trickled from the head of his cock. He rubbed it around his crown, staring at me while he did so. I bit my lower lip hard and a small, embarrassing whimper leaked from my throat. He seemed to be quite stimulated by that sound because he released another growl and moved the head of his cock to my sex. His deft hands nuzzled his erection between my folds, then slid it up and down like he was lubricating me.

"Don't even need it," he murmured as he stared at me. "You're crying for me, Keid." He notched himself in place and leaned forward, preparing to push past my entrance. I blushed as his gaze became more intense, but then it softened tremendously as a tender look replaced his fierce countenance.

He lowered his head to kiss me, but instead of pressing his lips into mine, he murmured five words, releasing them to brush past my lips and settle into my soul. "I love you too, Keid."

I sobbed in euphoria, and on those words, he gently rolled his hips to ease his length inside me. Tears streamed down my face again, and I couldn't help it. We'd finally come together. After all we'd suffered, we managed to find ourselves right where we were intended to be.

I lifted my legs to wrap them around his hips, wanting to feel as much of him as I could, and Ferrer pumped to gradually fill me. He was being so mindful of my soreness, and it deepened my affection for him. "I'll go slow," he murmured into my temple, then kissed it. His voice was thick, and for a moment, I thought we'd both end up crying.

"Thank you," I whispered, unable to keep my lip from trembling. I was so vulnerable right now, but I felt so safe. My body wasn't used to it at all.

Ferrer pulled his hips back, dragging his cock along my wall until he was halfway out, then pushed slowly in again. I hummed in pleasure from the gentle stretching and slid my hands up into his hair to massage his scalp. He groaned and drew his length out before easing in again. He swelled little by little as he became progressively more aroused, and he hissed into my neck when I rubbed his pointed ears.

I raised my brows as I ran my fingers up them again, and he spasmed, pushing deeper into me as he came. His cry was muffled as he lightly bit my neck, careful not to pierce my skin. I sighed in pleasure as he released against my inner wall, deeply satisfied by his primal claiming. I wanted it again and again.

"Careful with the ears," he rasped into my neck, grinding his hips into me as his climax ejected the last rope of seed.

"Alright, I will make a note to not be careful with them," I whispered through a grin, feeling deliciously, delightfully feverish with gratification. I never thought it could be rapturous to give a man or male so much pleasure, and the power I felt from it was dizzying. It was yet another gift that Ferrer had given me—one he hadn't realized he'd given.

He chuckled into my neck and kissed slowly up it, stopping at my ear to lick its shell. He slowly started rolling his hips again and released a breathy noise of pleasure that sent cold, glorious sparks of electricity down my belly to settle between my legs. I pressed my hips up to receive his next glide in, moving with his rhythm to lose myself in him.

His slow, sensual pace drew me into a state of carnal delirium, and I found myself lightly clawing at his back for release.

Catching onto the signs, he reached between us to caress my clit, mindful that heavy grinding would be painful right now.

I arched and mewled into him as he murmured his admiration. "If only you could see yourself now," he whispered between aroused pants, rubbing carefully around my clit. "I'm going to think about this sight every single time I'm away from you." His words sent a thrill through me, and I dug my fingers into his back, finding a solid grip on his taut muscles. "In meetings… on patrols… or just when I'm waiting for you to wake in the mornings in the bed we'll share."

Oh gods. The hot swell came out of nowhere, and I was assaulted by a blaze that rolled through my sex and shot up my body. I hissed and nearly squealed through my teeth as I tried to climax quietly. My arms and legs shook as I yanked Ferrer down into a tight embrace, clenching down on his length. He growled and seemed close to losing control, pumping through my contractions until he spent his seed again.

We writhed together, two pale bodies locked tight under dim candlelight. His lips landed on mine again, sending my heart careening to join the fabric of pleasure that'd encircled us. My sex throbbed like an accursed pulsar, radiating delight in its spin. I was left breathless in its wake and collapsed under my male when my orgasm faded into warm darkness.

Ferrer dragged his cock out slowly, groaning quietly as he settled next to me. I turned into him, pressing my body as closely as possible to his sweaty form. He flexed me against him, and I just knew he felt as I did. I didn't need to mark him to know his deep contentment. I could hear it, see it, and feel it. I knew it was real.

"I cannot wait to bring you home, Keid," he whispered into the top of my head. "Whatever happens before that, I'll keep you and our offspring safe, I swear."

"I know, my mate," I whispered, nuzzling into his chest as I drifted into sleep. I finally, thoroughly believed him, and I would protect him too.

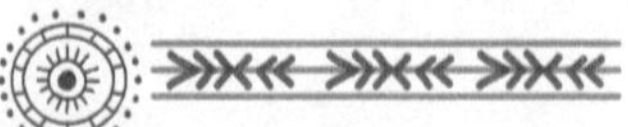
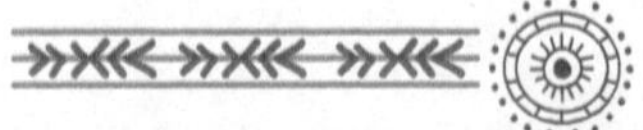

# Chapter 28

## Keid

A knocking at the door disrupted my complete bliss, and I clung on to Ferrer when he tried to get up to answer it. He chuckled and pried my fingers off him to address the visitor. My head popped out of the blanket when I realized he was going to open the door without pants, but the voice on the other side was male. I breathed a sigh of relief and flopped back onto the warm mattress that was still radiating Ferrer's body heat.

"That was our guard, a dragon-shifter," Ferrer said quietly, slipping his pants on before crouching by the bedside to look at me. "He's to take us to eat, then have an audience with the mothers. I suppose that's the role those rot-witches have here. Elders, mothers, whatever. Great-great-great grandmother seems more appropriate."

"Right," I croaked with a smile and sat up, licking my lips. Ferrer sweetly handed me my canteen, and I took a long draw of water. Vain fluttered down to land on my lap, and I smiled at the cute little thing. She truly was a little beam of starshine. Iron's nickname was apt.

*And then a new collar?* she asked. *I feel naked.*

"Well, we can't have a bat feeling naked," I asserted, scooping her up to pass to Ferrer while I dressed. "I will get started on it immediately. Ferrer has…" I hesitated and looked over at him, feeling a swelling of warmth in my heart. "Donated one of his feathers."

*I know. I heard,* she chirped.

"You did, did you?" I uttered, clearing my throat as I pulled my tunic over my head.

*All of it.*

I blew out a heavy breath and accepted that she'd been awake. Perhaps it was impossible to be quiet enough for her. She'd been around it in the woods. Why would it be different here? "Right."

*Was it good?* she inquired innocently. *You feel prettier now?*

Ferrer burst into laughter as he opened the door for us, and my face ruddied into a hot mess. "Er… yes," I replied shortly and whisked out into the hall to meet our escort, hoping to avoid follow-up questions.

*Vain, you're pretty too. Just reminding you,* Iron added, not wanting to be left out of the topic I very much wanted to drop.

*I would agree that they are both pretty for their species,* Marrow added. *Keid is lovely and Vain is a particularly cute little creature.*

*I know,* she chirped happily.

The chatter in my head was distracting, and I forced myself to smile at our guard, who was standing tall in the hallway, wearing the same style cloak as Eriu. It was cold down here, and I wished that I had a cloak too. Perhaps I should have brought my blanket along.

"Sunlight preserve you," the male said politely, briefly greeting us before turning to stride down the hall. He was a little older, perhaps in his middle age, but his gait was intriguing because he moved a bit like he'd come from high society. He also seemed, however, to be lacking an arm, and I was curious about his story. Eriu did say they took in strays.

When he kept looking over his shoulder at me, Ferrer drew me closer to him and growled a warning. The male laughed and pulled at the neck of his shirt and cloak, showing a mating mark.

"Please," he drawled with a lazy smile, "she merely reminds me of someone I used to know."

"A daughter?" I asked, frowning.

"In a way, Miss Keid," he said with a laugh. "A twisted way."

"You know our names, and you've yet to introduce yourself," Ferrer said flatly, moving me to his other side to put himself between us. I let him do it. It's not like the dragon-shifter wasn't making me uncomfortable.

"I've come here to start fresh," the male responded in a darker tone. "I won't scandalize you with my sordid past." He opened a large door and gestured us into what looked like a communal dining hall. It was bustling with activity, and the people inside looked anxious. Eriu must have made the announcement already…

"Thank you for bringing us," I muttered, trying to be polite to the stranger.

"Of course. Ah! My dear, you are radiant this morning," he said, becoming distracted by a cranky-looking woman who came to greet him. "Please join us."

The woman did a double-take when she saw me, then glanced at the dragon. "Almost thought that was her for a second."

"It's the hair," he said, kissing her on the cheek and leading us to a table laden with food. Ferrer continued to glare at him and act like a shield as he filled his plate with anything that had bone still attached to it, which wasn't much. I wondered if they had any blood in the back; otherwise, he'd have to go hunting later. There was no way he'd agree to feed on me, even a little bit. I didn't need a mark to know that.

Unfortunately, the dragon and the woman joined us at the table to eat. Were these two mates? I was confused, but if she had somehow managed to mark him… maybe…

"Um…" I said, clearing my throat awkwardly to get her attention. "How did… How did you mark him?" I asked the older woman, not even sure if she was a witch. My question very nearly came out in a squeak. It was probably very rude, but I wasn't going to be here much longer.

The woman's face soured more than its natural state, but it was the dragon who answered, snorting at my question. "Oh no, this one?" He chuckled, pulling at his collar again. "This one left me. Turns out once you lose everything, you lose everyone."

"Everyone who doesn't matter," the woman grumbled, shoveling eggs into her mouth.

"You are as correct as always, my dear," the dragon said dotingly, sounding more aristocratic than ever.

"Oh," I replied quietly, feeling disappointed. Ferrer reached under the table to hold my hand, squeezing to let me know it didn't bother him. It kind of bothered me, only because I'd noticed a lot of women and females staring at my shirtless bat-shifter. A shapely wolf in particular had been eying him since we'd seated ourselves. I didn't like how she stared at his neck.

I frowned when I took a bite of bread and looked up at the strange couple. "Can you not get the mark removed?"

The woman rolled her eyes and shook her head, which irritated me quite a bit. It was a perfectly good question considering what Mushy had communicated to me. "It's not possible. I already asked the mothers here," she replied sharply, stabbing her plate like it was the dragon's past mate.

My eyes met Ferrer's in shock. "She lied?" I asked him quietly.

He looked stunned as well, but it passed quickly, and he shook his head. "Should we be surprised?"

"Do you think she lied… about my eggs?" I whispered fearfully. "Are you sure she gave them back? Are you sure I—"

"Trafficked eggs?" the dragon mused from across the table, listening to us. "How terribly clever. People like you are incredibly expensive in th—"

Ferrer slammed his fist down on the table, making everyone jump in surprise. The plates rattled, and several cups fell over at the force of the impact. I immediately put a hand to his arm, but he didn't seem to respond to it. The hall went mostly silent, but a couple tables continued chatting nervously.

"Impetuous youth," the woman grumbled, wiping at the table with a napkin.

Ferrer leaned across the table, hissing through his teeth. "Do not refer to her so disrespectfully! I am one insult away from ripping off that other arm! Now what are you talking about?" His fangs and claws were out, but the dragon didn't seem particularly perturbed. He simply dabbed his mouth with his napkin before responding.

"Albinos are worth a lot, or should I say 'were.' I've lost track of the slave trade. The darker markets will even pay well for body p—"

"Not a table conversation!" the woman next to him snapped.

"I was never involved, my dear," the male argued to placate her. He held his hand up in surrender. "Too messy."

I was sick. I placed my icy hands to my simmering face and stumbled away from the table, no longer hungry. Nausea roiled into my belly, like Mushy's blood stew boiling over a cauldron's lip.

"No… no, no, no," I moaned miserably and ran out into the blurry hall. The panic and pain was rampant. I needed to hide. I needed to escape!

My heart felt like it was going to give out; it was racing so fast. As I sprinted, the corners of my vision started to creep in, and I blacked out, falling to the ground without my near vision and balance to guide me.

*Keid! Keid! Keid!* Vain cried, fluttering to land by my face. Her tiny tongue prodded the tip of my nose, and I moaned through my blackout as I waited for my heart to slow and my face to cool.

"Find Eriu," Ferrer's voice ordered, and Vain flew off to fulfill his command. He dropped to his knees to slide my head into his lap. "Keid. Keid, can you hear me? Keid, oh gods, wake up!"

"—ogizing to do here," the woman's sharp voice reprimanded from down the hall.

"I am very sorry," the dragon-shifter said from afar, not coming closer because Ferrer had snarled loudly at him. "I spoke without thinking. Shall we get you to our doctor? Can she hear me?"

I mumbled a yes to both their questions, and Ferrer lifted me from the ground. The longer I was horizontal, the better I began to feel, but I was so tired. My lids were heavy and stayed shut until I was gently laid out onto a bed.

"—ew I was supposed to see her later, but what happened?" a female's voice inquired hastily from outside the room I was placed in, and I heard the dragon explaining the incident. Ferrer stayed at my side, holding my hand while I debated over whether I wanted to open my eyes or not. I was devastated.

Did I have children out there I didn't know about? How many? How old? Were they enslaved? Had they been freed by the dragons? Had they been… I shut my eyes tighter and moaned as tears slid freely down my temples to soak the pillow. Unlike last night, these were not tears of joy.

"Don't cry, don't cry," Ferrer whispered worriedly, wiping my face dry. "Have some water," he murmured, sliding his hand under my head to bring a glass to my lips. I took a couple sips, struggling to not fall into wailing sobs. Ferrer cupped my face and said, "Keid, listen to me. Look at me."

Compelled by his thick tone, I managed to pry open my eyes. I blinked the water away and stared at Ferrer's pained, but earnest, face. He grabbed both my hands and leaned down to lock gazes with me.

"Listen, we cannot change the past, alright? What we can do is inform your old coven and the dragons when we return so they can investigate. I was already thinking about that when Mushy exposed the theft. We'll find who's responsible, alright?" He shook my hands a little to get me to answer. "Alright, Keid? We'll do that as soon as we return. Alright?"

I nodded slowly, my vision occasionally blurring completely with fresh tears. I felt so violated, and I knew he could sense that. In a way, it was a relief that I didn't need to share my feelings. He was informed and could work with it.

My lip quivered uncontrollably as I fought against the deep, raking sobs that were dying to break out of my chest. I hadn't really thought about what had been done with the eggs since I'd had them replaced... but those weren't the original ones. The original ones were long gone.

Ferrer held on to me until the woman who'd been talking to the dragon-shifter finally entered the room. "Hello, I am Doctor Kazue Akira. You may call me Akira," she said in a gentle but brisk tone. "I'm sorry for the wait. We've had a great many panic attacks to contend with today..." She began her examination by feeling my pulse at my wrist. "How are you feeling now that you've gotten a chance to lie down?"

"Better," I rasped, barely making an effort to speak. I wanted to just disappear.

I realized she was a female shifter and not a woman when she leaned over to place her ear to my chest, asking me to take a deep breath. She listened for a moment, nodded, and checked my pulse at the wrist.

"I hear congratulations are in order?" she inquired lightly, smiling down at me as she checked my reflexes.

I nodded, trying to focus solely on the one child I'd wanted to make. I could barely process anything else. I was crumbling hard.

"Is the offspring alright?" Ferrer asked nervously, squeezing my hand with both of his.

"Oh, women's bodies are tougher than that," she replied with a smile, tucking a strand of black hair away from her large, tan eyes. "But I've got a witch coming to check so you can feel better about it, alright?"

"Thank you," Ferrer said on an exhale, and looked down at me, stroking my hand with a thumb.

As the doctor continued her examination, a witch came in to check my pregnancy. Her procedure seemed similar to what our doctors practiced, so I felt comfortable and safe, especially with Ferrer glaring at her. I honestly didn't know if I could trust a witch to take care of me ever again after this. A bat? Yes. They would want me to keep my eggs.

Destroyed trust… I'd only come back from it once. I looked over at Ferrer again, and he seemed to know what I was thinking. He leaned over to kiss my forehead and continued watching everything that was being noted.

"Well," the witch said as her hand hovered over my lower abdomen, "the egg has successfully implanted, so all looks well with the pregnancy. The one thing I don't understand is that your eggs don't match your age. You have way more than you should at this point."

"They were taken and replaced," I replied emptily and stared off into a corner of the room, looking idly at the bottles and devices stored on shelves. Ferrer explained it more thoroughly, but I barely paid attention to it. I didn't want to think about it. I'd suppressed my grief so violently that I felt nothing now, and I wanted it to stay that way.

## Ferrer

It really was taking everything in me not to go out and rip off that dragon's remaining arm. Yes, more information was always beneficial for investigations, but… I studied Keid's empty face as she rested on the hospital bed. I had to wonder if not knowing would've been better.

*No,* Marrow advised calmly. *It's good we know. If anyone has hurt her, she needs justice to be served. Now we know what information to bring to Leofwine. They can cross-reference with their slave cases.*

*Listen to the big boy,* Iron said, *but hey, we could still kill that dragon in the hall. Why can't we have both?*

*Because we'll get kicked out before Keid can recover,* Marrow answered, ever the voice of reason… until courtship was involved.

*Quiet. Speak privately,* I told them both, in no mood to listen to their chatter. My thoughts were already running rampant, and my feral mind was threatening to break free.

I could barely tolerate the idea that someone else's seed could've been combined with my mate's eggs. It made me sick. It made me jealous. It made me furious. It made me even more territorial of her. It made me want to keep her pregnant so no one else could take her between our pups. I felt a mad urge to destroy everything within reach. As much as I held on to Keid's hand to comfort her, I also did it in desperation to anchor myself. I was reeling.

The cat-shifter doctor approached Keid's side and said, "Alright, Keid. You're free to go. It was just emotional stress that triggered vasovagal syncope. You just fainted. Just rest, and you'll be completely fine." Akira moved to a stone cabinet and opened a drawer to pull out a large canteen. Handing it to me, she added, "I was asked to provide this for you. We had a couple volunteers come in earlier."

I looked into what she'd given me and raised my brows in surprise. They'd gotten people to donate blood. At least I didn't have to worry about my next meal. I could focus completely on Keid. "Thank you," I said simply, placing the chilled canteen on my lap.

A scratching at the door prompted the doctor to open it, and Vain flew in to land on Keid's chest. She crawled slowly up her tunic to settle in her usual spot on Keid's shoulder.

*Eriu is coming,* she reported timidly.

*Thank you, Starshine,* Iron said, sounding relieved.

"Are you hungry?" I asked her. No doubt Vain was incredibly stressed as well.

*Yes,* she squeaked with a sigh, and I patted my shoulder, partially to let Keid have some space.

"Come eat," I ordered, and the bat jumped onto me to feed.

Eriu eventually arrived, and she frowned at Keid's listless state. "I'm sorry to hear about what happened." Keid nodded slowly in acknowledgment but didn't reply. "I can't very well reprimand him for sharing his knowledge, but I did warn him to be more tactful when he's on duty." She sighed. "There's a lot to be untrained with him. Some backgrounds are more difficult to work with."

"What incubator did you scrape that one off anyway?" I muttered.

"Now, now," Akira intervened, raising a palm. "Everyone who's joined us is entitled to their privacy and anonymity. Let's not stress out my patient with further talk of it."

I nodded guiltily, massaging Keid's hand gently as I held it. Her eyes moved to look up at Eriu, who shoved her hands into her pockets and announced, "Well, the mothers are available, but it looks like you will want to rest more before seeing them?"

I glanced down at Keid, then looked up at the doctor, waiting for their opinions. Akira shrugged and said, "I told her she's cleared to go, but I'd advise against significant excitement. Water and rest would be best."

"I think now's a good time," Keid said quietly, her gaze moving from Eriu to the doctor. "I feel nice and numb now. I think I'd rather do it now than later."

Oh, I did not like that. "Keid, I don't know if that's a good reason to rush," I argued, trying not to sound angry.

"The longer we wait, the closer the rot-witches will be to us. Don't you want to leave as soon as possible with everyone else?" she asked.

Shit. That was a really good point. I stood abruptly and held a hand out for her, offering to help her get off the bed. She took it, and when I stared worriedly at her vacant face, she noticed and stopped moving. Her eyes stared at mine for a moment, then closed tightly. She whimpered, shook her head slightly, then slapped herself in the face—hard. Both Akira and Eriu gasped, and though I was shocked, I was more than a little angry.

"Keid! Why? Don't do that!" I shouted and gripped her hand before she could do it again.

"I can't afford to be this way now," she answered sternly, her cheek red from the impact. She glared up at me, but I knew it wasn't directed at either of us. The situation we'd found ourselves in was receiving the full brunt of her anger. "I need to snap out of it. I'm stronger than this." The last words were said under her breath as she scooted to the edge of the bed.

To say that I was thrown was an understatement. I had not expected her to pierce her wall of grief so quickly, even though it might be temporary. However, this was the woman who led the witches' liberation from the lions' dungeon. Maybe she was calling upon that determination. I truly had no idea.

Keid hopped out of bed with one hand in mine and gestured for Eriu to lead the way.

"Good woman." The doctor nodded approvingly and turned to clean up her office. "Come back if you need me. I will be here until the last minute."

"Thank you, Akira," Keid said, pulling at the bottom of her tunic to straighten it.

The dragon-shifter and his companion were waiting outside and fell silent when we emerged from the office. Keid held up a hand before they could say anything. "No. Thank you for informing me. I'll investigate." Her tone was clipped, dismissive, and a little hard.

"You may leave your post and join the evacuation," Eriu told him.

The dragon-shifter nodded in acknowledgment and turned on a heel, followed immediately by the older woman. I took an instinctive step after him, feeling my claws come out, but Keid jerked on my arm.

"No. Calm down," she ordered and turned to follow Eriu, trusting me to join her. I stared as the dragon-shifter rounded a corner, the flaring of his cloak being the last of him to disappear. My fangs itched to drain him dry, and my ears craved his screams, but I clamped down on the urge. Keid's potential anger outweighed the satisfaction of his death.

Eriu led us to a different area of the bastion, and I knew we had to be closer to the river because I could just detect a rushing noise coming through the holes in the ceiling. She opened a large, thin door and said, "This is our greenhouse."

Green it was, but plentiful it was not. A house it was definitely not. It was much bigger—a colossal cavern. The holes between the stalactites were larger, letting in a fair amount of light and possibly a little rain—if this region got any. Large grow beds took up most of the floor and were all full of crops, but most were in bad condition. Though some stalks produced fruit and vegetables, they were limp, thin, and underdeveloped.

The three rot-witches were crouched around a large, circular bed of compost with what I suspected was the sack of Mushy's remains. They had trowels in hand but appeared indecisive about their project. All three looked up as we approached, expressions inscrutable.

"Good morning, mothers," Keid said flatly, nodding her greeting.

"Earthlight preserve you," Cantharius replied solemnly and scooped a small amount of Mushy's remains into a burlap bag. She tightened the string and put it to the side, then waved for us to join them on the ground. I chose to remain standing, but Keid settled cross-legged on the dirty stone floor.

"Hi," Agabius croaked simply and tossed an earthworm into the central grow bed. Upon closer inspection, there were skeletal remains in the compost, and I curled up a lip in revulsion.

"What has you so perturbed, bat?" Cantharius inquired, not missing my expression.

"My people are not a fan of rot-witches," I retorted, sneering at the obvious answer.

"Why?" Agabius asked in a wheeze, tossing another earthworm.

"Ask her," I growled, pointing to Morchenta, who was sitting in silence like usual.

"Oh, we know about what the others did," Cantharius murmured, wiping her long, spindly fingers on the skirts of her old, faded dress. "We had nothing to do with it."

"You are unnatural," I added aggressively. "Cruel. You are decay at its core."

Morchenta began laughing, but it turned into a bout of wet coughing, and Eriu rushed forward to aid her. She glared furiously up at me, but Cantharius raised a hand to stop her.

"And what is wrong with decay? Rot?" she inquired. Why in the shitting stars was she asking me these questions? When I didn't reply out of sheer stubbornness and refusal to play her game, she continued speaking. "Did you know that we worship the Earth Gods and work directly with Their blessing? That we formed the Terran Coven?"

"There is much that is not known about you and for good reason. Your kind goes mad. You murder. You crave power. You destroy. No one seeks your kind out," I retorted heatedly. Keid looked up at me, but her gaze wasn't admonishing. She was simply observing. For some reason, her neutral acceptance calmed me, but I couldn't pinpoint why.

"It is hard to live so long and not go a little mad," Agabius muttered under her breath. "Morchenta is halfway there."

"It's remarkable how much attention is given to the stages between birth and death," Cantharius said thoughtfully and picked up her trowel to fill another burlap bag. "There is another half that is ignored—the stages between death and birth. I suppose it's boring. No flowers, no babies, no sex, no laughter, or fighting."

"Critical though," Agabius croaked in a whisper, tossing something smaller into the grow bed.

"What would happen to all the corpses, I wonder, without rot? What would happen to the soil if nutrients were never returned?" Cantharius asked no one in particular and reached out to run a finger down a stained bone that poked from the soil. She pushed it down, making sure it was properly buried this time. "Recycling—it's a job no one wants to do, which is why the Earth Gods used to protect us worshipers. No… our sisters ruined that for us."

"You mentioned recruiting," I prompted, crossing my arms over my chest. I didn't need their excuses, though her point made me uncomfortable. What I needed was information about the dangers we were facing. What if the witches turned east? What if they marched on my colony?

"They seek to remove the 'doubtful,'" Cantharius informed bitterly. "They are aiming for something and want no dissidents. The more witches they have, the better their chances will be… whatever that is."

"Aiming for something?" I inquired, furious at the vagueness. Certainly, they knew more than they were telling me.

Morchenta snorted and shook her head. Cantharius sighed, already fatigued and short of breath. She weakly waved to Eriu who nodded and held up a placating hand in return.

"I will give you the context you are obviously lacking. Perhaps you can share it so we don't run into others who will slaughter the rest of us, twisted by their misinformed and prejudiced minds," Eriu snapped in a cold voice. While frowning at me, she pointed at Keid. "You know the Earth Gods made the humans—your mate." I bared a fang, not appreciating her tone. "And you have to know now that we witches draw our power from our gods, from the earth. The Earth Gods are love. They give. In order to give, They must make, and you cannot make from nothing. It is why rot is just as important as growth. You say it like it's profane, and that is not only offensive, it's wrong. Rot is divine.

"Searching for a 'greater love,' ages ago, our sisters dug too deep into the darkness below our very feet," Eriu said bitterly. "They found something our gods tucked away, and I can't imagine it was meant to be found. Our coven was divided back then upon the discovery. Some of us wanted to leave its presence well alone, but the others wanted to explore its existence. Cantharius had described it to me long ago," she said, looking over at the fatigued, decrepit woman, "as similar to a realm's threshold, but whatever was on the other side was as interested in us as we were in them. I don't really know what they were thinking in wanting to get closer." Eriu shuddered, and I spied goose bumps forming on what little I could see of her wrists.

"Thought it was a gift," Agabius wheezed and pulled her shawl closer around her shoulders.

"The… whatever they were, were eager to come but had no way to move their bodies here, so the witches offered to host them out of sheer pious curiosity. We theorized that they learned how to open a door in their own minds to invite company. Cantharius believes it was a similar process to summoning a familiar, but… they would never share how it was done with those who wouldn't join them. The group of rot-witches was fiercely exclusive.

"Cantharius said that at first, it was just a desire to form a special section within the coven, but as it became more controversial…" Eriu lifted her hands in a shrug, trailing off for a moment. "Those who left their minds open to the things… these guests… lived longer and were more powerful, but they also rotted faster, became addicted to absorbing more power and easily lost their minds, leaving the entity to even sometimes drive the vessel until it expired. Everyone seemed to have a different reaction to these things. Some personalities merged completely with whatever had nested in them, but they all met with the same rabid end.

"They 'recruited' enough of the coven to drive the rest of us out for a number of reasons. Some called us non-believers, some didn't like our attitudes, some thought we weakened them, and some were even afraid of us. Perhaps some were manipulated by their guests, it's hard to say.

"We heard they'd migrated to the fae realm for a while, but it's not exactly known why. Apparently everything was fine with the Terran Coven and the other covens who worshiped the Earth Gods," Eriu said with a frown, and Agabius's eyes began leaking tears. "We were fine. Our coven didn't lack for anything. The downfall was pointless.

"Eventually they returned from the Realm of the Fae, but something had changed. They were furious, and they started hunting the rest of us down, forcing us to either join them or die. We ran and all the covens dedicated to the Earth Gods fell. We've been here for a while, and it's been quiet up till now. We're not warriors. We have no fighters in our coven. It was not our way and still isn't. We do not force death. Things should rot at their own time as fate decided.

"You know," Eriu added with a sneer at me, "only a tiny percentage of our coven chooses to be rot-witches, which is something you dedicate yourself to in your senior years. Only the most pious choose to dedicate to that extreme, but those who do, our most powerful, are too fragile to fight."

I scowled at her in return but kept my mouth shut. I knew the other side of the story. I knew why the rot-witches had been forced out of the Realm of the Fae, and their response to the divine expulsion had been a brutal, unnecessary act on a peaceful people. Utterly unforgiveable.

I stared meaningfully at Morchenta, wondering if she and the others would ever share that half of the story. I wondered how regretful they were, if their claims of innocence were true. They could possibly be trying to save their own wretched skins.

Either way, Morchenta would not meet my eyes.

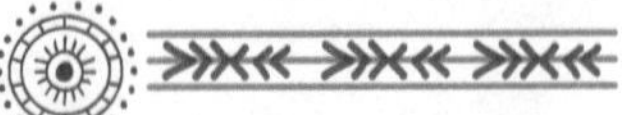
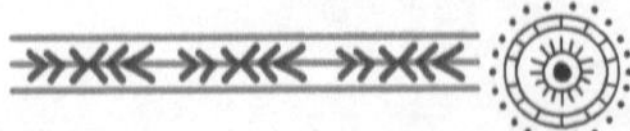

# Chapter 29

## Ferrer

Keid spoke up for the first time since arriving and asked what must have been a fiercely burning question. “One last thing… What did you mean by Mu— Cordycaris being dead? And what did you mean by her arriving back here in time?” I could admit that I was also curious about that.

Cantharius coughed wetly into her fist and spoke in a hoarser voice. “She’d manage to send word by a bird years ago that she was dying and wouldn’t make it back to deliver supplies. We’d sent people out to retrieve her body, but like we said, they never returned.”

“The occupation…” Keid surmised as she stared at her fingers. “Many died, but perhaps some are slowly making their way back here. If they’re alive, they’ll have to be informed of the coven’s move…”

Eriu hastily continued for Cantharius, offering a ratty kerchief for her coughing. “It sounds like Cordycaris invited something into her mind from the other realm, something that would bring her body back here if she died. I suppose it’s possible she was still alive and just hung in there until the end with its help… So, you could have been either dealing with her or… something else. Maybe both. We'll never know."

"Oh gods…" Keid murmured in horror, putting her fingertips to her lips. The goose bumps spread across her skin, mirroring the ones prickling down my back. Who had we dealt with? I felt Keid's sorrow and fear, then crouched to wrap an arm around her. She leaned into me, desperate for comfort. "Is there a way to know? What was she like?"

"Playful," Agabius croaked quietly. "Pious but liked breaking rules."

"We've all probably received her customary butt slap at some point," Eriu said wryly, looking both nostalgic and sad at the same time. I met Keid's watery eyes. The corner of her lip twitched when she looked at me, and I kissed her forehead softly. Perhaps Mushy had been in there somewhere until the end.

"And about her being back in time?" Keid prompted. "She also didn't have supplies on her…"

"Her supplies were her very body," Eriu murmured, then glanced warily at us, likely expecting judgment. "She was on a mission but tried to deliver herself in time after absorbing as much magic as she could. You must have noticed the dead environment around this place." Keid nodded slowly but looked upset at the revelation. "Our mothers," Eriu said, gesturing to the three rot-witches, "erected it, blocked our gods' presence. It was done to keep the other rot-witches out. We rely on outside soil to keep our rot-witches alive and sustain our people. It is hard to send out for it, but we are forced to on occasion.

"Also," she said as she gestured to the grow bed, "anyone who passes away may choose to donate their bodies to our compost. As you can see, our crops are not doing well with the nutrients we have left. We must ration our magic and try to help them grow, but… we are starving for reserves."

The story struck an unwelcome chord of sympathy in me. They were trapped much like my people had been and had suffered hardships. I didn't want to feel pity, but it was pulled from me, likely helped along by Keid's swell of compassion.

"How did she die?" Eriu asked, looking hesitant. "Did she… die well?"

Keid gave me a meaningful look and folded her hands in her lap. She was letting me decide, but it was an easy call to make. I had to take advantage of this. I released Marrow's broad wings, making everyone balk in surprise.

"Her last act was to remove my curse. I still have my bat soul, but my sky soul has been freed. Please tell me there's a way to lift my people's curse since she lifted mine," I asked, getting straight to the point I wished I'd brought up earlier. They'd better not die before being able to answer. Eriu looked confused, and I imagined they had not yet shared their dark secret with her.

"So, there is a way," Cantharius murmured, rubbing her temples with her ancient, yellowed claws. She seemed much more alert after my explanation—they all did.

"Recompense." Agabius coughed, and Morchenta gurgled something unintelligible.

"There is no time to research it," Cantharius replied to whatever Morchenta had said. "It would have been nice to regain favor with our gods. It might have been enough to protect our people again."

"Protect… now… more… imp—" Agabius began saying but fell into a hacking fit. Her voice was becoming quieter the more she tried to talk. Morchenta coughed and reached over to rub her back.

"We might have… enough now," Cantharius wheezed, "thanks to Cordycaris. Earthlight preserve her soil." Everyone capable of speaking, except for me, echoed that prayer.

"No," Eriu pleaded, her change in countenance being abrupt and extreme. "It can't be your time yet!"

"We've decided," Cantharius said resolutely, gesturing for Eriu to come over so she could stroke her hair in affection.

"Wait, what do you mean?" I asked, suddenly hyperalert. If there was a way to free my people from their curse, this was the first time it'd felt like a real, bloody possibility!

*No, no, no, no, no!* Iron gasped.

"They're n-not lowering the dead area," Eriu said through furious tears, her face flushing crimson. "They're keeping it up so they can continue to slow down the approaching rot-witches to give people more time to evacuate. They won't be able to escape with us. They're going to die here! It's pointless! We'll have enough time!" She crawled to Cantharius's feet in her appeal.

Lightning splintered down my spine. "No, you're bloody not!" I flared in fear and shock. They couldn't die, not when I just discovered a chance for my people! "I will bloody carry you all out!" I shouted, jumping to my feet to loom threateningly over them.

Morchenta started laughing, gently placing a hand on her knee to hold herself up in her mirth. Agabius sent a tired look to Cantharius, shaking her head in amusement.

"They're too fragile!" Eriu yelled, moving between me and the rot-witches. "Don't you dare touch them!"

I paced the floor, digging my claws into my skull as I tried to think. No, no, no, no! Arms wrapped around my chest, and I froze, feeling the comfort of Keid's mate touch. She held me as my hands slid to my eyes. I didn't want anyone to see me cry.

In a moment of madness, I grabbed my mate and ran.

Either my mate didn't protest or I couldn't hear her over the screaming of my heart, my mind, and all my three souls. I nearly flew to our room, tracking my way back by scent alone. Slamming the door, I retreated to an empty corner. I squatted with her in my lap and hid us in a shivering tent made by Marrow's large wings.

I then proceeded to cry at the top of my lungs. Keid did everything she could to calm me, but there was no resolving the utterly brutal chaos that'd taken over my mind. Perhaps I'd called things torturous in the past, but this was almost as bad as the thought of Keid rejecting me.

"Ferrer," she said softly, forcing me to cry a little more quietly so I could hear her. "Ferrer, please… tell me what you're feeling. You promised you would."

I had, that was true, but I struggled to do it. My brain didn't seem capable of forcing anything past my throat but sobs and throat-rending screams of agony. I buried my face in her shoulder as my body shook with strips of torn nerves. She rubbed my back fiercely, warming the skin around my wings with her touch.

"My love, my male, my forever mate," she whispered in a quieter tone, forcing me to stop crying altogether because her voice was becoming further buried. I needed her and the beautiful names she called me by, so I went silent. Only my body remained in its uncontrollable state of shaking. "Please tell me."

Her adamance was a force that was hard to deny. I was so controlled by her wants in my need to have her forever.

"I'm hurting. My mind is splitting," I croaked out in a voice husky from the strain I'd suffered it. "I need to keep you safe. My offspring is in danger too. I don't want to send you away with the others. I don't trust anyone to keep you safe but me. I'm afraid. I need to go with you. I need to stay here. I… My colony… oh gods, my colony!"

Tears continued to stream from my swollen eyes, dripping onto her skin and soaking the collar of her tunic. "And the witches… The thought of having to protect rot-witches goes against millions of years of hate being drilled into my people. It goes against the very core of my being. The thought of fighting rot-witches terrifies me! They are so shitting scary! They are so powerful! My body… my mind… Keid, I am suffering! Rage, sadness, anxiety, fear… It is bloody torture!"

"Oh, my love," she crooned and slid a hand up into my hair to massage my scalp. The act soothed me a little, but it wasn't enough. I gripped her tighter, wishing I could hide from my existence under her skin. The world as it was now; it was intolerable!

"Keid," I whispered, at my wit's very end. "Keid, what do I do?" I clenched my jaw tight, grinding my teeth together to hold back a weak sob. "This could be my people's only chance! I can't lose you though. I just got you! My offspring… the first of our colony in so long… so very long."

Gentle hands turned me to face her, and though I was panicking, seeing her strong face did me good. She slid her hands up to my chest, as though willing me to slow my breathing. I tried, I really did, but I was too stressed. What if this was it? What if this was the only opportunity to free my people—to let them be who they were intended to be by our gods?

My stomach churned as she stroked my heaving pecs. "Keid," I begged, searching her periwinkle eyes for the answer. I needed her. I couldn't think right now. I saw disaster around every turn.

"Breathe first," she whispered, reaching up to cup my cheek. "In and out, my handsome mate. In and out. Slow and steady. Yes, that's right. There you go…" She coached me through my panic. Every single time she called me her mate, it filled my spirit, and I clung to our future together. I held on to the reality that I'd been paired with a woman who was letting me lean on her right now. I felt so weak…

Keid pulled on my head to rest our foreheads together, and we went through one more round of synced breathing. My shoulders fell lower with each exhale, and my mind slowly cleared. It wasn't by much, but it was better than it had been minutes ago.

"I desire to stay and save them," she decided. It was in a whisper, but her words were steady, confident. I opened my mouth to protest vehemently, but she interrupted me. "Ah-ah. You will hear me out as I've heard you out." I shut my mouth out of respect for her, but I would not let her stay. "You know I have lived a life with struggling," she reminded me, and I nodded my recollection. "Will your colony embrace me, my love?"

"They will love you as I do," I replied in a thick voice. "We respect… no, we admire star-kissed. I know you don't like the name and the notion, but it is in our culture, and it is how I answer your question. I will spread your preference, but you will be embraced, especially as a fated mate. You will be cherished as one to help us expand our population. It will be a warm, loving home... I know it, so I swear it to you."

"Then you understand why I want to give back what will be a lifetime of love," she replied, moving her hands to massage my tense shoulders. "I cannot put myself before the benefit of so many."

"No..." I said, falling into sobs again. "No, Keid... no, no, no..."

*Please...* Iron added, unable to stay silent during this exchange.

*She could be right though, and we have the upper hand,* Marrow argued gently. *Others might join. We could take them by sur—*

"No!" I shouted, making Keid wince, and I withered in regret. "I'm sorry, I'm sorry," I whimpered into the side of her head, nuzzling a heartfelt apology.

"Ferrer, listen to Marrow," she said, moving my head once again to meet her gaze. Iron felt bitterness at being ignored but kept quiet this time. "It would be foolish to ignore the chance at real success. Imagine our long lifetime together after this. Imagine us living in happiness with many pups. Perhaps some of them will be hatchlings instead. We could have beautiful birds and butterflies in our family line. Our colony would be flourishing, no longer reliant on blood—no longer reliant on donations to survive. Isn't thriving better than surviving? We could have everything we've ever dreamed of. Your colony could have everything they've ever dreamed of..."

"Keid..." I repeated, torn by the pictures of the future she inspired.

"Don't forget," she pressed, "you were put in a position of responsibility. That puts us both in a position to put the colony's best interests first. They've elevated you in trust of that."

I loathed that she'd made that argument. I'd always put my people first. It was why I'd risked following a witch and a rot-witch at the very start.

"Please," I begged, wishing that she'd fight to run instead of stay. My legs gave out, and we sank to the floor. I felt so weak right now. I leaned against the wall, closing my eyes because I couldn't bear looking at her sincerity. "I… I will tie you up and make them leave with…" I couldn't finish the sentence. "I… I'll leave with…"

"No… we won't be doing anything like that," she responded gently, seemingly unoffended by my mad, aggressive assertions. "Use that father's instinct to protect our family's future. Use that instinct to protect your colony's future. Don't you want cute little vultures?" Her voice held the hint of a smile, forcing my eyes open again. Iron, surprisingly, was no longer offended but resigned to her words.

*Our offspring won't be forced to drink blood,* he remarked half-heartedly. *They have a chance to live normally... I am not abnormal... but I understand the need to be who one was meant to be.* I hated the hurt in his voice, but Iron understood the truth. He had a right to be himself but so did Marrow. If my offspring had their second souls trapped… it did bother me that they'd never be who they were intended to be. I hadn't considered the fact that Marrow had still been born. No one had known; there'd been no way to know.

"I…" I began saying, crumbling under everyone's words. I wiped the tears from my soaked face, and Keid helped to clean up my cheeks and chin.

"Thank you," she murmured, somehow knowing what I was about to say but couldn't bring myself to utter. She tilted my head and laid the softest kiss on my lips. "I love you so much. I want the best future we can have. We will win this, and we will survive it, I promise you. I think that wretched Mushy put us on this path for a reason. She never wished ill upon me."

For some reason, the mention of that stupid old hag made me smile. Perhaps I hated her a little less. I could only hope that she'd known everything by scrying the future without a mother's permission. I could only hope that she wanted us all to thrive, not just survive.

## Keid

"How does one kill rot-witches?" I asked as we entered the greenhouse again. The four witches were still there, and Eriu's head snapped up in surprise. She clearly hadn't expected us to return.

"Get to them before they get to you," Cantharius mused unhelpfully. We approached the group, and Ferrer tried to remove his hand from mine, but I wasn't having it. He could have forced it out of my grip, but he didn't. It made me hold my head higher for some reason.

"How do you anticipate their approach of the bastion?" I inquired, placing my other hand on my hip. I tilted my chin up, knowing that faking the body language always helped to inspire the real thing. I would be confident!

"You're serious, aren't you?" Eriu asked on a breath. "Why?"

"It's selfishness," Ferrer muttered, his voice raw from crying.

"It's to everyone's benefit," I corrected, meeting the witches' eyes in turn. "We will defeat your enemies and subsequently request your aid in freeing the bat-shifter colony from their curse. I believe that exchange is more than fair."

"It is," Agabius stated in the loudest I'd ever heard her speak, though it caused her to dissolve into a fit of coughs. By dissolve, I did not mean actual dissolving. That would have been a tragedy.

"We agree to those terms," Cantharius promised, speaking for everyone. No one seemed to have any issues with that.

"Now," I said, asking for a better answer, "what to expect."

"They'll likely send a sleep curse ahead, like always. We have no countermeasures for it that won't harm us," Cantharius replied wearily.

“That’s a non-issue,” Ferrer said, and I turned my gaze to him.

“It is? How?” I asked at the same time as Eriu, who said something similar in response.

“It is not to be discussed. I will not inform anyone of its nature. It is part of the deal,” Ferrer stated, slashing a hand through the air to punctuate his immovable stance.

“That is fine,” Agabius wheezed, waving her own hand in dismissal.

Ferrer seemed to relax significantly after that, but I continued to stare at him. Was I included in that part of the deal? Would he never tell me? I was burning with curiosity.

I dragged my eyes from my mysterious mate and voiced my next question. “What then? Will they move ahead of the humans or will they hide behind them?”

“They’re no longer who we used to know.” Cantharius coughed weakly. “I cannot say. They used to be ones to come forth ahead of all in a show of arrogance.”

“I see,” I murmured, placing my fingers to my lips in thought. “What about how they do warfare? Do they die like everyone else?”

Eriu held up a hand so Cantharius wouldn’t try answering. The old rot-witch was struggling with her breathing after coughing so much. “They die by a sword as much as anyone else. They’re fragile, so if they’re even pushed hard enough, depending on their age and state, they could break.

“As far as warfare goes…” Eriu continued with a shrug, “they are partial to curses.”

“I’ve seen them take over the bodies of warriors…” Ferrer informed from my side, his voice heavy with nausea.

She crossed her arms and shivered. “That’s only if they get the opportunity to place the curse symbol on them.”

“Which could have already been placed on their shackled people,” I pointed out to Ferrer, who nodded gravely. “If those people attack, it’s likely not by their choice, especially if they were shackled. That’s an obvious sign of slavery.”

"We don't have the resources this time to remove the symbols safely," Ferrer rumbled unhappily, referring to his last encounter, I supposed. "This could get bloody if we can't reach the rot-witches quickly."

"Unfortunate," the younger witch lamented, aggrieved by the potential loss of life. "They might very well be old coven members."

"We will simply have to do the best we can," I stated firmly and pointed at the ground with a stubborn finger.

"Might not… direct," Agabius grunted, failing to speak coherently. When Morchenta gargled something, Eriu nodded. How she understood that… it was impressive.

"She said they might not come from above. They could even blast their way through the dirt should they choose to sacrifice a rot-witch."

I frowned and shook my head, disgusted. "Alright, that is good to consider." I rubbed my temple and glanced around the greenhouse. My first idea was promising, but I needed guidance. "I require a botanist," I informed Eriu, who sighed and helped Morchenta to her feet. I raised a brow as the doddering old creature waddled toward me with a prodding gesture. Ferrer stood aggressively close to me, and I ignored it. He would be the way he was.

"What is your hungriest crop?" I inquired, wording my inquiry very specifically. I didn't necessarily mean the one that was suffering the most. I needed the crop that required the most nutrients, though it could very well be the ones that were dying.

The rot-witch wandered off and took me to a section of the cavern that hosted a variety of grains. I spied some wheat and even corn, and they looked rather sad indeed. It was actually convenient, because these plants' seeds were easy to access. Since it was autumn, some crops had already been harvested, but I was able to find a good number of abandoned grains sprinkled among the soil.

"Thank you, Morchenta," I said to her in dismissal. "That's all." My mind had been running nonstop since Ferrer's emotional collapse, and I was already forming bits and pieces of a plan.

I collected a variety of seeds, then looked for the crop that had wilted the most. I needed potential hunger and current hunger, then I needed a vining plant… Maybe they had grapes.

*What are you doing?* Vain asked curiously.

"I am deriving a way to slow the rot-witches. If Mushy was any indicator of soil fertility, seeds could potentially be attracted to them. I hope to make them hungry enough so they could slow and perhaps eat through them. The rot-witches are basically walking fertilizer at a certain point." I glanced up to find all four witches watching me, and I quickly added, "No offense."

I'd somewhat shut my emotions down, but it wasn't necessarily by choice. My brain often did when it dove into problem-solving, so I'd occasionally catch myself saying something insensitive. I'd have to do better.

Agabius laughed at my apology, and Cantharius squatted with a pained expression to pick up a burlap sack. She handed it to Eriu who walked over to me, offering the small bag with Mushy's remains. I took it with a degree of reverence, knowing now how important it was.

"Here is your share of the rations," Eriu said quietly, humbly. "I will speak to the remaining people here and see if we have any volunteers. I suppose I am staying as well. I cannot let them die alone…" Eriu glanced back at the witches in resignation. Perhaps she expected to die, but I wouldn't let her.

Morbidly curious, I peeked into the burlap sack and found nothing but rich earth. Mushy had indeed become one with the Earth Gods… I wiped a numb tear from my eye and pressed my lips into a grateful smile… or maybe it was a grimace. It was hard to tell.

"Thank you," I whispered to both Eriu and Mushy's remains. I wouldn't let any of it go to waste. With her soil, I could make the seeds a frightful force. "Vain," I said to get her attention.

*Yes?*

"Please do drills with Ferrer on improving your dropping aim while I work on my enchantments. If they are wearing shoes, I'm worried that leaving the seeds on the ground won't trigger them. I don't know… I don't want to risk it. This is too important. I'll also be making you a collar well before they arrive. I think I know what to prepare for."

*Yes!* Vain chirped, and I smiled faintly at her good attitude. She didn't take offense and was able to focus on the plan. I loved that about her. Results were what mattered.

I gathered the seeds that I needed, collected some withered samples, and found a bunch of mature grapes that would work nicely. The hybrid I had in mind was attainable!

"Where is the doctor's office?" I asked Ferrer, not recalling the way there. He grabbed my hand and led me out, scenting his way back to where we'd been. I cleared my throat on our return and held on to my current determination. I couldn't think of things that would weaken me. I'd cry after all this was over. I'd grieve another day.

Ferrer knew what I was struggling with, and his grip tightened as he led me back to Akira. When we entered her office, she looked up at us in surprise.

"Welcome back," she blurted with a wide-eyed blink. "Are you feeling unwell again?"

"No, I am fine, thank you," I replied politely, then looked around her office. "I am looking for a place to work on an enchantment. Have you a space with some light? I might need some tools too."

"Oh," she replied, looking further surprised. "Yes, ah…" She stood from her stool and opened a side door. "I have another office you may use. You may help yourself to whatever you find… I take it… that you…" She didn't finish asking her question as she tilted her head. It looked like she wasn't sure about her assumption.

"I am going to stop the rot-witches," I affirmed, but Ferrer growled softly.

"We are," he corrected, his voice gravely and insistent.

"We are going to stop the rot-witches," I said and smiled up at him. Ferrer closed the door behind us, rudely shutting out a speechless Akira. I didn't bother chastising him for it. It wasn't the time to think about small things.

"I will do as you ask with Vain, but don't think that Iron isn't losing his mind about her going close to the enemy," he said, sitting across the table from me. I laid out the seeds and considered the order of enchantment.

"He loves her too, doesn't he?" I asked, looking up at him with a half-smile.

*I...* Iron fumbled, not sure what to say. Ferrer was frozen, also not knowing how to answer my question.

"I think it makes sense," I replied before Iron could make Ferrer spontaneously combust. "She is practically my beast."

*It could be cheating,* Vain replied uncertainly. *I wouldn't do that to you, Keid.*

I shrugged. "It doesn't bother me, Vain. You and I are joined at the souls. I'll let you know if you ever mate and if I end up in a ball of agony," I said with a laugh and arranged the seeds in a different order as I studied them.

"I don't think now is the time for this conversation," Ferrer muttered, his cheeks and pointed ears red from either embarrassment or frustration. "Keid, we must speak about the curse evasion."

I sat up straight and raised my brows. That was right! "Yes, please tell me about that. I have no idea what you speak of. Aside from knowing and being strong enough to perform a counter-curse, it seems impossible."

Ferrer opened his mouth, then shut it abruptly. He checked outside the door and growled to find the doctor still in the other room. When he looked around the office, he snatched up a pen and started writing something down on the parchment. I frowned as he wrote.

"Ferrer, I can't read that. Is that in another language?" I asked. He froze and looked sharply up at me.

"Shitting stars! Yes, it's fae. Clots! They said they had to translate the documents at the recognition grounds for our guests, but… I didn't think…" He scrubbed his hands over his face before ripping up the paper. Whatever he needed to impart required privacy.

"One minute, my love," I said and made my way around the room, enchanting the walls, ceiling, and floor to keep in all sounds. If that female was a shifter, she'd easily be able to hear our words. "This room is now safe from ears and scrying."

Ferrer seemed to flush in pleasure at my term of endearment, but he looked uncertain still. "What about the rot-witches?" he asked slowly, staring at the wall.

"Magic is simple. A spell is either broken or not. If they break it, I will know. There is no bypassing without breaking," I stated and reached over to take one of his hands in mine. "Trust my expertise."

He sighed and let himself sink into the chair, nodding his acceptance. When I started giving his hand a little massage, he began to speak. "What I'm about to tell you is our colony's most important secret. It is critical that you share it with no one, Keid. Do not write it down, do not utter it to another, do not speak it aloud ever. Can I trust you with that?"

"Yes," I replied, surprised by his intensity. I had no desire to break Ferrer's trust… ever.

"I know I can trust you," he said in an exhale and covered my hand with his other one, sandwiching it. "I just have to ask."

"You must be required to." I smiled gently when he chuckled tiredly.

"Yes… Anyway," he said, looking down at our hands before meeting my eyes. "The bat-shifters are immune to curses. To put it extremely briefly, we've been so thoroughly cursed with what the rot-witches have done that we've developed an immunity to all other curses. You may want to test me now, just to make sure that Mushy didn't break my immunity as well."

My jaw dropped as he spoke, and his smile spread a little bit at my shock.

"Is that true?" I asked unnecessarily. That was… That certainly did change things!

"And… our blood can break curses. I plan to keep you awake with it, but you'll have to drink it. I… have a strategy you won't like."

"Oh." My lips puckered at the news. I wasn't upset about the drinking part. I was upset that if people found out about the nature of their blood, the bats would become hunted for it. No wonder it was so closely guarded! I drew my brows and chewed on my lower lip. "What's the plan?"

"I will have you fill your mouth with my blood, and every time you feel you're about to be cursed, I need you to swallow some of it. If we're separated, and I can't get blood to you in privacy…"

"Oh…" I murmured, nodding slowly as I absorbed his idea. "It is hard to say when a curse will hit, but I suppose it's the only way. I imagine you don't want to put it in a flask…" I already knew what he'd say. I didn't know why I bothered asking.

He shook his head sharply. "If anyone gets their hands on it, it's a serious problem."

"I know, I know," I said quickly, nodding vigorously in placation.

"Your mouth is the only place I trust," he said in a grave voice, but then we both broke into stupid, crazed laughter. My mind was filled with the voices of our other souls, who joined in on the nerve-racked, madness-induced mirth.

Oh gods, starlight preserve us all…

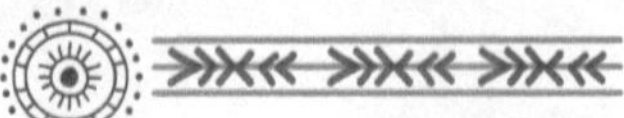

# Chapter 30

## Ferrer

After our bout of laughter, Keid tested my curse immunity.

"I don't know how, but you've retained it," she marveled, pinching at the hand she'd tried numbing three times. "Are you quite sure you can feel this?"

I snorted and jerked my hand away before she could retest again with something sharper. "It's not like I understand curses any better, mate," I said, relieved.

"Maybe it's the evolution that occurred parallel to the curse," she mused, resting her head on her palm. "Your kind lived with the curse for so long. I would love to study it more. Maybe Mushy had isolated the curse and managed to separate it from the magic immune system you've developed…"

"Well, you'll get every chance to test later," I replied, trying to call upon her optimism. We had to survive this. "I'll make sure you have your own office with everything you need."

Her smile was warm as she stared at me, and I hung on to that expression on her face. I wanted to engrave that look into my memory. I needed whatever comfort I could get for the day or two ahead of us. My nerves were drawn taut.

“Let me work here, love. Best take Vain to a more open area for drills. Use pebbles but try to find light ones. What I will be creating will not be heavy,” she said and cleared paperwork from the desk to make more room.

I hesitated, not wanting to leave her side in the slightest. “Keid, we’ll just… practice in here? Or maybe you could enchant where we need to go?”

She shook her head. “No, I need to focus. I will be fine here. Akira is in the next room, Ferrer. Vain absolutely needs the practice. We can’t afford to miss our targets.”

Anxiety splintered through my nerves, forcing my claws and fangs out instinctively. I dragged my sharp nails though my hair, unable to do as she asked. “Keid…”

She got up from the table and prompted me to stand. Reaching for the back of my neck, she drew me down for a kiss. I met her lips with mine, and the tension slowly softened, but it didn’t evaporate. I groaned miserably when she pulled away and stared at me.

“We have to trust each other right now. There is too much to do. We can only succeed if we believe in each other,” she said, her brows drawing into a tender expression as her gaze flickered between my eyes. She was asking me for her trust. It wasn’t her I distrusted, but perhaps she didn’t see it like that.

I swallowed hard and leaned my forehead into hers. “I will find more guards,” I said, my voice going hoarse once more.

“Ask Akira about it,” Keid said, moving her hands to my arms. I nodded and stepped away from her. My body screamed at me, threatening to go feral with my decision.

*Help,* I asked Iron and Marrow. *Help me stay sane,* I begged.

*On it,* Iron said.

*We will prevent it,* Marrow acquiesced calmly. I honestly wasn’t sure if Iron would have been enough, and I was grateful for the third soul's help. They were both pulling their weight, and it was encouraging.

I took a deep breath and tried to still my shaking. Leaving a final kiss on Keid's cheek, I left the office and addressed Akira. "I need extra guards to… keep her safe," I stated, massaging my sore throat. "I need trustworthy people…"

Akira nodded in understanding. "I will wait to see who stays and make an inquiry. Until then, you can rest assured that I will protect her." The doctor smiled flatly and extended her claws.

Gods knew what Akira's history was, but I chose not to question it. If she was an experienced fighter, then I wouldn't snub her. "Thank you," I replied, cleared my throat and departed with Vain on a shoulder.

I chose to return to the greenhouse and bristled at the sight of the one-armed dragon-shifter; he had returned. He stood calmly by the entrance and put distance between us when I approached. My claws were already out, but I asked my beasts for restraint. I couldn't afford to lose control.

"Staying?" I inquired dispassionately. The dragon nodded but continued to forgo any talking. "Admirable," I snapped and strode away from him. I could appreciate bravery, or perhaps he had a death wish. It mattered not.

I searched through the crops and gathered handfuls of seeds similar to what Keid had collected. I handed one at a time to Vain and moved unpredictably about the greenhouse, testing her agility and ability to anticipate movement.

"You've got to drop it ahead of the target!" I lectured when she released the seed where I used to be. "It takes time for the seed to travel downward!"

*Right, right,* she replied breathlessly and continued practicing. I knew I was moving faster than a rot-witch could, but the better she got at it, the better her chances would be at succeeding.

"Also make considerations for airflow," I added when the seed managed to just bounce against my elbow. "Well done!"

*That's what… one out of fifty?* She sighed in disappointment.

"Take a break, Vain," I ordered. "We'll pick up again in a little bit. You're making progress."

*You really are,* Iron added.

*I guess...* she muttered.

She flew up to the cavern ceiling and chose to rest by a stalactite, hidden in its shadow. I glanced around and noticed more people gathering in the greenhouse to talk to the rot-witches and Eriu. The dragon-shifter's partner had joined him, seemingly deep in discussion over some strategy. We'd all have to come together before the attack because we couldn't afford to have fifty plans occurring simultaneously.

A familiar scent hit my nose, making it wrinkle in distaste. It wasn't the rot-witches' potent stench but something else I'd encountered in the dining hall earlier. The wolf-shifter who'd stared at me had apparently volunteered to stay behind and was approaching me for some reason.

"Playing around with a bat?" she asked with a smile. "Cute."

"Not as much." I side-eyed her warily. "Need something?"

"No," she drawled and leaned on a post by me.

*Tell her to go away,* Iron hissed.

*She is trouble,* Marrow added.

*Nothing I can't handle,* I replied dismissively.

"I might want something though..." she said after a while, giving me a meaningful look.

"Save your breath. I have a mate," I snapped and made a shooing gesture with a hand.

"I don't see a mark," she argued, pursing her lips as she nodded to my neck. "We could die tomorrow. Don't you want to live a little?"

"Get out of here," I growled, feeling my feral mind start to twitch. If she pushed any more, I'd potentially find my claws in her throat.

"We all come here with our dirty pasts. I'll ignore yours if you can." She shrugged and came closer.

I turned to keep from breaking her neck. If she wouldn't leave, then I'd have to go.

*Vain, we're leaving,* I called, summoning her from the ceiling.

*Coming...* she replied with a sigh.

Turning my back on the she-wolf had been a huge mistake. She leapt onto my shoulders and dug her fangs into my neck, attempting a marking. Bats were fast, and it was only due to my speed that she'd not managed to completely bury them. I cried out in horror and launched her off me by releasing Iron's wings.

*Get to the bloody doctor!* Iron screamed at me as I staggered. I looked down to find rivulets of blood streaming down my chest. Wait… had she…

*We're holding back the venom together, but go! Go, go, go!* Marrow cried, and I knew that if he was panicking, I was in deep trouble.

Nearly out of my mind with fear, I sprinted to find Akira and burst into her office. "Help! Help, help, help!" I shouted and lifted her clear out of her seat. She gaped at me, then her eyes found my punctured shoulder. "A bloody shifter tried to mark me! My beasts are holding back the venom, but I can't let… I can't let…!" I began hyperventilating, and Akira forced me onto the bed for examination.

"Lie down flat!" she warned. "Stop moving!"

Keid burst from the other office, her face whiter than I'd ever seen it. Simultaneously, the office entrance opened, and the dragon-shifter's companion marched in with a grave face. "I saw it," she muttered and came to the doctor's side, who was cautiously observing my injury.

"What happened?" Keid asked, and when she saw the state of my neck, she crumbled into tears. "No!" she shrieked, making the woman and female jerk in surprise.

*It hasn't sunk in yet,* I told her quickly over a mind-link. *Iron and Marrow are holding it back.*

"Don't even bother trying to express it; it gets absorbed too quickly," the woman said.

"It's not usually helpful with other venom either," Akira muttered anxiously. "Would excising work if done before it's settled? I have no idea what the threshold is between the soul and flesh…" She grabbed a set of tools from a drawer and began sterilizing in haste.

"There's not enough research on it…" the woman said crankily.

*Wait!* Iron said. Simultaneously, a weight lifted off me.

*It's gone!* Marrow squawked.

I pushed Akira's hand away before she could make an incision, and I sat upright to pay attention to my body. Was it gone? I held up a hand, asking for silence as I focused my senses.

The assault was over, there was no doubt about it, but what had caused it to disappear like that? I listened to my body a moment longer, but everything had calmed. It was as if nothing had happened.

"Ferrer?" Keid sobbed, unable to wait in silence. I held out an arm for her, and she came barreling into me. Clinging tight, she stared and waited for me to speak.

"I'm safe," I murmured, in shock. "I don't know how, but it's gone. Her venom is gone… just like that…"

"I had a feeling he'd do that…" the woman said darkly and gave a humorless laugh.

"What?" I inquired, mildly alarmed by her tone. I rubbed my chest as my heart jumped from shot nerves.

She pinched her lips and waved away my question as if it bored her. Akira silently blotted at my neck, cleaning and sterilizing it just in case, and I allowed her to do so. I felt dirty after that wolf had placed her lips on me.

How had I allowed a female to surprise me like that? I would have never expected… I placed a hand to the bridge of my nose, pinching it to suppress my growing fury. The experience had been both humbling and humiliating. I'd been the one in danger by leaving Keid's side. I could hardly believe it.

With the turning of my back to a stranger, no matter how fast I was, I'd almost become entangled with another soul for the rest of my life. I didn't even know how that'd work. I'd never heard of anything like this occurring. This place was too welcoming to strangers.

The woman opened the door when there was a knock, and the dragon-shifter glanced in, looking unconcerned. When his eyes landed on my relieved face, he nodded slowly and smiled almost gleefully at his partner.

"You did it, didn't you?" she inquired sourly, shaking her head at him.

"Some people are not safe to keep here," he answered frankly. "If I'm to guard the mothers, I must be strict."

"What did you do?" I asked as Akira finished dabbing an ointment on my neck.

"Killed her." He shrugged, then left without another word. What?

"He'll say it's because she wasn't safe to keep around, but he did it to save your ungrateful soul. Don't forget that," she muttered to me and left to follow the dragon-shifter. I stared at her departure in slack-jawed shock. He'd what?

"That would do it," Akira said thoughtfully as she cleaned her tools. "Killing the shifter before her venom sets in. That leaves nothing to tie you to. You won't even suffer the pains of losing her because you weren't marked in time." She spoke so casually of it, but I was still in shock. He'd… what?

"Good!" Keid snarled angrily, and I looked down at her in astonishment. She must have felt my eyes on her because she turned her face up to glare at me. She was flushed red in outrage. "I'm glad she's dead!"

I didn't know what to say to that, so I just pulled her closer as she wept. What in the shit had just happened? I slid slowly off the bed and guided her into the office where she'd been working. "Thanks, Akira…" I uttered in subdued gratitude and closed the door behind Keid and me.

I sat down and Keid immediately climbed into my lap, distraught. I stroked the back of her hair, and the act soothed me as much as it comforted her. She echoed my deep sigh as I released it, and we both made an effort to gather ourselves. I briefly summarized the encounter to her dazed face.

She straightened to stare at my shoulder, looking deeply upset. "Will this scar?" she asked bitterly, thumbing the area around it. "Gods, I cannot believe this… Who could do such a thing?"

I shook my head. "No, it'll be gone in a day without a trace."

She frowned, and her face adopted a dreamlike expression. Her thoughts were far away from this place. I knew what she was feeling, but I didn't know what she was thinking. Tilting my head, I was about to inquire, but she spoke first.

"Scarmaster…" she muttered, looking like she'd bit into something distasteful. Meeting my gaze, she explained, "The lions… they used to scar their cubs when they came of age. They cut them every day so the wound would eventually scar."

"That sounds unpleasant," I replied hesitantly, not certain I knew where she was going with this. "It does take a lot to scar a shifter…"

"What if…" she said, then stopped and bit her lip. She traced the skin on my other shoulder, and guilt wafted from her soul. Ah, I understood now.

"Yes," I answered the question she couldn't bring herself to ask. "I want you to do it."

"You don't even know what I was going to say…" she protested, her guilt now joined by a heavy fog of shame.

"How do you wish to mark my skin?" I asked plainly. "Want to write your name?" I smiled, trying to encourage a laugh out of her. She merely stared at my shoulder and continued to feel terrible about herself. This wouldn't do. Today had been too emotional already. It seemed like we'd been bombarded with one thing or another since arriving.

"I shouldn't have to," she whispered. "I shouldn't be worried about this…"

"Let's think logically about this," I said, taking both her hands in mine. "A scar will deter this from ever happening again, but I promise you I won't let my guard down again. I just... I couldn't believe..." I was at a loss for words. The absurdity of a wolf trying to mark me like that... It was unrealistic. The bitch had almost raped my soul from me. I shuddered, startling Keid.

"Why am I worried about myself? I'm so sorry this happened to you!" she lamented and cupped my face. "What are you feeling?"

"Honestly? I feel violated," I said quietly. "I feel dirty." I frowned and cleared away the lump that was trying to form in my throat. She hadn't succeeded. Keid and I were safe... I had to hang on to that. We had too much to worry about right now.

"That... that..." Keid pressed her lips together, as though not wishing to speak ill of the dead. I placed a finger on her lips and shushed her. I didn't want her to say anything she'd regret later. "I'm sorry..." she murmured, and I traced her lower lip as she spoke. These were the lips I wanted on me. "What do you need, Ferrer?"

"You read my mind," I whispered with a forced smile. When she pouted, I specified my desire. "Every single day, I want you to bite both my marking spots until I bleed. I want your teeth marks on my shoulders until they scar. I know you lack the venom, but I still want everyone to know I'm mated to you."

She looked dubiously at my shoulders. "I don't know if I can bite that hard... Have you seen yourself? You're carved from solid rock."

I wasn't sure if she'd intended that to be funny, but I laughed at how she'd delivered the words. Her mouth twitched as she met my gaze. "Humans eat meat," I said wryly, gently poking her chin. "You've got a jaw that can do it."

"You trust my mouth?" she replied smartly.

"Absolutely." I drew her face in for a kiss. "Shitting stars... we will need peace and quiet after all this," I murmured into her lips, and she melted against me, whimpering her desperate agreement.

*Yes, please,* Iron muttered.

*We are all being tested,* Marrow moaned, malcontent and ruffled.

I wasn't really sure I could handle anything else thrown at us today. The attempted marking had shaken Ferrer and me to our very cores, and I felt a desperate need to be close to him. Unless it was required to engage with the rot-witches, there was absolutely no way he was leaving my sight again until we left this place, and I believed he was on that very same page with me.

"We're going back to our room," I said, moving my lips from his in reluctance. "I will work there."

"We need to discuss our part of the strategy with Eriu and the others first," he said with an equally reluctant sigh. "There are others gathering in the greenhouse, and I'm concerned some planning may be occurring without us."

"Ah…" I murmured, feeling my stomach knot with anxiety. I didn't want to go back to where he'd been assaulted, and I was sure he didn't either. I moved off his lap regretfully, thinking that it was too bad the bulge in his pants was going to waste.

Getting lost in each other would have helped the both of us. My stolen eggs, his turmoil, the assault… it was too much. We both felt deeply violated. I believed no one was built to absorb all that in a day, and it was a cursed miracle that both of us could still function, but perhaps that was the nature of necessity. We were fighting for our future offspring and for our colony. Thinking of the children I chose to have gave me strength to keep crawling.

We arrived at the greenhouse to find a large crowd of what I couldn't believe were volunteers; there were so many of them!

Ferrer parted the mass with his intimidating frame, holding tightly to my hand as I stayed on his heels. He needed me right now as much as I needed him.

"Cantharius!" Ferrer barked over the throng's chatter, and I quickly noticed why he hadn't addressed Eriu. She was currently busy burying a fresh body in the central grow bed. I averted my eyes and shivered. I hated myself for it, but I was glad the wolf was dead. She'd hurt Ferrer and almost took him from me. Of anything anyone had ever done to me, that was the most unforgiveable, and I struggled to find pity.

Cantharius turned from several other witches, looking wretchedly tired. I bit my lip, hoping she wasn't exerting herself to the point of injury. We needed her for the sake of the colony, but I also wouldn't wish harm on her. She seemed to be a decent person.

"Yes?" she croaked, rubbing her milky eyes. Her wild grey hair was vibrating from her fatigued shaking, and I sorely wished she'd sit.

"I need to know that if there's planning, it's occurring with what I've said in mind," Ferrer said tersely, obviously still uncomfortable around her. "If I wake Keid, can she wake everyone else from that curse?"

"You know how to lift a basic sleeping curse?" Cantharius wheezed at me, her voice seemingly raw from speaking. I nodded, and she copied the movement in a slower fashion. "Then she can wake us. Make sure you wake the witches first so they can work on the others," she continued, speaking first to Ferrer, then me.

"Then I suggest everyone stays together and away from any point of entry when we anticipate their arrival. It'll allow more time to wake them while they're prone," Ferrer advised.

"Nothing but interruption can keep them from casting it again," Cantharius warned with a cough. "Be warned."

Ferrer nodded grimly. "Understood. Keid and I will be retiring to our chamber so she can continue her work uninterrupted. There is much to be done in the next day or two, however much time is left."

"We have…" Cantharius coughed again, and I worried at my lip. She needed rest. "We have several familiars we can send out to check." As Ferrer turned to leave with me, she rasped, "I'm sorry about the wolf."

Ferrer glanced back over his shoulder, his countenance holding an odd mixture of surprise and bitterness. "You are far too cavalier about who you allow in."

She shrugged, a movement that was barely noticeable. "We do our best. She had a history, and it was our mistake for allowing her a chance despite that."

"A mistake that almost took my soul from my fated mate," he snapped harshly, then pulled me away with him. He gave me an apologetic look after jerking me a little rougher than he'd intended, but I just patted his arm comfortingly. We were both worn ragged.

When we arrived at our guest room, I grabbed my bag and Mushy's remains, then settled on the bed, deciding to continue my work in comfort. I placed the seeds down and studied them, recalling exactly where I'd stopped before hearing Ferrer's earlier cries.

My beautiful male climbed onto the bed next to me and Vain fluttered to roost, looking exhausted. The poor thing must have been working hard. My gaze moved to Ferrer when he pulled up my tunic so he could slide his hand under it. His palm stopped on my belly, and I watched him relax significantly. His eyes closed as he rested on his side, and he brought one of Iron's wings out to fold over him like a blanket. The sight of his desperate need for comfort and self-soothing tugged at my heart. I couldn't wait for all this to be in the past. We had far too much healing to do.

With his reassuring presence next to me and his calming hand on my stomach, I worked as quietly as possible, preparing an arsenal of enchanted seeds. I was brutal with the spells, making the creations as hungry as possible, and it was fortunate I had Mushy's remains to not only strengthen the spells, but to give them an example of what to attack. The rot-witches were obviously pre-soil, but I made allowances for that.

I glanced up at Vain while I worked. Another reason I was glad to have Mushy's remains was because I didn't want to tax my familiar any further. She could enhance my magic, but I needed her to save her strength for the actual encounter. I couldn't bear losing her, so I made sure that she only needed to focus on one thing. I believed in her. I knew she could get in and out fast enough while they were surprised. We had to trust everyone to do their part or this plan would be at risk.

---

It was late in the evening when I finally completed my seed enchantments. My head was pounding from the strain of puzzling them out, and my vision was bleary. At least food had been sent to me, and Ferrer had been able to feed from the canteen of blood Akira had provided. He continued to remain relatively calm after drinking his meal, to my mild disappointment. It was just as well; I needed to finish my projects as soon as possible.

When my fingers went to Ferrer's donated feather, a stern, large hand reached across to intercept me. "You need to rest, mate," he grumbled drowsily. "You've been doing this all day and night."

I let my shoulders sag in surrender. "I suppose you're right. I'm just anxious to get Vain's collar done. The timing will be tight, and I'm worried."

"I know," he said softly, opening his eyes to gaze up at me, "but you'll work faster tomorrow if you're rested."

"You're right, you're right," I replied, submitting to his logic. I blew out the candles and crawled under the sheets where he joined me, shifting away his wing to enjoy the softness of a real blanket.

"I love you so much," he whispered as he pulled me into him.

"I love you too," I echoed, meaning every word, and I hoped we'd be around to say it a million times more. I had to believe.

## errer

An explosion in the middle of the night startled me out of my sleep, and dirt fell like hail upon us. I rolled on top of Keid to shield her from the cave-in and spread Marrow's wings in an attempt to cover us both. Shaking her with urgency did nothing. Yelling her name did nothing. She was unconscious, and the realization that the rot-witches had arrived far too early sent a flood of adrenaline through my bloodstream.

What happened next was additionally unexpected. My feral mind flared to life, and a rage I'd never known before came to a boil under my skin and deep within my bones. Claws and fangs erupted from me in high alert.

*Kill them!* Iron snarled.

*Wake her first!* Marrow snapped uncharacteristically. *Bleed yourself, Ferrer!*

I sat Keid up when the dirt stopped raining on us, brutally sliced my arm with a fang, and placed the cut against her mouth, prying her jaw and lips open to receive my blood. I let her head fall forward as I tried to get her to swallow. "Come on, Keid," I urged her sleeping form, "wake up. Wake up, mate! It's time!"

Her throat worked just enough to pull down some blood, and it wasn't long before her eyes fluttered open, heavy and confused. She pulled her mouth from my arm, and her head lolled backward, forcing me to support her skull until she was fully alert.

"Love," I said, brushing her hair from her face and wiping excess blood from her lips, "you need to get up. They're here! They're early!" She shook her head and raised her hand to slap herself. I grabbed it and growled. "And will you stop doing that?"

"Help me," she croaked, pointing to the floor. I supported her as she climbed off the bed and stood on her own two feet, albeit a little wobbly. I tried to stop shaking from my instinctual rage so I wouldn't scare her, but it was impossible. My body wouldn't calm until the threat was gone. "I need…" she said faintly, blinking heavily as she became more awake. "I need… what do I need?"

"You cannot send Vain out," I asserted and rushed to collect the small thing from the support beam, which had protected her during the explosion, thank the gods. "You need to wake her though."

"Oh, Vain!" Keid bemoaned and took her from me. The blood bat was fast asleep. Apparently, the curse targeted every living thing in the bastion. "I failed you!"

"We couldn't have known. Something must have happened last night to speed them up. We should have had more time!" I growled, stroking her arms as I waited for her to wake the blood bat. I needed to get going, but we had people to wake too. Shit! The anger festered inside of me, waiting for the first enemy to cross our paths. My mate was being threatened and so was my offspring. The invading witches would be wormy soil within the hour; I promised myself that.

Vain flared to life in Keid's palms, seeming dazed. I caught her when she ran off and caged her in my fingers until her mind caught up with her body.

*What? What…*

"We have to get going," I said to Keid. "You need to wake the others! Give me the seeds, Keid! I will slow them down!"

"No!" She gasped, fumbling for the seeds by the table. "You can't go alone!"

"We have no choice!" I growled. "You ask for trust, and now we have to exercise that!"

She balked at my tone and argument, then handed the seeds over to me with a distraught expression. I shoved them in my pocket and handed Vain back to her. We pushed away dirt that had jammed the door and squeezed out, but I tripped over something I hadn't expected to be on the other side.

"Bloody clotted dragon!" I cursed, catching myself on the other side of the wall after stumbling.

"Was he guarding us again?" Keid asked, then crouched by the older, one-armed male to wake him.

Though I was excessively angry, I bit back spiteful words. I owed him my bloody soul and couldn't bring myself to insult him. I bristled as Keid lifted his curse, not liking my pregnant woman close to any male right now, and paced restlessly until he was awake.

"What… the Sun God… happened?" he asked, wiping a layer of dust and dirt from his face. I lifted him off the ground to his feet and pointed to where I'd heard the explosion.

"You're coming with me. The rot-witches got here early, and we need to slow them down while Keid wakes up more of the volunteers," I growled. The dragon's eyes snapped wide open, and he stared down the hall as if expecting an army to come around the corner any second.

I moved to Keid before she could run away, grabbed her aggressively, and crashed my lips into hers. She whimpered in surprise, and I growled into her mouth, tasting my blood and remembering what I'd almost forgotten. Spreading my wings to block the dragon's view of us, I reopened my wound and pushed it to Keid's mouth. She sucked on my arm until she had a mouthful of blood, then looked worriedly up at me as I backed away from her.

"I love you!" I announced fiercely, then turned and ran from her, trusting her to wake the others as fast as possible. I had witches to slaughter.

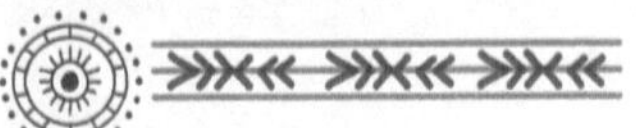

# Chapter 31

## Ferrer

I raced down the pitch-black earthen halls, almost leaving behind the dragon-shifter, who needed to breathe fire to see where he was going. When I slowed down just a little, he caught up to me and whispered, "Have you been in a battle before?"

"Yes," I replied through my teeth. "Unfortunately, we'd been the invaders, so I'm inexperienced with this side of things."

"Pardon me"—he laughed quietly as we turned a corner—"but I disagree. I think you can put your mind in your enemy's shoes now."

"I do not and could never think like a rot-witch!" I snarled at him, my claws twitching at the insult.

"Not even to protect your woman? Pity," he drawled.

"Do you have a death wish?" I spat, glowering at him. His words had twisted my stomach. The male had a way of jarring me with unsettling truths, and I wished I could simply ignore them. Unfortunately, they clung like sticky cobwebs.

He laughed darkly at my question. "Wouldn't you love to know?"

I growled to signal the end of the conversation. He was riling me up again, and I needed to focus. We followed the dust in the air, and I listened intently to chase distant echoes. There would be no one awake on this side of the bastion. I'd found the invaders.

"Wait!" a voice cried from far behind us, and the dragon slid to a halt. Whoever had spoken was far away down the halls from where we'd run. I slowed and glared over my shoulder, almost too furious to heed the command. The voice called several times for a halt before the speaker appeared. It'd taken them far too long to catch up to us. This obviously wasn't a shifter, and I recognized the annoyed voice.

The dragon's companion jogged breathlessly up to us, her face bright red from exertion. She bent over, and the dragon rushed to her side, murmuring words of comfort as he patted her back. "Are you joining us on the front lines, my dear?" he inquired curiously. He was obviously not concerned about her safety. He was either extremely confident in her ability to hold her own or didn't care as much about her as I thought.

"We cannot wait," I snapped at them and took off once more, my instincts screaming at me to run. Ignoring the reckless pulling of my feral mind was too difficult, but apparently, so was ignoring the woman. Stone jutted up in front of my foot, causing me to trip for the second time this night. I stumbled and regained my balance, then whirled in fury. "What the shit?" I raged as quietly as possible.

The dragon caught up to me with the witch in his arms and nodded ahead of us to keep going. "She said wait. She did warn you," he remarked. I was seething, but I held it together, knowing three people were better than one.

The voices ahead loudened, making us slow our approach. The doorway the voices were coming from led into a cavern bustling with activity.

"Watch out!" the dragon's companion hissed beneath her breath and pointed to the floor. I stepped back hastily and spotted some kind of symbol embedded in the ground. "That's to detect trespassers!"

"They're the trespassers." I flexed my fingers, fighting my feral mind for control. I was shaking almost violently now, and Iron's wings could no longer be contained. We were crackling with a need to fulfill our new role.

I worked my way around the image and peeked past the doorway to see how many had already arrived. The cavern here, infested with dramatic stalactites and stalagmites, looked to be some kind of storage room, but the humans inside were ignoring the crates stacked against the wall. I scowled when I spied four rot-witches among the fumbling, tired humans, barking orders through threads of spittle.

I held back a gag because the rot was almost overpowering here. The stench of these old, decrepit creatures was so much worse, and I wasn't sure if that had to do with their numbers or their state of corruption. I forced my mouth into my arm and dry-heaved when another rot-witch waddled in from the hole they'd blasted in the wall, carrying a half-rotted leg she'd casually strewn over a shoulder.

"Delightful." The dragon sighed next to me, seemingly not as affected by the smell, but I did detect the thickness of nausea in his whispering throat. "What now?"

They were all squinting as they held up their torches, and that was a sign to me that I stood a better chance if the room was plunged into darkness. Underground allowed for absolute darkness. Not even starlight could reach this place. "Witch," I hissed over my shoulder at the cranky woman, "can you snuff out those torches?"

"There was a time when the young never doubted their elders," the woman glowered at me. "I can, you fool, but then we won't be able to see! Not even this one!" She jerked her finger at her companion, who looked bored with the conversation.

"I can make light for us, my dear," he drawled, scratching the greying stubble on his chin.

"I don't need light," I gritted out through my teeth, "and you need to stay in darkness until you're swarmed, then sweep with your fire, understand? Don't let them get past this doorway! I'm going in when those torches go out!"

"Those could be slaves though!" the voices of several strangers came from behind us in hushed tones—a male and a man. Keid and the witches must be waking more people and sending them with shifters to find us.

"Look," I whispered, pointing my finger at everyone as more gathered at our hiding place, "if you want to try to save them, fine, but know that if you let this line crumble, and they get past you, putting my pregnant mate at risk, I'll end you when this is over!" My voice was thick with both my beasts' presence. I knew my feral mind was close to taking over, and Iron was working hard with Marrow to keep me grounded. I was holding on by a thin thread of blessed, internal starlight.

"Best believe him," the dragon said lightly, giving me an appraising look. I snorted at him and turned to peer around the corner again. The humans were putting stretchers together, obviously looking to carry out those they wouldn't be killing. How did they even decide that? Did they wake the witches one at a time and give them the choice of life or death? I sneered at the sight. Disgusting.

"Snuff those torches," I ordered the witch. She sighed, but with that huff of annoyance, all the torches died. There was no great wind that swept through the cavern to blow them out but rather a waning, shrinking death had taken over every flame, as though starving them all of air.

With cries of alarm pouring from the room, I slinked into the cavern, clicking to see with my ears. The noise was slightly confusing my echolocation, but I was able to make sense of the chaos as I got used to it. I dug my fingers into my pockets to grab the seeds and sought out the rot-witches.

"Did we trigger something?" a nearby rot-witch wheezed, and I focused my attention on her, making sure I wasn't getting close to anyone else. I fingered the seed for a moment, aimed, then threw it at the ancient wretch.

The seed stuck to the witch's skirts like a bur and immediately reacted to her proximity. Curling, reaching vines burst from the tiny, innocent-looking seed like ravenous hands and latched around her throat first, hardly allowing a single gurgle to pass her lips. I took a step back in surprise, then turned my head away when the vines penetrated flesh. I couldn't waste time enjoying her painful demise. I had to find the next one. I'd adapted quickly to the noisy environment, but I had to go faster.

"I don't know. Gamanata? Gamanata?" another rot-witch hissed. I spied her whirling about in the dark, blind and in search of her dead comrade. "Speak up!"

"Someone's here!" another rot-witch screeched, her voice laced with a touch of madness.

"Impossible!"

"Get those torches lit!" another hissed, and the humans fumbled in the dark to relight the cloth-wrapped branches.

"So fucking slow!" a rot-witch to my right cursed and lifted her hand to potentially cast some spell. Perhaps it was to light the torches, but I moved through the panicked crowd and flicked a seed at her. She soon fell to a viny, bloody death as the plant feasted on her rotten corpse.

*Brutal,* Iron whispered. *I love it.*

*Our mate is dangerous...* Marrow added with a mix of trepidation and awe.

I picked my way through the room, doing everything I could to not alert them to my presence or location. The witches were hastily relighting the torches with spells now, realizing that something lethal was occurring in the dark. The dragon's companion continued to snuff every torch that ignited, but as I approached my third target, I was finally spotted. Her torch flared to life as I tossed a seed, but she managed to let out a screech, and an earthen wall jutted from the ground to block my projectile.

"Bat?" she screamed and stumbled away as she erected more walls. I held words of rage back at being discovered, not wanting them to pinpoint me with sound. Before the third witch could erect dirt above her, I sent a prayer to the Sky Gods and tossed several seeds over the wall, hoping one would land on her. I breathed a sigh of relief when her gurgling death reached my ears, and I backed off to find cover in case a torch relit before I could close in on the fourth. This was about to get a lot more dangerous.

"Where? The skies' children? They've returned? Where, Cortellus? Cortellus!" the fourth rot-witch hollered, then dissolved into a coughing fit.

"Find the sleepers! I'll take care of the bats!" the last witch said, keeping a tight hold of the leg she'd swung over her shoulder. "If Mantegazz is here, drag her rotten ass out too!"

Flares of firelight illuminated the room, and I cursed under my breath, ducking behind the wall of earth the dead witch had erected. Glancing over to the door, I could see that the humans were charging the dragon-shifter. He was sweeping with fire as promised, but the compelled slaves couldn't retreat. The members of the coven would occasionally wrangle a slave to remove their curse mark, but it was a muddy, messy effort, and the dragon was quickly becoming overwhelmed. His companion had stopped focusing on the torches, which was just as well. His sweeping fire was bound to expose me anyway.

"Don't like light?" the fourth rot-witch shrieked as she looked around the room for me. "I'll give you fucking light!"

A brilliant ball of blue fire flared to life in the room, and she laughed when her arm detached from her shoulder. "Worth it," she rasped and grinned gleefully, waiting to find a bat cowering from the brilliant display.

That wasn't me anymore, was it?

I reached behind me to feel around the cluster of stalagmites. I couldn't chuck a seed that far considering its light weight, but I could throw something much larger…

*Help me out, you two,* I asked my beasts in desperation. It was going to take a colossal effort to snap this thing from its base. With two beast souls though, I might be able to do it.

*Alright, big boy,* Iron said to Marrow. *One... two...*

*Three!* Marrow finished.

I planted my feet against a stone lip and pulled on the giant stalagmite with all my bloody strength plus the might of both beast souls. My muscles strained and shook violently as I yanked at the formation, willing it to break free. My mind fixated on my mate and offspring as I struggled with it. Fear was leaking through my fury. I couldn't let the humans get past the dragon and the volunteers. I had to stop their onslaught! If one of these witches had been the ones to curse the group, I had a fifty percent chance of stopping the charge… If only the bloody, clotted witches were standing together!

With a resounding, deafening crack, the ancient stalagmite snapped from its base, and I careened backward under its weight. My back hit the earthen wall, and a bone in my wing snapped. I gasped through the white-hot pain and raised the column, catching sight of the dragon's startled face as I prepared my throw. I used my stumbling momentum as I came out from behind the wall to swing the column of rock in the direction of the cackling rot-witch, screaming through pain and rage.

She barely saw it coming before she was crushed. Rot splattered around the stalagmite, and at her death, her entire body decomposed before her companion. The remaining rot-witch released a terrifying screech that spoke of dark, hoary things hiding behind milky eyes. All the hairs on my body stood on end, and I retreated, knowing I'd be dead if she was able to focus on me.

*Shit! Move, move, move!* Marrow cried, and his wings seeped through Iron's to fix the broken bone. I cringed and tried to ignore the weird prickling of quills forcing their way out of skin that didn't normally have feathers.

"What the fuck are you?" She lumbered after me, raising her claws in a gesture that would have normally had me pissing my pants. I raced to put the dirt wall between us, and a jet of fire slowed the rot-witch enough to give me a moment to think. I felt around in my pocket for another seed and grimaced when I realized I only had two left.

"Sleep! Sleep! Sleep!" the rot-witch roared, and by the number of thuds that hit the ground, I knew that the bastion's volunteer army had fallen to the curse once more. I hazarded a glance around the space, and was surprised to find the majority of her humans asleep as well. Had I freed them by killing the right witch, and she'd been forced to knock them unconscious with everyone else? Or maybe she'd just gotten sloppy...

The only ones left standing looked to be a handful of normal witches working with the rot-witch, and they proceeded to march toward the doorway where we'd made our stand. One aimed her knife at the unconscious dragon's neck, and my heart leapt into my throat. I knew that if I went out there, the rot-witch would kill me on sight.

I owed him my soul, but... my mate... my offspring. I dug my claws into the dirt as I slowly avoided the approaching, stalking creature, completely torn over the decision I had to make.

I tried to take a step toward the unconscious dragon when the witch split his skin with her blade, but my feet wouldn't move. My feral mind wouldn't let me risk anything to step into the open. If I died, who would protect my mate and endangered offspring? They'd be on their own here!

My claws dug into the sides of my head, and I released an uncontrollable, guttural scream of frustration. Why? Why? Even now, the evolution forced upon me was getting in my way! I was freed from the curse, and yet the rot-witches continued to control me through the echoes of their actions.

I lurched forward, but I didn't know where I was going or who was leading my body. All I knew was that I wouldn't be able to save the dragon—whether it was because of timing or ability. There was no getting there without dying for it. The rot-witches never cast recklessly. If she aimed to hit me, she aimed to kill. My body's instincts knew it, and it wouldn't let me try a clotting thing.

*Iron! Marrow!* I screamed internally and moved my claws from the sides of my bleeding head to the dirt wall in an attempt to push my way toward the dragon. My wings flapped haphazardly, feeling out of sync with my body as my beasts fought against our newly adjusted feral instincts. In my peripheral vision, I could make out the bizarre combination of feathers and bat skin as they both came out in their struggling.

Whatever blood in my face hadn't trickled out from my self-inflicted cuts drained from the sound of footsteps behind me. In immediate danger, my body allowed me to leap into a roll, but when I put pressure on the base of my half-broken wing, I yelled in agony and scrambled to put stalagmites between me and the rot-witch. An explosion of dirt sandwiched the air where I'd been, nearly crushing and entombing me.

The creature shrieked her frustration at my evasion, and a small clump of her scalp slid down the side of her face, forcing her to rip it away in rage. The enemy witch who'd just pricked the dragon's throat stilled and looked up at something on the other side of the doorway, distracting the rot-witch as well. Using all the speed I had as a bat, I snapped a smaller stalagmite from its base and threw it at her when her head turned. Though her attention was drawn for just a heartbeat, it was all I needed.

The small column hit her hip, and she staggered backward, nearly falling to a knee. I had no idea what damage had been done to her hip, but this hag was sturdier than the others. Shit!

Just beneath the rot-witch's chilling shriek came the sound of new footsteps racing down the connecting hall. A bat dove into the room and attached itself to the witch's face for just a moment before jumping off to find me. What had to be the staff-like handle of a broom clubbed the witch where Vain had just been, and the woman collapsed to the ground. Keid appeared in the doorway and lightly slapped the next witch's legs with the pole, causing her to fall over somehow.

Terror met my fury at its very peak, and I ran out to keep the rot-witch's attention. My mate was now in danger, and I was bloody well going to draw attention away from her pregnant body.

*Seeds? Seeds left?* Vain cried as she flitted past me, and I tossed the remaining two into the air. She impressively caught them both with her maw and a foot, then spiraled down to attack the rot-witch, who'd had me centered in her sights. I had nothing now. I was completely exposed.

Unfortunately, the rot-witch had seen Vain's approach and batted away the first seed with the leg she was carrying. The seed violently germinated, and starving vines darted into the limb like snakes. The decrepit hag abandoned the leg, startled by a tendril that'd made a grab for her, and spun on rickety heels to run. As Vain made her turn to try again, the rot-witch dashed into the entrance they'd created, turning the tunnel into a desperate exit.

"Vain, don't!" Keid screamed, her eyes wild with terror as she bludgeoned the next witch. "Don't follow her! Let her go!"

Vain ignored her and darted into the tunnel, screaming, *No! No! No!* Her tone said it all. She didn't want to fail again. She didn't want this one to get away from her.

*Vain!* I shouted as I ran to help Keid with the last ten witches, slaughtering them all in a brutal sweep before they could get to her—these minor witches didn't intimidate me. Nothing scared me like the nigh corpses. The remaining invaders were swiftly razed, and I was flecked with human blood by the time I got to the tunnel.

A force threw me back, white filled my vision, and an explosion hit my ears.

*No!* Iron's cry was deafening as a puff of dust and debris sprayed from the massive hole in the wall. Keid ran past, which propelled me to get back onto my feet, though the effort had me crying in agony. That impact might have broken a couple more bones. It was hard to tell when parts of my body felt numb from shock.

I stumbled into the partially collapsed tunnel to find Keid digging through the dirt, sobbing and screaming her familiar's name. Both my beasts restrained my feral mind as violently as possible while I worked to help search for the little blood bat. All my body wanted to do was take Keid and leave this dangerous place.

Every nerve, muscle, tendon… everything yelled at me, but I kept pushing rocks and soil aside until Keid finally uncovered the small creature. I grabbed her shoulder and leaned over to look at the state of the little thing, but Vain was limp.

"She's not breathing! She's not breathing!" Keid shrieked and ran out of the tunnel with me at her heels. She fell to the dragon's companion's side and lifted her curse as fast as possible. I checked the dragon's neck, and though he was bleeding profusely, I didn't think his windpipe had been cut.

"I'm… getting… Akira," I groaned and started running down the hall, trying to scent my way back so I could look for the doctor. It took several minutes to hunt her down, but I found her unconscious with the rot-witch mothers in a small chamber adjacent to the greenhouse.

I threw her over a shoulder, grunting in pain from my fresh injuries, then grabbed what looked like a medical kit and raced back to where I'd left Keid. Cold sweat dripped into my eyes and poured down my back as I fought the searing pain of fractures. Just… needed… to… get… back…

I stumbled to a stop when I reached Keid and an awake, cranky witch who was hovering over Vain. Keid, pale, shaking, and sweating, watched her while putting pressure on the dragon's laceration. I laid Akira down by her to be woken, making sure she was within reach.

Keid gestured to another body, which I brought over to her so she could wake. That witch came to, clambered deliriously to her feet, and stumbled over herself to start waking the others one last time. The room was full of moans, groans, and cries of pain as the bastion's people and the witch's slaves were roused.

Leaving others to help Keid, I wandered around the cavern with a hand over my sore ribs, making sure that everyone who was supposed to be dead was properly expired.

My feral mind finally slipped through and managed to take control of me, driving me to quickly kill two half-dead enemy witches instead of allowing me to interrogate them. No one who was a threat to Keid was to remain alive. With my tattered body draining me, I was too tired to fight instinct. It didn't care about taking captives, only keeping my mate and offspring safe in the moment.

I was drawn back toward the collapsed tunnel, but I couldn't detect anything past the dirt. Had she escaped? Had the hag been crushed in the cave-in or had she been killed by Vain's last attempt?

"Ferrer!" Keid called to me, her voice thick with grief. Concern flared and gave me one last burst of energy, so I rushed to her side only to find her rocking a breathing Vain against her chest. The woman, my woman, was crying her eyes out as she looked up at me. "She's alive! They saved her!"

Iron's isolated presence in my mind was struck senseless. His relief, Marrow's relief, and my relief were all combined into an overflowing pool of messy, desperate emotions. I fell to my knees and mindfully pulled them both into my arms, unable to keep a wheezing whimper from escaping my throat. I covered the top of Keid's head in kisses as I fought tears. If I started crying, I wouldn't bloody stop.

Everything around our small sphere of solace was muffled. Grief and joy echoed around the cavern as some were revived and some were covered in old cloth for burial. There was nothing to be done for those who'd been burned to death by the dragon's fire. Hopefully the bodies were still identifiable, but I couldn't bring myself to look.

Once Eriu had been found and awoken, she'd taken charge of the entire situation. Not only had she sent volunteers out to retrieve the evacuees, she'd ordered a couple familiars and shifters to search for any signs of the missing rot-witch. One was still unaccounted for… but if the ancient wretch had somehow survived, I suspected she'd have to recover somewhere first. There was no way that she'd left this area completely intact if she'd used a heavier spell to collapse the cave.

Eventually, Keid helped me stand, and we wandered back to our room in a haze, desperate for rest. I was adamant that we'd done our part, and they had plenty of people to assist the injured. Eriu seemed to have things in order. My mate didn't argue; she was completely fixated on Vain and me.

Grabbing some supplies from Akira's office first, Keid laid me down on the bed and started addressing the fractures in my half-bat, half-ossifrage wings. I couldn't shift them away until they were more healed, and fortunately, she was already aware of that.

"I know it wasn't in your control, but I have to thank the gods above and below for your experience treating shifters," I grunted out as she carefully folded and bound my wings after setting several bones.

"Prepared me for you," she said tiredly, but I heard the small smile in her voice as I rested on my stomach. "Looks like Iron and Marrow got tangled… Such a strange sight. And gods, you might be purple, green, and blue for a day," she murmured as she cleaned me with a soapy cloth. "I suspect one or two of your ribs might have a small fracture, and what happened to your head?"

"Better than orange," I mumbled, then answered her question. "That was self-inflicted… kind of. I was warring with myself. These new instincts are hard to control, Keid…"

"Ah… I wish you hadn't done that." She sighed, wringing the cloth before dabbing at my temples.

"What matters is that you're safe now." I stared at her from the corner of my eye.

"I am going to make the most powerful fucking collar for Vain," she stated in a thick voice, on the verge of crying again. Before she could go back into blaming herself, I reached out to lay a hand on her thigh. She bit her lip, wiped a tear from her cheek, and continued to tend to my injuries in silence. I glanced past her to Vain's recovery spot in an old towel Keid had found. The blood bat was sleeping off her wounds, but if the witches said she'd be fine… then I'd have to trust that.

Trust… it was hard to come by, wasn't it?

"What are you thinking?" Keid inquired, sniffling. I felt her turbulent emotions and suspected she was asking for a distraction.

"I was thinking about trust… That's enough, Keid," I said, moving the blood-pinkened cloth away from my tender skin. "The rest will heal on its own. Iron and Marrow will fix it all."

Keid lay down next to me and cupped my cheek with a cool hand. I closed my eyes and sighed, letting her mate touch soothe my body, heart, and soul. "What about trust?" she inquired, staring into my eyes with her lovely periwinkle ones.

"Those we think we know…" I answered slowly, releasing a heavy exhale. I started over, struggling to find the right words. "I find myself not trusting my instincts anymore, Keid. It's… unnerving."

"Your feral ones?"

"No," I murmured, slowly reaching out to stroke her upper arm. "I feel like I can't judge people correctly… not anymore. I misjudged you… these people… that wolf… even that bloody Mushy."

She laughed weakly at the reference to the hag we'd known for many torturous days. "To be fair," she returned wryly, "I had trouble trusting her as well. I just had less invested at the time."

The reminder of her suffering was sobering, and it hurt me deeply to recall it. She seemed to see it in my eyes because she wiggled closer to offer me more comfort. I clung to her the best I could from my prone position. "I'm worried I won't be able to protect you and my family if I can't trust the right people," I confessed, shutting my eyes tightly.

"You trust me, though, right?" she inquired sweetly, tucking a strand of hair behind my ear.

"I do… especially after watching you wield a broom handle. What in the shitting stars did you enchant it with?" I asked, feeling my cheek tug in sudden amusement.

Keid's light, beautiful laughter lifted my soul, and she answered, "Numbing. I swear it's the only spell I can remember when I fall into a panic."

"So, they just succumbed to dead leg?" I chuckled into the mattress for a moment, then smiled over at her tired face.

"Well, like I said… you can trust me and Vain. I will help you decide who we can trust, and we will both keep our family safe. The colony will also. We can only do the best we can, love," she said, returning to her original question. "We live… we learn…"

"I knew I could trust your mouth…" I thumbed her lower lip, tracing the stain of my blood on it.

"There are other things it can do." She smirked uncharacteristically as she closed her eyes. She'd changed so much since the day I met her.

"That sounds familiar, but my recollection is a bit fuzzy."

"I'll refresh your memory when we get home."

"Home…"

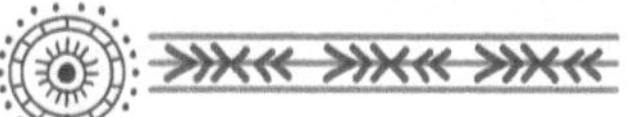

# Chapter 32

## Keid

"You stupid, irresponsible…!" a voice similar to mine cried as I entered the colony's great castle with Ferrer. Slippers slapping on stone was my only other warning as my twin sister rounded a corner and flung herself into my arms, pushing me back a couple steps. With the wind knocked out of me, it took several heartbeats to reply in kind.

"Rude," I wheezed flatly and stabilized my footing, aided by my mate's hand on my lower back. Despite my serious tone, it felt good to hold her again. The bond unique to us always seemed to recharge a different part of my soul, and it warmed from her show of affection.

Her male stalked over but kept his distance, giving my male a dubious look. "You're back," he stated uncomfortably, but I detected relief in his body as his shoulders dropped. He came a little closer as other bat-shifters arrived, his courage bolstered by their presence.

"I'm behaving now," Ferrer said wryly to him.

"Oh! I never introduced you," my sister said excitedly to me and pointed to her bat-shifter. "This is Borredan!"

"I… recall," I said with an arched brow, trying not to picture the two of them in the position I'd last witnessed.

"And what was with that note you left in my bag?" my sister raged, slapping my arm viciously. "I hated it! I'll always need you!"

Ferrer's hand twitched in my peripheral vision, and I warned my sister. "Best stop smacking me, Tsisana…"

Her eyes flickered from Ferrer to me, and a question formed on her face. "Did he… redeem himself?" She sent him a sour, disapproving look.

"A thousand times over," I said softly, placing a comforting hand on her arm before glancing up at the other bats who were patiently waiting for my reunion to pause. Mildly intimidated by their lineup, I moved closer to Ferrer, who slung an arm around me in a possessive move.

"Don't think our chat is over," Tsisana mumbled and reached her hand out to a smitten Borredan, who immediately came to her side.

"These are some of our coronels," Ferrer presented, gesturing to the two males and a female who'd arrived. "Ettor, Castanon, and Luzia. Nofre is away with his mate on urgent business, and the others are around here somewhere. I think they might be visiting Queen Hekla still."

"Correct," Ettor supplied promptly. "You must be exhausted. We've prepared a larger chamber for you as your note requested."

"It seems like we have a great deal to talk about. Shall we meet in several hours after you get settled?" the bat named Castanon inquired, clasping his hands behind his back.

"No," Ferrer said flatly, swiping his hand in a sharp gesture. "We have to discuss some things now so I can send word back to the dragons. I'm anxious to give the coven an answer." The bat hesitated, then glanced down at me. "You can go rest if you like, Keid. I don't want you pushing yourself…"

His attentiveness was heartwarming, but I shook my head. "No, I definitely want to attend this meeting. I'll rest later." I could see Ferrer mentally kicking himself, but he sighed and chose to trust me.

"Well, you won't need to send word because they're here," Castanon informed, and Ferrer's brows shot up in surprise. "They've been here for a day, anticipating your return with… what's his name? Twigbeer?"

"Leofwine," I corrected, pressing my lips together so tight that I was certain they'd turned white.

"He was joking." Luzia snorted. "Castanon's humor is slowly returning as we're getting used to our new life here. It, admittedly, needs some work. It is drier than baked blood."

"They didn't want to send representatives?" Ferrer asked, sticking to the topic at hand. "Surprising."

"Slaves were involved, and you know how their queen is. She's keen to hear directly from you and Keid," Ettor explained. "They also ran into a rot-witch in that region a while ago and are curious about it as well. Events could be connected."

"Ah," Ferrer replied simply as the bats entered a room. My mate held the door open for me, and I beamed up at him. He was so fucking sweet to me now! We'd truly come as far as we'd traveled—significantly.

We waited at the large table while the leaders of the dragon's kingdom were being summoned. The bats took turns approaching Ferrer's seat to study his wings around its bandages, murmuring sounds of awe at the strange sight. No doubt they'd be quite surprised when they could finally witness him shift into his sky form. Marrow was probably itching fiercely to introduce himself too.

I nearly jumped out of my seat when the door opened. A large male and his shorter female waltzed in to take a seat after greeting the room. I'd seen the king and queen of the dragons before, but they still filled the room with their presence, something I didn't think I could get used to. Despite the casual, almost boyish cut of his tousled hair, King Keyon's dominance was palpable, and there was as much strength as there was elegance in his movement.

This wasn't a king who lazed about on his throne all day—that much was obvious.

Queen Elpis had a fresh, open, and joyous countenance that belied the conservative appearance of her veil and thorned crown. Her eyes kept sliding to Ferrer's bound, healing wings, and her hand twitched on the table. I knew she was practiced in some form of medicine, so perhaps she was curious about his injuries. I hoped Ferrer would let her look at them if she offered. He said his wings itched like crazy, and I knew he wanted to free them as soon as possible.

"Starlight preserve you," King Keyon said, folding his hands on the table. It was a classy greeting. Though his kind worshiped the Sun God, they knew the bats did not favor the daylight. The queen echoed his words with a smile, then set her brows straight as we got to the matter.

"So, as you know, Keid and I did not make the rendezvous that Leofwine had set u—" Ferrer began but was interrupted by Leofwine trying to make a silent entrance. He was followed by a red-faced Adelais, and they both promptly took a seat. "Up." Ferrer cleared his throat and continued. "They tracked us to the surviving members of the Terran Coven, and we informed them of the attack."

"We're sending people to retrieve the slaves and the bodies of the slaves who've perished," Queen Elpis said in a somber voice, "but we'd appreciate you helping in gaining their trust. They are rather timid and insecure for a coven."

"They have taken in a number of individuals who might not have the cleanest history," I told her, feeling very shy in front of so many important shifters. Ferrer groped under the table to hold my hand as I spoke. "It's understandable that being on the run for so long has made them jumpy regarding strangers. They're also protective of their members' anonymity. I will do the best I can… I plan to work with them further…"

"I scented someone familiar, by the way," Leofwine muttered to King Keyon. "He'd left before we arrived, but we'll talk about it later."

"In regards to another trafficking matter," Ferrer said in a dark tone that got the table's attention immediately, "Keid and I discovered something horrifying that I was hoping you could look into for us." He gave me one last look, and I prompted him with a nod. We'd already discussed it, and I didn't want to be the one to say it. It was too painful. "Keid was told that she was barren by her old coven, but we learned that her eggs had actually been stolen. Someone suggested they may have been trafficked due to her nature."

The reaction at the table was mixed but collectively upset. I swallowed heavily, and my sister's gaze locked onto mine. My eyes burned with unspent tears, but I managed to keep the drops at bay. She mouthed a question, looking distraught, but I waved her away, telling her without words that we'd discuss it later.

"However, someone managed to return her fertility… as we are very much expecting, an—"

The table erupted at the news, the mood shifting from anger to joy in half a heartbeat. My sister dissolved into tears and tackled me from her chair. Oh Sky Gods, I was getting physical and emotional whiplash from this meeting.

"I don't believe it! Your dream, Keid! Your dream! It's coming true!" She gasped into my shoulder, rocking me in excitement. My sister might have a little more spark in her than I did, but I'd never seen her this energized in my entire life… except for when she'd met her fated mate. I held her calmly and smiled into her neck, doubly pleased to find the marking Borredan had left there.

"This is excellent news," Ettor was saying, and I turned my head in my sister's embrace to listen to him. "We have others who are expecting pups, and I'm delighted that we'll be registering you both as well. We're already interviewing for doctors and midwives."

"There seems to be a good one with the Terran Coven survivors, but I'm not sure if they'll part with her," I noted.

"Back to what I was saying, not that we don't appreciate the well wishes," Ferrer said, waving off a smirking Luzia who'd ruffled his hair. He ran his fingers through his locks and sighed. "We can't say when her eggs were stolen, but it was likely during a routine checkup," he growled, "and she may have offspring out there that we don't know about…" Ferrer left his question hanging and stared meaningfully at the dragon rulers.

"We'll look at our records of Reborn, freed slaves, and arrange a team to do some tests if we find any possibilities," Queen Elpis offered, looking a bit ill. "That is horrible. A horrible thing to do to a female… or woman. Such a violation."

"I was hoping someone could investigate my coven too," I asked in a quiet voice and sent a desperate look over to Leofwine. "I know we were just liberated, but if anyone ever returns to old habits…"

"We're a bit stretched for resources at the moment, but I'll scrape something together, yes?" the spymaster proposed, looking over at his king. Both rulers nodded, appearing quite upset and deep in thought. "We'll have to collaborate with the cats, since it will be in their territory. That will help."

"Thank you," I whispered and relaxed against my sister. A great deal of pressure rolled off my shoulders. My case was in good hands, I was certain of that. I'd give them everything they needed to know.

"And finally, we need to discuss the survivors of the coven," Ferrer asserted, tapping the table with a finger.

King Keyon crossed his bulky arms. "Who are being escorted to your borders as requested… under heavy guard. We're protecting our people as much as we're protecting them."

"I wouldn't expect anything else," Ferrer replied with a shrug.

"Rot-witches at our border?" Castanon inquired, tensing. A muscle in his jaw twitched as he stared at Ferrer.

"They're offering to find a way to break our curse, Castanon. They warned it could take years, but it's an opportunity to free ourselves," Ferrer returned, attempting to keep his calm as the other bats bristled.

"It's obvious that it's possible," Ettor said, looking both wistful and sick as he gestured to his wings. "I don't know if our people can tolerate their presence though. That's... You know it's not simple for us to..." He raised his hands helplessly.

"If you think my travels were anything but easy, you've got another think coming, Ettor," Ferrer replied sharply. "I know very well how hard it is to fight your instincts. I nearly pissed myself a dozen times."

"It was a struggle," I affirmed, moving from my sister to place a calming hand on Ferrer's shoulder. "He did manage. Would it be that intolerable to put them at a distance? They don't have to stay here. As long as it's a protected location... It's all they ask for."

"What about one of our islands?" Luzia suggested as she leaned back in her chair. "We've got a couple that are large enough."

"Surround earth worshipers with seawater?" Ettor inquired dubiously. "Would they agree to that?"

"It'd be hard to reach but close enough to send supplies to," she said with a shrug. "Does anyone really want to pass up a chance to break the curse because we're a little uncomfortable? You're all clottin' mad if that's the case. It'd be the most idiotic decision in our history."

"It's just a discussion, Luzia," Borredan grunted irritably, and Ferrer pushed her tilted chair with a finger, making her scramble to grab the table before she fell.

"Well, I think the discussion is over," she replied in a rush. "I vote we take them in, protect them, and reap the rewards of a lifted curse. I'd love to try new foods."

A snorty laugh burst from Queen Elpis, and she swiftly covered her mouth to muffle her mirth. Her mate's cheek twitched, but he remained silent.

"A vote to bring them in provisionally while we sort out the details? I'm sure the dragons don't want to wait at our border with them for longer than necessary," Ettor proposed with a sigh, rubbing his temples. "We can use the tents we received for the recognition event."

The vote was unanimous; all were in favor, and I almost fainted against Ferrer. This was phenomenal news, and I couldn't wait to share it with the mothers and Eriu. Fatigue washed over me as much of our agenda was addressed. The time that'd been spent with both Mushy and Ferrer now seemed like a surreal fever dream.

"I trust we can pick up the rest later?" Ferrer asked the room, likely sensing my exhaustion. "I'd like to get Keid to a bed before I go feral." He winced and held up a hand to interrupt scattered chuckles. It was the last thing I saw before I covered my face in embarrassment.

*Oh gods, Ferrer.*

"It's n-not what you think," he added with a nervous laugh.

"I'd forgotten about that," Castanon murmured as he relaxed in his chair. "That's going to make things interesting around here as more mates become pregnant. Everyone will be on edge."

"We'll manage," Ettor said. "I'm just thrilled that we're on our way to rebuilding our population. Welcome, Keid. It's wonderful you've returned safely. You'll find a good home with us."

I peeked through my fingers to find the room staring at me, and I found myself calming. Perhaps my new family would be larger than I thought. Yes, I've finally found the place I belonged—belonged and loved. Ferrer squeezed my hand, and I stood to follow him, ready to sleep for an entire month.

## Ferrer

When I'd arrived back home at the colony, I promised myself that my clotted, emotional ass wouldn't cry again for another fifty years or so. Opening the door to Keid's and my new set of chambers broke that resolution. My woman gasped and ran into the first room, a sitting room, and turned in circles, unable to decide which direction to explore. She wove between crimson tufted armchairs and a large, glossy tea table made of redwood.

"I thought we told the queen not to be overly generous with the family suites," I said in a rough voice and wiped a moist eye. I swallowed hard and tried to ignore the stinging in my nose. Bloody shits, I had to get ahold of myself!

*Look at this nest!* Marrow marveled in delight. *What beautiful furniture. Where will our hatchlings—er, pups—be?*

*Yes! Bring on the pups!* Iron crowed.

Keid laughed and looked for a spot to place an exhausted Vain. She was much improved, but after a long, multi-day dragon flight and a meeting, she was fast asleep. My mate grabbed a soft fur that'd been slung over a chair and spread it out on the tea table for the blood bat.

*Thank you...* she murmured drowsily and closed her eyes once more. Iron ached to see her so drained, but we were all relieved that she had a place to recover now without further interruption. Keid and I would give the two bats time together soon if they wished.

I toured the rooms with my enthusiastic woman and smiled at the sounds she was making at every little discovery. The place had a calm elegance about it, with warm beige walls, black accents, redwood floors, and crimson furniture. Keid was beside herself when we discovered the nursery. It had been fully stocked in advance, and I studied the window, which had thick curtains to thoroughly block out daylight if required. I glanced over at my woman and wondered about what was within her. Would it need these curtains?

My curse had been lifted, but what about the life developing inside Keid? Our young had been conceived before my curse was lifted, so would they still be cursed? Would our second one be freed from the curse? I could only hope that it wouldn't take the rot-witches years to unravel Mushy's secret cure. I didn't want any of my offspring enduring what I'd suffered.

Keid turned to me, somehow knowing what I was thinking. All she did was meet me at the window and pull my head down for a soft kiss. Her lips were just as enthralling as the first time she kissed me, and we stood there for a while, sharing a quiet moment with embracing mouths and arms.

"Whatever they are, they will be loved and happy," Keid said in a gentle voice, pulling away from me. Her words were a promise, and it comforted me to know that she believed them. Yes, they would be; I'd make certain of that.

She grabbed my hand, and we wandered around the rest of the suite, daydreaming and nightdreaming about all the possibilities. Keid spoke of the enchantments she wanted to put on their plush toys, and all her ideas kept me smiling. I had a feeling our offspring would enjoy having a witch for a mother.

In the bedroom—a large space with a four poster that Keid was convinced was much too fancy for her—we found a catalog on a side table. Fortunately, it was in both fae and human so we could read through the explanation.

"We'll order you new clothes first," I said, frowning as I pinched the fabric of her travel-abused tunic.

"Curses," she muttered, looking down with a laugh. "Yes, please!"

"Then let's be done with this tattered thing." I grinned and yanked the fabric over her head before she could protest. She yelped and I lifted her so I could wash us both in the luxurious bathing room before retiring.

"This is all from the fae?" Keid asked sleepily as I settled us both between the sheets, naked and scrubbed clean. I turned my woman's back to me, needing to stay on my side, and drew her close so I could curl around her.

"Mm-hmm," I hummed, squeezing her with my answer. "Our savior appears to be spoiling us… I will have to thank Queen Hekla personally. She'll want to meet you…" I yawned and nuzzled into her hair, breathing in the scent of birch I could properly enjoy now. I was worried that being around rot-witches for so long had destroyed my sense of smell. "We will do that after we sleep for a bloody month."

"Goodness," Keid murmured, "that's intimidating."

"You will like her. She's driven, like you." My words made her soul glow with happiness, and I was enjoying her new ability to accept compliments without arguing. Her self-esteem was indeed blossoming now.

"Th—" she started timidly, but there was a knock on the door, and I groaned, not wanting to get up again. I slid out of bed, resisting Keid's playful clutching, and went to answer the door.

A she-bat was on the other side, one of our castle runners, and she handed me a letter before turning on a heel to run her next errand. I closed the door and frowned at the envelope as I returned to bed. Keid rolled to face me, and I delivered the letter to her.

"It's for you," I said, raising my brows to mirror her expression. We were both surprised, and I rested my face on her shoulder as she opened and read what was on the parchment. It was not in fae.

"Dear Keid Semira, or perhaps Keid Galvan, your presence is requested by Her Majesty, Ragna Rhydderch, The Wolf Queen and The Vessel of the Earth Gods, at her royal castle. Please seek audience with Her Majesty at your soonest availability. The bat-shifters and fae will assist you in finding the closest realm door to make your travel as short as possible. From the office of The Wolf Queen; Starlight preserve your road." Keid's wide-eyed gaze slid over to find mine, and I didn't need our bond to know that she was withering from physical and emotional exhaustion.

"Day after tomorrow," I said firmly, grabbing the letter and tossing it into a corner of the room. "Get it over with." Keid whined and turned to curl into me, and I chuckled. "I know, I know. I have a plan. When we get back, I won't answer the door ever again." Her laughter was mixed with a whimper, her tone slightly delirious as she scooted as close as she could.

"That better be a promise…"

Ferrer and I chose to sleep through the next day and woke at the following dawn to make our trip over to the lycans' royal castle at their capital. I was admittedly a little grumpy at having to travel again, but at least the bat-shifters now had horse stables manned by, well, men. Horses were not fans of shifters, so I was grateful that they'd acquired mounts for their humans—and fae too, I supposed.

Ferrer walked along with me, keeping a little distance between himself and my bay mare. He was on edge again about my safety, which dismayed me, but there was no avoiding it. This was our very last trip for a while; we were both quite adamant about that. I desperately wanted to relax and enjoy my pregnancy in some peace and quiet.

We met with a fae representative who took us through several fae gates, which was a horribly dizzying experience, but at least the horse seemed to be used to it. She was remarkably calm, and I did enjoy giving certain muscles a break from walking. My bottom would be a little sore from riding, but it was a worthwhile trade.

The exiting gate was quite close to the castle of The Lycan King and The Wolf Queen, so we enjoyed a brief trip through a woodland weeping with vibrant autumn leaves. Ferrer collected some as souvenirs, marveling at the golds and reds like a young child. Though he had to stay covered like me, I loved the joy he got from daylight now and could listen to him talk about colors for hours. It made me see the world so differently, and I appreciated that.

We didn't have to wait long for an audience with The Wolf Queen, thankfully, and were whisked into a sitting room by a blond shifter. The choice of location was surprising, as we'd both expected to make our appearance in an audience chamber before two thrones. It wasn't the case.

"Welcome, Keid," a lovely brunette she-wolf said from a tea table. Her green eyes sparkled, and her cheeks were rosy, slightly plump from what I suspected was a mix of a healthy diet and a pregnancy. I'd seen it hundreds of times on lionesses. She nodded to my mate. "Greetings, child of the Sky Gods."

We both sat at her gesture after bowing and saying our own words of greeting, but I had a hard time tearing my eyes from the intimidating lycan who stood behind her. Ferrer was having a particularly rough time under The Lycan King's dominant aura, but he did a remarkable job not starting any murder. I reached to hold his hand and squeezed it in reassurance.

"Welcome," the king of both lycans and wolves, King Zorian, said gruffly. "You're currently addressing the Earth Gods, not Their vessel, Ragna Rhydderch."

I immediately stiffened, and this time, Ferrer squeezed my hand.

"There is no need for fear, child of Ours," the Earth Gods said through The Wolf Queen. "Have some tea. It is safe for your miraculous pregnancy."

Ferrer's growl was quiet but loud enough for everyone to hear.

"It's not poisoned, but don't drink it if you wish. No one here will be offended," King Zorian said with bulging, intimidating crossed arms.

"Thank you, Mother and Father. Last time I drank something questionable, it restored my fertility," I said with an amused smile as I reached for my tea. Ferrer frowned but didn't interfere with my decision. I wouldn't disrespect the royalty here, and I didn't doubt the claims of this being the actual vessel. To sit with my gods, I wanted to enjoy this experience. Already, I was soothed by Their presence. Somehow, They settled my shock and discomfort.

"We wish to thank you for assisting our cornered devout," the gods said. "We are greatly concerned by current events, seeing how 'Mushy' tested Fate's wrath."

"Wh-what do you mean?" I asked, alarmed. I placed my teacup back in its saucer and sat up straighter. I didn't ask how They knew about my nickname for Cordycaris. They were everywhere.

"Scrying without permission and making decisions based on what had been seen," They answered calmly. "No doubt you realized how she learned the things she knew—Ferrer's true nature, for one thing."

My mate nodded in my peripheral vision, and I bit my lip before asking my next question. "What… Are you afraid that Fate will do something?"

"None of us know Fate's actual plan. Our daughter is the closest to Fate, but She can only gleam so much. If Cordycaris changed something that was meant to happen, We don't know if Fate will intervene. It's one reason you've been summoned. We wished to warn you in person."

"Oh dear," I murmured, keeping myself from voicing profanity before my gods.

"Shit," Ferrer growled.

"Is there anything we should do?" I asked worriedly. This was adding so much more stress to what was supposed to be a new, peaceful life.

"Just be mindful," the Earth Gods said, tilting Ragna's head to stare at me and my mate. "We do not wish to see Our devout die and were pleased by the outcome. We have not seen Our true devout in a very long time, not since they went into hiding."

"Mindful?" My voice held more dismay in it than I wanted to express. Now what the fuck did that mean? I didn't want to be responsible for Mushy's actions!

"I see this warning has distressed you more than intended," They stated plainly. "We'd hoped you'd see Our warning as a blessing. Though We don't normally interfere with Fate, know that We intend to protect all Our children as much as possible. There may yet be wiggle room. Do not let this weigh on you. Enjoy your life, child of Ours. You've earned your happiness."

"Have… your original devout earned your forgiveness? They said you stopped protecting them…" I asked hesitantly, not sure it was wise to bring up their complaint.

"Nothing will change. All parents must release their children's hands at some point," They answered, and for the first time, there was just a hint of sadness in Their words. It was subtle, but it was there. "We may have done so prematurely. We were so disappointed in their coven."

They sounded like true parents in that moment, sad and regretful with the choices Their young had made. It lasted but a heartbeat before They returned to Their neutral countenance. "With the help of Our daughter and pairing those We've asked to be paired, We hope for a better future. Time will reveal the outcome. In the meantime, you've earned your joy. We will keep a benevolent eye on your family line. You and Ferrer have earned Our blessings with your shared victory."

"It was not as single-handed as all that…" Ferrer murmured thoughtfully, "but we accept your blessing with deep gratitude." I smiled over at him, comforted by his humble response.

I agonized over my last question, once again worried about insulting Them. The gods knew; however, and They gave me a prompting nod. "Speak without fear."

"Is… Is there a way for humans to mark their mates?" I asked, cringing internally as the words left my mouth.

"We anticipated this query," They replied, turning Their head to stare thoughtfully at Ferrer. "Marking was something Our daughter designed and the other gods copied. We are love at its origin, child. Original love needs no such validation. True partners know each other on the deepest levels without such soul ties. Our daughter likes to force things; We do not."

My heart plummeted, but in a way, I understood Their message. I didn't really feel like I needed a mate bond to know Ferrer. It was only really a problem when I worried about someone taking him from me.

"What if…" I cringed visibly and stared over at Ferrer in desperation, struggling to speak my fears. "Someone else…"

"Mortals cannot seek loopholes with gods. Once a shifter claims one of Our children, their soul is… how would We word it? Locked. No one can take away a human's mate."

"So, she died for no reason," Ferrer said flatly. "One tried. Her venom wouldn't have taken? It would have cleared out?"

"It would not have taken. I advise you to not suffer over the repercussions of her actions. Some do not deserve another chance," They replied, and King Zorian shifted uncomfortably behind his queen. "Calm yourself, lycan." If the king didn't like the gods calling him out like that, he didn't let it show. Despite his initial fidget, his face remained hard. I wondered briefly what the story was there.

"That's a relief…" I breathed, feeling my posture slump a little as another weight rolled off me. I couldn't bear sharing Ferrer with another shifter if someone decided they wanted him. That would utterly crush us both.

"Is it something you truly want? I can award this bond as part of your reward," the gods offered, making both Ferrer and I freeze in our seats. I shakily took a sip of my tea to give me an extra moment to think. Did I want that? Did I want something I wasn't designed to have? Did I want access to Ferrer's feelings and more? It almost seemed to be a step back from the trust we'd built in each other. It had been hard won… Would accepting this blessing be an insult to that? Being able to mind-link him would be helpful…

"I…" I stammered to fill the silence in the room, but the Earth Gods held up Ragna's hand.

"You may decide at a later date. Come back here if you choose to receive it. You have all the time in your lifespan. I would recommend birthing your young first. We do not want to risk complications. This is not a normal request."

"We'll wait!" Ferrer blurted loudly, grabbing my hand with both of his. "We'll wait… We'll talk and… we'll wait."

"Wise decision. Is that all?" the Earth Gods inquired, glancing from me to Ferrer. "If that is all, We will depart for now."

It almost came out in a squeak. "My eggs…?" Was I pushing my luck here?

"That is Fate's work. Nothing I can intervene in," They replied impassively. "Look to the dragons for your answers. Was that the last item?"

My mind went blank, and I sent a questioning look to my mate. He shrugged and said, “I… I think so?”

“You know where to find Us,” They reminded, and the room seemed to lighten instantly, like a colossal presence had departed. Well, it had, I supposed. In Their wake, I wondered how many had just left. They spoke of Themselves in singularities and pluralities. Perhaps that was the nature of two minds as one, another reminder that Ferrer and I didn’t need to tie souls to move together.

The Wolf Queen blinked fiercely, then gave me a bright smile. “Well!” She shifted awkwardly in her seat, laughing a little at the tension in the room. “My name is Ragna,” she said and held her teacup out for me to clink with mine, so I hastily did. “Would you all care for some scones and sandwiches? I’m starving!”

“Keid, and yes, please,” I introduced with a nervous laugh, and her lycan mate finally sat down to join us for tea. A wolf, a lycan, a bat, and a witch. It very much sounded like the beginning of a joke.

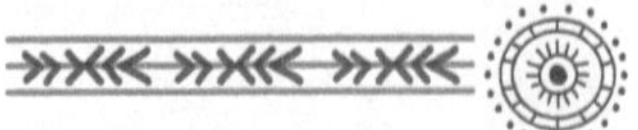

# Chapter 33

## Reid

"It's all so surreal," I murmured as Ferrer and I returned to our home, our family suite in the colony's castle. "Is it safe to breathe again?"

Ferrer closed the door behind us, dropped our travel bag, and scooped me off the ground. A satisfied sigh slipped through my lips, and I leaned against his shoulder as he took me to our bedroom. "Please keep breathing," he said in a low voice and unnecessarily, but sweetly, helped me get undressed. I was delighted to find that some clothes had already been delivered to our closet for me, and I snuggled into a soft nightgown.

"I don't recall the last time I wore something so comfortable," I groaned happily, crawling into bed with a luxurious stretch. Ferrer roamed about like a restless, windblown cloud, cracking the balcony door for fresh air and starting a fire in our bedroom's wood-burning stove. When he rushed out to fetch us dinner, I stared at the silent redwoods that stood like giant guardians outside our windows. If I leaned over enough, I could just make out the twinkling of stars through the boughs.

I smiled at their winking, feeling like they'd seen all and were as satisfied as I was. The Sky Gods would be nice to meet someday. I wondered how different They were from the Earth Gods. I still had a hard time believing I'd spoken to Them… I suspected it'd take a week to process what had been such a brief conversation. Now that I wasn't facing Them, I thought of a hundred more questions. That was the way of things, wasn't it?

The door opened and Ferrer came in with a large tray. Kicking the door shut with a foot, he climbed into bed and served me first with an incredibly serious expression on his face. My mouth hung open in a half-bewildered, half-amused grin as he focused on presenting my chicken soup.

"Are you alright?" I asked with a short laugh.

"I'm just glad you're home and safe now." He sighed and slowed his movements. When I stroked his hair from his face, he seemed to finally unwind. A shaky breath left his lips, and he settled next to me with his own food. "You have no idea what it's like with these new instincts. It's like every bloody shadow is a threat. I was on high alert the entire time. It's such a relief to be back."

"It's good to be home," I said in a soothing voice and spooned some chicken broth into my mouth. I placed my free hand on his arm and rubbed his firm muscles to show my genuine gratitude. "Thank you for giving me a home." I sniffed and rubbed an eye, feeling overwhelmingly happy. My gaze traveled around the room, and I pictured our future here. "I can just see a little shifter running into the room because they had a nightmare."

"I'll beat those nightmares into a pile of bones," he said around his mouthful of food.

I smiled at what he was eating and asked, "No more blood?"

"Not if I can help it," he grunted out, snapping a bone with his teeth to swallow a smaller piece.

"Sky Gods," I swore with a shake of my head. "Remind me to never put my finger into your mouth!" I winced as he cracked another bone in half. How was he not chipping his teeth?

"What? You don't trust my mouth?" he mused with a grin, glancing roguishly through a lock at me. I snorted at our returning joke—one that was born out of a moment of madness and shot nerves.

"I suppose it has done good work in the past," I admitted with a giddy blush as I worked through my soup.

"Only good?" Ferrer sobered and held his bowl to mine. "A toast for Mushy?" He was remembering the same night I did. I clinked my bowl against his and gave him a fond smile. He's grown so much. I was blessedly proud of him.

"To Mushy…" I said and leaned over him to peer into the next room, looking for the pottery I'd requested. There she was—er, some of her, I guess—resting on the mantel in a sealed urn. "May she rot in peace."

"Rot in peace," Ferrer echoed and bent down to nuzzle into my temple. I leaned into his affection and reveled in this perfect moment. It was only us and our gratitude. "I love you," was his whisper before he finished the last of his meal.

I ate quickly too, wanting to be curled up in his arms as soon as possible. With the lights out—except for the stove's firelight—we clung to each other, savoring the beginning of forever. Even our breaths felt like they'd synchronized by the time we'd fallen asleep.

Like that night so many nights ago, Ferrer pulled up my clothing as I drifted out of a dreamless sleep. His broad palm moved in slow circles on my hip, and I sighed in pleasure, loving to be woken by his touch. This wasn't a pestering for sex; my male just wanted to be closer, I could tell.

I wiggled out of my nightgown, the object of his discontent, and he rumbled an appreciative growl as I scooted back into him. Even though he wasn't pestering me, it didn't mean I couldn't pester him. He was mine to pester now, especially with his instincts mellowing him out a bit.

He hummed happily and ran his palm up my side to pull me closer, then buried his face in my hair. No words needed to be said. We were in a moment of blissful unity.

I turned in his arms and slid my mouth to his in a lazy, seductive maneuver. His satisfied sigh turned into a groan when I slid my leg up his to rest over his hip. He knew an open invitation now when one was given. Though it was easier to be bolder in the darkness, I was feeling much more confident now. It was hard to deny his reactions to my body. Something about him making me feel beautiful helped me act… beautiful. I couldn't be sure if that made sense, but it was what it was.

"You are bursting with starlight," he murmured into my lips and deepened our kiss, sliding his tongue in to flirt with mine. My heart fluttered at the pretty words, and I took them at face value. He meant them, and I knew they meant I was beautiful. Ferrer thought I was beautiful, and I believed him. I was beautiful.

As he said, I was bursting, and if it wasn't with starlight, it was absolutely with love. I rolled my hips forward to nudge his slowly swelling erection, and his hand moved to cup my face as he fell into our kiss. A long, drawn-out groan squeezed from his throat, and his breath caught in his chest.

"I still can't believe this is real. It'd been so lonely waiting for you," he whispered into my mouth as he moved his hand between us. His hips pulled away, giving the head of his cock room to slide down my abdomen. A trail of precum was drawn along my skin until he finished angling down his erection. Ferrer's breaths grew heavier as I helped guide him to my entrance, lifting my leg a little to prepare for his push.

"Ah…" I sighed out as he put pressure against my threshold, then slipped his cock past it.

"So wet, Keid." He gasped into my cheek, kissing it while we pressed our hips together. He pulled my leg over his arm, and he reached down to get a handful of my bottom, gripping for purchase. "How is my woman so ready in the middle of the night?"

"Isn't that when bats come out to play?" I inquired, breathless.

"It's obvious that's when you come out to play." He hummed and rolled his hips to push his hard flesh deeper.

"And I was just waiting for my bat, so…"

"Clots," he hissed as he finished burying himself in me with a thrust. "Keid…"

I stared at his face in the dark, illuminated by wild flickers of orange and yellow. I brushed a strand of hair away from his eyes again, knowing I'd do that a million more times in this bed before we passed on and returned to our gods. His eyes locked onto mine in the dim lighting, and I knew he could see me much better than I could see him, but I didn't need light to see him.

We stared at each other as he began to rock slowly, moving just enough to massage his head with my channel. My lips parted in a silent sigh as he made love to me. For just a heartbeat, I worried about his broken wing, but then I noticed that his dressings were gone, and his wings had been shifted away already. He must have gotten fed up with the bindings in the middle of the night, and it looked like they'd healed enough to be put away, thank the Sky Gods.

I spread my fingers along his back, massaging his muscles while I stared into his mindful gaze. He looked at me with such affection now. His handsome face with its fae-like features were entrancing, and I found myself so fortunate that this would be the last face I'd see every night before falling asleep.

"It was worth the wait," I whispered, echoing words he'd said so many nights ago. I moaned softly into his gentle and slow penetrations. "You were worth the wait." If holding on for over three decades was what it took to have him enter my life, I could happily accept that. I would have endured it again.

Ferrer's face turned tender from my words, and his brows drew inward. He rolled on top of me and covered my mouth with his, kissing me with everything he had to give. I wrapped my arms around him as I took his tongue and his cock, moaning in delight from his attention. His mouth and hips worked to give me his love, and I absorbed all of it, knowing it was for me and only me.

"Keid, love, mate," he whispered as he released my lips, "I want you to bite me… like we discussed…"

"We haven't discussed the marking…" I replied, momentarily confused by his words.

"That's… separate. I don't think… it'll be visible… if the Earth Gods do it for you," he murmured between breaths, then shivered and groaned. He fell into a steady pace over me, rocking his hips to pleasure us both. "You still don't have fangs… or venom glands…"

That was true; I didn't have either of those things. I brought Ferrer's lips down to mine again, tears leaking down my cheeks. He was willing to go through the pain and pleasure every night until my bite mark was permanent… He wanted to show everyone that he belonged to me. It wasn't necessary, and he still wanted it!

I didn't know if I could possibly feel any more joy. I released him from his kiss and nodded. "I will. I'll do it." I was still dubious about being able to get him to bleed, he wasn't exactly a well-tenderized steak, but we'd find out shortly enough.

He growled excitedly, and his entire body shuddered as he increased his pace. "Sky Gods, yes!" As he lurched over me, I wrapped my free leg around his hip to spur on his pace.

His enthusiasm, as always, sent a flare of heat and pleasure through my body. My nerves vibrated with excitement, and my sex clenched around his invading member, eager to return the favor. I didn't need the bond to feel him under my skin, in my veins, and around my soul. I felt him, I tasted him, and I breathed him. He was mine. Mine.

His sweat dripped down onto me, puddling with mine as he thrusted, moving progressively faster with his heaving breaths. Spurts of electricity danced around my stomach from the thrill of his taking and the stimulation between my legs. His grunting, the wet slapping, and the sound of the jostling bed provoked my senses, finding carnal arousal from the noises he made as he searched for our pleasure.

"Oh, Ferrer." I gasped, arching and raking my fingers through his hair. Like only he could, he'd relit the dead star inside of me, encouraging the buildup of a silent nova. He moaned in gratification and increased his pace. I could feel that he continued to swell, becoming more excited by the moment. He stretched me wider as that accursed log slipped wetly into my heat, and I jerked him to me, wanting to feel his entire body rubbing against mine.

He hissed into the pillow next to my head, stimulated by my pulling, and began bucking to find release. Fingers found their way to my clit, and I turned my head to moan into Ferrer's ear. I fondled and licked his earlobe, making him shake and groan uncontrollably.

"Shhhh, Keid!" he cried and uttered carnal sounds into the pillow as his fingers fought for my satisfaction. We were a tangle as we tried to get the other to reach completion first, desperate to give our partner the pleasure we wanted them to have. I loved Ferrer so much. I wanted him to have it all.

Knowing I was about to win, I pushed back on the swell of pleasure my mate was inducing and bit down on his shoulder—hard. Ferrer screamed into the pillow and slammed his hips into mine, lurching as he spent his seed. I bit harder, trying to draw blood like he'd asked. My male was writhing above me, crying out the ecstasy that I gave freely.

Once blood was present, the oddest snarling whimper escaped his throat as he doubled down between my legs, not to be outdone. The warmth flooded my core, and I viciously released his shoulder, positioning him aggressively so I could bite the other one.

I returned his scream as my teeth met his flesh, knocked senseless by the orgasm Ferrer had kindled. It was a white-hot flare that engulfed me like a nova. Blood welled between my lips and his skin as I bit savagely, grateful for the muffling lest the whole castle hear us.

Ferrer had captured both my hands under his claws now and crushed our mouths together as he came again into me. My hips bobbed up against his, greedily milking out the seed. Our voiced pleasures were a muffled tangle in our mouths—trapped beneath our tongues—and our hearts felt just as enmeshed.

My contracting, massaging core and his spurting cock went through their last motions until he collapsed, mindful enough to keep his weight from crushing me. He gasped for air next to my head, and I wrapped my arms tightly around his sweaty back, dizzy from soul-deep satisfaction.

"Blood… clots…" He panted, his expanding chest pressing against my breasts upon each gasp. "That was…" He swallowed heavily and licked his lips. It seemed like he couldn't find the words for it. That was…

"Deeply… flattering," I breathed, finishing his words with my own interpretation. He took a minute to gather himself, then propped himself up to dab at my bloody mouth. He looked rattled, like he'd just eaten something bitter.

"Gods, I taste terrible. I'm so sorry…" he said between breaths, trying to wipe my face clean. I laughed as he worried over me and nearly fell out of the bed in his haste to fetch me water. Granted, I was not a fan of drinking blood, but tasting it hadn't been as bad as I'd anticipated. I wouldn't mind repeating it until he scarred. His reaction to the bite was a bit addictive too. Honestly, I looked forward to doing it again later.

"I think that's why they gave us red sheets." I flashed a lazy grin as he returned with a full glass of water, which I quickly drained and set aside, happily quenched in all ways. "You're all such messy eaters."

His smile was warm; Ferrer was beaming like the sunlight he could now appreciate. "Hopefully not for long… thanks to you…" He laid me back and wrapped me in another embrace.

"And you…" I murmured, nuzzling under his chin to get closer to my other half.

"… and Mushy…" I could still hear his smile in his words, his breath, and his pulse. "Whatever trouble she brought, she brought you to me… No matter what, Keid, my love, my mate, it was worth it." We couldn't stop repeating that fact.

"It was," I whispered, then laid a kiss on his lips that told him how very happy he'd made me before we both fell asleep once more. With a partner to share a romance for the rest of our days and a family in the making, I'd have to find new dreams to dream about now.

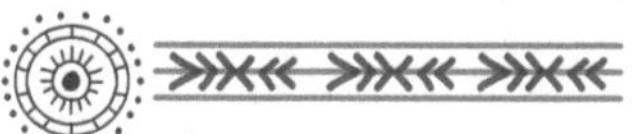
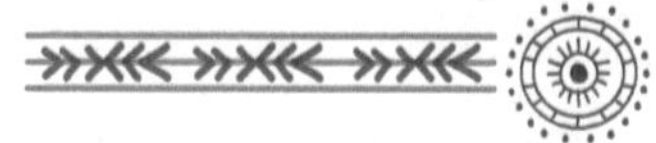

# Epilogue

## Ferrer: Months later

"Breathe," I encouraged, feeling the most helpless I'd ever felt in my entire life. There was practically nothing I could do during the birthing process, not with Akira and Amat—who was one of our bat-shifter doctors.

*Push?* Iron supplied somewhat helpfully. It was the most coherent he'd been all day, which meant that his wits were likely returning, but I couldn't say that mine had. Marrow had been working hard to keep him in control because he knew I wasn't doing much better.

I cracked my spine uncomfortably and tried to keep my bat's wings out of everyone's way to the best of my ability. A much more emotional beast than Marrow, Iron had tried to come out once, so I'd allowed his wings out instead to let him feel like he was more present. There was no way I wasn't going to be here as a supportive presence for Keid.

She was as calm as you'd expect, but she was sweating a lot, and I kept running to our bathing room to re-dampen a towel with cold water. I knew she was worried about what the offspring would be, but we had to get through this, and I did everything I could to appear confident so she could be comforted by that.

"Relax," Amat said, sitting back to wait with Akira after a second close observation. "This is natural. Her body knows what it's doing."

*Yes, you all need to calm down! It's not helping!* Vain snapped furiously. I had no idea how she was looking so bloody relaxed.

*I thought I was being calm!* Iron replied wildly.

*I'm trying to stabilize two males here,* Marrow lamented. *Amat is correct. Her body knows what it's doing. There are no signs of complications.*

"You're doing a fine job helping us, Marrow," I said and smiled over at Keid's pained face. I leaned over to kiss her cheek, and she nuzzled me in turn, making my heart swell. Touching her helped slow my heart rate and breathing, and I knew it aided her as well.

"I hope it's healthy," she worried. "It must be a bat, but… what if…"

"What I can see through the dilation looks normal, Keid," Akira said and patted her knee soothingly. I was glad that we'd transferred the leopard cat-shifter from our island coven. She'd found a replacement and visited on occasion, but it was useful to have another doctor from another species here; we were getting many mates from all territories and were still looking for a dragon expert. Amat said that different perspectives were always helpful, especially in unusual cases like ours.

"Time has flown so fast," Keid murmured with tears in her eyes, and I lovingly wiped them away with a thumb.

"Our family will grow quickly." I grinned and kissed the worry lines between her lovely alabaster brows. Her frosty lashes fluttered as her periwinkle gaze studied me.

"I'm glad this happened. We'll have a second one soon enough."

"And I'm sure they'll be best friends," I replied quietly.

*Don't know about that,* Vain said in a manner unusual for her, but that was expected. It wasn't like the rest of us were acting normal.

"Are you ok?" Keid asked Vain, reaching over to hook her thumb with her pinky finger.

*Yes, yes,* she replied quickly and dismissively. *Worry about yourself.*

"Goodness," Keid murmured, and I scrubbed my hands over my face. I couldn't wait for this to be over. The entire room was strung tight with tension… except for the two doctor mates, who had relaxed smiles on their faces as they went about their duties.

"Honestly, at this point, we both don't need to be here. I think this is going well," Amat said, turning in his seat to place a kiss on Akira's cheek. "It's well past dawn and our usual bedtime. You can go rest if you wish, mate."

"Are you kidding me?" Akira replied with a feral grin. "I must see how this goes. I'm far too curious!"

"This is not an exhibit!" Keid reminded her a little harshly. I sandwiched my mate's hands with mine, and my woman bit her lip, feeling regret and remorse. "Sorry, Akira."

The small leopard waved her hand with a chuckle. "I've been yelled at during deliveries every single time and not always for the same reason."

There was a larger flare of pain over the bond, and I nearly fell out of my seat. Keid released a gasp, and I clung to her as hard as she was to me. I didn't think she had the strength of grip to numb my hand, but she was certainly trying.

"Oh, here we go," Amat said, scooting his chair closer to the table.

"Oh! I see the head!" Akira added.

*This is taking forever,* Iron nearly sobbed, and Marrow shushed him. I had to admit that my ossifrage was really pulling his weight here.

It was deafeningly quiet in the room as the pup began its slow entry into this world, and I tried not to hold my breath; I needed to stay conscious!

*Breathe, Ferrer,* Marrow reminded me.

*I'm not the one who needs to hear tha—* I lied and swallowed hard, feeling mildly embarrassed about how bloody terrified I was, which was equal to my excitement.

*We all need to hear it,* Iron interjected weakly.

Somehow, appearing simultaneously quickly and slowly, a small bat head began wiggling out of Vain.

Keid and I scooted closer to her familiar's little birthing station, a small mesh wall over a soft folded towel. Vain was hanging upside down—which was right side up to us—and had curled her wings and tail inward so she could eventually catch the newborn with her webbing. My woman placed a hand over her mouth and wept at the sight of the little emerging thing, which utterly destroyed my self-control. Tears spilled down my face as Vain did the best she could to encourage out the tiny pup, licking and scratching incessantly at her stretched skin.

*Oh Sky Gods, oh Sky Gods, oh Sky Gods!* Iron cried, making my eye twitch because it felt like he was flapping wildly about in my head.

"Am I noticing what I think I'm noticing?" Akira murmured to her male, who nodded thoughtfully and fluffed up the towel under Vain, just in case the pup fell.

"This is... groundbreaking," Amat replied and released an emotional laugh.

"I'm not imagining it?" Keid whispered through a scrunched-up, tear-covered face.

I shook my head to answer her the best I could, at a complete loss for words as the bat pup squirmed and struggled to get free. The more I saw of it, the more I couldn't believe it. I'd never seen a bat pup, since our offspring were born in their human forms, but this pup, though properly bald as newborn were, was much lighter than its mother.

The pup had albinism.

"How?" Keid sobbed through her hands, which were cupped over her mouth as she struggled to breathe properly. "How is that possible? What are the odds? Not only does that mean you carry the gene, Ferrer, but… the odds of Vain carrying it…?"

"We'll… We'll ask the coven mothers…" I answered and sniffed wetly. I dragged Keid onto my lap as we watched Vain birth her pup. "Th-that… that… could also be your pup too, Keid… Oh gods. I hadn't expected…"

"I… I c-can test maternity… when it gets bigger… I've done it before…" she choked out in shock.

"Guess familiar souls are joined like shifter souls," Akira murmured. "Your pups, Keid, will be Vain's as well. I've never, ever seen a familiar pregnancy before." She shook her head in awe, looking more tranquil than her mate. "From my time spent in the coven… well… usually witches who get their familiars are quite old, and their partners either aren't compatible shifters or interested in breeding. This is an entirely new scenario. This has never happened to my knowledge. The night of conception, you said you didn't feel the 'cheating' pain when Vain went flying with Iron like you and Ferrer allowed?"

"N-n-no. I didn't feel like anything was wrong. I j-just went to sleep and Ferrer came to bed later. W-we both felt fine."

Keid was bawling into my shirt at this point, trying to muffle her sounds for Vain's sake. I held her tightly as she soaked my chest with her tears. A smile cracked its way onto my face as I kissed the top of Keid's head.

"Do you think," I began in a thick voice, "Mushy wasn't supposed to give you your eggs back?"

Keid looked up at me sharply, blinking with wide eyes that looked a little more purple than blue in the warm lighting. "Are you saying that the Earth Gods gave me Vain as a workaround to have your pups?" Her gaze darted back to Vain. "But she's birthing a bat…"

"I don't know," I sputtered with a bewildered shrug. I was just as much in shock as her about this entire thing. "Mushy helped you get her so… I don't know if you would have still acquired her on your own or…"

"Oh, Fate is so confusing! I wish I knew if we'd actually been thrown off course by Mushy." She moaned as quietly as possible, turning her face back into my chest. I slid my hands down to palm her very pregnant belly, lovingly holding our new pup's younger sibling-to-be. It'd been a little over five months now, so Keid had several more months left before her own delivery.

My mate looked back up at me with a distraught expression. "What if Fate wants to take my child back? What if I wasn't supposed to have her?" she mouthed, trying to not let Vain hear her anxious question. The blood bat wasn't paying attention to what we were saying, fortunately, and Iron and Marrow were busy encouraging her delivery.

Her words instilled a chill in me, but I shook my head aggressively and hissed under my breath, "I don't care. Fate will not get our pup!"

"But if Mushy changed things, what if Fate wa—"

"No!" I mouthed back fiercely. "I will keep this family safe and so will our gods, Keid! Do you trust me still? The Earth Gods Themselves said They'd watch over our family line! Believe in Them!"

She nodded through tears, her mouth strained tight and quivering. I could almost taste her deep, desperate terror, and it was bitter, too bitter for such a benevolent day. I tilted her chin up so I could kiss her lovingly, then angled her face to look at her familiar. A little thumb had poked out along with the head, and it was wiggling about frantically.

"Look, it's waving," I murmured to my mate, trying to make her smile. It worked. Keid's near hyperventilation had turned into quiet laughter as she lifted her fingers, wiggling them in turn at the blind newborn. "Reminds me of the day Vain was born, writhing about in the dirt like a lost little mole," I said softly to her, rubbing her belly slowly and mindlessly.

"You saw that?" she asked, laughing lightly in surprise.

"Mostly. I definitely saw you digging her out. First time I saw you naked too," I admitted with a grin. She gasped but was too laden with joy—and some mild concern—to pretend to be appalled.

"Do you think it's a shifter then?" Akira asked her mate.

"If it's the same genetics as offspring produced by Keid and Ferrer, it's possible…" Amat said, pursing his mouth in thought. "I'm guessing we'll have to watch as it develops. If the pup remains this way, perhaps if and when it turns eighteen…?"

"Oh Sky Gods, I have so many questions," Akira muttered thoughtfully. "Will the human mind arrive then or the beast mind? Who will be the dominant mind?"

Keid addressed them in a lowered voice. "Can we not discuss this now? I feel like we're stressing out Vain…" I did indeed feel the small blood bat become increasingly irritated and anxious.

*You are stressing me out,* Vain verified as she continued to urge out her squirming offspring. I repeated her assertion and the doctors acquiesced, falling silent. Keid and I quieted too, except for the occasional word of support.

Somewhere between a half an hour and an hour later, Vain finished birthing the small white bat and successfully expelled the placenta. Iron was cursing rabidly at me, wanting to get out so he could tend to the female he also very much considered his mate.

"Soon, Iron," I said sternly as Keid and I moved a tired Vain to her small section of the nursery. The pup was properly latched and nursing while the blood bat mother slowly moved to hang upside down once more.

"Do you know, Vain?" Keid inquired quietly, placing a bowl of blood I'd supplied by her resting place.

*Female,* she replied tiredly. *Female pup.*

"Oh!" Keid whimpered and placed her hands over her mouth again. Her swell of emotions tugged me down with her, and I bloody started crying again too. Shitting stars.

*So... Aludra?* Marrow inquired curiously, wondering if they still planned on using one of the names Vain and Iron had saved. It was another blue star's name that Keid had later recalled, and Vain had jumped on it immediately. Iron had voiced no opinion in that moment because he still couldn't believe he'd impregnated her. We'd all been baffled by his surprise at the time. Though Vain was a familiar, she was still a functioning female...

*Aludra,* Vain said firmly. *Our Aludra.* The blood bat's head swiveled a little as she looked for Keid. *Can you please leave one of your used shirts here? I want her to get to know your scent too as a mother, just in case she isn't picking your scent up from me.*

Keid became even more of an emotional wreck from those sweet words and rushed out to fetch something she'd previously donned that had a good amount of her scent on it. A balled-up tunic was pushed down into Vain's little recovery nook, and I raised my brows in surprise.

"You kept that thing?" I asked.

"It's clean," she said with a smile. "I just wiped it across my skin. I'm plenty sweaty." Keid released a light laugh. "Besides," she continued and leaned her head against me as she stared fondly at Vain, "I like to think it's lucky."

"Could very well be," I mused, pulling her against me. My heart was comfortably swollen with love now that the new addition to our family had come safely into the world.

A knocking on the door had my mate, my woman, the love of my existence, withering against me. "That would be my sister," she whispered and closed her eyes like she'd been defeated.

*No visitors,* Iron remarked heatedly. *Actually, let's leave the room. I'll come out later. Starshine needs rest.*

"It could also be Luzia... or any of the other coronels actually," I murmured, and we left the room so Vain could get comfortable while nursing. "They'll have to wait to meet her—our Aludra."

"Our Aludra…" Keid echoed, rubbing tears from her eyes. It was pointless though; my fated mate couldn't stop crying.

I entwined our fingers over her belly once more and chuckled. "Eldest of our family and the firstborn to the colony."

There was no describing the reverence I felt from my woman as I spoke. All I could say was that it matched the intensity of passion found in my heart. I couldn't wait to see the one growing within my Keid so they could meet our little pup—our little Aludra.

The End

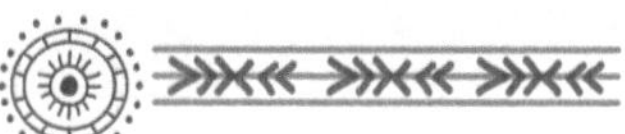

# Author's Notes

Why this book was written:

As I've said before, I started writing years ago as exposure therapy for my childhood sexual assault. I will not discuss it here because it's already explained in the author's notes of *The Mistake and the Lycan King* and *The Dragon Knight and the Coveted*.

Keid: She is the part of myself that struggles with an inner injured child. For a number of reasons, she worries about perception and works daily to separate herself from emotional reality. She is the mirror of the pain I feel about my appearance, scars, height, and more and my sense of belonging in society. In addition to serious and lifelong issues with my own physical traits, I also do struggle to look at faces, and though I've improved, I'm just not there yet. Specifically though, as a child, I avoided faces because I was terrified of seeing two things on other people's faces: interest and disinterest.

Contradicting interest & disinterest: Very weirdly, despite the deep injuries I sustained to my self-esteem, I had this dread that every man who interacted with me was interested in me. Illogically, this was not the case with any crushes I developed growing up, because I believed I was too tall and unattractive. Due to the fear of being hunted, I avoided eye contact with anyone and shut down, trying to seem as aloof as possible. It was probably the crossing guard that first triggered that behavior. From daily abuse, bulling, and the irrational fear of unrealistic interest, I felt perpetually like prey. All I could really do was avoid human interaction, turn off my emotions when I could, and hang on to what did make sense. If I didn't look at anyone's faces, I wouldn't see sexual hunger, disinterest, or sneers. Denial was my shell, even against things that didn't exist. Sometimes, I wonder how many opportunities I missed growing up because of that.

Coping with Keid's rewards: I feel like of all the books in the series I've written, the ending of this book was the hardest for me to cope with. After putting her through familiar trials, I gave Keid everything that she craved that I currently want and have given up on. Maybe I made her too much like me in that regard. Anyway, she deserved it, she earned it, and I wanted her to have her happily ever after. I don't like writing tragedies or bittersweet endings because I need as much positivity as I can gather toward healing. If my characters struggle and find happiness, it gives me hope that maybe I can get there some day despite hopelessness. The problem is that, for me, happiness feels more impossible by the day. At this point in time, many human relationships trigger my despair: seeing mothers with children, partners, entire families. It makes leaving the apartment difficult.

All I can do is keep myself afloat with my therapy, try to heal with the help of my care team, and do what gives me both joy and relief: writing about growth through adversity. What little pain I feel is worth the journey with every story, and I feel an accomplishment I've never felt with anything else. It gives me air. It lets me breathe. It helps normalize what gives me pause. I stumble across breakthroughs and epiphanies.

Ferrer: He is the part of me that struggles with letting go of old ideas. It's hard to grow out of things like prejudice born from fear, desperate survival, and hurt. It's hard to let go of ideas that have been drilled into me since I was a child, some ideas that have even spanned across generations. Still, I'm comforted by reminding myself that there is a difference between feeling prejudice and acting on prejudice.

Not every issue I have with myself has what I consider a good reason for being there. I know I'm not a bad person for having specific anxieties because I know I won't ever act on them. I *know* better. They exist because of trauma, and I see them as emotional reflexes that need to be trained away. I know that some instincts are at odds with my reason and rationale. I know what good is, I know what honorable is, I know what kind is, I know what right is, and the more I work with myself, the easier it will be to sweep away the negatives that were programmed into me from a young age. That's just more exposure therapy.

I believe that momentary bad thoughts do not necessarily make a bad person. Bad actions are what cause problems and pain, but a person can halt bad actions and do the best they can going forward. It might not make up for anything in the past, but the world might be a better place from there on out.

Mushy: I had not expected for Mushy to get as much love as she did, but I went into this book with the goal of making her, well, weirdly fantastic. I wanted to make an absolutely revolting character full of some of my best heartwarming memories—memories around or feelings inspired by three women who I loved when they were alive. As you saw, this book is dedicated to my late grandmother, who embraced a little insanity with laughter. The butt slapping was inspired by a friend's grandmother, who always treated me like her own. She always sent us off that way, playfully. Also, my mind kept going to a certain elderly celebrity when I started writing. I did not base Mushy off of her, but I think some of her no-fucks-given attitude snuck in. Mushy came out completely as her own entity, made entirely of love, filth, and absolute chaos... with a side of ambiguity.

Fun facts: As with many of the bat-shifters, Ferrer's name is inspired by old Spanish and Catalan. Ferrer (the meaning is related to an ironworker or blacksmith) worked beautifully because iron is needed for healthy blood. Iron is Fe in the periodic table of elements, which is short for ferrum (Latin for iron). So Ferrer is a nod to the element that is needed for healthy blood. His bat, Iron, is also a nod to the same thing. It ties in with Keid's resentment toward being called 'bloodless.' Ultimately, Ferrer turned, in the end, into a source of well-being for her which she learns how to accept. Her emotional anemia fades away. Through his eyes, his journey, as his own prejudice fades, as day colors come to him, she learns to see her beauty.

Vampire bats are communal, smart, and thoughtful mammals that do actually feed other hungry members of their colony. The ones who share regurgitated food find themselves more likely to receive food from another bat on another day if they were not successful in obtaining a meal.

According to some studies, vampire bats can run up to 2.5 mi (4 km) an hour and can jump up to three feet in height. I did base bat-shifters as much as I could on the animal itself, in subjective and relative ratios, rather than on the stereotypes of the common vampire. It's why I've made my bat-shifters so mobile. I think the acrobatics are incredibly impressive and unexpected for such tiny mammals. As mentioned in *The Packless and the*

*Fae Prince*, I picked the white-winged vampire bat for Ferrer's species, which is why he has bits of white in his hair and wings.

The only thing I did not really touch was the vampire bat's tendency to form harems, as scientifically defined, in nature. It just didn't fit well with their lore, so I left it aside for the time being. I do, however, see Luzia potentially forming a harem of males (it's not clear what the word would be for this, as 'harem' does not appear to be correct, and I probably will come up with a new term derived from etymology) in her own time. She's really enjoying her freedom, and it almost feels out of my hands. Sometimes characters get away from me.

Albinism and trafficking awareness: While I do not have albinism, someone important to me did, and I've spent a great deal of time studying the genetic condition and its history in different countries and cultures. The issue Keid faced with trafficked tissue is not isolated to her. It's a reference to a persecution that countless people with albinism have encountered worldwide, in modern times and throughout history. I cannot bring myself to talk about the body part trafficking atrocities committed, which are among the hardest for me to comprehend. At this point in time, certain countries have made improvements in protecting individuals with albinism, but there is a long way to go in preventing murders and disappearances—heartbreakingly long.

I feel like I do not need to say this to my readers, but I'm compelled to write it here regardless: wherever you are in the world, I implore you to not be silent. If you see something, say something.

And finally, don't forget to embrace your inner vampire bat. Feed someone today, and they might just feed you tomorrow.

Starlight preserve you,

Asha Nyr

www.ingramcontent.com/pod-product-compliance
Lightning Source LLC
Chambersburg PA
CBHW030809310726
48980CB00006B/436/J

* 9 7 9 8 9 9 2 4 7 3 9 2 6 *